CARTER REED

TIJAN

Cover image designed by Lisa Jordan
www.lisajordanphotography.com.au

Edited by Amanda Su, and Jocelyn Ginty
jocelynginty.editing@gmail.com.

Interior Design by Angela McLaurin, Fictional Formats
https://www.facebook.com/FictionalFormats

This book is dedicated to my readers. Seriously, you guys are amazing! There's so many of you that have supported me and fought for me, even if I've been misunderstood at times. I'd also like to dedicate this book to my other half. He's always there for me, and will always be there no matter. It goes both ways, J.

Douchebag's here.

That was the first thought that went through my head as I crept into our apartment. It was my apartment—*mine*—and I had to slink inside because my roommate's boyfriend was a pervert. I always snuck in when I saw his car in the parking lot, but this time was different. They were in the living room and my roommate cried out. I heard the slap next as he backhanded her and that stopped everything. I couldn't move, but I could see them. Then he growled at her to shut up before he went back to his business. She still whimpered, but quieted as he kept thrusting into her.

I couldn't look away.

He was raping her.

Sickness blasted me. I couldn't believe what was happening in front of me.

He kept thrusting as he held her down in front of him. His legs held her trapped and he was leaning over with one of his hands holding both of her wrists together. He kept going. My roommate lay there in surrender. He had defeated her, broken her, and I was witnessing it all.

Vomit and hatred spewed up in my throat, but I clamped them down. They wouldn't burst out of me, not when I had a chance to do something that I knew I would regret. But even with that thought, the decision had already been made in my mind.

Mallory cried out again. Her agony was heart-wrenching. My hand trembled before he ordered her to shut up again. Then he thrust harder, deeper. He kept going, clueless as to who else might've been in the apartment.

This was my home.

This was her home.

He was not welcome, but he didn't care. He kept going into her. Then he growled in pleasure. The sound of it went straight to the pit of my stomach. I wanted to spew my guts once more, but instead my eyes hardened and I went to the kitchen. There was a whole drawer of knives, but none of them would do. Not for him.

I went past the kitchen and knelt at the floorboards of our patio. I removed one of them and gripped the box that I knew my brother would've hated to know I had. Another scream ripped from behind me and my resolve grew.

My arm didn't shake.

I found the gun my brother had never wanted me to know about. I gripped it and lifted it free from the box before I put the floorboard back together. Then, with my heart going slower than it should've been and clearer eyes than I should've had, I turned for the living room again. The sounds of his thrusting continued. The couch slammed against the wall with each thrust. My roommate cried out with each movement. It never seemed to stop, but I held on tighter to the gun before I turned the last corner.

He had readjusted them. He sat her up against the wall as he kept pumping into her. Now her head bounced against the wall. She was pale as a ghost; fresh tears fell over the dried ones. Her eyeliner streamed down with them so that her face was streaked black, with bruises starting to fill in the rest of the space on her face. Her cheek was already swollen and red from where he had slapped her. There were cuts at the top of her forehead. Blood streamed from them. He had sliced her and pulled her hair out so much that it bled.

Her eyes met mine over his shoulder. A whimper left her again, but his hand slammed over her throat once again. He squeezed with more and more pressure, her mouth gaping open for oxygen. As he gripped tighter, his hips jerked even harder. He was getting off on it. Then she started to thrash around—she couldn't get any air.

He squeezed harder.

When her eyes started to glaze over, I saw a flash of something in them. It was meant for me. I knew it. And my hand held even tighter to the gun as I lifted it in the air.

I felt his gurgle of release before I heard it. I felt it in the air, through the floor, through my roommate. It didn't matter. I knew he was near to climaxing and nothing had ever disgusted me more, but my hand was steady as I held the glock. Then I removed the safety and I cleared my throat once.

He froze.

He didn't look around. He should've, but he didn't.

I waited—my heart starting to pound, but he just started thrusting once again.

"Jeremy."

My voice was so soft, almost too soft, but he froze anyway and twisted his head back to look at me. When he saw what I held, his eyes went wild—and then I shot him.

The bullet hit the center of his forehead. I wasn't surprised when Mallory started to scream, still in his hold. His body held her against the wall even as he slumped. He would have kept her in place if not for her frantic hands pushing him off. His body fell to the ground, as much as the bones and tendons allowed. His knees were still bent, but the blood seeped from him slowly. It formed a pool underneath, and as I stood there, it grew and grew.

Still screaming, Mallory scrambled from him and collapsed to the ground not far from his body. She scooted against the wall until she found the farthest corner and curled into a fetal position. She was sobbing, hysterical, as more screams ripped from her throat.

I went to her, but instead of soothing her like I should've, I put my finger to my lip and made a ssshing sound. When she quieted, I whispered, "You have to be quiet. People will hear."

She nodded but gulped for breath as her sobs grew silent.

Then I turned and slid to the space beside her. I couldn't look away from him. The pool of blood encircled him now. It seeped under the couch.

Absentmindedly, my hand found Mallory's exposed and bleeding knee. I patted it to soothe her, but I couldn't tear my eyes from him. I had killed him. I had killed someone. I couldn't think it or comprehend it, but everything was wrong. I should've been at the gym. I should've been trying to flirt with the new trainer, but I had been tired. I skipped the gym, just this once, and came home instead. When I saw his car, I almost turned around. I hated Jeremy Dunvan. He was connected to the local mob and he treated Mallory like crap. Still, I hadn't gone back to the gym. I figured I could sneak inside. They were always in her room anyway.

Jeremy's face had fallen towards us somehow. I remembered

that she had shoved him away from her so his body bent at an awkward angle, but his eyes looked at me. He was dead so they were vacant, but he could still see me. I knew it. A shiver went down my spine as I looked the guy I had murdered in the eye. He was damning me to hell with those eyes.

"Em," Mallory sobbed.

This time her crying broke through my walls. The sound was now deafening to me. My heart picked up. I worried that they could hear in the next apartment, maybe below us or above us. They were going to call the police. We should call the police, but no—I had killed someone. No, I had killed Jeremy Dunvan. We couldn't call anyone.

I found her hand and gripped it hard. One of them was cold and clammy. Mine. My hand was pale while hers was warm with blood. I turned and saw she had her other hand to her mouth. She kept taking gulping breaths as she tried to contain her sobbing.

"We have to go."

My voice sounded harsh to my ears. I flinched from the fierceness in it.

She nodded, still sobbing, still gulping, still bleeding.

"We have to go." My hand squeezed hers. "Now."

Her head jerked in another nod, but neither of us moved. I didn't think my legs worked anymore.

Everything after that was blurry, only remembered in flashes.

We were sitting in a gas station parking lot as we looked at each other. Mallory needed to be cleaned up. Did we go to the hospital? Did I need a camera to prove that she'd been raped? Then she started crying some more, and I remembered who I had killed. Jeremy's father would come for us. No police would help us, not when half of them worked for Jeremy's father, who worked for the Bartel Family. His body would be found in our apartment, I hadn't the stomach to dispose of it.

The bathroom was connected to the outside so I had to get the key. She couldn't be seen like this. One of the two lightbulbs didn't work so the lighting wasn't the best, but I used my phone as I inspected every bruise on her body. She was covered from the top of her head to the two large welts on her calves. When I saw them and looked up, she whispered, "He kicked me."

I got Mallory sunglasses and a scarf to cover her head. She looked like she was from a different country, but it hid the damage. No one spared us a second glance as we went into a diner and ordered two coffees. My stomach growled, but I couldn't eat. Mallory's hands shook so much she couldn't pick up the cup so both of our coffees grew cold as we sat there. I'd grown numb long ago, but her lip still quivered. It'd been quivering for hours now.

It was past midnight. Neither of us ordered food. When the servers changed, I ordered a new coffee. This time I could finally sip it. Mallory gasped. My eyes shot to hers and then I felt the warmth in my mouth. I had burnt myself, but I barely felt it. After my second cup, I waited ten minutes before I picked it up. I knew it wouldn't burn me then. Mallory still couldn't pick hers up.

It was morning now. Both of our phones rang, but we only looked at them. I couldn't speak. I could barely order more coffee from the new server. Mallory's lip had stopped quivering, but I knew her hands still shook so she kept them in her lap. Then she choked out as she reminded me to go to the bathroom. We went together.

We were back in the car again. The staff had started to whisper about us so we left. We didn't want them to call the police, but now we didn't know where to go again. Then Mallory said, "Ben. We can go to Ben's." I looked over. "Are you sure?" My hand was so cold. I barely felt the steering wheel when I turned the car around. She nodded, some tears slipped down again. She had started crying when we left the diner. She said, "Yes. He'll help us. I know it." So we went to her co-worker's house.

The force of what happened hit me full blast after we had been at Ben's for a few hours. He opened the door, took one look at Mallory, and swept her up in his arms. She'd been sobbing ever since, and now all of us were huddled around his kitchen table. He draped a blanket over both of them at some point, but I couldn't remember when.

As she told him what happened through her sobs, I slumped in my chair. Jeremy Dunvan. He had been living twenty-four hours ago, breathing. Oh my god. I had killed him—I felt punched in the stomach. No. I felt like someone tied up my hands and legs, threw me in the highway and waited as a bus ran over me, and then ran over me again. And again.

I was going to die. It was a matter of time.

Franco Dunvan worked for the Bartel Family. They killed my brother. It was my turn now. Icy panic seared through me. I couldn't hear Mallory anymore. It had been in defense. He was going to kill her. He'd already been raping her. I killed him because he would've killed me too, but it didn't matter. As I started struggling to breathe, I tried to remain logical. The police wouldn't have helped. Why did we take pictures of her bruises then? What did it matter? None of it did. We ran. We should keep running.

"We have to go, Mals," I choked out.

She looked up from Ben's chest. He wrapped his arms tighter around her, and if possible, she paled even more. "We can't."

"We have to." They were going to hunt us down and kill us.

"Please, Tomino, please." My brother had begged for his life, but they shoved him to his knees and took a bat to him. AJ watched me the whole time. As he stared past the alley where they found him, we both knew they couldn't see me. He made me crawl behind a vent before they saw him in the alley. My hands gripped each other as I kept myself from crawling out and helping him. He shook his head. He knew what I wanted to do.

"Emma!"

I jerked back to the present and saw Ben frowning at me. "What?"

Everything seemed so surreal. It was a dream. All of it was a dream, it had to be.

He snapped at me, "Christ, the least you can do is be there for her." Then he pushed off from his chair and stormed past me.

What had happened?

"Carter's going to come for you."

I went back to that alley. I heard my brother warn them as he gasped for breath. He was choking on the blood, but they laughed at him. They fucking laughed!

"Whatever. You're a nobody, Martins. You're a waste of space. Your boy's going to get the same as you if he comes after us. In fact, we want him to come to us, don't we, boys?" Tomino had spread his arms out wide and the other three snickered with him. Then he lifted the bat once more.

AJ looked at me. He mouthed the words, *"I love you."*

Then the bat came down at full speed.

I fell off my chair and was slammed back to the present again. I was on the floor now.

"Jesus, Emma. What the fuck's your problem?" Ben grabbed my

arm and hauled me up. He pointed to the bedroom. "I finally got her to sleep and now you're going to wake her up? Do you know the hell she's been through? I can't believe you. Have some consideration."

Have some consideration?

I yanked my arm away from him and glared back. "Are you fucking kidding me?" Was he? He had to have been. I shoved him back and then followed to get in his face. "I killed him, you asshole. I killed that rapist for her. I saved her life!"

Now I needed someone to save mine.

TWO

When I woke, everything was groggy. Nothing made sense, and my back was killing me. It protested when I uncurled from the ball I had formed and spasms shot up. I nearly screamed, but threw my hand over my mouth to muffle the sound. I couldn't make a sound. A sixth sense instantly reared, but then I frowned as different noises came from behind me. A pot clanged against a pan, and there was a sizzling from something being fried, which was quickly covered with a curse before the fire alarm went off.

I rolled over as I found myself on half of a mattress, pulled into a corner of a living room. Peering over the two couches in front of me, that boxed me into the corner, I remembered.

We were at Ben's.

Mallory had been screaming and crying. Mallory had been raped.

I dropped back to the mattress with a thump.

Jeremy Dunvan.

Panic swelled in me, but then the front door burst open. I jumped back and screamed. I kept screaming when it banged shut and people ran to the living room. And, even as I saw it was a friend, I couldn't stop the scream.

"Jeremy."

My own voice haunted me. The bang of the gun came back and I felt the kickback in my hand again.

"You have to be quiet. People will hear."

With an anguished gasp, I closed my mouth and fell over. Bending forward, I buried my head into the pillow. Another scream rushed through me. What had I done with the gun? Oh god. There was evidence. I couldn't remember where I had put it.

Soft hands touched my shoulder. "Emma."

I heard Amanda's voice, one of the few that I trusted. She knelt beside me and gathered me to her. "Come on. Lift up." Her finger slid underneath my chin, and she raised my head. I gasped for breath, but I couldn't breathe. My entire body wrenched forward, and I started to pound my chest. The panic swirled in my chest. It was suffocating me. Oh god. The gun.

Slap!

My head snapped to the left, but I never felt the sting from her hand. It was enough to pull me back so I could breathe again. I looked back as I felt my pulse slowing down and grasped Amanda's elbows. "Thank you."

She brushed back some of her blonde hair and smiled. It was a gentle smile, but I didn't care that it was from pity. I grabbed her and held on with all my might. She had no idea, she couldn't have, but she was there. I drew in a ragged breath.

"Amanda." Ben stopped in the doorway between the kitchen and living room. He had a white apron tied around his waist and he was shirtless. The jeans he wore underneath were wrinkled and ripped at the knees. They looked like he had slept in them, but then I saw the tear streaks on his chest and realized that he had slept in them. He had held Mallory during the night.

She waved a hand to him. “We’re fine. We’ll be there in a second, okay?”

He narrowed his black eyes.

I frowned as I saw how his black hair was messed, like a hand had run through it over and over. I saw the red nail marks on his chest and I shot to my feet. “Are you kidding me?”

“Emma.” Amanda shot to her feet beside me. She tried to block me, but I pushed aside all 98 pounds of her.

“You slept with her?! You had sex with her last night?”

He frowned and scratched at his chest. My eyes narrowed as I saw more scratches, long and red. They ran the entire length of his skinny torso. They stuck out against his pale skin. A different sickness came over me. It gurgled up from deep inside and threatened to spew out, but I couldn’t move. I could only look in revulsion.

He sighed as his hand lifted to his hair. It fisted around a clump of his black strands and pulled at them before he took another deep breath. His shoulders slumped then and the hand dropped to his side. “What do you want, Emma? She didn’t want to feel him anymore. She wanted to feel me. She wanted another man’s touch.”

“Did it work?” I spat out. I already knew it hadn’t.

His head fell down. The towel he held in his other hand slipped to the ground. Then he lifted bleak eyes to me. “She’s been crying ever since.”

“Ben!”

“Oh, come on, Amanda.” His arms went wide. “You weren’t

here. I was the only one. I didn't know what to do. Mallory was a complete mess the entire night and this one," his hand pointed at me, "was a zombie too. This was the first sign she was alive since that night. I thought I needed to take her to the hospital too."

My heart stopped. "You didn't."

"No." His eyes flashed with disgust. "But I should've. You should've. She shouldn't be here. Both of you shouldn't be here. You shouldn't be hiding—"

"They're going to kill us!"

"Who?" he yelled back at me. His hands were in fists, and he raised them both in the air. "Who, Emma? Who could possibly be this dangerous that instead of going to the hospital, you come here—"

"The mob, you idiot!" I lunged for him, but Amanda wrapped her tiny arms around me. Her feet dug in and I was swung back to the couches. I fell over them, but scrambled back to my feet. My hair fell to cover my face. I threw it back and heaved at him. My eyes were wild. Red-hot fury coursed through me, but it was when he stepped back that I realized what I must've looked like. Crazy.

I drew in a deep breath and tried to calm myself.

Shit—it was hard.

"Where is she?"

"Sleeping." He folded his arms over his chest, and his chin tucked down. "And she's going to stay that way. She needs to sleep, Em. She has to start healing, and she's going to need all the rest she can get."

I raked my hands through my dark hair. I wanted to pull it out. I wanted that pain to sear through me. Any suffering would do, anything strong enough to rip out the pain from inside of me. Then I cried out. A gasp/half-gurgle ripped from me as I sunk to my knees.

God, could I be more dramatic, but holy hell. I was going to hell. They were going to kill me.

"Emma." Amanda was at my side again. She urged me back to my feet, and we both moved to curl on the couch. I wasn't a touchy-feely person, but I clung to her in that moment. I needed all the strength she was giving me.

The chaos was bouncing inside of me, ricocheting around at a rapid pace. I couldn't stop it. I couldn't center myself in order to force all those emotions away.

"Emma."

I closed my eyes when her soft hands came to my face. She lifted it up and started to inspect every line of exhaustion there was. Then she said in a gentle voice, "You should clean up, hon. Let's go to the shower. I'll help."

I shook my head. It wouldn't do any good.

"Come on." Her hand cupped my elbow, and she started to pull me up. Her grip was strong.

Ben was rooted in place as he watched us. His gaze was stark and the hand that ran down his face couldn't hide the exhaustion. I saw that he could've fallen over alongside of me. We were a mess, both of us, but then I caught sight of the closed bedroom door. The sick laugh in me shriveled up suddenly. None of us were in as much of a mess as she was.

Mallory. He had raped her.

An image of her broken eyes stared back at me as his hips thrust into her.

I flinched from the sudden flash, and this time the vomit really did come up. Rushing into the bathroom, I dropped to my knees. Frantically, I threw the toilet seat up just before everything pushed out of me. I did it again. And again. More came after that, and by the end, I could only hang onto the toilet to keep from falling down.

I was going to die.

"Oh, honey. Emma honey." A cold washcloth was pressed to my forehead as Amanda knelt beside me. She wiped something off before she pressed it on my cheeks and then swiped beneath my lips. "You look a mess, but it'll be okay. Everything will be okay."

I closed my eyes tighter. I didn't want to see the rest of the pity in her eyes. I couldn't handle it, not from her. Her eyes were so crystal blue, no emotion could hide in them. I had to clear it all away. Mallory needed me. And then, as I continued to think of my roommate, I shoved the rest of my fear to the side. When I opened my eyes, I turned and finally looked Amanda in the eyes. Unlike her baby blues, mine were dark, nearly black, and she couldn't see anything. She wouldn't see the effort it took me to keep from vomiting more garbage.

I was contaminated.

"I killed a man."

"I know, honey." She bent and rested her forehead against mine. Her hands continued to wipe the washcloth over my cheeks. "We'll get through this. We have to."

"How?"

I winced at the tremble in my voice. I was weak. Pathetic.

"They're coming for me, Ems. You need to be strong. You hear me? You have to be strong."

My brother's voice was in my head. Those memories wouldn't help me now.

Amanda frowned at me. "What?"

"Nothing," I muttered as I lifted an arm and tried to push her away, just a little. I needed room to breathe.

"No matter who knocks on the door, you don't answer it. You

don't trust anyone, no one except Carter. Go to Carter. He'll take care of everything. He'll take care of you, Ems. I promise."

I gritted my teeth. I had to stop thinking about my brother.

"EMMA! GET OUT HERE!" Ben bellowed from the living room.

I shot out to yell at him for yelling, but then I heard the reporter's words and froze.

"Jeremy Dunvan is believed to be missing." A picture of him flashed across the television screen. He was laughing in the photograph, smiling with a carefree look to whoever snapped the image. Then the reporter filled the screen with a somber expression over her face. Her eyes were sharp as she frowned into the camera. "If you have any information about the whereabouts of Jeremy Dunvan, call the number that is scrolling over the bottom of your screen. Again, if you have any knowledge at all about what might've happened to Jeremy Dunvan, please call this number."

She continued to recite the same message. The police were notified by Jeremy's father, Franco Dunvan, earlier in the morning that his 32 year old son had gone missing when he didn't return home the prior evening. She recited it over and over again. I started to feel sick. More pictures of him came up. Some of them were with his friends. He wore a softball uniform in one, another with a beer in hand. All of them made him look friendly, handsome— not at all like the monster that I saw twenty-four hours ago.

A strangled sound came from Ben as he gaped at the television. One of his hands was twisted in his hair again. The other clutched the remote to his chest. His eyes were frantic. "I thought you said—" He stopped. His mouth closed, then opened again, then closed once more. His chest puffed up as he blinked rapidly for a second. "Holy shit, Emma. What did you do?"

My eyes narrowed and I lunged for him. He reared back as fear flared over him, but I swiped the remote from him and turned the television off. "He was raping her. He was killing her. He would've killed me too." I stopped and swallowed over a knot in my throat. My eyes started to swim. "I did what I had to do."

Ben gestured to the television again. His arm shook before it dropped back to his side. "Franco Dunvan. They said Franco Dunvan. Do you know who that is?"

"Yes," I hissed out. God yes. I blinked back more tears. I sure as hell knew who had ordered the hit on my own brother.

"If you ever need anything, go to Carter."

I shook my head to clear the last words my brother spoke to me before he rushed from our apartment. I followed him. He hadn't wanted me to, but when he caught me in the alley, it was too late. They appeared at the end and he lifted me so I would be hidden.

I forced the memories away and spoke to Ben, "I told you this last night."

"The day before yesterday."

"What?" I stopped everything.

"The day before yesterday," Ben murmured, lost in his own thoughts. "You came here two days ago."

A whimper came from me. He'd been dead for two days now. Wait—was it? Time didn't make sense anymore to me. But he was right. I always went to the gym after work at 5:00, but that day I got off early and skipped the gym. It was two nights ago when I killed him.

I had slept for almost twenty-four hours. I blinked in surprise. Had Mallory? I looked up quickly, but Ben shook his head. "She only fell asleep an hour ago. She hasn't slept at all, neither have I."

Oh.

Amanda reached around me and took the remote. The

television was turned back on. As she sat on a couch, Ben sat beside her. Both of them settled back with determined looks on their faces. They were going to watch the news. They were going to hear all of it. And then, with my stomach clenching into a thousand knots, I went back and curled on the couch.

I tried to ready myself for what I was going to hear.

"Authorities will be conducting a thorough search for Jeremy Dunvan and we've learned that federal authorities will be brought into the case. They believe that Jeremy Dunvan's disappearance may be connected to a string of mob feuds. Now," her voice grew clearer. "We've been told from credible sources that Franco Dunvan, the father of Jeremy Dunvan, is a highly ranked member in the Bartel family. Federal authorities have been trying for years to get evidence against Mr. Joseph Bartel to indict possibly thirty members of their criminal organization."

"Now, Angela," a deeper voice spoke this time.

"Yes, Mark?" She was so chipper.

"Do the authorities believe this disappearance might be connected to the feud between the Bartel family and the Mauricio family?"

There was so much excitement in her voice. "While we haven't been told for certain that they're heading the investigation towards the Mauricio family, it certainly seems likely. The government has long tried to get evidence against Carter Reed, someone they believe is a high official in the Mauricio family."

My heart stopped. I turned to the see the screen now. There was a picture of him.

I sucked in my breath.

I'd forgotten how clear his blue eyes were or how powerful the glare he sent to whomever had taken the photograph. He looked ready to kill whoever was behind the camera, but then another picture came next. This one was him in a black tuxedo as he got out of a black car. He had lifted a hand to block his face from being pictured, but they had been quicker. A sneer curved at the top of his lip, but even through the grainy image and blurred lines, the striking features were unmistakable.

"Go to Carter."

AJ's words floated back to me, but I couldn't. I probably should've, but there was no way. He had been my brother's best friend over ten years ago. He had joined the Mauricio family after AJ's murder and, from what I heard, killed all of those that were a part of my brother's death. A shiver went over me the first time I was told that, and those same shivers were felt again.

Our city was big, but in that world, it would never be big enough. Word spread fast and everyone was soon calling Carter the Cold Killer. He didn't kill only those that ordered the hit; he killed the actual shooters, the back-up guy, the driver, and even the messenger who passed along the hit. He took all of them out, moving faster than anyone could imagine.

While I was in high school and went from foster home to foster home, I saw him a few times. There were random moments when I'd be waiting for the city bus and he would come out of a restaurant. He was always surrounded by other men, big and burly guys. They scared me then, and I knew they would scare me now.

Then in college, since I attended a local one, I caught glimpses of him at nightclubs when I would go with my friends. I never asked for special treatment, I never even knew if he remembered me, but I knew which clubs he owned. Most of them were popular ones, ones my friends wanted to go to anyway, but I liked to see if I could get a glimpse of him. When I did, it was the same—always at a distance.

The same men surrounded him, but there were times when he had a woman with him. They were always beautiful, almost too beautiful to be human. He got the best.

I sighed as more images of him went across the television screen. With any story that might've been connected to the local mob, his picture was always broadcasted. The media loved him. He was gorgeous with striking cheekbones, blue eyes that reminded me of a wolf, and dark blonde hair. All of that plus a six feet two lean build with muscular shoulders.

No one knew that I knew him. I didn't dare tell a soul. If they did...I bit my lip as I considered it now. Would Mallory ask me to go to him? If anyone could help me, it was him. But this? Did I trust him with this information? That I had killed one of his enemies?

"You don't trust anyone, no one except Carter. Go to Carter. He'll take care of everything. He'll take care of you, Ems. I promise."

It hurt to swallow, but when I opened my eyes again—Mallory was in the bedroom doorway. A blanket was wrapped around her frail form. Dried tears caked over her cheeks and she gazed back at me.

He broke her.

I saw it in that instant.

Then I made my mind up. I would go to Carter, but if he wouldn't help me, I'd help myself. I wanted to kill the bastard all over again. If his father came after us, I would protect her. I would protect myself. Carter rose among their ranks when we were kids. He did it to avenge my brother. If he could do that, I could keep us alive. I had to.

When I got out of the cab outside Octave, I faltered for a moment. What the hell was I doing? The crowd was lined down the block as they waited to get inside Carter Reed's most popular nightclub. It was the most exclusive, but it was also the roughest. When my life had been more normal, prior to forty-eight hours ago, my friends and I enjoyed the more vanilla of his nightclubs. They played techno music, mixed with the pop hits, and the crowd didn't make me envision BDSM occurring in any shadowed corner of the club. With this club, however, there was a reason why so many wanted to get inside—it ensured confidentiality. A lot of celebrities would sweep through and were ushered to their private boxes, floors above the actual dance floor. But there was also another crowd, the criminal crowd, which made it so secretive and exclusive at the same time.

Anyone could go to Octave with the assurance that whatever happened in Octave stayed in Octave. There must've been security that swept the club on a regular schedule. Carter wasn't stupid. He was far from stupid. While some of the rougher customers might feel they could get away with anything, there was a limit.

Even though I'd only been inside Octave once, I couldn't be completely sure about my suspicions. I knew Carter. He had never sanctioned that stuff when we were kids. Still, a lot had happened from then till now. As I swallowed over a dry throat, I was fully reminded. I had killed a man and now I was hoping Carter would help me.

"Miss," the cabdriver honked his horn at me. "You gotta pay, lady. This ain't a charity ride."

"Oh." Fumbling through my purse, I found the money and handed it over. As he started to leave, a laughing couple stumbled from the club and climbed through the door. I still hadn't closed it. His on-service light was switched off as I heard the guy mumble an address before he started sucking on the girl's neck. Then the cab drove off, and I was left on the curb.

Great.

Again. What the hell was I doing?

I eyed the line waiting to get inside. Most of them were dressed with next-to-nothing while I wore a long-sleeve shirt over jeans. Granted, Amanda had to lend me her jeans, so they stuck like glue to me, but I was covered. There was no way I was going to get into that club, not like this. So I took a deep breath and saw how long that line was. It'd be hours before I even got to the door. As I bit my lip, I considered going around the line and approaching the four large hulks in front of me. As one glanced at me, I saw the flat look in his gaze. My gut told me that others had tried and been rejected. I sucked in my breath—they might even ban me from the place. Then all hope would be gone.

As a large black Sedan drove past the club and turned into the back alley, I started to follow. Could I get in through there? But no. The car slid to a stop and four more men rushed the back door as it was opened. A man and a woman hurried out and through a side door. She'd been giggling, wearing a flashy red dress, and the guy had a business suit on. The door shut with a resounding finality as the bouncer pounded twice on the roof. The car took off and those four guys resumed their stances before the door.

Just then, the door opened again and another big guy walked down the alley towards me. I gulped. This was it. This was my chance. As he started past me, I reached out for his arm, but my wrist was grabbed before I made contact.

I froze. My eyes bulged out as I saw that he had a vise-like grip on my arm. His eyes were hard, almost too cold.

"Yeah?" he growled.

I gulped again. I tried to keep my knees from buckling. "I-I—"

"Spill it, honey. You have five seconds."

Oh god.

I swallowed over a basketball in my throat. "I—I know Carter Reed. Could I—I mean—is he-?"

He smirked, the harshness of that look slithered down my back. "You and everyone else, honey. You wanna talk to him? Go to the end of that line and wait your turn. But," his eyes slid down my body and up. "You'll be wasting your time. You ain't getting inside dressed like that. You've got a damn fine body, but you gotta show skin. You ain't showing any, honey."

My stomach fell to the ground. This wasn't how I thought it would be, but who had I been kidding? Carter Reed probably didn't remember me anymore, much less give a damn about helping me. But I didn't know what else to do so I wandered down the block and then turned the corner. I sighed. The line went past another block.

There would be no way I would get inside, much less even close to the door.

My phone buzzed at that moment, and I checked it. It was Ben. **Where the f are you? Mal's going crazy. Crying and stuff. Might go to the hospital.**

I quickly thumbed a response back. **DON'T! Can't. B smart. Will kill her and me.** I sent it and then another one. **u 2.**

U need to come back. She needs u.

As I read it, tears threatened to spill, but I walked all the way to the end of the line. I heaved a ragged breath. This was what she needed. If I had to wait all night and through the next day, I would. I had to see Carter. He was our only real hope.

I responded to him. **Mite be gone awhile. Doing something to help. Trust me.**

She's flipping out, Emma! Get back now!

I felt more tears coming, but I couldn't let them spill. This was on me. No matter her emotional trauma, I had to do this to ensure that we both lived. Ben didn't understand that. He was thinking of the here and now, how Mallory had cried through the rest of the day and how Amanda and I had to help her shower because she'd been so sore.

Her cuts and bruises would heal. The soul would as well, though it would take longer, but what I was doing would make sure that she had a chance to heal.

I texted back once. **U won't hear from me for awhile, but I'm doing this so we can stay alive. Phone will be off for awhile. Sorry...**

As I started to power my phone down, a text flashed at me before my screen went blank. **Bitch!**

I rolled my eyes. Mallory knew how to pick 'em.

The line moved at a snail's pace. A few times bouncers would roam up and down the line. They would pick some of the better-looking girls and lead them to the front. As the hours went by, I noticed that they would pick eight girls to two guys. I checked my phone a few times and when it was around two, the line had shortened enough so that I was finally around the corner. I watched as cars drove up and people would hop out and dash inside. It seemed like an impossible job for me to get there, much less close to Carter. But every time I considered leaving, I remembered Mallory. The image of Jeremy with his hands on her throat flashed in my mind. I couldn't go anywhere else.

I had to stay and wait it out, but two hours later when the club finally closed, I hadn't moved farther down the line. Most people left, but a few stayed like me. One of the girls in front of me told the other that celebrities would stumble out. Sometimes they would peruse the line and pick a girl to take home. Her friend squealed in excitement.

Sure enough, as everyone started to leave, celebrities swooped out just as the girl said they would. However, they didn't linger to look over the line. They had girls with them.

An hour later, after everyone had finally left, I was the last in line.

I had no idea where to go.

The bouncer from earlier came out of the door. He noticed me and frowned. He came over and asked, "You crazy, girl? What are you waiting for? We don't hand out numbers for the next night. You have to come back, and get in line. Maybe you should come earlier next time and dress a little less, if you know what I mean." He sneered at me. "You'll have no problem getting inside."

"I need to see Carter Reed."

His head went back, and he rolled his eyes. "Are you serious? You're still on this?" He laughed. "Do you know how many girls come up to me and say they know the boss? I mean, really, take a guess."

I stiffened under his amusement, but I had to endure it. This was the only way. "I do know him. He was best friends with my brother."

"Say what?"

I looked back up and spoke clearer, "He was best friends with my brother. I haven't talked to him in years, but something's happened. AJ told me to go to Carter if I ever needed something. He said he would help." My throat burned. "I have nowhere else to go."

He heaved a deep breath as he looked me up and down. Somehow, I saw a twitch of pity enter his eyes. Then he mumbled under his breath, "I can't believe I'm doing this. What was your brother's name?"

"AJ Martins."

I didn't blink. I didn't stutter. My brother's name was spoken with respect.

One of his hands came to the back of his neck as he stared again, long and hard. He rotated his head around before his hand fell abruptly back to his side. "I can't believe I'm doing this." But then he took out a radio and pressed the button. "Rogers, you still there?"

He let go of the button.

"Yeah. What's up?"

He shook his head, but he pressed it again. "Can you get a message to the boss for me?"

"What about?"

He cursed under his breath, rolling his eyes. "Can you ask him if he knows the sister of AJ Martins? I've got her on the street; she keeps asking to see the boss. She's been here all night."

"I'll radio him right now. Hold on."

The next two minutes were the longest in my life. I held my breath as I felt the bouncer's eyes on me. He never looked away and at one point muttered, "This could be my job, you know, honey. I could get canned for even asking him this question. He doesn't mess around."

I swallowed. I knew exactly who Carter really was.

Then the sound of static came over the radio before Rogers' voice replaced it with, "Boss said to bring her in and set her up in the penthouse. He's coming in quick for this one."

Relief flooded me, so much that a whimper came out of my mouth and I almost dropped to the street. My knees hadn't stopped knocking since the bouncer first radioed his colleague.

"Hey, easy there." He caught my arm as I started to fall and pulled me upright. All the disbelief and sarcasm was gone. He was the epitome of professional now and before I had a chance to thank him, he was leading me inside Octave.

The last time I'd been in there everything had been dark. My college roommate dared me. Her boyfriend was a bouncer so he snuck us inside. I'd been scared to go, but Rosalie told me that she was wet between her legs at the idea of that nightclub. When we had gotten inside, I understood what all the rage was about. There were flashing lights, but the rest of the club was completely dark. As we went through all the hallways and mazes, circling the real dance floor, there were hidden corners around every bend. More than once we would touch couples in the throes before we even knew they were there.

Once we got to the dance floor, we never left. Hypnotic beats sounded from the walls, floors, ceilings, everywhere. And since the club was so large, Rosalie and I stayed attached to the hip, but it had been worth the one night of risk. I'd never done drugs, but as we danced the entire night, I felt like I had.

A shiver of anticipation went through me as I remembered the rest of the night, but instead of the darkness from then, the club was flooded in light now. A few bartenders remained behind their counters as they were drying off their glasses and a few waitresses were huddled in another corner with a wad of cash between them. As the bouncer led me down a back hallway, a few girls whisked by us going the other way. Their hair still looked styled, and heavy make-up covered their faces. They wore the same uniform, a piece of black string that crossed all over their body. A larger piece of black cloth covered their breasts, but one girl let it hang free. Her breasts bounced as she hurried down the hallway, but all of them had a cold glint on their faces.

The bouncer murmured under his breath, "They're the dancers. They like to head home as soon as they've finished with the private boxes."

I didn't know what he meant, but nodded as if I did.

We went through a bunch of hallways, then up some stairs. When we entered a tunnel, I grabbed his arm. "Where are we going?"

The sound of traffic beneath was loud so he leaned close and kept me going. He yelled over the sound, "Boss owns the hotel behind the club. He said to take you to the penthouse so we're going to the hotel. You'll wait up there until he can get into town."

Into town? Carter wasn't even in town?

We neared the end of the tunnel and he pushed open a heavy door. As it slammed shut behind us, everything was suddenly quiet.

Too quiet. Red plush carpet lined a hallway that had gold trimmings on the doors. There was even gold on the doorknobs. I tried to remember what hotel was connected to the back of Octave but couldn't. It looked expensive.

The bouncer took me to the elevators. A man was inside, wearing a grey uniform. No words were exchanged, but he pressed a button at the top. Then we waited. We went up ten floors before the doors slid open to expose a hallway with a bench and one door to the side. The man from the elevator halted the doors before he walked past us. He opened the room for us and returned to the elevator. The doors slid closed, but the bouncer didn't move from the hallway.

I looked at him in question. What was he doing?

He gestured to the room. "You're supposed to go inside."

"What about you?"

He indicated the wall. "I wait until you leave."

Oh.

And then I went inside to wait for Carter Reed.

FOUR

I walked into the penthouse with my heart pounding, my chest tight, and my hands ice cold. They should've been sweating. I felt like I was having a heart attack.

I drew in a deep breath. Was this what I really wanted to do? Carter Reed was a killer. He was connected to the mob. I never knew how important he was to the Mauricio Family, but I knew he was powerful. AJ had always known that Carter would be someone. He boasted about it to me. He would tell me that Carter was going places, that he had the smarts to make a name for himself. Well, he had—a big name.

The place was huge, but none of the lights were on. For some reason, I didn't have the urge to search for a light switch. Through the glass patio doors, the moonlight shone inside and highlighted some couches that were in a circle, set below the rest of the penthouse in a middle valley. A fireplace was beside one of the couches. I doubted it was a real one, certainly looked like one, but I didn't know how that was possible in a hotel. I stepped down the two steps and curled into a ball on one of the couches. Then I hugged a pillow to my chest and waited.

My heart was still pounding. It hadn't slowed down in days.

I didn't know how long I waited. It felt like hours, it could've been minutes. My phone was with me. I could've checked the time, but I was reluctant to turn it on. After Ben's last message, I had turned it on and off at random moments, but it had remained off since the guard took me inside Octave. For some reason, I enjoyed the silence. Though I was scared and my pulse was still skyrocketing, I drew in another shuddering breath and felt something else. Sheltered. I felt safe, holed away in some glitzy penthouse. It was a relief to be away from what happened and what I had done.

The first tear dropped to my hand. I stared at it, detached from myself. I hadn't realized I was crying and I didn't feel it on my hand. My hands were folded over the pillow, and as I stared, more tears joined it.

How could I cry and not feel it?

I couldn't take my eyes from the growing wet spot on the pillow. It was soaked before long, and then exhaustion settled in. My eyelids grew heavy and I couldn't keep them open. My head went down, but I jerked back upright. The pillow was clasped tighter to my chest and I sat as straight as I could. It didn't matter. My head fell backwards this time and I caught myself at the last moment. I gasped again and tried to stand, but after I swayed and started to fall, I grasped the top of the couch and then gave in.

My head rested on that soaked pillow and I curled around it. It wasn't long before I faded away.

Something woke me, and I stirred briefly, but sleep overtook me again. I folded back into the darkness. My bones thanked me. Then something woke me again. My eyes flicked open and I saw a dark silhouette. It stood above me. An alarm in the back of my mind told me to wake up, defend myself, but my body didn't heed the alert. I slipped back into a deep slumber. It was heavy. It was welcoming, and I succumbed to it.

When I woke again, it was still dark out. That couldn't be, but I saw a clock in the corner. It said 8:00 o'clock. I had come in around four in the morning and it wasn't eight in the morning now. I drew in a breath; I had slept through the entire day. Scrambling, I searched my pockets. No phone. Panic pressed tight into my chest as I ran my hands over the couch cushions, then around and underneath them. Still nothing. I sat upright and peered into the darkness. Where had my phone gone? It wasn't on me, it wasn't in the couch. I dropped to my knees and felt on the floor. Again, nothing. Then I started to fumble around until I found a lamp. When I tried to switch it on, no light came out of it.

Was it broken? But no, it couldn't have been.

"Where were you when AJ was mugged?"

The voice came from above me and behind me. I knelt on the

floor as my heart started to pound. Oh god. What was this? My phone was gone. The place was in darkness on purpose. Carter didn't trust me? I sucked in a breath. Was he going to kill me?

He repeated, even quieter, "Where were you when AJ was mugged?"

Thump. Thump. Thump.

My hands started to shake again and my palms grew sweaty. I rubbed them over my pants and opened my mouth, but nothing came out. A choked sound ripped from me.

"I asked you a question."

My eyes clasped shut. He had stood, wherever he was. I could tell it was him, but his voice was colder. I'd known him most of my life, but I'd never feared him. This was the Cold Killer. He was in the same room as me. I had sought this out.

"He wasn't."

I waited. One second.

Then two. Then a minute.

He was so quiet. "Who mugged your brother?"

I spat out, "He wasn't mugged. He was killed."

My chest was heaving as I remembered that day. A sick helpless feeling came over me. I couldn't do anything. I wanted to, I wanted so desperately, but AJ shook his head. He didn't want me to help, but for a moment I considered it. I thought about crawling out from behind the vent so I could die with him, but I knew they would've done something worse to me. So I stayed.

The old sobs were there again. I felt them climbing up, ready to come out again. I gritted my teeth and pushed them back down. I wouldn't cry, not here, not if this Carter Reed was going to kill me. He wasn't the same guy that I remembered. That Carter never would've done this to me, set me up, isolated me, and then started an interrogation.

"How?"

"How what?" Anger was starting to boil in me now. How dare he?

"How did he die?" He never reacted. His voice grew colder, quieter, each time he asked. He wasn't human. He didn't sound like it.

"With a bat!" I yelled at the dark room. "A fucking bat. They killed him with a fucking bat and I saw the whole thing."

I bent over and pressed my forehead to my knees. I had hoped that they would be cold, that they would cool me off, but they weren't. My jeans were warm and sweaty. I could smell traces of blood still on them, though I had showered...hadn't I? I didn't remember anymore. Was Mallory's blood still on me or was that Jeremy's? Was their blood ingrained with me now? I gasped for breath. A part of me wanted to still have Jeremy's blood on me. He deserved to die again. He deserved to die a worse way than a bullet to the head.

I didn't know how long I stayed like that. The room remained in silence and then it was flooded with light.

I fell to the side and closed my eyes against how sudden it was. It blinded me. When I opened them, with my chest still heaving and my heart still pounding, I still wasn't ready to see him. But there he was. Carter Reed.

I stopped all thinking, all feeling, as I took in the sight of him.

He was perched against the glass wall, his arms folded over his chest, and his icy eyes focused on me. They were piercing blue, like a wolf's, and he never blinked. Not when I roamed over the rest of him. His dirty blonde hair had been kept long when we were kids. He would tuck it behind his ears and let it grow until an inch above his shoulders. That's how he liked it, he told me once. It was cut short now, but it suited him. A vacuum effect had taken over my oxygen. I couldn't seem to get enough as I realized that the last few times I had seen him didn't do him justice, not when I saw him up close and personal now. His high cheekbones led to an angular face, which moved to lips that seemed perfect. He had long eyelashes that were curled with a natural perfection that females longed to have. He straightened against the wall, but still remained against it. His shirt slid across his chest and shoulders, across the canvas of muscles. He had sculpted his body into a weapon. He had done it on purpose.

Shit. He was perfect. And he was a killer.

I wet my lips and then gasped as I realized what I had done. I couldn't have done that, not here. No way. But I had, and a small smirk appeared on his face. He knew the reaction he was getting from me. I tried to stomp it all down, but it didn't. I became wet between my legs and a slow throb started.

I tore my eyes from his. It took a concerted effort from me, but then a low, smooth chuckle came from him. "No one knows how AJ died except his sister. I needed to make sure it was you."

He had to make sure? He was wary of *me*? The irony wasn't lost on me. He was the killer. I was not. But no, I sobered at that thought. I was a killer too.

"Yeah, well...it's me."

He pushed up from the wall and strolled around to the openings of the couches, two steps above me. He gazed down at me, and then gave me a brisk nod. "Stand up."

I did. Reluctantly.

His eyes slid up and down me. It was an intense perusal, slow and steady. He didn't miss a thing. His eyes lingered on my knee, where I knew some of my tears had fallen before I stopped them. Then he instructed, in that same cold and detached voice, "Turn around."

My eyes shot to his. "No."

"Turn around, Emma."

Waves of desire washed over me when he said my name. I gasped against them. I didn't want them, I didn't want that. I sucked in my breath, he couldn't know. Clenching my jaw, I turned my hands into fists and pressed them against me. I willed my own body not to betray me, but I still turned around. Different waves of humiliation came next. I was the cow being led to slaughter. I felt poked and prodded as he continued his silent inspection of me.

"You've lost weight." He waved to the kitchen. "There's pizza up there, if you'd like."

I clamped my mouth shut. My stomach growled and I salivated at the mention of food. When had I eaten last? I couldn't remember—in the diner, after we had killed Jeremy. No, after *I* had killed him. I had tried to make myself eat something, but I couldn't. I needed something in my stomach, but anything else would've been vomited. I filled it up with coffee instead.

I moved past him for the food, but he caught my arm and pressed me against him.

"No!" I didn't want to be touched. The image of Mallory being hurt flared through me, and I yanked my arm back, but he wouldn't let go. Then I was lifted and pushed against a wall. He held me trapped in his arms. "I said no!" I tried to lift my legs to kick him, but he had me paralyzed within his hold. As I seethed and lunged at him, only my stomach lifted from the wall. It didn't matter. He held my arms above my head, and moved them both into only one of his hands. His legs were pressed against mine. I couldn't move at all now. My heart was racing, but I whimpered. My breathing grew shallow and the ache between my legs was almost unbearable now.

He lifted back, just an inch, and looked up and down my body.

My chest kept heaving. He could see my breasts through my shirt, but he didn't touch them. I bit down on my lip. I wanted him to touch them. I wanted the feel of his hand there, but I couldn't ask that. I couldn't let him know. A small whimper slipped past, and his eyes shot to mine. A small flicker of shock was there. It was gone instantly.

Then he stepped back. As soon as his hands released me, I crumbled to the floor. I should've kicked at him, something so he would know not to do that again, but he was quicker than me. He always had been. He would've done it again. I would've been pressed against the wall once more and my body couldn't handle that. Everything was a mess inside of me.

He moved back a step. "What's happened to you, Emma?"

I couldn't look away from him. He held me captive. My heart wouldn't stop racing.

"You're like a feral cat."

My knees came to my chest and I wrapped my arms around them. With a groan, I tucked my forehead against them. I wanted everything to go away. I wanted my brother back. I wanted no Jeremy in Mallory's life. And I didn't want Carter to have become this man in front of me. Shame filled me next as the throb picked up again. God, how could I want this man? He was cold, detached. He killed others.

So have you. A nagging thought whispered in the back of my mind.

The pizza box was thrown beside me. The smell overwhelmed me. My mouth salivated again and my stomach clenched. I reached for it without thinking. I shoveled a slice into my mouth, then tried to get more in. I was so hungry.

After the third slice, I choked back the vomit. My stomach growled again, but in agony this time. Then I shot to my feet and looked around, panicked as I felt more vomit spew inside of my closed mouth.

Carter pointed to a side door and I burst through it the next second. I fell to my knees around the toilet and emptied everything back out. More and more kept coming up, even more and I wondered how that was possible. There was nothing in my stomach. It was like my body wanted to erase everything as much as I did.

When I stopped, with my mouth covered in vomit, I rested my forehead against the lid and gasped for breath. I felt so weak, so helpless in that moment.

A glass of water was placed beside me. A gentle hand brushed some of my hair back as Carter lowered himself to the ground. He gazed back at me, but this time it was the old Carter. The killer from before was gone. He gave me a small grin. "I'll take care of you."

Relief soared through me and my body gave way. But before I slid to the floor in a crumbled heap again, he caught my arm and hoisted me to his lap. Then as I curled into him, his hand went back to my hair and he brushed it back. Slowly, with my heart still pounding, I rested my head against his chest and felt his other arm came around me.

Finally.

Carter cleaned me up. He lifted me, sat me on the bathroom counter, gave me mouthwash, and held the glass so I could spit it out. After I was given more water, he carried me back to the kitchen table. This time, he gave me the crust from one of the pizza slices. With stern instructions to nibble on it, he left for awhile.

I didn't know what he did, or where he disappeared to. I knew he was in the penthouse, I could hear him on the phone, but that was all I cared about. He wasn't leaving so I picked up the crust and started to do as he said. I nibbled on the piece of bread until the entire thing was gone. Then I waited, and when nothing came up this time, I grabbed another piece of pizza. This time I tore some of the toppings off and nibbled on those.

I almost groaned at how good they tasted.

It'd been so long since I had real food inside of me.

"How are you feeling?"

He stood beside the counter, watching me. A blank expression was on his face and I couldn't stop the shiver down my back. He was a stranger again. This was the Carter that I didn't know, and I wondered where the old one went before I remembered the phone call. It must've been the phone call that changed him.

"I'm fine."

He frowned and took the seat across from me.

He moved like a ghost and folded into the seat with a grace of a panther, one that stirred with purpose.

"What are you thinking, Emma?"

I jerked at my name. It was foreign to me. The sensual way he had spoken before was gone. It was then that I realized he had done it on purpose. He wanted to invoke desire within me so he had. Was everything about him a weapon? His voice, his eyes, his body, his mind?

I looked down at my plate. "You've changed."

"Yes," he sighed. "I suppose I have. Things were," he hesitated, "easier back then."

I looked back up.

He amended, "Relatively speaking, I guess."

"You guess?" Anger flared up in me. AJ had been addicted to gambling and drugs. He owed the mob money and they killed him because of it. Our parents had been absent since before I could remember, and Carter hadn't had it easier. With a drunk as a father and an addict as a mother, he spent most of his nights on our couch. For as long as I could remember, he always had bruises when he would come over.

I spat out, "You must be remembering things differently than me. Things never got easier, it just changed."

A small chuckle set the hairs on the back of my neck upright. He sat back in his chair. "Things were easier for me, Emma. I didn't have to worry about killing people."

My eyes narrowed. "Are you trying to scare me?"

He leaned forward. "I'm not the same boy who needs somewhere to sleep anymore. Looks to me like our roles have changed, Emma." A hard wall slipped over his face. "Why don't you tell me the real reason you're here? You sought me out. Here I am. What's your crisis?"

I sucked in my breath. If only it were that easy. I shook my head. "Are you kidding me?"

"Did I say something to offend you?" A faint glimmer of a smile flared, but it was gone. His eyes fell flat again. "You came to me. You tell me why."

I opened my mouth.

"And you can drop your attitude. I don't tolerate it from my men. I won't tolerate it from you, whether you knew me in the past or not."

I closed my mouth and sat there stunned. He was right. I wouldn't talk like this to another in his position. The Carter I had known was no longer. I saw that now. I realized that now. Pushing up from the table, I knew I'd made a mistake. "I'm sorry. I need to go."

"Stop," he ordered.

I fell back down, but it wasn't because I made a conscious decision. My body reacted to his command. He said it and I obeyed. I sat for a second, blinking in a daze, as I comprehended what happened. It was so instant, so quick.

As anger boiled again, I leaned forward. I was ready with a scathing comment, but he sighed.

His eyes softened. "I haven't heard from AJ's little sister in ten years. I'd like to know the reason you're here now."

Oh.

All the anger, resentment, and foolish feelings vanished. I remembered my reason and the nightmare flooded back. Panic and desperation were my friends again. They clung to me. I struggled to find the words. When my arm started to shake, he seemed to grow colder. His eyes darkened and anger stirred in them.

"Who hurt you, Emma?" His voice was sensual, but there was an underlining tone of icy disdain.

Fresh shivers wracked me. My eyes clasped shut. What had I done to him? I felt his hatred. It gutted me.

"I can't help you if you don't tell me what happened."

I choked out, "But maybe you'll hurt me."

"I would never hurt you."

"Promise?" I held my breath. I was depending on him, everything centered on him. Mallory needed him. I needed him.

"I promise."

Relief washed over me and I sagged in my chair. My throat choked up. Then I whispered, in a hoarse voice, "I did something."

He nodded.

My insides tightened. I couldn't say it. It'd be real, but I already had said it out loud. Still, Carter was different. Once he knew, I couldn't undo whatever would happen next.

"What did you do?" He softened his tone.

He was persuading me now. He wanted me to confide in him. If only it were that easy. I could just open up and share my problems to him, but no. Was this the right decision? Could I trust him? I didn't know him anymore. He was the Cold Killer. I hadn't known that man from before. I only knew the boy he'd been.

"Emma."

I looked at him. The tears blurred him in my vision.

"I know you're debating whether or not to tell me what happened, but if you're here with me then I'm your only choice. I know you. I remember the smart girl you were. I was always proud of how you handled yourself. You were a survivor, all those years ago. I knew it then. I know it now." He leaned forward. A glimmer of the old Carter shone through to me. "You have to tell me. I won't hurt you. I've already promised you that."

I nodded. He was right. He was so right. He was the only one. But I couldn't look at him. I hung my head and whispered, "I killed someone."

"Who?"

There was no reaction. Just a question. The ball of fear in me loosened. "He was hurting my roommate."

"Who did you kill, Emma?"

He said my name so that it felt like he was caressing me with it. I relaxed a bit more. It was easier to speak. "He was raping her when I went into the apartment." Then, I closed up. I couldn't say. He was the mob. Carter was the mob. Carter would hand me over.

"Who was raping your roommate?"

I shook my head again. "I can't say it."

"You have to." Gone was the softness. He had hardened again.

I jerked back in my chair. The stranger sat across from me once more. Now I knew for sure, I had to get out of there. I tried to swallow over the knot of terror that was lodged in my throat again. I looked for the door. I could make it—there was a guard out there. My eyes swung back to Carter. I would have to stop him. He couldn't alert the guard about me. But how? I had no idea.

His phone rang from a room. He must've left it. When he turned, I bolted for the door. It was my only chance.

He caught me around the waist. I made it to him, but that was as far as I got. As he picked me up with one iron-clad arm, he said over my struggles, "You're being ridiculous, Emma."

I kicked harder. "Let me go!"

"No."

My arm fought free and swung at him, but he deflected the blow and adjusted so he held both of my arms against my side. He carried me into a bedroom. I tried kicking backwards towards his groin, but he just grunted and moved his thigh so it was wedged between my legs. As I kicked again, he raised his leg higher so I was straddling him. My feet swung, but only touched air now. I was helpless so I used my last resort. My head went forward and then, as I bit my lip, I rammed it backwards.

"Oomph." He twisted to the side, a low chuckle sounded into my ear.

"Agh!" I tried hitting my head to the side, but I didn't have the angle to do any damage. "Carter! Let me go!"

As he chuckled again, he sat down on the bed while he still held me in his arms. My back was pressed against him and he tightened his arms around me. One shifted up so he could use his shoulder to keep my head close to the side of his. I couldn't do a thing. Then he murmured into my ear, his breath caressing me, "You're still the fighter AJ raised. He'd be proud."

That sent another burst of fight through me. I tried wiggling, thrusting, but nothing. He sat and held me until I stopped. I had moved lower on his lap somehow. "Let me go, Carter. Please."

In a flash he twisted and I was on the bed now. He straddled me instead, with his legs on each of mine and my hands were raised above my head. He held them with one of his, leaving his other free to grab my chin. He forced me to look at him as he loomed above me. His body wasn't pressed down on me. He held himself in the air and stayed there, suspended, as he searched into me. I felt him trying to pierce my thoughts so I closed my eyes.

His hand gentled on my chin and he whispered, "Emma. Please."

Oh god. Something coursed through me at his softness. I looked without thinking and was caught by his gaze. He had captured me, my body and mind. As a sob rose in my throat, my body betrayed me. It softened underneath his holds. The fight was leaving me and it was being replaced with desire. I was aware of the few inches that separated us. A throb started between my legs. It wanted him to press there, against my core. It was starting to ache.

As my body weakened, so did his holds. His legs moved to rest beside my legs, one of his knees remained pressed between mine. I fought to keep from squirming. I wanted his knee to move further up. I wanted to press down on it. Then I gasped as I felt a gentle nudge under my chin. As I blinked through a sudden onslaught of tears, he moved further up the bed so his face was above mine. He lowered so I felt his breath against my lips. His eyes were raking over me; a few lines were wrinkled around them as he looked with concern. A small frown appeared over his mouth.

"Tell me what happened." His plea was so soft.

I broke. This wasn't the stranger anymore. This was Carter, the boy I had grown up with. I flung my arms around him and pulled him down. Instead of fighting, I clung to him now.

He wrapped his arms around me and rolled to his side. He patted my back and tucked his head into the crook of my neck and shoulder. I felt his lips brush there as he repeated, "You have to tell me. I won't hurt you. I will protect you."

A shudder went through my body. At last. Those were the words I was desperate for. He moved his hands, one sliding down to my hip and the other cradling the back of my head, he pressed into me. The last of my reserve fled then. A gasp escaped me and I pressed against him. I needed him.

"Emma."

Shame flooded me. He knew. What kind of person was I? Fighting, running away, and then starting to tremble in his arms?

His hand started to caress my hip. His fingers slid underneath my shirt and moved under my pants' waistband. He held me there, his hand splayed out. I tried to resist, but I wanted to wind my legs around him. I wanted to pull him on top of me and feel his hand between my legs. But I didn't do anything. I lay there, still, as my heart pounded inside of me. He could feel the beat against him. The thumping drowned everything else out.

He pressed a soft kiss to my forehead and raised himself up again. He looked down at me. The plea in his eyes was still there. As he brushed some of my hair from my forehead, he asked, "Do you not trust me?"

I nodded. "I'm scared of you."

A small grin appeared at the corners of his mouth. "You are?"

"I don't know who you are anymore." I couldn't believe I was admitting any of that, but I needed to trust someone. I had to if I was going to survive what I had done. Feeling a little bit brave, I touched his chest. My hand spread out like his was on my back. His heart was steady. I murmured, "I know who you are. I know you're the Cold Killer. I know what you did for AJ." A tear slipped from the corner of my eye. It fell unheeded. "I always wanted to thank you for that."

He tensed. "You need to tell me who you killed."

I'd been looking at his lips, wondering distantly what they would feel like pressed to mine, when I heard the cold tone in him again. All the warmth and desire fled from me. I tensed as well and my gaze snapped back to his. My chest surged up in a small gasp as I saw nothing in his eyes. There was no amusement, no softening, nothing.

He was the stranger again.

My hand fell away from his chest. I lay beneath him, but he retracted his touches from me. He scooted to sit on the edge of the bed.

My chest started to ache. He couldn't leave. I needed him.

"Enough with the games, Emma. Tell me who you killed." He turned back. His eyes were like ice again. "I would like to help you. You and AJ were my family. I would do anything for you, but you're wasting my time."

He was right.

I sat up and moved so my back rested against the headboard. It was time. The new Carter and my old Carter were the same person. I didn't need to be scared of this new one. He was the ruthless one, the one that I needed help from. "I killed Jeremy Dunvan."

He clipped out, "Where?"

"In my apartment."

His head nodded once. "Stay here." And then he left.

SIX

Carter was gone for a long time. I waited, but after I ate a little bit more, I curled up on the bed. As soon as I pulled the comforter over me and snuggled into the pillow, I was out. I had never fallen asleep so fast. When I woke, the penthouse was still dark. He hadn't come back. That affected me more than I wanted to admit, even to myself. But, with a stab of disappointment and something more, I looked around for my phone. When I found it along with my purse, I headed out.

I didn't know what to do. He said to wait, but for how long. I couldn't sit around for too long. What if he never came back?

I sucked in my breath as pain sliced through me. He said he'd protect me, but if he never came back, did that mean I was on my own? Either way, I'd been away from Mallory for too long. She needed to know that we would need to make our own decisions. We'd have to leave. That was all there was. It was the last resort, but we were out of choices. Carter had been a long shot. I could see that now.

When I stepped out of the penthouse, there was no guard. That only reaffirmed my decision. Carter had changed his mind. We were on our own.

When I got into the elevator, I remembered that we hadn't come from the lounge so I wasn't sure which button to push. There was a B and a 1, so I pushed the B to take me to the bottom floor. We had come in from the nightclub, a back entrance. I didn't think I could find my way back that way, but when the doors slid open, I saw that I was still lost. B didn't stand for bottom floor. It was the basement. I stepped out but then thought better of it—too late. The elevator closed behind me, and when I pushed the button again, it didn't open back up again. After waiting another five minutes, I realized the doors weren't going to open so I turned to peruse the basement.

Standard basement. Grey cement, big posts, and lots of shiny expensive-looking cars. I walked down an aisle and caught sight of a red sign in the far corner. Exit. With a sigh of relief, I headed that way. When I got to the door, it was massive and heavy, but I pushed through. I found another small set of stairs in front of me and felt a bit like Dorothy with the yellow-bricked road. However, as I went up two flights of stairs, I heard sounds from the street coming from behind an un-marked door. I shoved it open, slipped through, and found myself in a back alley. Heading to the closest road, I was where I had been two nights ago. There was a line to get into Octave. I recognized a few of the same people in that line, even the two girls who had hoped to get picked up by celebrities. They had the same eager look of desperation on their faces. One of them eyed me up and down, but as a sneer came to her face, I turned and walked the other way. I didn't need to return to Octave. I had already gotten my answer.

I took a cab, and when it pulled in front of Ben's, I heaved a deep breath. I didn't want to go in there. I didn't want to look in her eyes and see the agony that Jeremy had put in them. I didn't want to tell her that we would need to leave, but I had to. There was no other choice.

Since the door was locked, I knocked.

Ben swept open the door, a fierce scowl on his face. "Where the fuck have you been?"

I cringed.

He had a butcher knife in his hand with a death grip.

"Have you had problems?"

"Oh, you mean Mallory's nightmares and blood-curdling screams? No. No problems at all, except wait. You! Her roommate and best friend took off, didn't tell us where you were going, and she thought you had deserted her." After I stepped inside, he slammed the door shut. His scowl deepened. "Nice fucking friend you are, Emma."

"Emma?"

A timid whimper came from the living room. Mallory stood there, wrapped in a blanket. Her hair was messed, some of it stood up and the other side was frizzy. There were bags underneath her eyes and her lip, still bruised from him, started to tremble.

"Mallory." I wrapped my arms around her. I wanted to reassure her that we'd be alright. No matter how far we had to go, we'd be alive.

Her whole body started to shake as I hugged her. More sobs came out, and I could only hold her tighter. My hand smoothed her hair as I rocked her back and forth.

She grabbed onto me. Her hands formed into fists around my shirt. As tight as I was holding her, she clung to me even tighter.

"Please don't leave again."

I shook my head. "I won't. I promise."

Ben stood in the doorway of the kitchen, watching us. His scowl softened and showed his fear. Then his eyes darkened into something that looked like panic before he turned away. The sink was turned on later and sounds of doing the dishes came next.

"She hasn't been sleeping much." I saw Amanda in the bedroom doorway. She gave me a sad smile, but I saw the same exhaustion that Ben had. She was in a blue tee shirt and a different pair of jeans. When she noticed that I was looking at her clothes, she lifted a shoulder up before she crossed her arms over her chest. "I went to work yesterday and grabbed some clothes for everyone." She glanced towards the kitchen. "Ben didn't go in. He was too scared to leave her. Every time she tries to sleep, she only gets an hour. Always wakes up screaming from what...," she hesitated, "he did to her."

Ben cleared his voice behind us. A towel was clenched in both of his hands now. "Can you get her to sleep a little?"

Amanda looked back at me. She shifted on her feet, uncomfortably. "She needs you or me to be with her. I've been..." She glanced over her shoulder at Ben. "Ben's tried, but she won't let him touch her. So I've been..."

I got it. My stomach twisted, but I nodded and led Mallory towards the bedroom. After an hour of lying in bed with her, holding her, she fell asleep. I waited another hour to make sure she stayed asleep. Her breaths were even and deep so I snuck out. When I went to the kitchen, Ben looked exhausted in a chair. His shoulders drooped down, and he had bags under his own eyes. A cup of coffee sat in front of him, but when I touched it, it was cold.

His coffee pot was empty. "You want another pot started?"

He jerked his head up, as if seeing me for the first time. "Oh.

Uh. Yeah. Thanks." He ran a hand over his face, waking himself up. "She's asleep?"

I dumped the little bit of coffee left down the sink and refilled it with water. "Yeah. It took an hour."

He nodded.

"Is Amanda still here?"

"No." The exhaustion had turned into a glaze over his eyes. "She went home for a break. She'll be back tomorrow. I think she said something about getting new clothes or something."

After pouring the water in his coffee pot, I rummaged through his cupboards, looking for his coffee grounds. "And maybe food." His cupboards were sparse except the huge bin of ground coffee beans. I put two healthy scoops in the machine and hit the button. It wasn't long before it started to gurgle to life.

"Yeah, I haven't gone to the grocery store in awhile. I've been too nervous..." He trailed off, lost in thought as he stared at the table.

"Too scared to leave?"

He jerked his head in a nod. "Yeah." A sad laugh left him. "I'm a grown man, and I'm terrified. I can't step out the door. I'm afraid they're out there, that they know, they're watching. And her." He glanced in Mallory's direction. "I can't touch her. I tried to help her when she asked. She didn't want his touch, but now it's mine that disgusts her."

"No, it's not. It's his. Trust me. You did help her. You *are* helping her."

He lifted stricken eyes to me. "I've been an asshole to you. Why are you being nice to me?"

I shrugged but huddled back in my chair. I understood. "Because you want to help her but don't know how. I understand. Believe me."

He shook his head with his eyes closed. "I have no idea what to do, Emma. None whatsoever. She has to go to work. *I* have to go to work. I called and covered for us, but that'll give us a week. We have to figure out how to clean this mess up in a few more days." He looked towards the door again. "I'm so scared to go out there. You have no idea."

"I do. I really do."

Then he sighed. The momentary truce ended as he pushed up from the chair. "I'm going to clean up. That's all I've been doing. I just clean. Clean the dishes, clean the table, clean the floors. I have to do something." A bitter laugh escaped him. "I gotta clean myself. I'll be in the shower if you—if she needs me."

He was scared to step outside that door, but that was all I wanted to do. "I'm going out on the patio for some fresh air." Maybe a new idea would come to me, but as he ignored me and left, I didn't think it would come to me.

As I sat on his small patio, curled on one of his loungers, I couldn't shake the idea that maybe I should go on the run. Mallory didn't kill him. I did. He'd been hurting her. He hadn't been hurting me. She could offer me for her safety, and I would be long gone.

My stomach rolled over and over. I felt nauseous, but I hugged myself harder. My arms pressed tighter to my stomach. It didn't matter. I wasn't going to stop the unsettled feeling inside of me. It wasn't going to go away. I had tried with Carter. He left me so that gave me one other alternative. I would go away. Mallory would be safe.

With my new decision made, I was in no hurry to leave. I stayed in that chair for a long time. The night air was cold and I knew my body was shivering, but I didn't feel it. I couldn't. All I could focus on was the next step. Where would I go? How would I go? I needed money. I knew that much, but I didn't have enough set aside. My job was better than all of theirs, but it still wasn't enough. The little in my savings wouldn't be enough. Ben and Mallory both worked at a fancy clubhouse. They didn't make enough to help me at all. Amanda was a teacher. She might've had a little bit, but I knew she worked in the café during the summer to make ends meet.

I was on my own.

I sat outside for a long time. Ben came to the patio door and peered through it. When he saw me, he came out and gave me a blanket, but I didn't leave the chair. I didn't want to move, not yet, but I took the added warmth he offered. I wrapped the blanket around me, and he went back inside. The lights turned off and I was left in the dark again.

"I told you to stay put."

I gasped and jumped in my seat.

Carter appeared around the patio's corner. A fierce scowl was on his face and his eyes glittered in the moonlight. He was furious as he sat across from me. He was dressed all in black, black pants and a black sweatshirt with the hood pulled over his head. It shadowed his eyes. It made him look even more dangerous.

My throat went dry. As he had turned to pull out the chair, I saw a bulge from his back. Was that a gun? Of course, it was. This was Carter Reed. He killed. That's what he did.

"What are you doing here?" My heart picked up. If he was there, did that mean...?

"I came to get you." He leaned forward. "I told you to stay put. I came back and found you gone. I don't like that, Emma, not one bit."

I glanced towards the patio door. What if Ben came out? I didn't want him to know about Carter.

He sighed from irritation. "Are you worried about your boyfriend?"

"Ben?" I was stunned. He thought, but no—Carter was here. He was sitting across from me. I couldn't wrap my mind around that. "How did you get here?"

Determination gleamed from his eyes, but there was more. A darker intent was in there, one that made my heart beat even faster.

"You came to me for help, then you left. What did you want, Emma?"

"What did I want? I wanted you to help me."

"Why'd you think I left?" he remarked. "So I could help you."

Oh.

I fell back in my chair. Of course he had left to help me. I was an idiot. "But when I woke up, you weren't there. I..." How long was I supposed to have waited? My heart skipped a beat. What if he set me up? I was in the perfect place, left alone until he led Franco Dunvan to the front door.

"You what?" he snapped. "Let's go. You're coming with me."

"No!" I shoved back my chair and surged to my feet. I couldn't leave. Mallory—Ben—Mallory. "I can't leave, Carter. I have people depending on me."

He was around the table in a flash. His hands grasped my elbows, and he pulled me against him. He was tense. His body was hard, but I couldn't stop the soft intake of breath as I touched all of him and the same yearning from before started inside of me. I wanted to press back against him, get even closer, but I shook my head. I needed to clear those thoughts.

He bent down to me. "You think he's going to help you? You came to me, Emma. Not him." His breath caressed against my skin.

I closed my eyes. I was already softening against him.

His hands tightened and pulled me closer to him. Every inch of him was pressed against me. I felt him between my legs. He whispered as his lips were pressed against my neck now, "You killed Dunvan. It's your hands that are dirtied. Your boyfriend won't save you. Come with me. I'll protect you. I can keep you safe."

I shuddered in his arms. I wanted to go with him. Was it that easy? But no, what about Mallory? "My roommate. He was hurting her."

He shook his head. His lips clamped together on my skin. I felt his teeth scrape against my neck, just slightly.

I gasped and arched into him. I couldn't stop myself.

"She'll be safe. She didn't do anything. It was you. They'll want you and I can't protect you unless you're with me. Come with me, Emma."

Oh god. He hadn't left me. I thought he had. I thought he abandoned me, but he hadn't. The relief of that weakened me. I felt myself crumbling, but Carter held me up. His hand shifted as he slid one around my back. It moved underneath my shirt and slipped inside my pant's waistband. He kept me anchored to him with that hand.

I wanted it to move. I wanted his hands all over me.

I wanted him.

I needed to stop thinking like that. I couldn't forget my situation. My head was pressed against his chest and I opened my mouth. My own lips brushed against his sweatshirt. He shuddered from the touch as I murmured, "They'll hurt Mallory. He was hurting her, Carter. I killed him to save her. She didn't turn me over. They'll know that and they'll come for her."

He shook his head. His other hand wrapped around me. "They won't. They won't know, but you have to come with me."

"But Mallory?"

"My men have already taken care of it."

Wait, what did that mean? I tried to pull away. He wouldn't let go of me. "Carter."

He tightened his hold. His muscles twitched against me from the movement. "I have men watching your roommate. Your apartment has been cleaned. Your friend can go on with her life. Franco Dunvan won't connect his son's disappearance with her."

"So I'm free too?" My voice hitched on a sob. Hope flared inside of me.

He stopped talking. His chest moved up and down against me. His hands tightened their hold. "You need to stay with me—"

I shoved back to force a few inches of breathing space as I looked up. "You just said—"

His cold eyes glittered in the dark. They narrowed, and a shiver went over me, but I couldn't look away from his intensity. I was starting to crave it. His mouth was flat as he spoke, "I can't protect you if you're not with me. You can live your life, but I want you to live with me."

"With you?"

"Until it's over."

"Until what's over? You just said it was over."

"We don't know for sure. My men will watch over your roommate and your boyfriend, but not you. I want you near me."

"But—"

Then he clipped out, "I won't protect them unless you come with me."

"You won't?" Panic stirred inside of me again. He had said, but we needed his protection. They needed his protection. His hand reached up to cup the side of my face. I flinched. It was so tender, so gentle, but his words had been so harsh. I needed Mallory to live.

Then he whispered, "You're AJ's sister. I have to protect *you*, Emma."

Guilt speared me. He was right. AJ would've wanted that. But Mallory—I looked up. "You'll watch over my friends? Mallory will be safe?"

He nodded.

"Your men will watch her? I won't go with you unless you promise to protect her. That's my final word."

He nodded again. He was so tense. "My men will watch her, but as long as you're with me."

I knew what I had to do. "Okay, Carter. I'll come with you."

-CARTER-

Carter jogged back to the car and slipped into the backseat. He didn't look over, but felt his associate's disapproval. He didn't care. When he didn't say anything, the older associate asked, "What did you tell her?"

His reply was short. "She'll live with me."

"You're a fool."

Carter had the man against the door in a flash. His hand was at his throat and he held him paralyzed within his grip. The older man didn't fight. He knew better. Neither said a word. It was a standoff between the two and Carter waited until he sensed the acceptance in his associate. "You will express your judgment when and only when I ask for it. But with her, I will never ask for it."

He held him for another few beats before he released him. Two other guards sat in the car with them, but no one made a move or sound.

After the car traveled a few more blocks, the associate remarked as he rubbed at his throat, "I've known you a long time. I've never seen you like this."

"She's different."

"She must be."

Carter didn't respond.

The associate waited another few blocks. "What did you tell her about the others?"

"That I'll have men watching them and protect them as much as I can."

"So you lied to her." He started to scoff his disapproval again but caught himself. He straightened abruptly, his hand still at his tender throat. "You know you can't protect her friends, even if you have men watching them. The second a Bertal shows up, our men have to scatter. They can't know about our involvement. It's too soon."

"I don't care about her friends. I care about her, and she'll be safe."

"What happens when she realizes you've lied to her?"

"She'll accept it. She'll have to. The second Dunvan entered their lives, no one was safe. And when she pulled that trigger, she became the hunted. Not them."

"You sure she can handle all of this? You know how ugly it's going to get."

Carter sighed and remembered the look on her face when he saw her sleeping in the penthouse. She'd been exhausted and starving, but she'd been at peace in that moment. He hadn't the heart to wake her so when he returned and found her awake, he was a coward. He remained in the shadows as he interrogated her as he would one of his enemies. He had to know and he did. He told his associate now, "I pushed her, Gene. She has fight, more than I did when I started. She'll handle it."

She'll have to or she'll die.

Carter kept that thought to himself.

SEVEN

“I don’t understand.” Ben wrung his hand through his hair. It stuck up in the air. “You’re leaving now? It’s the first night she slept through. She didn’t scream once. Mallory needs you here.”

I looked over to the couch where she was huddling. She sniffled and wiped a tear away from her eye, but she didn’t say anything. She hadn’t said a word since I told her that we were protected. She didn’t ask me how I knew or what I meant, but she nodded. She never said a word, not even when I told her that I had to go somewhere else. But she looked away and a tear slid down. I pulled her in for a hug and tried to reassure her again.

It was so hard. I couldn’t explain. Carter didn’t want them to know about him and I didn’t want them to know either. Carter’s connection to me had to be kept a secret. I didn’t know why, but I felt it in my gut. But how did I explain things to them when I couldn’t explain anything?

Mallory had hugged me back. She’d been on the couch since.

Amanda looked confused as she sat beside Ben, who paced in the kitchen, but she remained quiet as well.

My phone vibrated. It was a text from Carter. **A car is outside for you. Take your time with your goodbyes.**

"Who was that?" Ben asked. His eyes were wild as he grabbed fistfuls of his hair again. "I don't understand this, Emma. I really don't. You need to be here for Mallory. She needs you."

"Ben," Amanda spoke up, calm and sad. "Read between the lines. She's done something for us. Emma would never leave unless she had to. Now she's saying we're safe and we don't need to worry anymore. You're not stupid. Think about it."

"But—" He stopped with his hands still in his hair. His eyes went to the living room and didn't move. "Mallory needs her. That's all I can think about."

"I'll be fine." The words were whispered and all of us whipped around. Mallory pulled the blanket tighter around her. Her eyes were wide and full of fear, and her lip trembled as she cleared her throat. It was like she was fighting for her voice. "I'll be fine. I will."

Ben started forward. Mallory held a hand up to stop him. He skidded to a halt.

Then Amanda coughed. "Well." She blinked rapidly with shock on her face. "That's that, then."

I couldn't look away from my roommate. She tried to summon a small smile. It was so tiny, but it was there. She whispered now, "I'll be fine, Ems. Don't worry. Do whatever you have to do. I know you helped us somehow."

"That's it?"

I stiffened.

Outrage came over Ben as he looked between us. "That's it?! Are you serious?"

"Ben!" Amanda chastised.

His voice softened, but his eyes were still wild. "I can't believe this. I can't believe any of this. What the hell is going on here?"

I grabbed the bag Amanda brought with clothes.

We had divided the rest earlier and left a pile in the bedroom for Mallory. Carter said she could go back to the apartment, but when I told her she could return home, she withered into a ball on the bed. I knew then that we weren't going to be roommates again, not for a long time. So I had hugged her and whispered that I would contact the landlord. I would take care of everything, the packing, getting all of her stuff put away until she knew where she was going to be. When I told Amanda those were my plans, she said she would help. She would stay for a while to help Mallory get back on her feet.

I made Mallory promise that she would go to counseling. She shuddered as I said it but nodded a second later. Then she curled back into her ball again. Amanda and I shared a look as we finished folding up her clothes, with mine already in my bag.

And here we were. Ben was freaking. Amanda was still quiet but confused. Mallory seemed to have withdrawn into her own world again.

It was time for me to go.

I walked to the front door with a heavy heart. I didn't know when I would see them again. As I reached for the handle, there was movement behind me. Tiny arms wrapped around my waist, and I turned to hug Mallory back. She whispered against my chest, "Be safe. I know you're doing this to help me."

I nodded, unable to speak. This was harder than I thought it was going to be. I squeezed her so tight.

Ben and Amanda came to the doorway. His hand was still in his hair. He hadn't let go. Amanda tried to give me a reassuring smile, but her eyes flooded with tears. She turned away. I sighed. I had to go. That was all there was to it. They would be safe, so I had to go.

"Okay." I pressed a firm kiss to Mallory's forehead before I opened the door. "Be good. Be safe."

She stood there, looking lost.

A gurgle ripped from Ben's throat. He stood gaping at me. "You're *really* going? I can't believe this."

I jerked my head in a nod. A ball of emotion was in my throat, big and too thick for me to talk again. Then I left. Tears blinded me, but I didn't brush them away. I didn't look back as I strode towards the big black car waiting for me. A driver got out and opened the car. I flung myself in and turned away from the door. I didn't look. I couldn't.

As the car pulled away, I still couldn't look back. Carter wasn't in the car waiting for me, and I was glad about that. I felt like I was going to the dark side. Even as I thought about him, my body started to throb with need. I shook my head. Carter was dangerous. He couldn't have so much power over me. When we knew Franco Dunvan wasn't going to come for me, I needed to leave him. A foreboding sensation started low in my gut. It grew the closer we got to Carter's home.

When this was all done, I would have to leave. I knew it, otherwise he would destroy me. But when the car pulled into a basement garage and stopped, my heart skipped a beat.

A rush of dark excitement went through me. The thought of living with him, being with him, sent my heart into a tailspin. He already had too much power over me.

Then the door swung open and a guard was there. He was Goliath in a dark suit. He could've been a professional wrestler with a strong jaw, bald head, and bland eyes. There were bulges underneath his suit coat. I knew enough to know those were guns. Then he indicated the elevator. "We'll show you to your new home, Miss Martins. If you would follow me."

With my bag in hand, I stepped out on unsteady knees. The door closed behind me. Another guard had shut it. He could've been a twin to the first one. He followed behind me as the car pulled away. Then we were in the elevator. The first guard pushed the top button.

"Are we..." My voice was hoarse as I asked, "Where are we?"

The first guy turned to me. "You're at Mr. Reed's private residence. You have the top floor."

My eyes bugged out. The top floor? As in...the whole floor? "Does he own the whole building?"

"Yes, ma'am."

There were six buttons in the elevator. This building had six floors to it? I knew Carter was powerful, but how powerful was he really? He owned an entire building as a home, in a city where no one owned a home like this.

When the elevator stopped and the doors opened, it was similar in layout to the penthouse. A small hallway led from the elevator to a door. A bench, light, and mirror were in the hallway with an opened closet to the side. Empty hangers hung in the closet. As both guards crossed the hallway and stood at each end of the bench, I wondered if it was the same set-up as before. They stayed until I left? But the other guard was gone when I left Carter's penthouse.

"You can go on in, ma'am." The first one gestured to the door. His arms crossed in front of him and his shoulders relaxed in his dark suit.

I took a deep breath and went inside.

Unlike the penthouse, which had been housed in darkness, this floor was bathed in light. The floors were marble white, the walls white behind bright wall decorations. A long table was in the middle of the room. It was also white. All of the walls were floor to ceiling windows. The city spread out around me as I circled around the floor. I couldn't believe that this was where I would be living.

A stairway led down at one end to the floors below. The entire building was brightly lit.

Then I looked around my floor again. There were two bedrooms. Each of them had a private bath. I had my own living room set-up with two white couches around a fireplace that had candles inside of it.

"How were the goodbyes?"

I swung around. Carter stood at the top of the stairs. Gone was the dark sweatshirt and pants. He was dressed in a pristine-looking suit now. It was grey with blue lines that matched the blue in his eyes to perfection. A tie enhanced the colors even more.

My mouth watered. "You look nice."

He frowned. "You don't want to talk about your goodbyes?"

I drew in a breath and looked away. "Are you going somewhere?"

He sighed, but then moved towards me. "I have some meetings I have to get to."

Of course. That made sense. I had waited until Amanda returned after work to say my goodbyes. He was in the mob. Their work probably happened during night-time hours. "Oh. Okay."

His frown deepened. "I'll be back in the morning. If you need food or anything, you can ask Thomas or Mike."

"Those are the big guys out there?"

"Yeah." A small grin appeared.

I drew in my breath. His face transformed, even from that small change. I had seen it before, but it was still startling to see it again.

He was beautiful—there was no other way to put it. His eyes darkened as he heard my reaction. He moved a step closer and reached for me.

I reacted, stepping away from him, before I realized what I had done. I gritted my teeth together. I wanted his touch, but I feared his touch at the same time. A storm exploded inside of me from the dueling needs.

His hand retracted to his side. "Okay." His smile softened. "If you need anything, you can call me." He gestured to the long table behind me. "There's a new phone there for you. It's safer for you to use that one, not your old one. Your old could be—someone could be listening in."

Oh. My brows furrowed together. Did that mean Dunvan knew it was me?

"It's just safer. Use this new one."

I looked back and was caught. I couldn't look away. He had moved closer to me, within touching distance now. His voice grew quiet. "Franco Dunvan has no idea about your involvement. I have a phone company that'll keep your line safe. I can't guarantee that with your other phone. This would be a favor to me. It'll make me worry less about you."

I jerked my head in a nod. I was overwhelmed with so many emotions.

"Emma," my name came from him in a soft whisper. He reached out and his hand slid to the back of my neck. He cupped my head and then stepped closer, almost pressing against me.

I closed my eyes as I felt him. My arms twitched. I wanted to wrap them around him and pull him to me, but I couldn't. So I hugged myself harder. I hadn't even realized I'd been hugging myself from the beginning. He pressed into me. His breath teased against my lips as his forehead rested on mine.

His other hand lifted and thumbed the corner of my lips.

I gasped, my mouth parted.

His thumb slipped inside, just an inch.

Before I could stop myself, my tongue darted out and swiped against it.

He whispered again, "Emma." He drew in his own breath, tensing against me.

"Sir." A different voice broke us apart.

Carter's eyes were dark with desire as he stared at me, but then he cleared his throat. "Be right there, Gene."

"Sir." And then the door shut beneath us.

"I have to go."

I nodded, trembling before him.

He groaned and reached for me. Instead of feeling his lips against mine, where I wanted them, he pressed them to my forehead. He whispered against me, "I'm glad you're here. AJ would've wanted me to look out for you."

He tore himself away and was gone within seconds. I was left in a mess behind him.

Was that all he was doing this for? For AJ?

My phone vibrated in my pocket. I pulled it out and saw it was a text from Amanda. **Ben keeps walking in circles. He can't understand any of this. We ordered a pizza and he pulled a knife on the kid. Or he tried. It fell and almost sliced his toes. He's a bumbling idiot. What did you leave me with?**

I grinned. **Make him go for a walk tomorrow. It would do him good, Mals too. Good luck. Hide the knives.**

Now you tell me. Hope you're ok wherever you are.

I struggled for a second. My hands shook, but then I took a deep breath. Everything would be fine. I knew it. **I am. You too. Take care of Mals for me.**

Will do.

After I looked at the new phone Carter left for me, I texted her the number and said I'd be using that number from now on. When she said that she had programmed it in and would give it to Mallory, I relaxed a little. She hadn't questioned it. I'd been worried about that, but Amanda and Mallory hadn't questioned a lot of what I had done over the last week. They trusted me. That was the truth. They knew I would take care of them, and I had.

I looked around my new home.

I shook my head. This was my new life, at least for now. With that final thought, I grabbed my bag and went in search of my bedroom. My priorities were to shower and then get a good night of sleep. Everything could go back to a normal routine.

But as I went into the master bedroom and saw the king-sized bed in front of me, I just wondered what my new normal routine would be. I didn't think it would be anything like my old life.

My first night was spent in a restless sleep. I didn't know when Carter would come back. I didn't know what he expected of me. Did he expect something more? Was I in his home for a reason, other than to keep me safe? I had closed my bedroom door, but when he got home I didn't know if he would come to me. Or maybe I wasn't there for that? Every time I thought I heard something, I jerked awake and my heart would start hammering in my chest. Then nothing would happen, so I would relax back in bed.

The last time I looked at the clock it was nearing five in the morning. When I woke, groggy, it was after eight in the morning. Three full hours of sleep. I looked around the spacious room, and everything rushed back at me. I sat upright, fully awake with no grogginess at all.

Unsure what to do or where to go, I slipped on a robe from the closet and headed downstairs after finishing in the bathroom. As I rounded to the second floor, I heard water running and coffee brewing. Then came the smell of bacon, causing my nose to twitch and my stomach to growl.

When I reached the kitchen, I braked. Instead of the grey suit from the night before, Carter stood in front of the stove in jeans and a plain tee shirt.

My mouth watered, and not from the food. Tee shirts had never looked that good before. Then my eyes widened as I realized what I was thinking. I'd never learn.

"Good morning," he drawled, relaxed and composed. He had showered and his hair was still wet so the ends curled a little bit.

It was adorable.

Then I grinned to myself. Carter Reed was not adorable. Hot and dangerous, but not adorable.

"What is it?"

I shook my head. "It's nothing."

"Take a seat." He indicated a counter. "Would you like some breakfast?"

I saw a box of Wheaties, bagels, orange juice, and a few eggs on the counter. "Breakfast of champions?"

He grinned at me. A bolt of warmth went through me. Goodness. I needed to get a handle on myself. It was moving into the pathetic zone.

"I was at the gym this morning. Breakfast helps me fuel up for the day. Help yourself." He caught my eyes. "To anything."

The gun at a horserace went off and there went my heart. It was thundering like a herd of hooves. I managed out, "Uh, coffee?"

His grin widened. He knew full well what he was doing to me, but he turned towards the stove again. "Or I could make you an omelet?"

"Oh. Uh." My stomach rumbled, but I shook my head. "Coffee is usually my breakfast, or a breakfast bar on the run. I hit the snooze too much and am always late for work." I grimaced. "Or almost always late."

He checked his watch. "What time do you start work?"

I snorted. "After last week, I doubt I have a job there."

"Are you sure about that?"

My eyes had wandered over to the coffee, but now they whipped back to his. A deeper look caught and held me breathless. Then a suspicion started to grow. "Carter, what did you do?"

"What makes you think I did something?"

I studied him, but there it was. I saw it again. There was a spark of amusement in his wolf-like blue eyes. I sighed. I was starting to realize he could do anything, and getting my job back was probably something he could've done in his sleep. "You know Mr. Hudson, don't you?"

His grin widened. "No, I don't know Mr. Hudson. Who is he?"

I couldn't tell if he was lying now. "He's the Head of Beverage Sales. I'm his assistant."

"Oh." He lifted his orange juice and took a sip. "That's good to know."

Why was I getting frustrated with him?

He glanced at his watch again. "When did you normally have to be at work?"

"Nine in the morning." I narrowed my eyes. "Why?"

"You're going in like that?"

I glanced down at myself, in the robe with my bare feet poking out. Then I heard what he said again and my head whipped up. "You got my job back, didn't you?"

He took another sip of orange juice. "I don't know Mr. Hudson, no, but I am sparring partners with Noah Tomlinson."

My eyes bulged out. "You know Noah Tomlinson? He owns The Richmond, Carter."

"I know." His grin grew wicked. "He owns all of them."

I couldn't talk, not for a while. The Richmond was a ritzy hotel, with a chain that spread nationally and internationally. It had global success and Noah Tomlinson started it all. Wait—did he say sparring partners? Feeling dizzy all the sudden, I reached out for the counter to steady myself. My hand slipped, and I would've fallen off my stool to the floor had Carter not caught me. He grabbed my arm. It happened so fast. I couldn't look away from his hand as it was wrapped around my arm. He righted me back on my stool before he stepped back.

"Good reflexes," I noted, breathless. "I'm sure that comes in handy when you're sparring against an MMA Champion."

Carter grinned and shrugged. "It does have its benefits." Then he gave me a pointed look. "You are going to be late if you don't get ready."

I still couldn't believe any of what he said.

"Emma."

Work. Late. It was after 8:30 now. Oh god. I shook my head. I was getting dizzy again. Then I choked out, "Noah Tomlinson didn't have enough money to start all those hotels at once. He got the money from you, didn't he?"

Carter lifted an eyebrow. "Your job is still there, but if you're late, I can't guarantee it'll always be there."

He didn't have to say any more. I raced upstairs and emptied my bag onto the bed. When I couldn't find anything that would've been appropriate, I wanted to scream. But then I looked at the closets and I wondered.... I swept it open and gaped. Well, that wasn't true. I would've gaped if I had enough time. The closet was full of designer labels and after I checked a skirt, I saw it was in my size.

I didn't have time to think about that coincidence.

Hurrying, I grabbed a white business skirt and shirt. There was another closet of shoes. I wanted to fall over in a faint. High heels, sandals, pumps, everything a girl would've wanted in shoes were in that closet. Giggling from all the emotions, I slid on a pair of Casadei shoes and then stopped in my room. How would I get there?

With my purse, the new phone from Carter, I headed out of my bedroom. My answer was standing in my living room, waiting for me.

One of the guards gave me a nod. "Miss Martins. Your ride is waiting downstairs."

Of course. I had a car waiting for me.

This was Carter's life. It was now my life, I guess.

We went down the elevator where the other guard had the door opened for me. I slid inside. One of the guards sat beside me while the other sat in the front and off we went. I didn't say a word. I didn't know if I was supposed to. I didn't know which guard sat with me, but I had a feeling that Carter wanted them around me from now on.

When we were close to The Richmond, my phone vibrated.

When you are ready to come home, push zero nine on your phone. Mike and Thomas will be waiting at the back entrance of wherever you are. Have a good day, Emma.

I stared at the phone for a long time. I couldn't look away from it. Home? To Carter? I was really living with him. It felt so intimate, my pulse picked up. A sizzling sensation went through me. This was my life. This was my new life. I had a car. I had two bodyguards. I lived in an extravagant home, with an extravagant man. I drew in a shaky breath. Could I handle this? This was all too...it was too much.

I sat back and counted to ten. An anxiety attack was coming on.

Four days ago, I thought my life was ending. Everything had taken a 180 degree turn.

"We're here, Ma'am."

I jerked out of my thoughts. The car had stopped and I scrambled out the door to find that we were at a back entrance. When the guard closed the door behind me, I looked at him, unsure what to do or say now.

He gestured towards the door. "This is where we will pick you up. Have a great day at work."

"I—thank you..."

He nodded at me and then waited.

Uh...

"You can go on in, ma'am."

"Oh!" Flushing from embarrassment, I hurried through the door. It was an entrance that I never knew about, but a time clock was next to it. I clocked in before I headed to the hotel's breakroom for coffee.

I ignored the workers at the tables. No doubt they had whispered about me and my week of no-shows, but as I got my coffee and headed out, I was surprised. There was no reaction. It was like nothing had happened, so I shrugged and headed towards Mr. Hudson's office.

When I got there, it was the same shock. I expected some comment from him, but didn't get anything. As I sat down at my desk, in my own little office two doors down from his, there was a pile of paperwork on my desk and my inbox flashed a number that would keep me reading emails all morning.

It was nearing lunch when I got my first clue.

Mr. Hudson said from my opened door, “How was your vacation?”

I jerked back, my heart pounding. He never knocked, not even a courtesy knock. “Vacation?”

I stared at my boss. It took me a moment to comprehend and then I sputtered out, “Oh. Um. It was good. How was the week here?”

Mr. Hudson stared at me behind his glasses and pinched the top of his nose. He was a big man, but bigger since he had stopped working out due to a back injury. He had gained fifty pounds over the last year. He carried it all in his belly now, which made him unhappy. Everyone knew Mr. Hudson used to think of himself as a player type of guy, but with his hair starting to gray and thin, he couldn’t keep up the image. Annoyance had his nostrils flaring and he clipped out, “The week was fine, would’ve been better if we had proper notice of your vacation.” His eyes narrowed and he lifted the top of his lip in a sneer. “Word came down from the top. You never told me you knew someone at the top, Martins.”

I straightened in my chair and lifted my chin. “The vacation was a surprise to me as well. I apologize for any strain it might’ve had on you or others.”

He huffed out, “You can thank Theresa for doing most of your work. She couldn’t do all of it, since you’re my actual assistant, but you can touch base with her. She’ll bring you up to speed on everything. We’ve got a big deal coming up. There’s a conference in New York. I want you there.”

New York? My eyes widened. I was going to New York?

“Is that okay with you, Ms. Martins?” There was an edge to his tone.

“Uh, yes, Mr. Hudson. Of course, Mr. Hudson.”

"Good." He rolled his eyes. "We have to present to Mr. Tomlinson in New York. I want you to do the presentation."

"What account is that, Mr. Hudson?"

"It's a new account. There should be an email about it. If you can't find it, ask my secretary."

"Alright, Mr. Hudson." I pasted a professional smile on. He couldn't know how much I wanted to strangle him. A new account? There was an email about it? He spoke to me like I was two.

With another eye roll and a disgusted sigh, he marched back to his office. I was left in my office with my hands digging into my desk. I wanted to get up. I wanted to follow him. And I wanted to do some damage. He had never talked like that to me before.

What the hell had been told to him? And by whom?

The only thing I could do was scroll through my email again, but an hour later I still didn't see what he was talking about. There was no email from him or any from the higher administrative offices so I pushed back my chair and went in search of Theresa Webber, another assistant that worked underneath The Director of Sales. I could've gone to his secretary, but she was slimy like her boss. As I got to Theresa Webber's office, she was frowning at her computer with a pencil between her teeth.

I knocked on her door. She jerked away from her computer. Her hands flailed in the air and the pencil went flying. She grabbed onto her desk to keep from falling off her chair. Her hair had been pulled back in a low pony tail, but half of it had come undone from her startled movement. With green eyes wide in surprise behind thin glasses and her shirt already half unbuttoned, Theresa groaned from embarrassment.

"Am I interrupting?"

"No, no." She waved towards a chair in front of her desk. "Have a seat." Her hand quickly did up the buttons on her shirt and she tried to smooth out her hair. She failed. Half of it fell down on her shoulder. The other half was still in the pony tail. "Sorry. You gave me a fright."

I hid a grin. Theresa was always like that. I didn't know her that well, but she had a reputation. Whatever she was doing held her concentration completely. A nuclear bomb could've gone off, and it wouldn't have fazed her. "What are you working on?"

"What are *we* working on," she corrected me. She gestured to her computer. "It's the account Mr. Tomlinson asked for you to present on."

My eyebrows shot up. Mr. Tomlinson asked himself? I instantly grew wary. What account was it? I hoped Carter wasn't a part of it, but I already knew he was. He had to have been. I held my breath as she gestured for me to come around to her side.

"See, here." She tapped the computer screen.

As I started to read, shock spread through me. It was an account to develop our own liquor as a brand. I shook my head. What did this mean?

Theresa must've sensed my confusion. "Mr. Tomlinson wants us to pitch this to the board. This bourbon's been a bestseller in the restaurant and bars. Other revenues are starting to request it. He wants it advertised as a product and distributed nationally. This is a big deal, Emma."

"How am I involved?"

She shrugged and went back to the computer. "Who knows why Noah picks who he does. He always has a reason and it always works. The guy is a genius."

Noah? I grinned at her. "First name basis?"

Her fingers froze and a blush spread up her neck.

My grin widened. "You know office gossip, Theresa. The little biddies are going to be over this like white on rice."

She wrinkled up her nose but the blush spread to her face. "Um, you know, it's nothing. I mean..."

My eyes got big. I'd been kidding, but there *was* something going on.

"Um." She shot me a pleading look before her looked down. Then she stopped and held her breath. "Oh, wow. Look at your shoes!"

My shoes? It was my turn to become flustered. I'd forgotten about the very expensive heels on my feet, and the expensive designer clothes that I was wearing.

"Are those Casadei?!"

"Um," I bit on my lip. "Yeah..."

"Oh my gosh!" She jerked her face down to peer at my shoes better. Her shoulders straightened, her back turned rigid, and she looked back up with a stone face. "Emma, those shoes aren't even out yet."

"How do you know?" I huffed out and fanned myself. It was getting warm in her office.

Because I know someone who's a shopper for Hagleys."

As she named a boutique that was known for being exclusive, expensive, and one of the 'it' spots for celebrities, I was going to faint. Of course, Carter would have a closet full of shoes that weren't even out to the public yet. I glanced down at my skirt and wondered how much money my outfit was worth? How much was I wearing?

I gulped.

Theresa had been eyeing my outfit as well. Her eyes were wide. "You look really nice, Emma, *really* nice."

I didn't like getting all this attention, but wait—she knew Noah personally. That was worth way more attention than my clothes. I jerked a hand towards the computer. "So what do I need to know for this presentation? Tell me what *Noah* wants."

She jerked back in her seat like she'd been burned. "Oh, of course." After readjusting her glasses, she ran a hand over her hair and then sighed. "It's going to be a long night. You have a lot to catch up on with this account."

Theresa wasn't kidding. I sent Carter a text to tell him that I would be staying late at work. When I didn't receive a reply, I tucked my phone away and didn't think about it. After reading more and getting a sense of what Noah Tomlinson wanted for his new pet project, I started to get excited. He wanted this new liquor to be a household competitor. I knew if this bourbon was a hit, there'd be more to come and I would be on the team. In fact, it seemed that Theresa and I were doing most of the grunt work. Her boss and Mr. Hudson were our supervisors, but we were appointed the lead workers.

It was a big deal.

When it was nearing seven in the evening, Theresa heard my stomach rumble and grinned at me. She pushed her glasses up and collapsed against the back of her chair. "What do you think?"

"What do you mean?" I was on the floor in the middle of three piles of papers. I'd been there for the last hour and didn't think my legs could work again. They'd fallen asleep forty minutes ago.

"Should we call it a night? It's your first day back from vacation. Talk about a killer, huh?"

She was joking, but I sucked in my breath. She couldn't have used different words? Then I forced out a laugh and tried to relax my shoulders. There would be permanent knots in them. "Uh, yeah. We can call it a night."

"I don't know about you, but I could go for a Joe's pizza right now. You up for a slice and a beer?"

I started to push myself up from the floor and once I was up, I threw her a rueful grin. I wasn't getting any younger. Then I saw she was serious and jerked upright. "Oh. Uh, sure."

I'd been invited for drinks by some of the other assistants in the hotel at other times. It wasn't a large group, but we were somewhat exclusive. A fair amount of people worked underneath us so my group of friends wasn't too big, but Theresa was in another league. She was the Assistant to the Director of Sales and now I knew that she knew Noah Tomlinson personally. I was taken aback by her invitation, but I couldn't turn her down. In truth, everyone was curious about Theresa Webber. She worked on all the higher accounts and she worked alone. She wasn't known to go for after-work drinks, much less a slice of pizza and beer.

She flashed me a friendly smile as she shut down her computer. "Good. I'll meet you there in fifteen? Or if you wait around, we can walk over together?"

"How about we meet in the lobby in ten minutes?"

"Perfect. See you down there."

When I went to my office and shut everything down, I grabbed my phone and stuffed it in my purse. I needed to go to the bathroom before I met Theresa in the lobby so I used the one on the first floor. It was always cleaner since it was the same one that the customers used, and it was beautiful. The tiling on the floor was top-notch, with separate sinks along the wall. Each of them had been individually customized as works of art from Italy. The Richmond was a work of art in itself. I was proud of Carter if he had anything to do with it.

"Oh. Hi!"

My head jerked up from washing my hands.

Amanda stood behind me, she had just come in. She was pale in the face and grabbed onto the wall to steady herself.

I whipped around and tried to grab her. I didn't think about it. I saw her foot slip and knew she was going down, but she caught herself against the wall.

She flinched away from my hand.

The smile fell away and my hand dropped back to my side. I wasn't used to that reaction from my friend.

"Sorry." She grimaced. "The last day hasn't been so easy."

My head fell down. Shame flooded me as I remembered what I had left behind. Guilt flared up. "I'm sorry, Amanda. I really am. I—"

She waved me off. "No worries."

I hesitated. "You were working at the café tonight?"

She nodded. "I picked up a late shift. They were cleaning our bathroom so I figured I'd use this one. You guys are right next door."

"Yeah." The guilt had settled in me. It wasn't going anywhere. "I'm really sorry I left, Amanda."

"Really, Emma. No worries. I mean it." She was firm now. "We know you did something to help Mallory, all of us, since we're all a part of it. You don't have to explain yourself."

I sighed. I left that life and stepped into some other glamorous life. Even my job seemed to have gotten better since Carter. "How's Mallory?"

"Uh," Amanda jerked forward. She went into a stall.

I waited until she had finished and came back out to wash her hands. Once she turned the water on, she soaped them up and rinsed before she looked up again. "Ben took her to the hospital last night."

"What?"

She waved at me again. "No, no, no. It's not what you think. He wanted her to get tested. They couldn't check for sperm since Ben had...you know..."

I looked away.

She lowered her voice and stepped closer. "He wanted her bruises and stuff looked at, to make sure she was healing alright. The hospital recommended a counselor and I think he took her to one this afternoon. Since you left, and, you know, you told us that we could have a life again, she's been better. You weren't the only one scared about what *they* were going to do to us."

My stomach twisted at the reminder. Franco Dunvan was still out there. He was looking for his son. Thanks to Carter, the trail wouldn't lead back to us. I nodded, my throat thick with renewed emotion again. "I'm glad she's doing better."

"Ben still wants me to come by every night, but she slept last night. She had a little food today and he just texted. He said she's watching some movies tonight. I was going to stop in and see if she wanted me to stay the night."

"That's good," I wrung out. I should've been the one doing that. I should've been sleeping with her, taking her to the hospital, making sure she got to the counselor's office. I shouldn't have been going to work again, working on a new project that would ensure my future, or even going to Joe's for a slice and beer with someone I always wanted to be friends with from before.

Things had changed so much. I felt like I had lost my old life.

"Emma?" The door opened and Theresa walked in, but stopped as she saw me. "The guys at the front desk said they saw you duck in. You ready to go?"

Amanda's eyes went wide.

Theresa noticed her and stuck her hand out. "Hi, you work in the little café next door, right? I'm Theresa Webber."

"Um." Amanda shut her mouth with a snap but took her hand. "I'm Amanda. Yeah, I work in the café. You work for Mr. Dalton, don't you?"

"Well, Emma and I both work for him now. We're on the same account." Theresa cheeks were pink from excitement. "I already love the work we've done together today."

Amanda swung her wide eyes to me, but I readied myself. There it was. I saw the realization settle in. The surprise had moved over and her eyes darkened from hurt. She'd heard me mention the higher administrative levels. I must've talked about Theresa since her boss was near the top.

I hung my head. I should've given myself up. Maybe that would've helped. But no, it wouldn't have. Things would've been the same and we wouldn't have had Carter's protection. She didn't know who I went to for their safety. Carter stressed the importance that they couldn't know about him. He had his reasons. I would trust in them. I would trust in him.

"Oh. I see."

Theresa frowned now as she looked between us. Her eyelids fluttered and I knew she was starting to figure out that something was wrong. She drew in a deep breath and gave Amanda a polite smile. "Well, it was nice to have met you. Are you ready, Emma?"

I nodded. I didn't trust myself to speak, not yet.

As we left, I looked back. The hurt had transformed into a glare, but I saw a small tear. Amanda flicked it away as she turned her back to me.

My heart dropped the farther I walked away from that bathroom door. I didn't know how or what had happened, but my friendship with Amanda wouldn't be the same. She knew something changed in my life and it wasn't the same type of change that had happened to them. Things got worse for them while things got better for me.

As Theresa led the way out the door and across the road to the popular pub, I made my mind up. I didn't know Carter's exact requirements, but I wouldn't forget my friends. I needed to see Mallory again. I had to make sure everything would be okay between me and her.

When we walked inside, I cringed as I saw the place was packed. It seemed that everyone needed a drink. A large portion of workers from The Richmond sat in the front. There were servers from the restaurant, clerks from the front desk, and a few of the managers. All of them looked up and all of them quieted when they saw I was with Theresa. She led me towards the back and grabbed a table in a corner. Across the room were the girls that I would usually grab a drink with. They paused when they saw who was with me now. A few of them dropped their mouths, but leaned forward to the others. The buzz in the restaurant doubled as Theresa waved down a waiter.

I needed a drink. Now.

As Theresa ordered a pizza for both of us, I nodded when she asked if she should order a pitcher of beer. As soon as it arrived, I downed my first glass.

"Oh, whoa." Her eyes widened. "Was I that hard on you?"

"No." A grin escaped me. "I'm sorry. Things have been pretty stressful for me lately."

"Yeah." She nodded. "I heard your vacation wasn't planned."

I had been reaching to pour a second glass, resolved that it was going to be my last drink for the night, but I dropped my hand back to my lap at her words. "What do you mean?"

"Oh." She shrugged as she sipped on her own beer. "Nothing, really. I heard that something bad happened and you had to leave town suddenly. A family crisis?"

"Where did you hear that?"

"I was in the office with Noah when he took the call. He called Mr. Hudson himself and told him that you were on vacation that whole week."

Oh god. I wasn't surprised, but I hadn't realized it had gone down like that. I looked at my lap with my mind whirling. Noah Tomlinson himself had taken the call? I jerked back up. "When did he get that call?"

"Oh. Um, last Friday?" She frowned. "Why?"

So much didn't make sense. I had not shown up at my job for four days. Didn't they have questions about that, but no, not with that explanation coming down from the boss himself. And he took the explanation from one phone call? I shook my head. Carter was more than a sparring partner to Noah Tomlinson. Maybe he was even more than an investor.

"You okay, Emma?"

"Uh, yeah." I tried to give her a reassuring smile. "I'll be fine. You're right. It was a family emergency. I—uh—everything is better now." I hoped everything would be better.

"Good." Her smile stretched from ear to ear as she leaned closer, across the table. "I have to tell you that I've been itching to work with you on a project like this."

"Really? Why?"

She laughed. "You've earned your way up the ladder. You're quiet. You're hard working, and you've lasted the longest as Mr. Hudson's assistant. He's so hard to work with. Anyone who's lasted as long as you have and not gotten the punt by him says a lot about you. Plus," she giggled, "if everything goes well with this new account, you and I both are going to be promoted."

"Really?" My eyes went wide. "How do you know?"

She sat back, still trying to quench her smile, and shrugged. "I can't tell you that, but I know it's a definite possibility. They've had their eye on you for awhile."

I sat back, dazed, as I heard her. I couldn't believe it. That meant—this was from me. Carter couldn't have helped me with this new account. If what she said was correct then I earned this new project and maybe a new promotion on my own, not because of him.

I wanted to celebrate. I was alive. I was going to stay alive and things were going to be okay.

I sat back in amazement as those realizations washed over me. I couldn't believe it. I mean, I could, but I couldn't. I hadn't thought about things at all in the last week, but here I was. I still had my job. I was going to get a better job, I hoped, and things were going to be alright. Mallory was getting help. Everything was going to be fine.

"You okay?" Theresa peered close to me.

"Yeah," I gasped. "Everything's great." And I meant it. I reached for my second glass of beer as the pizza came to our table.

"Let's cheer to that." She raised her glass.

Three pitchers later, our table had been joined by the girls that usually accompanied me for drinks. All of them were eager to know Theresa better since she seemed out of our reach for friendship. When they learned what account I had been assigned to, a few gave me heated looks from jealousy or anger. Laura seemed happy for me, but she was the nice one of the group. She was happy for everyone.

I had long forgotten to check my phone so I wasn't sure how late it was when a sudden hush came over the table.

I jerked my head up. "What?"

All of them were looking at me. No. All of them were looking behind me.

My eyes went wide and I knew. A knot formed in my gut as I took a deep breath before I turned, but then I relaxed. My shoulders dropped down and I let out my breath. It was only Mike, or Thomas. I wasn't sure. They both looked the same.

"Miss Martins," he spoke. So tall and goliath-like. I snickered at that thought. He could've been a gentle giant, but since he was security for Carter, I doubted it. He spoke again with a blank expression over his face, "Your ride is waiting for you outside."

"Your ride?" one of the girls hooted. "Moving up in the world, Ems. Hot new project at work and hot new ride."

Another girl laughed, "He's like a butler, for rides."

"Is he a chauffeur?"

Then someone whispered, "I think he's a Chippendale dancer."

The first girl hooted again as she slapped her hand on the table. "He's going to whip off his pants any second…any second…wait for it…"

Mike never blinked. He never reacted. He just waited for me.

I sighed. The fun was done for the night. "I should go, you guys."

"Oh, come on! Emma, don't go. We're just starting to have fun."

I shook my head. "I have work tomorrow." Theresa nodded beside me and I indicated her. "We have work tomorrow. We can't slack off like normal."

"Like we do, you mean!" The girl wasn't offended.

I grinned. "See you all tomorrow?"

"Wait." Theresa grabbed her purse and threw $50 on the table. "Can I get a ride with you? I can't drive home like this."

Oh, that was right. I started to dig into my purse to pay my bill, but Mike said in my ear, "It's already been taken care of, Miss Martins."

Oh. He paid my bill? But then I was distracted when I caught his quick glance at Theresa, who was waiting beside me. Comprehension flared and I glanced at him with the unspoken question. Could we give her a ride? Was that allowed? I was still fuzzy on Carter's rules, or even if he had any rules? Then I frowned.

Where had Mike come from? Had they been waiting outside all day and night? But they couldn't have known I was at Joe's with Theresa...could they?

Then I shrugged. What the hell? I was feeling brave and buzzed so I linked my elbow with hers. "Let's go."

She gave me a giggly smile in return and off we went. Mike followed behind at a more sedated pace. When we burst through the door, the car was waiting out front like he had said. As Theresa reached for the back door, I sucked in my breath. It was at that moment that I realized my mistake. Carter could've been inside, waiting for me and I knew he wouldn't be happy at my friend's discovery of him. When she slipped inside and there was no comment or greeting, I relaxed a little. Then I caught the bland expression on Mike's face and knew he would've stopped her if Carter had been inside.

I flushed. I was an idiot sometimes.

When I bent forward and sat beside Theresa, Mike folded into the seat beside me. We had to scoot over for him and Theresa giggled behind her hands. "It's like you have a bodyguard. Are we giving him a ride home too?" She patted my leg a few times, but then jerked forward. "Who's driving this car?"

I cringed. I didn't want to say it to her. I didn't want her to look at me differently. Who else had a driver and bodyguard?

Mike answered for me, "An associate of mine. It's a new car service offered by Joe's."

"Really?" She frowned. "I never knew about this before. I would've used this. A lot."

"It's only for the night, ma'am."

"Ma'am." More giggles came from her. She slapped my leg again. "I had one pitcher too many, Emma, but I had fun. Did you have fun? I think we'll make a great team for this account. Noah's going to be so proud of us. I'm glad he picked you for the account." She leaned close and whispered loudly, "I don't have a lot of female friends at work. Those girls were fun tonight. We should do that again sometime."

I patted her arm as she turned back to her window and asked Mike, "Do you need her address?"

He didn't look at me as he spoke, "We already know it. Thank you, ma'am, for asking."

I sat back, stunned. I felt snubbed by my own bodyguard. Had I been? Or was the beer speaking to me too?

Theresa lived in a newer building. As she teetered her way inside, the car waited until she had been let inside by her doorman. I sunk low in my seat. I was back to the home that wasn't home. It was then that everything slid back into place. I wasn't some fairy princess with new friends and a new job—well, kind of, but as we progressed across the city, I remembered my place. I had killed a man, and I was in hiding from his family. I sighed and closed my eyes. We would arrive at Carter's home soon enough, and I doubted I would have a restful night's sleep.

When the car dipped down into the basement, I didn't wait for Mike to open the door or even for the car to stop. I opened the far door and hopped out. I had hit the elevator button before Mike had his own door shut. Both of them hurried for me, but I stood back and watched as the elevator door slid shut. For some reason that made me feel better. I had escaped them, for a second, and in Carter's own home, but it was a little burst of victory for me.

My stomach twisted and churned. I didn't know what was wrong with me, but when the elevator opened to my floor, I stepped out into the little hallway with trembling legs and shaking hands. My palms were sweaty and my pulse had started to race again. It was Carter. If Mike wasn't happy with me then I knew Carter would be furious, but I had no idea why. What had I done wrong?

It was my life.

I could live how I wanted.

I tried to reassure myself that. Carter couldn't be mad at me. He didn't have control over my life. But it was a lie. My heart raced even faster and my body started to feel sick as I opened my door. Then I stopped in shock. My floor was dark. There were no lights on, and as I made my way towards the stairs, I couldn't see any lights on throughout the rest of the building either.

I was alone. There was no Carter.

I wasn't sure what to feel about his absence, and I refused to believe I was disappointed. Instead of dwelling on it, I showered and headed to bed. It was nearing midnight and tomorrow was a full day at the job again.

It was later, much later, when my blanket was ripped off of me and I jerked upright. I caught a glance at the clock. It was after four in the morning. Carter stood above my bed. His icy blues glared down at me. He was dressed all in black again with a hood over his head. It covered his blonde hair, but I couldn't notice anything more. I was caught and held captive by his eyes. They had turned into those of the stranger's and he was livid with me.

I scooted against my headboard, but didn't say a word. I didn't dare. I didn't reach for the blanket. I had gone to bed in a tight white top and I was in my panties, but I couldn't cover myself. I knew Carter wanted that. I remained still and took a quiet breath. I felt like the prey being caught by the predator. A wild animal stood above me, and then he took a step closer. His pants brushed against my bed. He was so close to me.

He bent down to the bed and placed his arms on either side of me. He grasped the headboard into fists but kept himself off of me. His knees never touched the bed as he bent forward. His breath brushed across my skin. He spoke in a low growl, "I was on my way to Greece tonight when my men called me. You disappeared tonight."

I drew in another breath. It left me shaking. "I didn't."

"You did." His breath tickled against my lips. He never blinked. The rage in him was barely contained. "You worked late—"

"—I texted you that."

His fists tightened on the headboard and his knee touched the bed now. It dipped under his weight, but he held himself above me.

My heart was pounding, but I couldn't keep his gaze. Too many different emotions were being stirred up inside of me. When I felt the throb start between my legs, I clenched them together and hoped it would go away. What was wrong with me?

"You sent me a *weak* text and then you never looked at your phone again."

I clamped my eyes shut. He was right.

"You were hiding from me."

Right again.

His breath hit me on the side now. He had moved and I wondered where he was looking now. Was he closer to me? The bed dipped again so I wondered if both of his knees were on it now. I was still trapped between his arms, but he was so close to me. The throbbing between my legs grew. I wanted him between them. I wanted him against me, on top of me. A small whimper left me before I could stop it. I bit down on my lip and tried to keep another from escaping.

His hand left the headboard and cupped my chin. "Emma."

Oh god. He had softened his tone. It was a sensual caress against my skin now. My leg moved back, just an inch. I opened for him.

"Emma, look at me."

I shook my head. I couldn't. He'd see.

"Emma." His lips touched the side of my mouth now and I gasped. I couldn't hold back anymore as I turned into him. My lips brushed against his, but he moved back, just enough so his lips only lightly touched mine. He didn't give in. He didn't press them against mine.

I wanted all of him, not just the soft feel of him.

He moved even closer and his other hand left the headboard. It slid behind my waist and he picked me up. My eyes burst open and I wrapped my arms around him without thinking. He lifted me from the bed and moved me to the dresser. He sat me on top, grabbed my legs, pulled me to the edge, and then fit himself between them. One of his hands braced against the dresser while the other went to my back. He pressed me against him, all of me against all of him. My chest was crushed against his and my lips fell open. The throbbing was so insistent now. I was wet, ready for him.

"Why didn't you tell my men you were leaving your work?"

I couldn't hear him. The need for him had a haze over my mind. I only felt him, how his heart was still calm while mine raced. The front of his pants burned against me. He had thickened, pressed between my legs, and I opened them wider. Then he drew in a breath. He stiffened against me and his head dropped to my shoulder. His lips skimmed my naked shoulder in a soft kiss. My hair was brushed back and he pressed another kiss to my neck.

I shuddered against him.

"Emma," he whispered now. "Why didn't you tell my men you

were leaving? They searched your entire building before they called me."

His voice grew insistent and I struggled to hear his words. When I finally processed his words, a small frown came to me. I didn't want to talk. Not then, not anymore. My voice had grown hoarse, "I forgot." My eyes widened, though the lust increased inside of me. What was he doing to me? "I forgot. Theresa mentioned Joe's and we went over. I saw..." Who had I seen? Someone had distracted me. "I saw Amanda and felt bad."

"Why did you feel bad?" His hand brushed more of my hair away and skimmed down my back. He cupped the back of my thigh and pulled me closer to him. I couldn't get any closer. I was plastered to him.

My legs opened again, even wider.

His chest rose against mine and his hand skimmed down my arm to my waist. He lingered on the inside of my thigh.

I was burning up now.

He repeated, "Why did you feel bad?"

My arms wound tighter around his neck. I stuck my head against his chest and said, my voice muffled, "Because I left them."

I left them for you.

I bit down on my lip from saying that thought out loud. He'd know how much I wanted him. I started to wonder if I had always wanted him.

"Oh, Emma." His hand cupped the back of my head and lifted me to face him. My eyes opened to slits as I peered at him. He was studying my mouth, his eyes dark with lust as he murmured, "They're safe. You're not. You need to be here with me, where I can make sure you're safe. You pulled the trigger. You're the one they want."

"Jeremy."

My own voice haunted me. The bang of the gun came back and I felt the kickback in my hand again.

"You have to be quiet. People will hear."

A sob escaped me and Carter lifted me from the dresser. My arms and legs wound around him, but my head dropped into his chest. Another sob came up and then another. I was crying as he lowered both of us to the bed again, but he held me as I continued. I couldn't stop crying. As the night progressed, I cried myself back to sleep in his arms.

-CARTER-

Carter sat on the edge of the bed. He watched her. She had cried in his arms that night and he wanted to murder whoever caused her the pain. He couldn't. She had already killed Jeremy, and Franco was a cancer. Struggling to keep his rage under control, he pulled out the nightstand drawer and studied his gun for a moment. It was his trusty friend, one that he had used so many other times when someone needed to disappear. He hadn't used it in a long time. He hadn't had to, but the temptation to take matters into his own hand was great. His arm shook as he tried to keep himself from reaching for it. It'd be so easy. He could slip out, no one would know. He would go to Franco and get into his house, but he couldn't. Franco's death was a political death. It had to be approved by his family. And even when he would die—and he *would* die—the Bertal Family would send another. They were all the same. They would do as Franco had done with Cristino. They would take over the last assignment and do more than they needed to prove their authority to the neighborhood.

That couldn't happen. When Franco died, it had to stop with him. No one could hurt her.

Carter shut the drawer softly and left for the gym. His hands needed to pummel someone so the boxing bag would have to be it. As he went, he was already thinking of ways to ensure that Franco's death would be the last of it.

Two hours later, he was still considering ways to cement her freedom.

ELEVEN

I woke from an empty sleep. His arms weren't around me. I didn't feel his legs entwined with mine anymore and when I turned over, I already knew he was gone. The clock said that it was after six in the morning. There were no other lights on, not that I could see, but I rose and grabbed the robe again. I pulled it on as I went in search of him.

I went through every floor and looked in every room. It wasn't until I got to the bottom floor that I heard him. A light was on and shone underneath a closed door, but I heard thumping from inside the room. As I opened the door, I saw him in the middle of a gym. His black pants were still on, but his shirt was gone and sweat gleamed down his chest. His hands were taped and he was circling a punching bag. There was blood on his tape. I tried to find where he had been hurt, but I didn't see blood anywhere else. Only sweat and muscles. They constricted and stretched as he continued to hit the punching bag, each illuminated in the stark contrast by the light. I wondered if there was an ounce of fat on him. It didn't seem likely, but then he stopped as he saw me.

He touched the bag to hold it as it swayed and his chest rose up and down from his breathing. His eyes narrowed when I stepped inside the room. "You couldn't sleep?"

I shook my head.

I didn't know what to do. I wanted to be near him, but I couldn't say that. What would change then? I held my tongue, though my hands fought against me. They wanted to reach out to him. My feet wanted to cross the room and I wanted to feel his arms around me again. I swung my body back to keep myself from going to him.

His pull on me was so powerful, too powerful. It scared me.

"Emma."

I jerked my eyes up to his and gulped. His eyes had darkened as he watched me. Lust filled them, but there was more to his darkness. There was danger in them as well. That was what kept me from going to him. He was so dangerous.

"You never looked at your phone, did you?"

I frowned. My phone? But then I remembered. I shook my head. No, I hadn't. And he'd been right earlier. I hadn't looked at my phone because I wanted to run from him. I wanted to hide from what my life had become. I wanted to forget everything, just for a night.

"Talk to me," he urged in a quiet voice.

I gasped as I heard a soft yearning in him. There was a pleading within him and my eyes went round. He was pleading me for something. Oh god. I couldn't stop myself. I crossed the room to him, but I stopped right before him. I didn't touch him. My eyes fell to his chest and it rose up and down in a steady rhythm. My hand lifted without my decision and touched where his heart was. My eyes widened as I saw my own hand in front of me. Why couldn't I stop myself when I was around this man?

"What are you thinking?" His voice grew rough. His heart picked up its pace underneath my hand.

I sighed to myself. It was soft and quiet, but it was everything. It was my surrender. I closed my eyes and I stepped into him. His arms wound around my waist and then my head rested on his chest. It was right to be in his arms.

"Emma. You need to talk to me."

I nodded, choked up now. My hand wound around his waist and formed into a fist on his waistband. As I bit my lip in a poor attempt to hold myself from jumping him, I lifted my head and gave him a fleeting smile. "I wanted to forget for the night."

He nodded, his eyes darkened even more.

I couldn't look away now that my eyes had connected with his. The words tumbled free now. "I wasn't hiding from you. I was hiding from everything. I'm sorry that your men contacted you and you had to come back from Greece."

My heart skipped a beat. He had come back for me.

I continued, stumbling over my words, "Everything is different, Carter. Nothing's the same. Even my job changed yesterday. It's all," *better,* "different. Everything is different. I'm different. I've changed and I," *don't know how to handle that*, "don't know what to do now."

I clasped my eyes shut against my thoughts.

"Hey." His hand skimmed up my arm to caress my cheek. "When my men called and said you had disappeared something changed in me too. I would do anything for you, Emma. I thought Dunvan found out about you and took you. I was ready to come back and start a war. When they told me you were having drinks with your co-workers, I could've gone back, but I didn't. I came home. I needed to see you. I had to make sure that you were okay. You were in bed when I got home. You were sleeping. You looked so innocent. I wanted to murder Jeremy Dunvan for what he did to you."

I shook my head. "He was hurting Mallory—"

"He hurt you too." An alarming tone came from him. "He changed your life. For that alone I will not stop until all of his men are in the ground."

My hands fell away from him. What was he talking about? I shook my head again. "You can't."

"I can," he growled. His hand flexed against my back and he held onto me as I had with him. "When you came to me, I wanted to torture Jeremy Dunvan, but I couldn't. You already killed him. His father won't stop, Emma. He's still searching for what happened to his son and they know about Mallory."

My eyes bulged out and I bent over. I couldn't breathe. Panic filled me.

His hand didn't move from me. He kept me chained to him. "They know he was with a girlfriend, it's only a matter of time before they find her."

I gasped for breath. It wasn't coming. Something was blocking my air.

"I can't protect her—"

I shook my head, fully panicked now. I gasped out, "You promised me. You said that—"

He jerked me against him. His eyes drilled into mine. "I said what I needed to get you here. You never would've left her if I told you the truth."

"NO!" I ripped out of his arms. Then I turned and started for the door.

"No," he growled as he grabbed my arm and pulled me back.

I struggled against him, but he lifted me in the air. He carried me further into the room, into the shadowed corners, and he pressed me against the wall. I was trapped again. I had nowhere to go. He held me up as he had held me in the bed that first night. His legs paralyzed mine and my arms were helpless under his hold. His chest was against mine again. He lowered his head to my neck. His nostrils flared and he skimmed my skin with his lips.

I shivered as sensations flared inside of me. But no, Mallory—I tried to struggle again, but it was useless. I was melting instead.

He whispered against my neck, "You can't go to her. You can't, Emma."

I whimpered. My legs started to soften.

"That man wasn't your boyfriend."

I shook my head, but it wasn't a question. Another whimper left me.

"I found out who he is and where he works. I know that he works with your roommate. He loves her, doesn't he?"

Another nod. Another submission. I groaned and my head fell against the wall. I was starting to need only him now.

Carter whispered against my neck, an edge in his voice, "That man would do anything for her. What do you think he would do if Franco's men took her?"

Agony speared me. I already knew.

"He would give you up in a heartbeat," he clipped out. "You know that. You know what he would do. He wouldn't even give you a heads-up, Emma. They would take her and he would walk into Franco's office without a second thought. And that *will* happen. Franco's men knew Jeremy was with someone, they're searching for her right now. As soon as they question her, and they will, your name will come up. If she doesn't give you up, he will." His hand had a cement hold on me. He was claiming me. "He will do that to make sure the woman he loves is safe. And I would do the same for you."

My heart stopped. Had he just—I opened my eyes and saw the stark need in his.

"I have been protecting you since you were a child, Emma. I'm not going to stop now."

It was for AJ.

My stomach dropped as I realized that. This was all for my brother. It was like he reached in and squeezed my heart. It was a painful hold that I couldn't stop. He kept squeezing as he continued, "My men have to know where you are at every minute of the day. They're going to come for you, Emma. It's only a matter of time, but when they do, they'll learn who is protecting you and it should stop them. Once they find me at your side, this becomes another matter. Franco Dunvan will take his claim to his Family Elders and they will make the decision on whether or not he can pursue retribution for his son. If they do, they'd be starting a war against me."

I blinked back tears. I didn't know what to think anymore. He was right, this was beyond me, but he was doing all of this for me. Then I shook my head and I cleared my throat. I had to think again. I needed to push all emotions aside. I had to focus.

I rasped out, "And what about your family?"

"What do you mean?"

I pushed him back an inch. He was a force in himself on my sensations. Already my body wanted him back again. "When Franco finds out that you're protecting me, it's not between him and you. Right?"

He nodded.

"And he has to go to his family for approval to come for me?" A searing pain stabbed me as I realized what they would do to me if that happened. I pushed past it. "So if he needs approval with his family, then don't you? Doesn't your family need to approve of you protecting me?"

His eyes softened and his hand touched my throat gently. He murmured as his thumb rubbed against me, "They already have."

"What do you mean?"

Moving closer, he rested his forehead against mine. "I've been protecting you since I joined the Mauricio family. You were why I joined them in the first place."

What? I—what? My eyes implored him for further explanation, but I couldn't speak.

He grinned to himself and moved to press a kiss at the corner of my mouth. He didn't move away like he had before. He stayed there and I felt his tongue brush against my mouth. "Those men were hunting you down after they killed AJ. They wanted his family wiped out. I killed them and then I went to Mauricio. Your safety was part of my condition to join his family. You will always be safe. That's been my first priority, even over the family itself. My elders know that. Anything I do for you will always be cleared with my family."

But—I couldn't think. What he said—it didn't make sense. None of it made sense. He had been protecting me this whole time? But—

He pressed a kiss to my cheek and sighed. His hand trailed down my arm in a caress. "I tried to keep you safe. I wanted you to live your life free, but when you came to me, I couldn't allow you that freedom anymore. You have to be with me. You have to stay with me and let the men know where you are at all times. I can't risk the chance that Franco might go against his family and take you without their approval. He's crazy enough to do that. And if he does, if he gets through my men," he shuddered against me. His arms tightened their hold on me. "I need you safe. I need to be able to contact you at all times."

I nodded and flinched at the same time.

"What's wrong?"

I couldn't tell him. I didn't even know. A storm erupted inside of me and as he explained more and more, the storm spread throughout me. Then I started to break down. I couldn't understand all of it, not the fullest extent, so I clung to the bits that made sense to me. I needed to stay with him. Franco Dunvan could still come after me. I needed Carter. That made sense to me so that's what I held onto.

"Emma."

I looked up as some of the panic started to subside. I could breathe again. I could think. But, my heart started to thump in my chest. His hand rested there, between my breasts, and my heart doubled its pace. I choked out, "I won't hide anymore. I understand."

"You do?"

"Yes."

Then he sighed and his forehead dropped back to mine.

I couldn't leave, not even if I wanted to, but I stopped thinking there. I couldn't think about the possibility that I was starting to not want to leave. I distracted myself and asked, "What about Mallory?"

He frowned. "What about her?"

"What do they know about her?"

He tensed again. "I have someone on the inside. He said they don't know much about her, but they know Jeremy had a girlfriend and they're looking for her."

"What if he had lots of girlfriends?"

"He did, but they know there was a girl he saw on a regular basis."

A lightbulb turned on. "Do they know her name?"

"Not yet."

My chest tightened as he held something back, and then I knew. My heart grew heavy. "But they will, won't they?"

He nodded. "I'm sorry, Emma."

"How long do you think?"

He gave me a sad smile. "I don't know. I don't think it'll be too much longer before they find Mallory."

A sob hitched in my throat. "Are they going to hurt her?"

He didn't respond.

I knew my answer.

Then he lifted me into his arms again, but this time his embrace was for comfort. He brushed some hair from my forehead. "They might let her live if she gives you up."

I couldn't speak. The pain was too much. For the first time, I couldn't believe that I hoped for my roommate and best friend to stab me in the back. Then she would be safe. Jeremy wouldn't be able to continue to hurt her anymore. I nodded. I was okay with that, if it meant she would be safe.

"Carter."

His arms tightened around me. "Yeah?"

"Would you sleep with me?"

"Of course." But as he carried me from the room, he didn't go to my room. He took me to his. The sun had started to rise so his room had some light inside, but I didn't look around. I kept my eyes closed as he placed me under the covers and slid behind me. He curled me back into his arms. "When do you have to wake up?"

"Eight o'clock." But it didn't matter. I never fell asleep, neither did he.

When his alarm went off an hour later, I rose from the bed and got ready for work. Carter handed me coffee and then we went to the car. He rode with me to work and squeezed my hand when we arrived. Mike, or a look-alike, opened the door for me, but I didn't get out. I stayed in the car for another minute. No one said a word. The door was held open, waiting for me, and then as my heart sank, I started to go.

Carter pressed a kiss to the corner of my mouth before I went. A tear fell from my eye, but he brushed it away. As I left, I knew that my entire life had changed and this was the first time that I accepted it.

The rest of my week turned into a routine. I barely saw Mr. Hudson, which was fine with me, and worked almost solely with Theresa on the new project. We took our breaks and lunches together. By the end of the week she was quickly becoming a friend, which seemed like a good thing when I stopped receiving text messages from Amanda. Theresa and I went to the café for bagels one morning and Amanda was working. She never made eye contact with me and, as I watched her, I saw there were bags underneath her eyes. I wondered if something had happened to Mallory, but I couldn't ignore Carter's warning. There was no going back. It was best for everyone that I stepped away from my old friends, best for them and for myself.

I missed Mallory. I missed Amanda. I even missed Ben, just a little bit. There had been some good times with the four of us on the weekends, so when Theresa suggested pizza, wine, and movies at her place I was excited to go. Carter had left town for the weekend. He hadn't told me where he was going, only that he would be back

Sunday night so I wasn't looking forward to spending it alone. I called him and relayed where I would be. He only said to make sure the men knew my plans for the evening. He had another guard added to my team. I started to realize the same men didn't work 24 hours of the day. They switched at regular eight hour shifts, but they all looked the same. I had been calling three different guys the name of Mike. The real one had a scar on the inside of his left hand and his eyes were darker brown than the rest.

When we stopped at Amanda's building, the real Mike sat next to me.

I let out a shaky breath, trying to calm my nerves. He gave me a reassuring smile before he got out of the car.

I waited inside.

This was their routine for me. The car would stop at the back and one of the guards would get out. He would start a sweep around the building and when he cleared it, the car would pull to where I would get out. Then the guard who rode beside me would walk around to my side of the car while he did another visual sweep of the surroundings. He remained at my door while he waited for the third guard to get into place inside the building and then he would open the door for me. Once that happened, I went inside and forgot about the men.

They were always around. I never knew where they were, but they were close. Carter told me one night over dinner that he trained his men to be ghosts. They were supposed to adapt and blend into any environment; otherwise, he wouldn't hire them for his security team. He never used them himself. When he left, he only had one man with him, named Gene. I never saw Gene, but I heard his voice a few times when he would call for Carter.

Gene was an enigma to me, but everything about Carter's life was a mystery to me.

When Mike opened my door, I gave him a small nod in thanks and walked inside. Theresa's doorman gave the guards a scared look, but he opened the door for me without a word. His hand trembled as he did so, and he flushed when he saw that I noticed it. I wanted to murmur my understanding, but I didn't. I ducked my head down and followed him to the elevator. He pushed the button for Theresa's floor and bid me a goodnight. He said that he would be announcing my arrival to her over an intercom from the front desk.

As with Mike, I gave him a nod in thanks as well, then stepped back and waited until the elevator stopped at her floor.

Theresa opened her door down the hall and stuck her head out. She waved at me. "Hey there! I've got a pizza on the way and two bottles of wine being chilled. I hope you like wine. I like the sweet stuff. I'm not a dry girl."

The ball of nerves inside loosened at her easygoing laugh. As I stepped into her apartment, I was taken aback by the warmth. It was a three bedroom apartment with a simple layout.

"You want a tour?"

I flashed a grin. "I'd love one."

"Here's the kitchen." She waved to the room we were standing in, with an island counter in the middle. "There's the living room." She had a white plush sectional sofa that curved around one corner of the room with a loveseat next to it. The wall was covered with a large flat-screen. She led the way through the living room and opened her glass doors that led onto a large patio. "Here's my balcony. Nothing special, but I like the view." It was over a courtyard that was in the middle of the surrounding buildings. A pool glistened up at us.

"And here's my bedroom." She took two steps and opened

another set of glass doors. We stepped inside to a large bedroom. She had matched her white comforter with the white couches in the living room. As she showed me her bedroom and the other two rooms used as an office and an exercise room, I noticed there were no guest bedrooms. The last stop was her public bathroom. She opened the door. "I've got a private bath off my room, but you can use this one. I never have guests so it'll be like your own bathroom whenever you come over."

A twinge of pleasure spread through me. She was already planning for the next time we hung out.

Her buzzer went off and she went over to it. "Yeah?"

The man on the other side spoke, "Your pizza is here."

"Okay. Let him up. I'll be waiting."

"Yes, Miss Webber."

She grinned and shook her head as she turned to me. "He always calls me Miss Webber. I've been living in this building since I was three. You'd think Jarvis would start calling me by my first name, but he never does."

"You've lived here your whole life?"

She nodded as she collected her wallet from her purse. "Yep. My parents moved in when my dad got a new architect job. Then after they died, I didn't want to leave the building. I did downgrade to this apartment, but I like this building. It's home. Known all the neighbors all my life. There's not much turnover here."

My eyes went wide. She downgraded? I could never afford a place like this, not with the salary I earned as Mr. Hudson's assistant. Then I comprehended the rest of what she had said. "Oh, I'm so sorry about your parents."

She shrugged as she opened the door. "It's fine. It was a car accident. I was told that they didn't feel any pain. A truck blindsided them."

I heard the hitch in her throat.

The elevator sounded its arrival and she stepped out to pay for the pizza. When he left, she closed the door behind her with a large steaming pizza box in her hand. I wasn't sure what to say. I understood grief and death, but I didn't understand her lifestyle. For the most part, I grew up in a one-bedroom with AJ. Mallory and Ben grew up with their parents, but they lived in poverty. All three of us had fought our way out of it. I'd been the most successful, but I would never feel comfortable in a home like this. Carter's was different. That was Carter's place, not mine.

"What about you and your folks?"

"Oh." What did I say? "Um, my parents have been dead since I was nine. I grew up with my brother."

"I'm sorry about your folks too. You must be close with your brother?"

I was. "Yeah." I forced a wide smile and changed the topic. "The pizza smells delicious."

She chuckled as she pulled out two plates. "Gotta love Sammy's Pizza, right? I grew up on it. My mom always ordered delivery. I think she had a crush on the delivery guy back then, but my dad never minded. It was the only time he could eat junk food. My mom was a stickler for healthy food back then. Not me. I indulge when I can. When the pounds start sticking, I'll have to stop."

I had to agree. She was stick-thin and after spending so many breaks and meals with her during the week, I knew she had a hearty appetite. I wasn't as blessed, but I never had a problem with my weight. My problem was not having an appetite like Theresa, something she had started to notice over the past week. I was determined to match her with pizza tonight, but as I made that decision she already gobbled a slice down as she searched for two glasses for our wine. I didn't think I stood a chance. However, I slid a piece onto a plate and took the glass of wine she offered.

That was normal, to indulge after a hard week at work and laugh with your friends over a glass of wine. This was all normal. I could be normal.

Carter wasn't normal, but I couldn't only have him in my life now.

"So what do you want to watch?" She indicated to the couches and soon we were both situated with blankets, the pizza on the table, and the second bottle of wine beside it. As I watched her gather everything, she flushed and murmured, "I get lazy once I'm on that couch. I don't like to get up. Don't judge me."

"Never." I couldn't contain the smile that stretched from ear to ear. Theresa was exactly the friend that I needed.

It was after the second movie and the second bottle of wine when someone knocked on her door. I fell off the couch, my heart pounding, but Theresa scowled at the door. There was no fear, there wasn't even surprise. She sighed as she stood from the couch, a little clumsier than normal. "Excuse me while I deal with this."

With this?

I slunk down on the couch so they couldn't see me, but I tried to peek over the edge. As she opened the door wider and I heard a masculine voice, my mouth fell open. Did Theresa have a boyfriend and not tell me? Well. I rolled my eyes. I hadn't been forthcoming about my life at all. I couldn't blame her for not sharing her personal life. Then I heard her snap, "Noah, you never told me!"

I gave up on peeking and fell to the floor beside the couch. That was my boss.

He growled from irritation and snapped back, "I did too. I told you about the family dinner last week."

"Yeah." Theresa held her own. "You told me, you never invited me. I thought you were just being a selfish prick, like normal."

"AAH! You make me crazy."

She snorted. "You do that fine just by yourself. I don't do a thing to make you crazy." Her voice softened. "Your mother must be so angry with me."

"Don't worry. She blames me, said I must've done something to piss you off."

"Look, come in. I'll call your mom and square everything away. I have company so I can't come anyway."

"You have company?" Interest and alarm spiked in his tone. "Who?"

"A friend."

He snorted this time, "You don't have any friends."

She growled. "I'd slam this door in your face if I didn't have to call your mother."

"Ookay," he mocked her.

"Whatever. Come in. Be nice to my friend." She turned around and grabbed her phone from the table beside me. As she bent, she flashed me an apology, but she spoke to the big guy who had followed her inside, "You might want to be professional. She works for you." And then she flounced out of the room, lifting the phone to her ear as she went.

I sat up. So this was Noah Tomlinson. I never met the guy but had seen photographs of him. There'd been a few from when he had been an MMA fighter and plenty from when he won the national championship. He wore jeans and a sweater that stretched across his chest in an impressive manner. The guy was huge, and as I caught his gaze, I knew he was intelligent. A cloud of suspicion and leering was in his gaze as he raked me up and down.

I expected the owner of The Richmond to stick his hand out, smooth back his hair, and become the sleazy smooth-talker most of the guys at the top level were. He didn't. His frown deepened and he leaned against the island counter in the kitchen. He folded his arms, making his chest seem even bigger, and scowled at me. "Who are you?"

He didn't know—but he must've. "I'm Emma Martins."

His eyebrows shot up and everything vanished. Shock and something close to panic came over him. He glanced to where Theresa had gone and, when he heard she was still on the phone, dropped his voice to a whisper. "What are you doing here?"

"I—huh? Theresa and I are friends. We're working together. *You* put us together."

He growled from the back of his throat. "I didn't expect this. I knew you'd work together, but," he glanced where Theresa was again, "she doesn't know your relationship with Carter, does she?"

My relationship with Carter? Did he? What relationship? "No, no one does." Well, he did. I narrowed my eyes. "What do you mean you didn't expect this?"

He frowned again. "That was my mistake. I'm sorry, but you really need to go. You should cut your friendship with Theresa too. She hates Carter."

My eyes threatened to pop out. She *knew* Carter?

He amended, "I mean, she hates the idea of him. She's never met him, don't worry, but she knows he's a friend of mine and connected to the mob. She doesn't approve of our friendship, and if she knew your relationship with him," he whistled and shook his head, "it would not be pretty. Trust me."

"How do you two know each other?"

He shrugged. "Family friends. Her parents were friends with my parents. We took her in when they died."

"Oh."

His eyes narrowed again. "You're not here trying to get her money, are you?"

WHAT?

But then I glanced around, she had money. I saw that from before, but I wondered how much she had. Then I remembered who I was living with and replied, "You think I'm scamming her for money?"

"Oh, yeah." He relaxed and flashed me a grin. It transformed his face. I saw why a lot of the females at work whispered about his deliciousness. He didn't have the classic model-like looks that Carter had, but when his mouth turned into a smile, it lit his face up and he was handsome in a manly and rough looking away. I knew that appealed to a lot of women. "I forgot your connections. Maybe she's scamming you?"

I could tell by how his mouth curved up in a crooked grin that he was kidding. I was a little insulted. I might've grown up with a scammer, but I never did cons. AJ never allowed it, and after he died, I was determined to be successful without resorting to low-level ways of making money.

"Look," his jaw tightened and his voice grew rough, "I really am sorry. I didn't mean anything by that, just that Theresa's been targeted before because of her money. She doesn't have a lot of friends because she's too damn trusting. I tell her to steer clear of everyone, but she tries every now and then. They never end well. That's what I thought before I knew who you were."

That would explain Theresa's lack of friends, but I couldn't shake his suspicion. He was covering up for it, but it was there. I didn't know if my relationship with Carter kept it there or made it worse? My gut told me that he would've been suspicious of me with Carter in my life or not.

"Okay!" Theresa returned with a smug smile on her face. She threw an arm around Noah's shoulders and bumped her hip into his. "It's all good with your mother."

He studied her with a slight sneer. "Tell me you didn't."

Her smile stretched from ear to ear. "I did."

I frowned.

He groaned. "Whatever deal you struck with my mother, I'm out. I have a date tonight."

"No, you don't," she laughed and poked him in the chest. "Well, yes, you do. With me and Emma." She continued, "Brianna got a job at Octave. I told your mother that we'd go and check on her."

"Brianna did what?" Noah exploded. "You did what?"

"Yeah, I did." Theresa struck a cocky pose with her hand on her hip. "And you can be damn pleased with me because I told your mother that we'd go and check on her. In return, she's not going to hold it against you that you didn't invite me to the family dinner tonight."

"What family dinner? Brianna wouldn't have been there." His jaw clenched as he said it. "She got a job at Octave? What the hell was she thinking? That place is dangerous."

Theresa frowned. "She's probably thinking it's the coolest job in the world. You go there all the time."

"I do not."

"You take me there all the time."

"Oh, yeah." But as his jaw continued to clench and unclench, his anger was obvious. "How the hell did she get a job there?"

"What do you mean? The owner probably lured her there. He's

sucking up to be your friend, Noah. He always does this."

Her voice rose a notch and his head slunk down. I got the distinct impression this was a fight they had often. My boss shot me a guarded look. There was also an apology there as Theresa started to talk more. "Why you're friends with someone like him is beyond my comprehension. He's bad news, Noah. He's nothing but a—"

"—Theresa," he interrupted and shot me a pointed look.

"Oh." She flushed and turned to me. "I'm sorry, Emma. I don't like one of Noah's friends, but that's not something you need to worry about. I'm really sorry. I forgot you were here." Then she blinded me with her white teeth. "Want to go dancing tonight? Noah knows the owner of Octave. I might not like the guy, but his club is hot to go to."

Oh dear. I wasn't sure how to react.

She misunderstood. "Oh, you don't have to worry. Trust me. I know the place can be dangerous, but whenever I go with Noah, we always get the VIP treatment. We get our own entrance and a private box. It's completely safe. For us."

When I didn't say anything, she grabbed my hand and squeezed it.

She gushed, "I promise you'll have fun. And it's not like we'll even see the guy. He's barely ever at the club. He's so important and powerful that he doesn't have time for his friend." As she said the last statement, her voice grew thick with sarcasm.

Noah rolled his eyes. "Can you stop griping? You've never met the guy."

She shot him a dark look. "I don't need to have met him. He's bad news, Noah. I don't know why you refuse to see that about him. He's only using you for The Richmond. You're the one who told me he wanted to buy some shares last year."

He shook his head and grumbled, “I didn’t say he wanted to buy shares. I said I offered him *more* shares.”

She straightened to her fullest height and squared her shoulders back. “You’re crazy for being friends with him.”

“Drop it, Theresa. You don’t know the guy. You don’t know my friendship with him. And,” he sent another pointed look in my direction, “you really want to hash this out in front of your newfound friend?”

That did it. The tension left her in the next second and she squeezed my hand again. “I’m sorry, Emma. I get so angry sometimes.”

I tried to give her a reassuring smile back. “Oh, that’s okay. We all have our…secrets, I guess.”

“Well, it’s not really a secret, but it’s not an argument that needs to happen tonight. I invited you over because I thought it would be fun. This’ll be fun too. You’ll come to Octave with us?” She gave me a puppy-dog look.

Well. This was going to be interesting.

I nodded, but as Theresa cheered and Noah frowned, I wasn’t sure how this night was going to unfold. When we headed downstairs and piled into Noah’s car, I saw my car parked behind us. Oh, great. I hadn’t considered what to tell Mike and the other guards, but when Noah pulled into traffic and my car started to follow, I realized that they already knew what I was doing. I only hoped Carter wouldn’t get mad about the change in plans.

-CARTER-

"Sir."

Carter glanced towards the door and saw one of his men. He stood from the table and left his business associates behind. When they stepped into the hallway, his man waited until the door was closed before he told him, "The boyfriend met with a Bertal."

"They found him?"

"No, sir. He went to them."

Carter's eyes whipped up. "Are you sure?"

He clipped his head in a nod. "Yes, sir. We held back, but when he returned to the apartment he had a briefcase with him."

"What was in it?"

"Money, sir."

Carter's eyes closed in a grimace. He knew what that meant. "Are you certain?"

"He opened it in the car. Vance got a picture of it. It looked like a lot of money too."

"Okay," he sighed. "Double the guards on her. Make sure they blend."

Carter returned to his meeting, but it took a few minutes before he was able to concentrate on what they were telling him. His mind was on Emma and what this meant for her. He didn't like it. It happened too fast for his liking. The time to tell her what was going on was nearing, but he didn't want that. Not yet. It was too soon for her to be as scared as she needed to be.

THIRTEEN

As Noah neared Octave, my phone buzzed. When I saw it was from Carter, my entire body grew warm. Theresa had insisted that I dress up. She threw a white dress to me. I hadn't expected much, but when I put it on, it was the perfect choice. It hung low on me. The ends of the dress touched my toes, but the front of it separated. Instead of an actual dress, it was two lengths of cloth. Theresa tied it around so each one covered my breasts and wrapped around my torso once. She declared I was a goddess and I had to admit that I felt like one. I was even more grateful now that I had listened to her advice. Tingles of excitement and nerves soared through me, but when I read it, a rush of desire made my head spin. **I'm coming back tonight. Finished my work in one day. I'm flying back now. Where are you?**

I replied. **Will be at Octave soon. Going with my friend who knows your friend. Noah Tomlinson.**

Thomas and Mike?

In the car behind me. I rode with Noah and Theresa, she's my friend I told you about.

Stay close to Noah. He can fight and will protect you. The guys will watch over you at the club.

"Who are you texting?"

My head jerked up and I almost dropped my phone as Theresa frowned at me. Her eyes fell to my phone and warmth surged to my cheeks as I fumbled to keep my screen hidden. I knew I was redder than red. I must've been a lobster because Theresa grinned and lifted an eyebrow. "Do you have a boyfriend, Emma? You haven't mentioned him all week. I want to know!"

I slid my eyes to Noah, who had tensed behind the steering wheel. "You didn't mention a few things yourself."

Her mouth clamped shut and her cheeks grew pink. "Point taken. Well done." She chuckled as she turned back around. "But I want to know all about him."

No, you don't. You really don't.

I looked in the rearview mirror and saw that Noah had been watching me. I could tell he shared my unspoken thought. From what I had been told and heard, Theresa would not like Carter's relationship with me. And yes, I frowned and hung my head. I just admitted to myself that there was something between us. I sucked in my breath and my hands started to tremble. My stomach churned and formed knots, but I had to admit that something was growing between Carter and me. He hadn't said anything outright to me, but he desired me. I knew it. I felt it, but during the past week, he never made a move.

He was always home when I returned from work. We had dinner every night. After that first night, I never used my bed again. When I got sleepy, he would lead me to his. He always held me in his arms and stroked my back until I fell asleep. There were a few times when I would wake in the middle of the night and he was gone. The first time, I checked the gym, but he wasn't there. I remained awake for the rest of the night until he returned after five in the morning. No light was turned on, but I heard him return to the room and slide back into bed with me. He drew me back against his chest and wrapped his arms tight until I felt his chest move up and down in a deep sleep. When his breath evened out, I fell asleep as well.

The second and third time when I woke to find him gone, I didn't search for him. I fell back asleep and woke again when he returned to the bed. I always snuggled back into his arms, and when I would leave for work in the mornings, he woke as well. He never seemed tired. He was always alert and he had coffee and breakfast ready for me by the time I made it to the kitchen. Then, he'd ride with me to my job.

Every morning he would give me a kiss as I left the car, but he never kissed me when we were at home or in his bed.

I will come to you and find you there.

I bit my lip. I could only imagine Theresa's reaction. **Maybe you shouldn't.**

Why?

Theresa is protective of Noah. She doesn't like you.

Has she met me?

I couldn't hold back my grin. He didn't even know. **No, but your reputation speaks for itself.**

She doesn't have to see me for me to see you. I will find you.

I wasn't aware of the breath I'd been holding until I let it loose. Goodness. There was a promise and something ominous in his last text. Every nerve was stretched tight and ready for him. The throbbing had started when I got his first text. It was too much for me by the last one. Carter was making me go crazy over the past week. I wanted him. It was to the point where I needed him. I couldn't think straight when it came to him.

"We're here."

As I looked out the windows, I was surprised to see that we had pulled into the alley beside Octave. Then I remembered the couple I watched from the street, as they were hurried through a side door into the club. When a door opened and two large men stepped outside, I knew it was the same thing. Noah opened his door and stepped aside as Theresa crawled over his seat and hopped out of the car. My door was opened and a giant stood next to it, waiting for me to do the same.

As I got out, I glanced around and saw that Mike stepped next to one of the guys from the club. He blended in with them.

"Come on, Emma," Theresa called from inside.

Mike nodded for me to go in so I did. He followed behind, along with three other men. As I joined Noah and Theresa in a small hallway, I saw another two men with them. She gave me a squeal and wrapped her arms around me for a hug. Her body was riddled with delight. "This is going to be so much fun." She whispered into my ear, "I'll never admit this to Noah, but I do like that he knows the owner sometimes. We always get the best treatment here and this place is amazing. I just don't want them to be as close as they are. The owner scares me."

I hugged her back, but shook my head. A week ago, I never would've thought Theresa was the kind to let loose and go to a club like Octave. A lot of things would've surprised me a week ago. And a part of me was getting riled the more she badmouthed Carter. I understood. She obviously knew he was connected to the mob, but she had never met him. And at that thought, a different anxiety filled me. What would she think if she did meet him? Would she not want to be my friend? Or would she want more to do with Carter? I wasn't a fool. I could tell that some of her reaction to Carter was from the intrigue and how the media portrayed him. Carter was seen as a real-life mobster from the movies. He had the smoldering looks, but he was out of reach for so many. He was too powerful.

"Ma'am."

I jumped at Mike's one word reminder.

Noah and Theresa had followed the other two guards down the hallway. They paused halfway and waited for me, frowning at me.

Mike and the other three guards stood behind me. I shook my head as I started towards them. Tonight was going to be interesting indeed.

We were shown into a box that opened to a shared dancing area with two other boxes. The six guards took up positions against the wall and were camouflaged by the dark shadows; after awhile it seemed as if they weren't even there. However, Theresa kept glancing at one of the bigger guys. She said to Noah, in an awed voice, "Your friend is really pulling out all the stops with you tonight."

She flashed Noah a knowing smirk, but he ignored her and frowned in my direction. We both knew the truth. They were there for me.

It was at that moment a guy came in and approached Noah. He oozed sleaze. He was dressed in a business suit. Everything was flashy about him. His hair was gelled into spikes. His teeth were perfectly white. This was the slicked-back type of guy I thought my boss would've been. The two shook hands and clasped each other on the shoulder. It wasn't long until Noah motioned Theresa over. The three of them talked for a few more minutes as drinks were brought in by two servers. Then, as I watched, Theresa laid her hand on the guy's arm and motioned for him to bend down. She whispered something in his ear, smiling at Noah the whole time, whose frown had reappeared. Then they were laughing again.

For some reason I wanted to melt into the background. I must've inched backwards without realizing it because a hand touched my elbow in a discreet manner. I jumped, turning to see Mike behind me. He gave me a small nod. "Ma'am."

I sighed, "Mike, you can use my name by now."

He gestured towards Theresa. "Your friend might be jealous, ma'am."

I grinned, but he was right. She wouldn't be jealous, but she'd be curious. He had heard her thoughts on Carter. All of the guards had heard.

"Emma, come over here."

Everything inside of me clenched, but I couldn't ignore Theresa. For some reason, I didn't want to be anywhere close to the other man. However, as she crossed and grabbed my arm, she dragged me over to them and squeezed my shoulders. "This is my friend, Emma. Emma, this is Scott. He's the night manager at Octave."

A seductive smirk appeared as he held his hand out for me. "Emma, it's very nice to meet you."

Noah snorted in the background.

With my skin itching, I shook his hand but released it as quickly as possible. I tried to smile so he wouldn't know how uncomfortable I was, but I couldn't stop the dark chill that went down my back. "It's nice to meet you too, Mister."

"Emma!"

What? I glanced at Theresa. Her mouth hung open as her eyes

had widened. What?

“Mister?” Scott grimaced but still grinned at me. “I haven’t been called that by anyone except my niece’s little friends. They call me Mr. Scott. Please, call me *just* Scott.”

I nodded but moved back a step.

Noah chose that moment to pinch Theresa’s side. She rounded on him, but he ducked her arm as he chuckled and moved at the same time. As he settled in front of me, blocking me from Scott, I knew the entire thing had been on purpose.

I was grateful.

He wrapped an arm around Theresa’s waist as he touched his drink to Scott’s. “So, I hear my little sister is working for you. How’d that happen?”

“Oh, uh.” Then Scott laughed, tipping his head back. “She came in here and asked for an interview. How could I deny the little sister of The Great Noah Tomlinson? She’s a good worker, Noah. You should be proud of her.”

Noah’s shoulder stiffened. “It’s her first night.”

“She’s been doing great so far. I’m sure she’ll be one of the best girls within a few months. She could move all the way up to bartending the privates pretty soon.”

“As long as she sticks to the bartending services, Scott.” A dark warning was in his tone.

“Yeah, yeah, of course.” A sick laugh left him. “What else did you think I meant? You don’t think I’d do that to your little sister, do you?”

“Does Carter know Brianna is working here?”

“Why would The Big Man know? That’s my job.” An uptight tension settled over the group. Scott’s tone turned sour. “I do the hiring and firing.” He paused for a beat. “You don’t want me to fire your little sis on her first night, do you, Noah? Theresa said you were here to check on her and make sure she was doing a good job. I'm getting the opposite feeling here. I know Brianna would be upset."

During the exchange, I had floated back to where I felt comfortable. It wasn't a conscious decision, but I relaxed when I felt Mike beside me.

Theresa gave both men a strained smile. "Come on, guys. I'm feeling thirsty. Scott, could you order some wine for us? I promised Emma that we'd have wine tonight."

"Already did." Scott never blinked. "It's on the tray behind you."

The two didn't look away as they stared at each other.

I couldn't take anymore and turned to Mike. "I don't want him here."

He nodded and pressed his ear. He murmured something and it wasn't long before someone cleared their throat from the entrance to the box. "Mr. Graham."

Scott turned in shock. "Gene? What are you..." His voice trailed off and his eyes looked past the man. "Is Carter here?"

I started forward to see what Gene looked like, but Mike grabbed my elbow and held me still. "Please...Emma."

I relaxed and stayed where I was.

"Can you come with me, Mr. Graham?"

"Why?" Scott frowned and glanced at Noah with a question in his eyes. "I'm here with friends, Gene. Whatever it is can wait until tomorrow unless Mr. Reed is here."

"Can you come with me, Mr. Graham?" The question was asked with a reinforced authority now.

Scott's shoulders sagged. The small battle was over. He flashed an apologetic smile to Noah and Theresa and nodded to them. "I'm needed somewhere else, but I'll try to get back before the night is over." He turned for me and frowned when he saw Mike's hand on my arm. "It was nice to meet you, Emma."

I gave him a small smile, but Mike never moved his hand.

Scott didn't move. He remained and stared at me. It was another minute before Gene cleared his throat again. "Mr. Graham." Then he shook his head and turned to leave. As soon as he left, Mike's hand fell from my arm and I felt like I could breathe again. I didn't know what it was, but I was jarred from his presence.

I looked up, "Mike, are you going to say something..." The question fell from my lips. He gave me a small grin and I knew that Carter already knew. It was why Gene had appeared, Carter's personal bodyguard. Then I frowned. "Is Carter already here?" But Mike had resumed his original bodyguard stance back up against the wall. He blended with the shadows to be invisible so I knew he wouldn't be answering that question.

"That was...odd..." Theresa was frowning to herself as she poured a glass of wine from the tray a server had left. She shook her head. "Oh well. Emma, would you like a glass?"

I nodded, relieved, as I crossed back to them. My knees were a little unsteady.

It was an hour later, after two bottles of wine and most of the time spent on the small dance floor, when Theresa went in search for the private bathroom. As I limped my way to our seats, Noah handed me a bottle of water and patted the chair next to him. I collapsed onto it, but I wasn't expecting what happened next.

"Thank you." He cast a glance over his shoulder to make sure Theresa was out of earshot. "I hate that guy. He makes my skin crawl, but I never knew if I could say something to Carter or not. I know you did that tonight."

Shivers went down my back again as I remembered his sick

laugh. "I just didn't like him."

"You shouldn't. There are rumors that he broke whores in for the Mauricio family."

My stomach dropped. "Why would Carter have him work here?"

He shrugged. "I don't know, as a favor maybe? He won't anymore, not if he gives you the creeps. I know that much. Thank you. You have no idea. He's been sniffing around Brianna for the last six months. I'm sure he had something to do with her getting a job here."

I nodded. I shouldn't have been surprised. "Why did you seem so happy to see him?"

Noah snorted, taking a sip from his beer. "You can't let a guy like that know what you really think of him, not until you're in the position to actually do something about him and I've never been in that position."

I nodded. That made sense, somewhat. I murmured, "Theresa seemed to like him."

"He's charming to most females." He cast me a sidelong glance. "You seem to be the exception. Thank god."

An image of Jeremy raping Mallory flashed in my mind. My hand flew up to my mouth as I felt vomit come up, but I took a deep breath and swallowed it.

"Emma?"

I recovered, shaking my head. "I'm fine." A dark feeling came over me. "I've seen men worse than him before." I would've killed Jeremy Dunvan again, if I was given a choice, but I would've enjoyed it the second time.

"Ma'am?" Mike was at my side. At my look, he corrected himself. "Emma?"

"Yes?'

"Your ride is here."

"My ride?" Carter. "Oh!"

Noah chuckled. "Go ahead. Theresa wants to stay out awhile longer. I can tell. I'll tell her you got a ride home. Tell Carter hello for me."

Nerves and excitement took over me when I realized what Mike was insinuating. I was distantly aware that I reached out and gave Noah's shoulder a squeeze as I rose, but then I was walking out of the box area and following Mike. I was barely aware of the five other guards that followed as I was led through a back maze of Octave again. This time the lights were still off and a memory rushed at me. It was the night I had come to the club with my college roommate. She had slipped away to find her boyfriend and I danced by myself until two hands slid around my waist. For one night, I gave in to temptation and I allowed the touch of a stranger. I never saw him, but I felt him, and I never experienced those sensations again until Carter. The same need I felt that night, that I felt every time I thought of him, rose with a powerful intensity in me again.

By the time I was shown through a door and into a darkened room, I couldn't control myself. I couldn't think straight. When I saw a shadow, and felt his hand slide around my waist as I had that night, I turned into him. I surrendered everything to his touch. Even before I said anything, I already knew that night had been with Carter. No other man ever made me feel as he had and being back in Octave opened the floodgates.

I wanted him even more.

FOURTEEN

"It was you that time before," I gasped as Carter's lips brushed against my neck. He lingered on my pulse. His tongue swept against it as I tried to turn around to him. I needed to feel him against me, between my legs, but his arms tightened around me. He moved behind me and pressed into me.

He murmured against my skin, "It was me."

I clasped a hand over his on the other side of my neck and held it there, claiming him, as I turned in his arms. His hand slid across the front of me and I saw him. His eyes were dark with lust and need. I knew he saw the same in me, but I didn't care any longer. I needed him, but I remembered that night. My roommate left and I'd been alone until I felt someone behind me. The liquor in me hadn't been enough to turn off all my inhibitions, but they had helped. My skin sizzled as I thought of that night again, how it had been him behind me.

He whispered against my skin as he lowered his head, "I was in the security room. I saw you on the cameras and couldn't help myself." His arms slid around to my back. He pressed a hand to my hip and anchored me against him.

I gasped as he pressed his hips into me, but then he lifted and carried me to the corner.

It was the same as that night.

He held me suspended in the air, so I wound my legs around his waist. I felt him even more against me and then his hands slid under the edge of my dress, to the inside of my thighs. He felt the string of my thong, in the apex between my legs, and started to rub against it.

Desire and pleasure rushed through me. I was feverish for him. I held on, urging him to do more. My hips began to move in rhythm with his hand and it wasn't long before he swept my dress up and his hand was against my skin.

"Carter," I whispered, my back and throat arched for him.

He placed a kiss there, licking.

"I need you inside of me."

He grunted, tightened his hold on my thigh, and slipped two of his fingers inside of me. They went deep before he pulled out and then pushed back in. As he continued, his tongue swept against my neck.

I gasped. My hips moved so his fingers slid even deeper.

Then he pulled my mouth to his, and his lips claimed mine. His tongue swept inside, brushed against mine, and then grew more demanding as his fingers continued their onslaught.

"Please," I whimpered. He'd held himself away from me all week. My body had been strained from wanting him, all damn week. I wanted him, not his fingers. I wanted all of him. "I want you."

His fingers continued their attack. They picked up speed, and I couldn't hold onto him anymore. It was building and building. I felt it nearing. Before it was there, so close, I shoved off the wall so only my head touched it. I pushed my hips against him and he growled at the last thrust before I exploded in his arms.

My body trembled as the waves washed over me. Carter held me up. I had gone limp in his arms. He pressed a tender kiss to my shoulder, then slid a hand underneath and cupped my breast.

I wanted my dress gone. I wanted his clothes gone. I wanted his body on top of mine and with nothing between us. As I gazed down at him as he still held me, he saw what I wanted and lowered me back down to the floor. Then he pulled me against him, pressed another lingering kiss against my lips, and whispered, "Not here."

My eyes closed and my head fell to his chest.

He pressed another kiss. "Soon."

My body had melted into liquid and I was a puddle at his feet.

His fingers helped smooth my dress back in place. When my hair was brushed back and I looked presentable, he grinned down at me and took my hand. His voice was hoarse, "As soon as we get home. You won't walk for a week."

I wish.

Images of the two of us flashed in my mind and I grew wet again. He was going to be the death of me. A part of me knew that once I felt him inside of me, it wouldn't be enough. I would want more. I would never be satisfied, and when he made me come, that'd only been the teaser. My body was primed and ready again. My hand slid down his muscular back. It felt all the ridges, all the dips and curves. A dark pleasure spread through me when I felt his muscles contract as he turned his head to see me.

This was mine.

He was mine.

He groaned and had me against the wall in a second. His hands grabbed my hips and positioned me at an angle before he slammed his into mine. I felt the bulge in front of his pants. That was for me. All for me. He bent over me and lowered his lips just above mine as he thrust against me.

I couldn't breathe. My hands held onto his arms. The muscles there also moved underneath my touch, as if wanting more.

"This," he growled in a whisper against my lips. "This is what I wanted that night. I couldn't contain myself and I had to taste you, but tonight is the night I really have you. You're mine, Emma. You always have been."

I nodded, so weak against his touch.

"Mine."

He was mine as well, but I didn't say it. Not yet, though everything in my body was aching for me to do so.

He took my hand again and led the way out into the hallway. People stopped and watched us as we left. I knew it was because of him. Carter was lethal. His body was carved and molded to perfection. His eyes were cold while his face resembled an angel's. Everyone knew who he was, where he had come from. Even the media went into a frenzy when he was seen in public. However, he moved like a ghost, how he trained his men to be, so those moments were rare, and this moment wasn't any different. His staff had seen him before, but they all went quiet in the presence of a deadly panther.

A wave of possession rocked through me. My legs shook as I remembered my climax. This creature who held my hand was mine, as I was his. I belonged to him and I gasped in silence as I felt his claim sink into my blood. It went deep to the bones. Everything in me belonged to him, and as I followed him through his club, I knew that I was becoming addicted to him. My hand yearned to touch his back again, to slide across his muscles and so much more.

I bit down on my lip. This ache wasn't going to go away. The ache between my legs and the ache that resonated deep inside of me grew every time I was with him, every time he looked and touched me.

A soft sigh left me and he glanced back.

I was scorched by his gaze. His wolf eyes saw into me. I was stripped bare to him, no matter what I wore or how many walls were around my heart. He saw through everything. His hand tightened around mine, and he lifted it. His lips grazed against the top of it. My eyes closed, the ache doubled between my legs at that soft caress.

"Sir." A man stepped out of the shadows. Another guard.

Carter stopped as he listened to what the man had to say. He spoke quietly so I couldn't hear, but both glanced at me.

"What?"

His eyes narrowed and darkened. His hold on my hand became possessive.

I asked again, "Carter? What is it?"

He turned, his decision made, and he curved a hand into the place between my shoulders blades. He started to walk with me down a hallway. As we got further along, I saw Mike waiting for us and then I recognized it was the same box where I had left Noah and Theresa. I dug my feet in. I didn't know what was going on, but I knew he was going to leave me there. Something came up and he needed to handle whatever it was, but I didn't want to be left behind.

"Emma?"

"No." I shook my head. "You're not leaving me." Not again.

He studied me, but then nodded. His hand tightened around mine again. My knees nearly buckled from relief as he turned to the man. "Get the information and call me. Do it quick."

The man went off; he didn't need to be told again.

He led me back through the hallways until we returned to the side entrance. It was our exit this time. A black car was waiting with the door open and Mike beside it. Carter gave him some signal because he left. As we drew closer to the door, he guided me into the seat by my hips and then slid beside me. When he reached to close the door, I jerked forward.

Theresa and Noah had been waiting behind us for their car. Her mouth was hanging open while Noah was frowning.

Oh no.

But the door was shut and the car took off. Carter had no idea what just happened or he didn't care. I had a hard time believing that he didn't know Noah was behind us.

"What?" Carter looked at me.

I must've made some sound. "Oh, it's nothing." It wasn't worth talking about.

He reached for my hand again and raised it for a soft kiss. "Emma, tell me."

The knots in my stomach loosened at his touch, but I shook my head. This was embarrassing in a small way. "It's really nothing."

"Emma," he sighed. "Is this about Graham? They told me you asked for him to be taken away. I'm sorry about him. I should've seen that situation ahead of time, but I didn't. He won't bother you again. I promise."

I shook my head, but I was relieved when I heard that. Then I told him, "Noah and his friend were waiting behind us."

"I know."

"You did?"

He nodded, his eyes lidded as he gazed at my lips. He reached up and ran his thumb over them. My heart skipped a few beats as his touch lingered. He leaned close and dropped his head, but he didn't kiss me. I was waiting, ready for it, but his hand pressed softly against my cheek. "I did, but I didn't think you wanted me to meet your friend."

"I just met her this week. She's Noah's friend more."

His hand tightened on my thigh. He pulled me closer to him. "Your friend too. It was her home that you went to tonight, wasn't it?"

I nodded. I was becoming flustered at how near we were to each other. I wasn't sure who was going to crawl into whose lap, but I was ready. I only waited for him to lift me.

"Then she's your friend too." He grinned, the sight was delicious to me, and rested his forehead on mine. "Anyone who disapproves of someone connected to the mob seems alright to me. You don't need to worry that I won't like your friend, Emma. If she's as good to you as she has been to Noah over the years, I have no reason to dislike her."

And there it was. That was what I had been fearful about, not what Theresa would think about Carter, but what he would think of her. It meant something to me that he approved of my one friend now. Actually, it meant a lot to me that he did—another change in my life. I had three friends who I considered family, but now it was Carter. It was quickly becoming all about him.

"What's wrong?"

I shook my head, my throat thick with emotion. I didn't trust myself. I would start crying. I was sick of the crying.

He cupped the side of my face and turned me to look at him. "Emma."

The kindness in his eyes was my undoing. A few tears trickled from my eye, and he brushed them away. His touch was tender.

"Carter," I wrenched out in a sob.

He lifted me to his lap and folded me against his chest.

The comfort I felt was home to me. I closed my eyes and burrowed into him. I stopped thinking and worrying about everything. I stopped fighting what I was feeling or how much hold this man had over my life. It wasn't only my life anymore, it was my heart. Even without the fear of Franco Dunvan, I knew I wouldn't want to leave him. It was like I had been watching him over the years and wanting to go to him, but I never had enough reason to. At that thought, reality hit me like a bucket of ice water. I sat upright on his lap and looked at him.

Concern and lust intermingled with him. He waited for whatever I had to say.

I sighed to myself. I should move away. I should protect my heart, but as I held his gaze, I couldn't. Different emotions battled each other inside of me, but all it took was one look from him. There it was. One look and I was pulled to him. I would always be pulled to him.

I knew it in my gut, like an anchor thrown into the ocean. The deeper it sunk, the more I knew. I was in love with Carter Reed. As the anchor landed on the bottom of my stomach, it resonated throughout me. Shockwaves soared over my nerves and tendons. My arms shook, even my legs felt the explosion.

And then I wondered, had I always loved him? "Carter."

"Mmm?" His thumb pressed against my lips, but he looked up again.

My voice grew husky. "How did you do it?"

He knew what I was asking.

His hand fell away and he leaned back against the seat, but his eyes never left mine. There'd been a soft playfulness in them before.

That fell away to be replaced by a chilling look. It was still intense, but he reminded me of the Cold Killer everyone talked about.

I started to move off his lap, but he kept my legs in place. They straddled him so I waited, content to stay where he wanted me.

"You want to know what happened after AJ died?"

I nodded. I needed to know. I thought I did, but maybe I didn't know everything. "You said they were looking for me?"

His hands tightened on my arms, an instant reaction to my words. He forced them to relax as he answered, "Yes. They were. Franco Dunvan is a monster, but I can't pretend that I'm not like him. I became like him."

-CARTER-

Carter gazed at her. She was so earnest. She wanted to understand and he saw that she needed to understand, but he still held back. Could she handle knowing everything? His man told him that Troy couldn't be reached. He was their confidante in Dunvan's organization, and he always got word back to them. But something had happened, or something was going to happen. The last communication they got from Troy was that the boyfriend had sold her out and Franco's men were looking for her.

She had to know, before it was too late. So he'd start from the beginning.

She needed to be ready.

My lungs strained against my chest. It hurt to breathe, but I bit my lip and listened.

"Franco didn't order the hit on AJ. Everyone thinks he did and he took the credit, but it was Cristino who ordered it."

I closed my eyes as a shudder went through me, remembering my brother's pleas. *"Please, Tomino, please."*

Carter's voice grew rough. "It was Tomino, his little brother, who did the hit." I felt his scrutiny as he added, "But you know that. You were there."

The image of Tomino raising the bat came back. It seared me.

"So was I."

Reeling, I tried to slide off his lap. His hold on my thighs kept me anchored to him. He pulled me closer and kept going, now in a whisper against my ears, "I was upstairs. AJ was coming to me and I saw it, but I couldn't do anything. I couldn't even get my window open long enough to yell down. Hell, not that I could've done anything, but I wanted to try."

He was there. My eyes were wide open now and unblinking, crushed against his chest. He was there. I couldn't get around that.

His hand started to brush my hair back as he continued, "When it happened, I couldn't look away. And when they took that bat to him, that was the beginning for me, Emma."

Oh god. A whimper left me. I burrowed into him now.

"I already knew I was going to kill them, but then, when I saw you crawl out from that vent, I snapped. You, you! You saw the whole thing. They did that in front of you, but I replayed it in my head. I realized that they didn't know you were there. They couldn't have, because," his hand shook behind my head, "if they had, they would've killed you too. Or worse. They would've taken you with them." There was no restraint now. His voice slipped and the icy rage he felt that day was in him again. "I killed all of them, Emma. I'd do it again. I *have* done it again. I went to Tomino's house that afternoon. I went from room to room and I sliced their throats. When that didn't work and there were too many of them, I used their guns on them."

My hands turned into fists on his shirt. My shoulders bunched together and I hated what I was hearing, but I had to hear it. A part of me wished that I had been there, that I had been the one enacting the revenge that I could only hear about. I was biting my lip, trying to keep everything in, and I tasted my own blood. But I didn't stop biting, I only bit down harder.

Carter's voice had grown distant as he remembered that day. He took a deep breath. His chest lifted up and down. "I'm not going to tell you everything. I don't need to add to your nightmares, but when I was done at the house, I went to The Blue Chip and shot Cristino. I shot him and his two drivers in his office. There were a few more that I didn't know about until later, but I still killed them. I killed all of them. For you."

There was a hitch in his voice, but I didn't move. I stayed pressed against him, biting so hard that blood trickled out. I felt it slide down my chin and knew it covered him as well. It didn't matter.

"You went to Mauricio after that?" I wrung out, my own voice was hoarse. It was painful to speak.

"I left The Blue Chip and took a cab to their warehouse. It was Farve who saw me first. I was damn lucky he did. I had blood on me by then. I don't know how I got it on me, I don't remember touching the bodies, but somehow it got all over my face. I'm surprised the cabbie didn't take me to the police. He could've. I was out of it by then, but yeah, it was Farve that saw me first. He remembered me from my dad. He'd been drinking buddies with him, but I knew he never approved of the beatings I got."

I remembered when Carter would sleep at our place; almost every night, he would slip in through the patio door. He had never spoken about it when we were kids, and since I had come into his life again, the topic hadn't been raised. I remembered one night when he had been laying on the couch, bruised and still bleeding. I never knew what to say. AJ ignored it; he did it because that's what Carter wanted. But I couldn't ignore it that night. I slept on the floor beside him. When I woke, his foot had slipped off the couch and rested against mine.

I didn't move for hours. I held still until Carter took his foot away. When he woke, he never said a word. He got up and went back to his home. Thinking about it now, a few tears for him came back to me, but I remained quiet. When he wanted to talk about that, I would be there for him.

"Farve vouched for me. He said I was a good fighter and loyal."

I knew the rest. They had taken him in and there had been more massacres left behind by him. When I was taken into social services and shuffled between foster homes, I still heard stories about Carter Reed, the Cold Killer. The stories had stopped by the time I graduated high school. It wasn't until my first year at college that I realized why, he had moved up. Octave opened, and a few more clubs followed.

Four years later Carter Reed had turned into a legend.

He held me now and pressed another kiss to my cheek. He whispered, "Franco Dunvan replaced Cristino in the Bertal Family. They found out that everything I had done stemmed from AJ's death. Everyone knew he'd been my best friend, so he wanted to put a hit on you."

"What?"

He nodded, his eyes were remorseful. "But they couldn't. What I had done was too big. The police were never pulled in because Tomino's house was their base for making sex slaves. The Bertal family hid everything and cleaned it all up, but Franco wanted to avenge Cristino to make more of a name for himself." Carter shook his head. "We heard his elders never allowed it. You were too young and you were an innocent, but that didn't stop Franco from trying. He just never made any outright moves that the Bertal Family could link back to him."

Everything in me hurt. It hurt to breathe. It hurt to feel. It hurt to think. It hurt to speak, but I rasped out, "They tried to hurt me? All my life?"

He nodded, framing my face with both of his hands. "I've been protecting you all your life, Emma. Mike and Thomas are only two in a long line of men that have been watching you. All your life. Since that day. This has all been for you." He frowned. "You were supposed to have a guard at the penthouse. He was taking a piss when you slipped past, but the others followed you." He laughed now. "I couldn't believe that one. He vowed he'd never piss again to me."

All my life? They'd been watching me? All my life? I couldn't wrap my head around that. Wait, did he mean—I sucked in my breath. "Did you know about Jeremy Dunvan before I came to you?"

He nodded, waiting for my reaction.

My eyes were wide-open and panic rose. My chest felt tight. Something was pressing on it. But—I shook my head. It didn't make sense. He knew, but how? Why had he waited for me to come to him?

I had looked away as I started to comprehend everything, but he turned me back to him. His eyes were tender, loving. His thumb brushed over my cheek. "My men took care of the body and the gun. That's why the reports said he was missing."

"But you never said anything to me..." I remembered the hysteria inside of me, the panic at what had happened, how Franco Dunvan was going to kill us. I gulped for a breath, my heart was racing again.

"I knew you'd be scared, but it was your decision," he murmured. "I've always wanted you to be free as long as possible, but when you came to me—"

"Did your men know I was at Octave?"

He nodded. "I was already coming back when they got the call through to me. I knew you were there and that you had decided to come to me." He tilted my chin so I was eye-level with him. "Finally."

"You did all of that for me?"

"I would declare war for you."

He stole my breath, again. It was becoming difficult to breathe around this man. I always felt like I was having a heart attack, and this was no exception. His hand fell down to my thigh and he trailed it over to the inside of my legs. As I closed my eyes and rested my forehead against his, his finger slid underneath my dress and slipped past my underwear for the second time that night. As I drew in a ragged breath, he pushed inside of me, all the way in. His breath was hot against my face, but I didn't move. I didn't want to move. He began to move in and out and I trembled on top of him. When he pushed a second finger in and kept the same rhythm, I opened my eyes. I was so close to him. He was gazing back at me, an intense look on his face as his fingers sped up.

I fought against making a sound, but I couldn't help myself. A soft moan escaped me.

A smirk came over him and he reached around the back of my head. He kept a firm hold there, but it didn't matter. I covered the small distance between us and touched my lips to his. A fuse was lit. It had already been lit, but when our lips touched, it erupted inside of me. I was burning up. His mouth opened and became more demanding. He commanded entrance. I gave it to him. I would give anything to him.

I loved this man.

I pressed harder against him. My hands clung to his shoulders, and I molded my body to his. I couldn't get close enough.

"Emma," he murmured against my mouth.

My tongue swirled up and brushed against his. "Carter."

It was at that moment the car swerved, throwing me to the side. I would've fallen against the door, but Carter caught me. He held me in place as he pushed a button on the ceiling. "Gene?"

The same low voice from the club came over the intercom. "Sir, there's three of them."

Carter held still for a moment, thinking. Then he slid me off his lap and pushed me until I was on the floor. A different look settled over him, a cold mask covered his face. He was no longer the Carter I knew, the one who held me and kissed me. This was the one who killed, and as that sunk in, everything changed. Time slowed until every second passed in rhythm with my heartbeat.

The car slowed.

Carter reached inside a hidden compartment and pulled out a gun. It was black, sleek, and lethal. It fit like a glove in his hand and he moved closer to the door.

Then he burst out, exploding out of the car.

I jerked up from the floor as our car slammed to a halt. Doors were thrown open, rocking our car from the force, as people charged from the front. Then I heard the screech of another car's brakes. Shouts were heard. Shots rang out in the air. Someone screamed.

I opened my mouth, trying to hear myself, but I couldn't. It was as if someone had thrown a veil over me. I could see out, but I couldn't hear, not fully. Everything was muffled. Then pain exploded inside my head, and as the ringing started to dull, I could hear again. I could hear too much now.

"Cart-" someone yelled. That sounded like Mike, was it? My heart was pounding.

I started to move closer to the door.

Bang! Bang!

I swayed to the side as someone flew against the car. Then, with a low grunt, he pushed off just as quickly.

"Carter!"

That was someone else, maybe Gene?

My heart was pounding in my ears as I moved even closer. My fingers grabbed onto the leather exterior, but I couldn't get a good grasp. I was still kneeling on the floor and moved over until I was at the edge of the opened door—*bang! Bang!*

I jerked back, eyes wide. My heart jumped up into my throat. It was right there, ready to burst out of me, but then I gritted my teeth. I was a part of this. I was the reason for this. I had to see.

As I stuck my head out of the car, three pairs of legs blocked my view. They had formed a living wall to my opened door, and I fell to the ground. A burning sensation registered with me, but it was so far away. I barely felt it. I would deal with it later. As I knelt there, I peeked between their legs. They had them planted with their arms raised and guns pointed outwards.

I saw Carter in the distance. He was behind a car that had stopped behind us. Another was left abandoned to the side. All of its doors were open and a fire had started from inside. As the flames leapt higher, smoke filled the night sky. It was becoming overwhelming, but I couldn't look away from Carter. A streetlight glowed above him, and I watched him lift a man to his feet, hit him with the butt of his gun, and let him fall to the ground, unconscious. Then he looked around. He looked calm. He wasn't alarmed like me. But no, he wasn't calm. He was enlivened. I sucked in my breath. His eyes narrowed. He raised his gun and thumbed off two bullets. A body fell against the front of the other car and slid to the ground. A gun scattered on the ground next to him. It slid all the way to our car and underneath. It was behind the tire closest to me and I reached for it.

I didn't know what I was doing. I just knew that I needed to help. I needed to do something.

As I gritted my teeth, I stretched my arm out farther. The tips of my fingers brushed the metal. It was hot and burned me so I knocked it to the side to get a better hold. When my hand closed around the handle, I felt myself being lifted back to my feet. The gun came with me.

Mike was startled as he held me in the air. My feet dangled and skimmed the ground. His grip tightened on my arm and I knew it would bruise, but nothing mattered except the gun in my hand. And Carter. Where was Carter? I looked again.

He was fighting another man. This one was twice his size. He threw a punch. Carter dodged it and jammed his elbow into the guy's face. As he stumbled back, Carter kicked at his knees. The man fell down, but Carter wasn't done. He raised his gun once again and brought the back end of it down with all his strength. The guy fell backwards.

Bang! Bang! Bang!

More shots rang out.

Carter looked over. His eyes widened when he saw me, now clasped against Mike's chest. Then he jerked his gun up and pointed straight at me.

I watched, in almost sick fascination, as his thumb pulled the trigger.

"Agh!"

Mike whirled. I went with him. We both saw a man behind us on the ground. Carter had shot him. Blood seeped from his forehead and his gun fell to the ground.

"Get her out of here!"

"Sir?"

Carter had sprinted back. He waved us off. "Get her out of here. Now."

Mike threw me inside and flung himself next to me. I was pushed to the ground before I realized what was going on and the car sped off.

"No!" I tried to get up. "Carter!"

The hand on my head tightened. I was held in place. He had half of his body over mine and he yelled in my ear, "He'll be safe."

"Carter!"

Mike shook his head next to mine. His voice softened. "He'll be safe, Emma. He wants you to be safe more than him."

"No!" I tried to claw at his arm. I needed to get free and get back to Carter. "We left him behind."

"No." He shook his head again. Both of his arms came around me now. "There's another car. He'll come with that car."

We had gone too far. I knew I couldn't get back to him so I listened to what he said. Carter would come with the next car. He had to. Everything would be fine, but as we went back to Carter's home, I looked down. The gun was still in my hand.

-CARTER-

Carter watched as two cars sped away with Emma in the back. She was safe. He kept telling himself that. She was safe. He needed to make sure there were no others and he was one of the best. He was needed there, not with her. Not yet.

There was a third car, and he sprinted over to it. The driver had been shot and slumped over the steering wheel, sounding the horn. Carter pulled his body back to silence it. Then he sensed movement in the back seat and ripped out a struggling man. The man swung his arm around, trying to aim his gun at Carter but it was knocked away. The man kicked out. That was blocked as well. He swung his other leg at him, but was pinned to the car. He couldn't do a thing but glare at his captor.

Carter stared at him. He didn't say a word. He didn't blink. His eyes were blank. They were ice-cold blue.

Gene hurried over. The taller, older man stopped and glanced around. He stroked his jaw. "That was the first hit."

"I'm aware." Carter glared at him. He threw the man to one of their guards and crossed to kick at one of the unconscious men. When he was rewarded with a moan, he hauled the guy up and threw him against a wall. "Who leaked her location?"

"We can interrogate them at the warehouse."

"No!"

"Carter." Gene stepped forward, placing a hand on his associate's tense shoulders. "We will do this. Go to your woman. Make sure she's okay."

Carter knew he was right. Gene was always right. It was annoying. However, while he would normally ignore the unwanted advice, he listened this time. He remembered Emma's face and how pale she had gone when she was lifted into the car.

He reached down, wound his arms around the struggling man, and snapped his neck. As he stood, Gene stepped back and asked him, "Did that make you feel better?"

"No." He glanced up, an impassive mask over his face. "We leave for Chicago tomorrow."

"Are you sure?"

Carter didn't answer.

Gene sighed, "There's another issue."

Carter snapped his gaze to his friend. His jaw clenched as he waited.

"The boyfriend went back."

Carter's shoulders grew even more rigid. "Tell me he went for money."

"There was no money with him. They're getting him hooked. They can control him better that way, if they still need him."

A savage curse came out, but Carter couldn't do anything about that. He repeated instead, "We go to Chicago tomorrow."

Gene never questioned him again.

"And call Noah. I don't want her going to New York. It's not safe."

Two of his other men had pulled up on motorcycles. He gestured for one to step off, and he climbed on. He turned the bike around and went home.

SIXTEEN

The car sped into the basement, and Mike carried me through a door. It opened to the gym, and we kept going until we were in the kitchen. After he set me down in the middle of the room, he swept it. Four more men followed and they went in opposite directions. They were checking the perimeter.

I couldn't form a thought, much less a decision, so I stayed and swayed on my feet.

"Clear."

"Clear."

"Clear."

"Clear."

"Clear."

I glanced around the kitchen and croaked out, "Clear in here."

Someone laughed somewhere in the building, but all seemed quiet as they filtered down to the kitchen area. Nope, only three of them did. Two were missing.

Mike said, “They took point outside your elevator.”

Oh. Of course. The elevator. Couldn’t forget the elevator.

“Emma.”

I turned. It was Mike speaking to me. Why was he the only one that ever spoke to me?

He gestured towards a stool that one of the other guys pulled out. “You look like you’re going to fall down.”

Oh. Then I swayed a bit more until the guy behind the chair took my arm and guided me into it. He pushed me up to the counter and I lifted my hands to rest on it.

“She has a gun?!”

The men whirled around, but it was Carter. He stood in the open door from the gym, and he was pissed. He rounded on Mike and pointed to the counter. “She has a gun?!”

He looked at a loss.

I sighed in relief. He was here. He was alive. He was furious, but damn he was hot. I couldn’t stop a blush from forming at my thoughts. Images flashed in my mind of us on the bed, in the car, on this counter. Yep. I bobbed my head in a nod to myself. I was in shock. I must’ve been because all I wanted to do was jump Carter. I didn’t want to think about those gun shots or the bodies we left behind, nope. Sex seemed like a better distraction to me.

“Emma?” Carter had come closer. He tipped my head up to his. “Where did you get the gun from?”

“The guy you shot.”

He frowned.

“His gun slid under the car and I reached to get it. I wanted to help.”

He softened and placed a tender kiss to my lips. He murmured against them, “Leave the gun. Go take a shower.”

I stayed. It wasn't to make a statement, I just didn't think my legs could work.

"Please, Emma."

I nodded. "I can't walk."

One of the men snickered again.

Carter shot him a dark look but slid his hands underneath my legs. He lifted me from the chair and my legs wrapped around his waist. Apparently, they worked enough to do that. When he turned and left the kitchen, I laid my head on his shoulder. This felt good. This felt like home. As he took us both to his bathroom, he set me back down on the ground. I stood there, motionless, as he opened the glass door to his shower. He padded inside what was more an entire shower room and tested the water until it was warm enough. Steam started to fill the room as he came back to me.

His eyes never left me. There was so much sadness in them. I touched his lips and sighed.

"What is it?" His voice had grown hoarse.

I shook my head. "All that bad stuff happened, but all I care about is being with you."

"Emma," he groaned.

"You killed more men tonight."

He dropped his forehead so it rested on mine. His breath caressed my skin. "I did."

My hand went to his chest where I felt his heart. It was strong, beating fast. "You were protecting me."

"Emma, if you don't want this to go any further, you have to stop now."

I looked up. I didn't say a word. He was giving me an out, but I didn't want it. I couldn't, not anymore. All I wanted was to be with him.

He saw my answer and his eyes darkened.

I held my breath as he stepped back and slid his hands underneath my dress. As his hands slid up, against my skin, he lifted it over my head. I raised my arms so it cleared my head and then he tossed it aside. My bra went next. With my breasts freed, he cupped one in his hand, his thumb rubbing over the tip. My heart was beating so fast. The ache for him spread through me, but I couldn't do anything. I stood there, wanting more, needing more. When he bent over and took my nipple in his mouth, I couldn't hold back a moan. My hands slid through his hair and took hold, but I was the one held captive by his mouth. He teased me, his teeth biting down gently on the tip as his tongue swept around the nub.

My back arched, giving him better access as my head fell back. The sensations blinded me. My desire was almost overwhelming and my legs began to tremble.

He kept kissing my breasts. One of his hands slid down the front of my body. As he cupped me and his fingers went inside again, he lifted me up so that my legs wound around his waist.

He stood to his fullest height. I was wrapped around him as he turned to walk into the shower. When he stepped underneath the water, I wasn't fazed. It didn't register over the fire heating up inside of me. He stroked in and out, fanning the flames. His teeth released my nipple, and he went in search for my mouth. I gasped, feeling his lips slam into mine, and he swept inside as his fingers stroked deeper with each thrust.

"Carter."

He kept thrusting. I kept building.

I slammed my back against the wall and dug my nails into his shoulders. I was almost there, just at the peak. Then it hit me full force and I cried out, unable to stop myself. I couldn't do anything.

Carter held me in place as the waves rode over me. Each one sent a pulsating sensation through me, and in the end, I was reduced to a puddle. It was then, when he saw that my orgasm had stopped, that he moved and sat me on a seat inside the shower. With heavy eyelids, I watched as he stripped off the rest of his clothes. The rest of my pants came next. As he bent to pull it from my feet, his shoulders bunched and bulged before me. I bit my lip, already wanting to touch him again. I wanted to feel those muscles against me.

Before he stood, he pressed a kiss to the inside of my thigh. I gasped as another burst of pleasure soared through me, but he stood and sent me a smug smirk. He was very aware of the effect he was having over my body. My eyes narrowed, a smart comment on the tip of my tongue, but he stepped back into the shower spray and the words died.

Hunger stirred in me as I watched the water slide over his body.

I thought earlier that he had molded his body into a weapon and I'd been right. He was perfect, from the cut between the muscles in his arms to how his obliques curved down his lean waist. Every muscle stood out underneath his skin. He was perfect.

He watched me as he washed himself. I couldn't tear my gaze away. By the time he was done, my body was brimming with lust again. The first orgasm had only intensified my hunger for him.

When he came back for me, he pulled me to my feet and stepped underneath the spray with me. He lathered shampoo into my hair and rinsed it as I stood touching him. I closed my eyes underneath his tender ministrations. Then he turned and washed my body, every inch. As he cleaned my core, kneeling in front of me, he glanced up and met my eyes in a heated look before he placed his mouth there. I gasped and surged to the tips of my toes. His tongue swept inside of me and a guttural moan was ripped from the bottom of my throat.

He held me anchored in place with his hands on my thighs as his tongue swept in and out. He nibbled and licked as I trembled, clutching him until a second climax swept through me, crashing over all senses in my body.

He swept me back up in the air. Temporarily sated, my head rested on his shoulder and I wrapped my arms and legs around him as he carried me from the shower to his bedroom. He lowered me down and then toweled me dry. I couldn't look away from him as he took care of me. His touch was loving. As he dried himself, I wanted him to slide into bed with me. I wanted to show him the same care, but he disappeared into his closet and came out dressed in black clothing.

"What are you doing?" My voice was raspy. My body hummed with pleasure and my eyelids grew heavy with each word I asked.

He came over and pulled the comforter from underneath me. As he tucked me into the bedding, he kissed my naked shoulder. His lips brushed against my skin. "Sleep, Emma. I will be back."

"Wait." Suddenly panicked, I caught his hand before he slipped away. "Where are you going?"

"I have to take care of some things. I will be back." He glanced out the door. "If you need anything, the men are here." He brushed some of my hair back from my forehead. "Sleep, Emma. You've been through enough tonight."

"Carter." I wanted him with me. I didn't want him to leave, but he was gone the next instant. As he turned off the light and shut the door behind him, I was left with my heart constricting in fear. I didn't want him to go, that was the bottom line for me. I wanted him with me. I wanted to sleep a night with him, especially after the night we just had. But, as I lay there for another hour, I knew he had things to do.

I wasn't going to get any sleep that night.

He didn't return for the rest of the weekend. Saturday passed, then Sunday. I spent both days wandering around the building. I sent a few text messages to Amanda, asking how Mallory was, but they went unanswered. I wasn't surprised. Theresa called me Sunday afternoon and asked if I wanted to come for dinner, but I declined. She saw Carter with me. She knew that I knew him and had kept quiet when she discussed him earlier. An explanation, albeit short and mostly fabricated, was needed to smooth out our co-working relationship; along with any friendship I felt was burgeoning. However, as I rose Monday morning and dressed for work, I didn't have the energy needed to dredge up a lie that made sense.

Mike had the morning off so a new guard was beside me. Two more were inside the home, while another two were outside the elevator. I wouldn't have been surprised if Carter had an entire perimeter around me. He extended messages through his men to me: that he was alright, that he wished me goodnight, and that he would return as soon as possible. I didn't know if they were actually from Carter or something he told his men to say if they sensed my growing restlessness. I had no idea, but I tried to keep myself from becoming angry. I knew he was a busy man. After an attack like we had, I knew he would have more pressing matters to attend to, but I missed him.

And I worried about him.

I'd been in my office for ten minutes before Mr. Hudson barreled through. He didn't knock. Again. "What'd you do?"

"Excuse me?"

"What'd you do?" He tossed a paper on my desk. "We were taken off the Bourbon account. What'd you do? Miss Webber requested it and since she's higher than you and her boss is higher than me, we got pinched. What'd you do, Emma?"

I picked up the paper and saw it was an email from the Director of Sales sent to Mr. Hudson. There it was, it said in three short sentences that the group had been reassigned. The team had two new names and we weren't on it. I checked the bottom of the page. It was sent from Noah Tomlinson himself.

I gulped.

Theresa really did have a problem with Carter, and she knew I was connected to him. Shit. We were off the account because of me.

"So?"

I lied, I had no other choice. "I have no idea, Mr. Hudson. Theresa and I were getting along fine. She even invited me over for drinks Friday night. I went to Octave with her."

He started a huff, but froze midway. "You went to Octave? You got into Octave?" He was taken aback. "Well now. My girls say that's the place to get into and you got in?" His head bobbed in some form of a nod, but then he frowned. "Well something happened between then until now. We're out. I want you to fix it. I want to be on that team, Emma. Make it happen."

I picked up my phone, ready to call...who? I had no one to call. Mallory was the one I usually called. If she didn't answer, I went to Amanda. But since the bathroom a full week ago, I hadn't heard from her, and Mallory had never been one to reach out. Who was my other friend? Theresa, for one week, and Carter but I couldn't even call him. He was off doing what Mike had termed, 'the clean-up' from Friday night's attack. I didn't want to know what that meant and judging by the grim set of his shoulders, I saw that he didn't want me to ask. But it made sense since there'd been no coverage of our attack. I checked the news over the weekend. Nothing.

I put my phone back down and sent Theresa an email instead. An automatic response came back stating she'd be out of the office all week. A few days passed with no results. It wasn't until Thursday, the day that I was supposed to be leaving for New York that I even glimpsed Theresa.

I pushed the button for the elevator, and it opened. My eyes popped out when I saw Theresa inside, with a pencil in her mouth and two large suitcases beside her. She was holding onto a large poster, but it started to slip out of her hands. "OH!" She scrambled to catch it, losing her other grip on the briefcase. It fell to the floor and opened, scattering papers, pens, folders, and flashdrives all over the floor. "Oh no." She bent and started to grab for her stuff.

I got in, hit my button, and knelt to help her.

"Oh gosh. You don't have to do that. Really, Emma." She gave me an awkward smile around the pencil still in her mouth.

I settled back on my feet. That wasn't the reaction I had been expecting. "Oh, no. It's no problem." I glanced down at some of the papers in my hands and saw the logo for the new Richmond Bourbon. The two suitcases seemed ominous next to her. "So you're going to the airport from here?"

"Oh yeah." She brushed her hand back and smoothed her hair from her forehead. It only pulled more out of the ponytail. "Since Noah added Allison, this week has been hell. I meant to call you the other day and see if you wanted to meet at Joe's for a drink after, but

I never got time to do that. I haven't had a chance to check my email. Can you believe that?" She groaned. "I know that once we finish this, I'll have a week's worth of email stuff to catch up. And that's on top of everything we're going to be doing *after* we present to the board."

"Wait." This wasn't making sense. "Noah pulled me?"

"Noah pulled Mr. Worthless. He didn't want your boss to get the credit so he added Allison and Harold instead. Talk about being ineffective. With you, we would've had a great week and had all this done by Monday. With her, I'll be lucky to get it all done by the time we walk into that boardroom. I wish you were coming, trust me."

"Oh." That was unexpected. "I thought it was you that requested the switch."

"Gosh no! I wish you were still on it. We could've been relaxing poolside with margaritas by now if you were on the project." When the last piece of paper had been picked up, Theresa stood, smoothing out her skirt and her hair. More strands were pulled from her ponytail. "By the way, who was the hottie getting into that car with you?" She laughed, "Next thing I know, I'm returning from the bathroom and Noah's says you got a ride home. Imagine my surprise when we leave later and there you are, holding hands with Mr. GQ himself."

Mr. GQ himself? Did she really not know? "Uh," I laughed. "It was kind of sudden."

Theresa snorted as the elevator slid open. "You can say that again." After she stepped out and saw that I remained, she caught the door. "Aren't you coming?"

My exit was a floor down. "I forgot something by the lobby. I'll see you next week."

"Oh. Okay. See you! Let's have wine when I get back!"

When the doors closed behind her, I was left with one very confused thought. What the hell had just happened?

I should've gone through the back exit I had come to use since Carter came back into my life. I should've gone home, but I didn't. Feeling rebellious for some reason, I went out the main entrance and turned into the café where Amanda worked. With a quick scan, I saw that she was working. She was placing cookies onto a tray for their display case so I rounded the counter and leaned against its side next to her.

She kept sliding the cookies onto the tray and ignored me.

I had sent another text earlier that morning, but it went unanswered. Again. I wasn't sure what she was doing, pretending I didn't exist, but I knew Carter advised against communicating with all three of them. He said they were a risk. They could hand me over to ensure their safety, but when I glanced over my shoulder, I saw Mike pretending to study the menu by the door and one of the other guards just came out of the bathroom. I was safe. I had no idea how they moved that fast, but they were good and since my visit to Joe's they had upped their surveillance over me.

"Amanda."

Nothing. She rearranged a row of the cookies now.

"You can't ignore me."

She sighed and moved an entire row of cookies to the side on the tray.

"Why are you mad at me?"

She shot me a dark look, moved the same row back to their original spot.

Okay. I got the message, but I wasn't going anywhere. I was tired of being alone. Since I got the boot from the account, the other girls I'd previously been friendly with had taken her cue. They stayed away. I didn't get a hello in the break room anymore so my week had literally been spent by myself in the office. Mr. Hudson hadn't come back to the office since he gave me that warning and his secretary only shook her head every time I popped in to see if he was in or not. I had sent Theresa emails and considered emailing Noah himself, but he was the Big Man. Before last Friday, I would've pissed my pants at the thought of sending him an email without having it approved by Mr. Hudson. I didn't think it was appropriate now.

Maybe it was my sorrows at disappointing my boss or thinking that Theresa had been the one to boot me from the account. I didn't know, maybe it was just that Carter had been gone all week and life felt lonelier to me now, but I missed Mallory. I missed Amanda and I even, only slightly, missed Ben. I wasn't going anywhere, not until she said something to me. "How's Mallory?"

The entire pan fell off the counter. As it crashed to the floor and everyone in the café looked over, Amanda knelt down and starting grabbing all the cookies with frantic hands. I knelt beside her, she was blushing. The back of her neck was bright red. She smacked my hand. "Don't!"

"Hey." My eyes lit up. "Hey!" She talked to me.

She cursed under her breath, reaching for the cookies that went the farthest. "Go away, Emma."

"No." I frowned. "Why?"

"Because Mallory and Ben are gone," she hissed. We were still on the floor. Most of the cookies had been collected.

My hand jerked and the few that had been in it were now crumbs. "What?"

"They're gone. Like you. You're gone too. Everyone's gone." She stood and brushed off her pants. "You should take that as a clue and stay away. *I* should take that as a clue and get a different job."

"I don't want to stay away," I mumbled. I felt ridiculous.

"Yeah, well, I don't care." She glared at me before she took the tray into the back room.

I followed. I heard a groan come from the bathroom hallway, but I didn't look to see if it was the guard or not. I didn't care.

When Amanda saw that I had followed her, more curses fell from her lips. She took the tray to the sink and wiped all of the cookies into the garbage beside it. "I know you texted on Monday, but I tossed my phone. Things don't feel right to me."

"You said that Mallory and Ben are gone?"

She jerked her head in a tight nod before she turned the water on. "Yeah. I packed all your stuff at the apartment and took a few things to Ben's on Sunday, things that I thought Mallory would want, but his place was empty."

"Empty?"

"They were gone. His clothes looked packed. He had boxes out in the kitchen with dishes. I went back Monday and everything was locked up. I tried the extra key, but they changed the locks. From what I could see, even his furniture was gone. They took off, Emma." The pan was in the sink and the water was on, but she didn't move to clean it. She studied me instead. "You look good. I'm glad someone's doing okay with this whole ordeal."

I stepped back, as if slapped, but she didn't know. She hadn't pulled the trigger, that'd been me. "I'm sorry that you got dragged into this."

"Into what?" she snapped. "Doesn't seem like anything happened. The body's been missing, who the hell did that? Then you left, now those two. It's just me. I didn't even know what to do with your stuff so I put it all into storage."

"You need me to pay for that?"

She shrugged, putting the pan underneath the water now. "It doesn't matter. Ben gave me enough money so it's paid for a year."

"Wait." I grabbed her arm. "Ben gave you money?"

"Yeah. Why?"

He wasn't the type to give money, much less have money. "Where'd it come from?"

"I don't know. He didn't say, just tossed me a big envelope and told me to take care of Mallory's stuff. I didn't question it. After you took off, I learned that maybe it's better if I don't ask any questions."

My eyes narrowed. "How'd Ben look?"

"What do you mean?" She grew weary now, more than she had been at the beginning.

"Was he his normal grouchy self?"

"When's he not his normal grouchy self?" She paused with the pan in her hand. "Actually, now that you mention it, he looked happy last week." She shuddered. "I don't even want to know what that means. I took the money and did what he said. I told you before that I would take care of your apartment. Two of my co-workers helped me clean and I left your keys on the counter. Your landlord seemed fine with that."

I nodded. I tried to tell myself that things were fine. I was safe. Amanda seemed fine, pissy, but fine. However, I couldn't shake what she told me. Mallory and Ben were gone. What'd that mean? That had to mean something. And Ben had money. Ben *never* had money. Something was off, well, considering the situation, something was really off.

She bit her lip, eyeballing me. "You don't look too good now. What's wrong, Emma?"

I jerked my head up. "Nothing. It's fine. Thanks for taking care of the apartment."

"Look," her shoulders dropped and her voice softened. "I'm sorry that I didn't text you or call you. You gave me that new number and I know you were never one to really call, but I was mad after you took off. I know you did something to keep us all safe and I know that I'm not supposed to ask what that was, but Mallory went off the deep end a few days after you left. She got real bad again. Ben wouldn't let me call you. He said that you deserted us so we would make do without you." She blew out a deep breath. "Anyways, so I was mad at you for a bit. And I missed you. I miss making fun of Ben with you. He's so weird sometimes."

I grinned, despite myself. This wasn't a funny situation, but I missed those moments too. "You said he was happy? What's Ben like when he's happy?"

"Oh, you know." She chuckled. The pan had been cleaned and put on the drying section. "He was walking around, strutting like some peacock that got laid by a swan. I dunno. He had some weird new walk, thrusting his hips around." More chuckles poured from her. "I know he thought he was hot stuff, but he looked ridiculous.

Like a plump turkey that got stuffed and liked it."

My grin widened, and I relaxed. I had missed this. I missed our camaraderie. "He thought he was hot stuff?"

"I caught him checking himself out in the mirror. I think he'd been jerking it, but I wasn't sure. He was all sweaty and his pants were undone."

"Gross."

Her nose wrinkled up. "Tell me about it. By then Mallory was starting to come around again. She thought he was stupid too, but it's not the same. She doesn't..." Her voice trailed off and a glimmer of sadness appeared before she looked away. Mallory wasn't me. She didn't laugh at Ben like we did.

"So," my voice hitched on a note. "Mallory was doing better before..." I couldn't bring myself to say it, that Mallory and Ben were gone. Oh god. I swallowed a knot in my throat. What did that mean? They had left. No one had taken them? My chest tightened. Had Franco found Mallory? But Carter hadn't said anything, he would've told me, wouldn't he? But then I knew—he wouldn't. And he'd been gone all week.

Just like that, my stomach dropped, and I knew something horrible had happened.

"Emma?" Amanda was frowning at me. She was pale now. "You don't look so good."

"I have to go." I turned on my heel and walked out of there. I would've run if it hadn't looked suspicious, but as I went, my heart dropped again. Everything had changed. Jeremy Dunvan changed everything. Carter was right. This had been done to me. I lost my friends because of what he did to Mallory.

My jaw hardened.

I was done with waiting and hiding. I had taken care of Mallory before Carter came into my life. I wasn't helpless and he needed to start telling me what was going on. This was my life too.

As soon as I cleared the cafe's entrance, I was whisked into a car waiting for me. Mike pushed me inside and climbed behind me. Another door shut in the front so I figured the guard by the bathroom sat by the driver. I glared at Mike and rubbed my arm, where he had gripped me harder than he ever had before. "Ouch."

He growled, then blanched and sat up straight. "Is your arm okay?"

"It's fine." I eyed him. I'd never seen Mike as anything other than professional, but he quickly switched, oozing it again. "You're mad at me?"

He stiffened.

I corrected, "You're all mad at me, aren't you?"

He didn't respond.

That was my answer. I sighed and scooted down. "I just missed her. I'm sorry." And I wouldn't do it again. I knew that much. They were only doing their job, and I had gotten mad. I was still mad, but I was going to take it out on Carter. And when I said take it out on him, I let out a deep sigh and knew I wouldn't say a word. He was protecting me. I shouldn't forget that and I had, for a little bit that afternoon.

"When you deviate into an unmarked room without us, you're going in blind. We were not prepared for the back room of that café."

Oh. Huh? "When you say unmarked, you mean...?"

"We've been over every room in your work building. We've even planned for the café, but you went into a dark room. We didn't have a guy in the back ready because we didn't think you would follow her. We thought you would stay in the front room."

"So a dark room is somewhere that you guys haven't mapped out yet?"

"Planned for."

"What's the difference?"

He grimaced. "We will be better next time. I promise."

I blinked at him for a moment. Why was he apologizing to me?

He saw my look. "If something had happened, if someone had grabbed you, it would've been our fault. We weren't ready. We have to always be ready."

"Oh." And the Shame of the Month Award went to me. I was flooded with guilt. "I won't go into rooms like that again. Would that help?" There was so much about what they did that I didn't know about. "Maybe you guys could help me learn about how you operate. I don't really know that much, except that Carter told me to call 09 for when I'm ready to go home. I never call it, but you guys always seem to know. He said you guys have been watching me for a long time."

He shrugged. "We have a blending technique, but you don't need to really understand that. We'll do better next time."

"Okay." I wanted to know. I wanted to help, but I sensed that Mike wanted the conversation to be done. I let it go.

It was later that I wondered about all the security guards again. I had showered, changed clothes, and my stomach was rumbling. When I heated up food, I saw one of the guards turn suddenly away from me. His hand grabbed at his stomach and I knew it hadn't been mine that was rumbling. I wondered when the last time these guys ate, but no—they must've had breaks at times. Still, I looked at the huge casserole in front of me. There was too much for me so I dished it onto three plates and handed one to the guy. A fork was next. He was startled, but shook his head. "No, ma'am. That's alright."

His stomach sounded again. I rolled my eyes and pushed it into his hands. "I'm not going to die in the two minutes it'll take you to eat that. Go ahead." I lifted the other plate. "Where's the other guy?"

He hesitated, but gestured with the fork to my floor. "He's outside by the elevator."

"Eat." I pointed to his plate as I started towards the stairs.

The other guard had a similar reaction except he dropped his radio. It hit the floor with a loud screech and he grabbed it, muttering apologies at the same time. I left the plate on the bench beside him and waved. "Have fun. Eat up." I scanned the small hallway. No Mike. "Where are the others?"

His head jerked up. "Ma'am?"

I sighed. Why did they all have to call me ma'am? "Mike and the rest of the guards. Where is he and how many are there? I'll cook something for everyone. They can eat it when you guys take your breaks."

I could tell he hadn't expected that. He almost dropped his plate. "Mike got called away for a transport and there are eight others."

Eight? Really? "Okay. I'll make more."

I didn't ask what a transport was. I was starting to figure out what they would tell me and what they wouldn't. Whatever a transport was made the list of Things Not To Discuss With Emma. But when I went back to the kitchen, I was surprised at how many guards Carter had enlisted. That meant there were ten security guards around me at all times. Ten...my stomach dropped and I sat down with a plop on the counter stool. I swallowed a lump in my throat. Ten guards. I had known there were a few, but ten—it was serious. My situation was serious. Carter wasn't one to waste anyone's time. Then I remembered what Amanda had said about Ben and Mallory.

My hands started to tremble.

I pushed that thought away before, but now I couldn't shake it. Something happened. I knew it. I could feel it. That same something could happen to me. Ten guards. All ten of them were trained and ready to take a bullet for me.

My stool started to wobble and I grabbed onto the counter. I couldn't hold on. My hands were shaking too much.

"Ma'am?"

I heard the guard's voice in the distance. Things were going black. He sounded far away. I thought he had been in the next room? Maybe he moved, and then the darkness covered all of me. Something crashed far away, and I heard his radio buzz.

"She's down...call the boss..."

EIGHTEEN

"Emma."

A hand touched my arm briefly. I jerked awake and was disoriented. A large black silhouette stood above me and I started screaming.

"Stop!" He bent further down. "It's me, Mike."

I gasped on my last scream when he turned on the light, but my chest was still heaving from the panic. My heart was pounding. I rolled over to dry heave until I started to calm down. I felt something cold against my arm.

"It's Carter. He wants to talk to you."

"What?"

The cold thing pressed against me again. "It's Carter. He's on the phone."

Phone. Carter. My hand streaked out and I grabbed the small cellphone. When I rolled over, I pressed it to my ear and asked, "Carter?"

"Hey."

Everything in me sagged in relief. His voice soothed me. In the distance, I was barely aware of a door clicking shut. I murmured back, "Hey."

He chuckled. His smooth baritone came over the phone and sidled over me, like another caress from him. I closed my eyes and snuggled deeper into bed. I didn't care how I got there, what had happened, all I needed was Carter. That was all I knew.

"They said you fainted. Are you okay?"

I grimaced as I remembered. "Yeah. I did."

"Why?"

"Because you weren't here. Because I think something happened to Mallory and Ben. Amanda told me they're gone and I think you know something happened to them. Because I'm tired of feeling trapped. Because I got booted off a great project at work and I don't know why. Because I miss Amanda. I miss all of them, even Ben." I felt stupid saying all of that and I felt even more stupid because it was coming out of me in a rush. I needed him. My hand shook as it held the phone to my ear. "Because I miss you and because I'm scared."

There was silence on the other end.

Another beat passed.

"I'm coming back."

Everything in me exploded, but I tried to argue with him. "No, I didn't mean for you to do that—"

"I'm coming home anyway." He sounded tired. "I have some business in New York, but I'll head to the jet right after." He paused. "I miss you too."

Warmth burst inside of me, but I tried to tone it down. I was becoming one of those gushy types. I hated those types, but I whispered back, "I'm glad you're coming back."

"You have to promise me something first."

"What?"

"Stop taking your anger out on the guys and making sudden changes."

Guilt sunk low in my gut.

"You can go wherever you want, just tell the guys first. They're good at their jobs, but sometimes they can't adapt fast enough. Please, Emma."

"I will."

"Good. How was your week?"

"It sucked."

He chuckled again. "I'm guessing it's not just because of last week?"

"What?"

"Friday night, Emma."

"Oh!" My eyes widened. I'd forgotten about the attack. How could I have forgotten? "That slipped my mind. I can't believe that..."

"Look," his voice dropped to an intimate tone. "I can't talk about a lot of things over the phone, but I'm making things happen. I'm making sure you're safe and someday you might not need all those guys around you. I'm trying, Emma. I'm doing my damnedest right now to fix it so you're going to be okay."

"But my roommate," I whispered back.

He sighed into the phone. "I can't make any promises about her. I'm trying, but you're my first priority, Emma. I promise you, this will all be over soon."

I clenched the phone tighter. "You promise?"

"I do. I can promise that."

I nodded and felt a tear fall onto the pillow. "Okay."

"Are you okay?" Concern filtered into his voice now. "Are you eating?"

"I got scared." The admission slipped me before I knew what I was going to say.

"I'm sorry, Emma. I should've been there."

"No, you said that you have things to do. You have to work. You—" *are doing something to make sure that I'm safe.* Even as I thought that, shame tore through me. He was right. I was angry that he left and that he stayed away for so long. I was angry that he hadn't called or texted. I was angry that he wasn't beside me, but Carter wasn't normal. This wasn't a normal relationship—and then I bolted upright in bed.

Carter and I were in a relationship.

The last time I'd been in a relationship—I squeezed my eyes shut. The guy had cheated on me, robbed me, and turned all of my friends against me. It was another reason why I was only friends with Mallory and Amanda. The few friends I had in college were snooty and disloyal. Mallory and Amanda seemed safe when I met each of them.

AJ and Carter had been my first family. The few friends I had in college could never be considered as family, but that changed once I met Mallory after I graduated. She became my family, and then Amanda was included. Ben got added because he never left Mallory's side for years. But now those three were gone and Carter had come back.

As I sat there, struggling to breathe, tears flowed down my face. Everyone left.

"Emma?"

I became aware of his voice. The phone had fallen into the covers and I grabbed it. "Sorry."

"Are you okay?"

"I'm fine."

"Emma."

"I am," I rushed out. "When are you coming back?"

"I'll be back tomorrow night."

"Good." I took a deep breath. "That's good."

"Are you sure you're okay?"

"I'm good." And I was, as long as I heard his voice, felt his voice, had him in my life—I was good, but it wasn't going to last. Nothing good lasted for me. He was going to go away. I just didn't know when or how it would happen.

"Okay..." He wasn't convinced.

I counted to ten, hoping he'd let it go. I couldn't spill any of the thoughts that were racing in my mind. They were too much.

"So what's this I hear that you're cooking for the guys now?"

My shoulders sagged. He had let it go. "Yeah, I felt bad. I'm going to cook for the whole group this weekend."

He chuckled, "I'm sure they'll love it, no matter what you cook."

I slid back under my covers. We talked for another hour, the longest conversation I ever had over the phone. I could've continued for another hour, but I told him to go to sleep after I heard his exhaustion. He sighed into the phone, "It's good to hear your voice, Emma. I've missed you too."

I couldn't hold back a grin. "Good night, Carter."

"Good night. I'll see you tomorrow."

"I'll see you tomorrow."

Then I heard the dial tone and laid the phone next to me. I slept with it beside me.

-CARTER-

When he put his phone away, his associate glanced up from the parallel seat. He asked, "Is she alright?"

"She feels frustrated and trapped. She doesn't know what's going on and it's making her angry."

The older man frowned. "She told you all that?"

"She doesn't know she feels all of that."

"But you do?"

Carter threw his comrade a grin. "I always do. I know things about you too. Would you like me to enlighten you?"

He started to open his mouth again, but Gene groaned, "Please don't." He paused for a second. "Are you going to tell her what's going on?"

"Not yet. I want to wait."

The older man lifted his phone. "I got off the phone with Christian."

Carter waited, more alert and quiet, if that was possible. When his comrade hesitated, he lifted an eyebrow. "Am I supposed to guess? Is this when you're going to question my intuitive senses?"

"Shut up." A grin slipped from the other man. He shook his head. Carter reminded him of his son. It was why he vouched for him when Farve brought him into the family. Carter never knew that and he didn't want him to know, although it was a fair assumption that Carter probably did. He treated him differently, but then again,

Carter Reed had demanded different treatment than the others. He'd always been better than the rest. He had proved that again with the feat he pulled off.

"Gene," Carter prompted.

"They're deliberating right now. We'll know the decision by tomorrow." He eyed the younger man. He seemed as unfazed and cold as always. "You're not worried?"

"Legitimate business is always good business. They won't pass on it."

"If they do?"

Carter turned back to his window. "Then I'll figure something else out."

Gene shifted in his seat, trying to stretch his long legs. He had no doubt Carter would find a different way. He always did. Then he cursed. The damn jets were so cramped, even the private ones could use bigger leg spaces.

It was the next day, at the end of my shift when I learned the real reason he was headed to New York. Theresa called me and gushed over the phone, "You're back on!"

"I'm back on what?" I grinned as I heard her excitement and pulled the office door shut behind me. As it clicked in place, I turned for the elevator. The whole day had been torturous. I knew that I'd see Carter that evening. The day went slower because of that.

"The Bourbon account. You're back on." She laughed. "Allison was horrible. She was so flustered by your boyfriend, she kept dropping everything. She almost dropped the computer equipment, but Noah sent her out of the room. So you're back in. That's great, right?"

"Yeah..." I frowned. "My boyfriend?"

"Yeah, about that." She turned serious. "Not cool, Emma."

"What are you talking about?"

"Carter Reed. Your boyfriend. The guy I saw you with at the club, but, stupid me, didn't realize was Carter Reed." She grew quiet. "Were you laughing at me? Was that why you didn't say anything?"

"What?" I punched the elevator button. "No. How do you know about Carter? I didn't think you had ever met him."

"What do you mean, how do I know? He's Noah's best friend and he owns some shares in the hotel."

"I thought you said Noah offered him shares and he turned him down?"

"He offered him more shares and he turned those down, but he already owns 32% of the business. I thought you knew that." She sounded sheepish, "Okay. I'll admit that I never believed Noah, but I'm realizing that I judged him wrong before I ever really met him."

I stepped inside the elevator and pushed my button. "Carter and I don't talk about that stuff."

"Oh."

I sighed in frustration. A headache was coming on. "Carter was there? He was in the meeting?" And that was why he was going to New York, not for me, not like he had said.

"Of course he was there. We had to present the new account to the board so that we can go through with making it a brand. You knew that?"

But I hadn't. I really hadn't. I sighed into the phone, "Look, I have to go. Can we talk about this later?"

"No, that's the thing. We're flying back now. We're on his jet with him. He's being nice, Emma. And he said that he wants to treat us tonight. I'm calling you to tell you to get your cute butt all dressed and sexified. We're going to Octave tonight, and we're going to be with the owner. Can you imagine what perks go with that? It's awesome enough just when Noah and I go there because Noah knows him, but actually being with the owner?! I'm really excited. And Brianna's going to be there too. We already asked. He promoted her once he found out that she was working there. I'm not sure what she does, but Noah's okay with her working there now. Obviously, your boyfriend did that for him."

"Stop calling him my boyfriend."

She grew quiet on her end, but the elevator opened on mine. I stepped out and headed towards my back exit. When the door opened and I slid into the backseat, Mike was next to me. He gave a small wave.

"I'm sorry," I groaned into the phone. "I'm irritated with him, not you. I shouldn't take it out on you."

"Oh. Well. You're still going to Octave tonight, right? Even if you're mad at him, you'll still go? Pleaseee?"

I grinned at how eager she was. "Yes, I'll go for you."

"And for him," she whispered into the phone. "Even if you're pissed right now, imagine the hot make-up sex. That man is one fine specimen, Emma. I know I should hate him. I used to, but I can't deny the sex appeal of that man, not one bit. If I wasn't so used to Noah and how attractive he is, I would've reacted the same way as Allison. Good thing I've got some immunity built up, huh?"

"You're horrible."

She laughed, "Just happy that you're back on the team again. Noah already told me that he's going to promote us both. He really doesn't want Mr. Hudson to get the benefits from this account so he's moving you above him. Mr. Hudson is going to be your assistant. You're the Head of Project Promotions now. Congratulations!"

"What?"

There was a grumble on her end before she rushed out, "Sorry. I wasn't supposed to tell you that. It was a surprise for tonight, but dress sexy. Tonight will be so much fun. I promise!" Then I heard her say, "Shut it, Noah. If I hadn't said anything, she might not have come out…I don't care…" Her voice grew clear again. "I'll see you later, Emma. See you tonight!"

It wasn't long until my phone lit up again. This time it was Carter.

I answered, "Calling to do damage control?"

He sighed, "No, but now I am. You're angry with me?"

"Were you sitting right next to her?"

"I'm in the back of the jet. They're in the front."

"But how did you—"

"I had the intercom open on her end. I could hear everything she said to you."

He didn't even sound apologetic. "You were eavesdropping on her."

"Yes, I was. And I'll do it again and again when it comes to you. I'm starting to realize that you have no idea the lengths I have gone and will go for you."

I shut up and sat back. Then I surrendered, "You weren't in New York for me."

"No, I wasn't, but I was in Chicago because of you, for you. I was in New York today for a friend of mine that asked me a long time ago to buy into his hotel so he could start up his idea. It was a good proposal and I invested. It was smart on my part, one of the first decisions I did independent from those my reputation associates me with. That decision and that money have allowed me to further expand and I am very close to becoming fully independent of those previous associates. Are you understanding me?"

I gulped. Oh yes. I was following along. I was suddenly a starving person given their first morsel of food in months. I was hungry for more. "You're coming back with them?"

"I'm coming straight to you."

Desire lit inside of me. The flame grew to a fire. "Hurry."

"I am." The raw need in his voice had me breathing hard. "Are you still angry with me?"

I grimaced. "I was never angry at you, not really."

"Good."

I glanced at Mike, who was studying his window with an intensity that told me he was very aware, and uncomfortably so, of our intimate conversation. I lowered my voice, "I have some things to tell you when you get here."

He hesitated on his end before he said, his voice husky as well, "As do I."

My heart picked up. My hand grew sweaty around the phone. "Okay then."

He chuckled. "Okay then."

"Did you get kicked me off the account?"

"Yes."

"Why?"

"Because it wasn't safe for you. I didn't want you in New York, not right now. You're safer there and in my home. And it wasn't ethical. Noah shouldn't have put you on that team in the first place. He knew I was on the board. He knew about my relationship with you. He was trying to manipulate me."

I was confused, again. "What are you talking about? He didn't think you were going to approve the product?"

"No. My previous associates have another product that would be its competitor."

"But you did approve it?"

"Of course I did."

My head was swimming. "This makes no sense to me."

He chuckled again. "This is my excuse to step away from the other product."

My chest felt constricted. "They'll let you...step away?"

"Yes, they will. I have done very well for those associates. They've known about my wish for independence and with a venture I insured for them over this past week, I have fulfilled any obligations they might've had for me to the family."

"Are you saying..." No, it couldn't be. People didn't walk away from that life.

"Yes, Emma. I'm free now."

I couldn't talk. My chest was heaving. My eyes were watering and I gripped onto that phone like my life depended on it.

"Emma."

"Yes?" I wrung out.

His voice dropped even more. "That's a good thing, right?"

"Yes," I breathed out. "That's a very good thing."

"Good." His voice broke for a beat. "We're almost there. I'll be home soon."

I couldn't say anything. I should've said good bye or safe travels, something, but the magnitude of what he had just told me hit me like a truck. I was bowled over at what that meant for both of us.

NINETEEN

It was five hours later when I got his text. **Something came up. I'm sorry. Will meet you at Octave tonight. The men are notified. They will drive you there at ten.**

I didn't text him back. Maybe I should've, but my entire body was humming. I had been waiting for him and now this. It wasn't long after that when I got a text from Theresa. **Meet you at Octave! So excited!**

I spent the next hour choosing what I was going to wear. I was going for Theresa and because Noah had promoted me and, as tingles raced through me, because I was excited to see Carter, even if it was later than he told me and not where we'd be alone. So as I headed downstairs, I ignored the shocked looks on the guys and even the raised eyebrow as Mike scooted beside me. I didn't want to admit that I was dressing for somebody, certainly not for Carter, but I was. My tan dress fit like a second skin. The fact that it resembled a corset was an added bonus.

As I walked into Octave and saw the reactions, I knew the dress had been perfect. However, when we neared the door to Carter's private office, I stopped walking. A fresh batch of shivers raced up and down my spine, but not the good kind. Scott Graham was approaching from the opposite end. As he stopped outside the door, he looked up and his eyes trailed up and down my body. His lips pursed together in a wolf whistle, but two of the guards stepped in front of me, blocking his view.

"Mr. Graham," Mike spoke up. He didn't move, nor did Lawrence—whose name I recently learned. Thomas also sidled closer to me. Scott tried to look around them, but this last maneuver put an entire human wall between us.

I had never been more grateful for those guys.

"Hi, guys. You're going to see the boss?"

Thomas pressed his ear and said something. I couldn't hear, but it wasn't long until I heard another voice speak up, loudly with authority, "Mr. Graham, Mr. Reed kindly requests that you leave his guests alone for the evening."

"What? But—"

"You've been relieved of your duty for the evening."

"What's going on here, Gene?" His voice rose in anger. "You can't tell me what to do."

"Actually," Gene spoke again, harshly now. "I can. You've got the night off, Scott. I suggest you go on your own two legs."

There was silence, and as it stretched onto another minute, the guys stiffened around me. The air grew thick with tension, but then a bitter laugh came from the night manager. "Fine. I'll go, but I'll be speaking with Carter himself about this tomorrow."

"He's expecting your phone call tonight."

The guys waited another minute before they parted before me.

Scott Graham was gone and so was the mysterious Gene. I felt like I could breathe easier again and drew in a deep breath when Mike opened the door and disappeared inside. Three guards from behind me followed him inside. It wasn't long before some signal was given to the guards beside me and Thomas nodded towards me. "You may go in, Emma."

I gave him a gracious smile. "Thank you, Thomas."

When I went in, I was taken aback. It was large and grandiose with its own dance floor that extended out like a deck to an apartment. There were couches on one side, a table set on the other, and a bar—Carter's office could've been its own apartment. When I looked to the side, I saw four doors and wondered if they were all bedrooms.

The other places that we had used didn't come close to this. The place was extravagant for a nightclub office. I thought I met Carter in his private box before, but now I wondered if he had a few of them.

The glass doors slid open and Theresa came inside holding two huge drinks in her hand. Her eyes went wide and her mouth dropped when she saw me. "Holy crap, Emma. You are hot!" Then a twinkle came to her eyes. "Planning something extra for tonight, maybe?"

I flushed. "I don't want to talk about that."

"You are." Her grin turned wicked and she pushed one of the drinks into my hand. "Can't say I blame you. That man is one fine specimen walking around on two legs. If I hadn't agreed to a date tomorrow night and if you weren't my friend, I would've thrown my name into the hat. He's gorgeous, Emma. You're very lucky to get to ride that man tonight."

"Theresa." I knew she had a little of a wild side, but this was a new Theresa to me. Then I realized how red her cheeks were as I fanned mine to cool off.

Noah came in around her. “She’s drunk.”

“I gathered.” So those two were going on a date?

Theresa snorted. She must’ve caught the look I skirted between them. “It’s not him. I met a nice gentleman this afternoon. He suggested drinks and it’s high time I got something from a man.” Then she threw a dark look to the side.

Noah rolled his eyes as he poured a drink from the bar. “A gentleman? He’s a dick. Just wait. You’ll see.”

She drew upright and her shoulders squared back. “I will see, now won’t I?”

He mumbled something under his breath as he went back to the dance floor.

Theresa glared at his back until he had stepped beyond our eyesight, then the corners of her lips curved down and her shoulders dropped. “He’s the dick, not Allen. Allen is a gentleman to me. Kind. Considerate. Not like Noah. He’s such an ass sometimes.”

“What happened today?”

Her lip started to tremble, her chin quivered, and a burst of tears came out.

“Theresa?”

She shook her head, unable to speak, and sat on one of the couches. I sat beside her, placing both of our drinks on the table. With one hand rubbing in circles over her back, I murmured, “What happened? Whatever it is, I’m sure it’ll be fine.”

“No, it won’t.”

“What happened?”

“He’s such an ass, that’s what happened.” Her head reared back up and she flicked some of her tears away. “We went back to my place when we got home. I was so excited you’d be working with me again, and I wanted to start celebrating early. Noah said to leave you alone until tonight so fine, we did. We had a few drinks and then," she took a deep breath as she flicked another tear away from her eye. Her make-up smudged. "And then we had sex."

I sat upright, my mouth forming a small o, but I wasn't surprised. "And it wasn't good?"

"No!" she wailed. "That's the problem. It was amazing. It was agonizing. It was everything those movies make it out to be."

"So what's the problem? Unless he didn't..."

"We did it twice, Emma." She turned to me, eyes still watering and her lip shaking. "I want to do it again, that's the problem. I want to do it till the cows come home, but he said thank you. He said thank you! Can you believe that? Thank. You." Her mouth stretched in irritation. "Thank you, like I'm some maid that cleaned his couch. Thank you. My ass, thank you. And then he suggested we go to the gym together. The gym!"

"I'm sorry, Theresa."

"Leave the girl alone about our sex life. She's got bigger problems to deal with than us," Noah barked from the doorway.

She sucked in her breath and surged to her feet. "That was a private conversation."

"Not real private when I can hear every damn word. Stop whining, Theresa. I have every intention of bending you over tonight."

Her mouth dropped and she wavered on her feet before she squeaked out, "You do?"

"Yes." His eyes sparkled from annoyance, and he pulled out his tie to toss on a table. "Finish your drink, get another one, and come out here to dance with me."

When he went back outside, Theresa's hand gripped mine and

squeezed. "I know I shouldn't be excited by that. I know it's against women's lib and all that, but I'm going to have sex with that man. I'm going to have sex with him tonight and every night after this, at least that's what I'm hoping."

I chuckled and swatted her on the booty. "Go for it, Theresa. Show him who's the man."

"I'm the man."

"Go tell him that."

Her smile was dazzling and she embraced me, holding me tight for a second. "Thank you, Emma. I'm so glad that I've gotten to know you. You have no idea. I don't make friends that easily and we clicked so well right off the bat."

I hugged her back, patting her at the same time. "Me too." But as she pulled away with an excited bounce in her step and joined Noah on the private dance floor, I lost the slight enjoyment I had for the evening. I had other friends. Two of them were very near and dear to my heart and I had abandoned them.

"What's wrong?"

I whirled around, and there was Carter. He was dressed in a black sweatshirt with a black shirt underneath. His pants were black as well. I had never been one to critique his wardrobe, but I knew enough to know that he hadn't come from the office. My throat had gone dry. "Where were you?"

His eyes switched from concern to an intense perusal.

I flinched underneath his scrutiny now, knowing he was doing what he always did. He was searching inside of me, trying to read what was wrong with me. His head tilted to the side, his wolf eyes narrowed with thoughtfulness, and his lips thinned. "You're mad I didn't come to you?"

His hand reached for my arm, but I flicked it away. "I'm

disappointed you didn't come to me. I'm mad because there are some things we need to discuss, things you've been keeping from me."

He stepped close to me, enough so he brushed against me and didn't move back. His hand circled to rest on my back, urging me even closer to him. A dizzying wave swept over me. It was always like this, the second he came into contact with me. Lust, pleasure, and so many other emotions blinded me until I only felt one emotion. Need. It was overtaking me again and my eyes closed when I felt his head bend towards mine. His lips brushed over mine, so softly, as he murmured, "I'm sure there are, but right now," his hand cupped the back of my neck, "we're here to celebrate you and your promotion."

My body melted into his. "I haven't been told the official news."

His lips pressed against my mouth, taking my breath away. His hand found mine. He interlaced our fingers before he whispered against my lips, "Then let's make it official." He turned to the dance floor and called, "Noah."

"Yeah?" He was leading Theresa inside by her hand. Both looked as if they'd thoroughly been kissed. When my eyes caught hers, she gave me a sloppy smile that told me two things. One, she was happy and two, she was indeed drunk.

Carter curved an arm around my back and pulled me close. He held a hand out—a drink immediately appeared in it thanks to an efficient employee—and he handed it to me before a second one appeared. He held that one in the air. "To a great new product for The Richmond Hotel and to Emma, who received news today..." He lingered as he gave Noah a pointed look.

"Oh, yeah." Noah lifted his drink higher. "You've been promoted, Emma, but these two already broke the news. Congratulations! You're now the Head of Project Promotions and you're partnering with the Head of Innovative Projects right here." His arm squeezed around Theresa. "Congratulations to you both."

Theresa giggled as she raised her drink. "Congratulations to both of us!"

"Thanks, guys." I watched as Theresa and Noah clinked their glasses together before taking a sip. She reached up for a kiss, but he batted her away. When her lips formed into a pout, he frowned, but yanked her back out onto the dance floor for privacy.

Carter and I watched through the glass walls as they kissed in celebration.

I chuckled, "Do they know we can see them?"

Carter pulled me to face him and bent his head down. His lips lingered on the base of my neck as he murmured, "I don't care. As long as we have some privacy." His hands gripped my hips, and he held me against him, anchored in place as his lips started to explore my neck.

I closed my eyes as a feeling settled in my gut. It wasn't one that I was used to, but it wasn't one that I would reject. It was peace. In his arms, surrounded by two new friends, I was happy.

Carter stayed by my side most of the time. He left for phone calls or when an employee would poke their head inside the office, but for the most part it was just the four of us. Noah's sister came a few hours later. She was a slim girl with platinum hair and twinkling blue eyes. There was a kinship between her and Theresa. As I watched them laugh together, their years of history were obvious and a small prick of envy came to me. When I watched the younger girl interact with her brother, that envy grew into jealousy.

I missed AJ. I missed the hugs. I missed the hair tussles. I missed how he told me what to do and I would ignore him. And I missed the time we never got. AJ died so long ago that I rarely thought of him, but I did that evening. When a few tears came to me, I let them fall freely. They were healing tears, ones that I wasn't embarrassed to show.

Theresa mouthed to me across the room, "Are you okay?"

I nodded. I was. I really was.

Carter returned from another call and saw everything. He took my hand, pulling me into one of the back bedrooms. When he flipped a switch, the lighting was soft and low, but I saw that it wasn't a bedroom. Two large couches were set up along with a sectional in the other corner. The wall was covered with a large flat-screen television. He turned it on, but muted the sound. It was of the club downstairs. Every minute the screen would change to another room in Octave.

Then he turned and studied me. The multi-colors from the television flashed over him, casting him in a changing canvas of shadows. It made him seem more alluring and dangerous. He asked, "What happened?"

I sighed. He always knew. "Nothing."

"Emma."

"Nothing," my voice rose.

He took my arm and pulled me close. "What happened?"

"Nothing." His hand tightened, but I didn't feel it. His touches were becoming a second skin to me. "It's seeing them out there."

"Did they do something?"

"No, it's their love for each other, and Theresa grew up with them. It's—"

"AJ."

At that one word, the dam broke in me. I had known that I missed him, but those earlier emotions were nothing compared to the storm that took over me now. I fell to the couch and Carter went with me. He lifted me into his lap and pressed a kiss to my forehead. He brushed my hair back and continued to do so. His touch was tender and soothing, but he was right. It was AJ. I missed my brother.

"I miss him too." Carter gave me a smile, but it was haunted. "We don't talk about AJ that much, but I loved him. I don't protect you because of him, though. I know you think that, but that's not why. I protect you because of you, because..."

My heart pounded and my eyes grew wide. Was he going to say what I thought he was going to say...? I waited, my breath held, but a guarded look came over him.

He started to look away, but I grabbed his chin. I held him in place. "Carter."

The guarded look slid away. "Yes?"

My hand tightened. "What were you going to say?"

"When?"

I moved so I was straddling him. His hand gripped the back of my hips. I was pressed against him, my chest to his, eye to eye and I lingered with my lips just above his. I whispered to him, "What were you going to say to me?"

His chest lifted and I felt the air that he drew in. My eyes closed. My breath went with him, into him.

He still didn't say it.

"Please," I wrenched out.

"Why?"

"Because I think I know." I hoped I knew. Every nerve in my body was stretched with want. I wanted to hear those words. The need was blossoming in my chest, ready to explode. "Tell me."

He grinned. "Tell you what? That I care about you? You already know that."

"Stop teasing me."

His smile slipped and his eyes dropped. They lingered on my lips, where I was teasing him. Then he said it, "I love you." Everything fell away in that moment.

My eyes caught and held his. My hand fell to his chest, and it stayed there, feeling his heart. He tilted my head back and pressed a kiss underneath my chin as he murmured, "I have always loved you." Another kiss. "I will always love you, Emma. There's been no other for me." His hand slid to the back of my neck and his lips moved back to mine. "Now, do you love me?"

I grinned against him, unable to hold it in. "You know I do."

His hand tightened behind me. "Say it."

"I love you." My body melted to his. I became one with him as I said those words. Then I said it again, because I could, "I love you. I always have."

His lips opened over mine, demanding his entrance. I gave it, because I needed all of him, as much as I could get.

The rest of the night was spent in a mix of anticipation, agony, and adrenalin. I was addicted to Carter and we couldn't go long without a touch or a look between the two of us. Theresa noticed something was different when we came back to the main dance floor. Her eyebrows went high and she crossed the room to grab my hand. "What happened?"

"What do you mean?" I was breathless. My body was still tingling with the knowledge that Carter loved me. He loved me. A new set of sensations rushed through me.

"Emma, I might be drunk, but I'm not stupid. You're glowing." Her mouth dropped. "Did you guys get it on in there?"

"No!"

She shrugged. "A bit kinky, but we are at Octave." She glanced at Carter as Noah handed him a drink. "And he's the owner. You could do it on the main dance floor if you wanted." She cringed. "Make sure it's clean, though, huh?"

"We didn't get it on." We had come close.

"Why not? I would if he were mine." Her voice dipped low to a seductive drawl.

Carter looked over. His eyes lingered on Theresa and narrowed before he turned back to Noah.

She barked out a laugh. "God, how many times does he get hit on? I was giving him the bedroom eyes, a lip quiver and everything and nothing. He's loyal, I can tell."

I stiffened. Should I get pissed about that?

Then she sighed, "I was wrong with all my rants before about him. Noah always said I didn't know what I was talking about and I should've listened to him." She gave me a wide smile. "I hope you have hot and dirty sex tonight, do it for me."

I glanced towards my boss. "I don't think I need to. I think you're going to be having your own tonight."

"No." She rolled her eyes. "I love Brianna, but she freaked out when she saw us flirting. Look at her over there now."

The petite blonde stood close to both men. When one of her hands lifted, as if to rest on Carter's chest, a bolt of possessiveness went through me. He was mine. Carter caught my look, curved the ends of his mouth up, and moved out of her reach. The hand fell back to her hip, but she stiffened and her head straightened upwards. He shot me a smoldering look as if to reassure me, but I blinked rapidly and shook my head to clear the need to go over there and drag the little girl away. It was primal, setting off the ache between my legs again.

Theresa sipped her drink and murmured, "Holy woman, another hot look from him."

"So his sister doesn't approve of the two of you?"

She grinned at me. "Nice subject change, but I'll take the bait."

She took a deep breath before sipping on her drink again. "Brianna is the princess in Noah's family. Everybody dotes on her and she's here, trying to prove that she can make it on her own. Of course, she's doing it so she can get their grandfather's inheritance. He made a stipulation that she had to keep a full-time job for so many years before she could touch that money. So this is her, trying to prove to everybody she can make it."

"You guys seemed fond of each other."

"We are. I love her like a little sister, which is probably why she freaked out when she saw me and Noah dancing together." A sad tone rose in her voice. "And if little sister isn't okay with it, then big brother won't do it. *Heavens* that Brianna might be disturbed by something. She's been through so much since their grandfather died ten years ago." Her sarcasm was thick at the end.

"So everybody does what she wants?"

"Yeah," she finished her drink and moved to the bar for another. "When their grandfather died, she had been with him. The next year was hard on her. She couldn't sleep. She was barely eating. She started drinking, doing drugs, all of it. Unprotected sex. To say that she put that family through a second wringer after losing their grandfather is an understatement. Noah will *not* do anything to jeopardize her health in any way."

"They're okay with her working here?"

"Are you kidding me?" She shook her head. "After the initial shock, they love it. She loves it. That's all that matters. They don't care as long as she goes somewhere and makes money. Plus, she got that promotion." When the bartender handed her the drink, she took a big gulp before setting it down roughly. "I know your man did that as a favor to Noah, but it didn't help her. Now she's got it in her head that the boss wants her. Look at her."

She had edged close to Carter again. Her head was tipped back, her long hair cascaded down her back, and her lips were pursed in an adorable pout. I gritted my teeth and tried to keep my fingers from shattering my glass.

"I'm sorry," Theresa groaned. "I love her. I'm just a bit sore because the night I wanted with Noah isn't going to happen now. I don't think it'll ever happen."

"She can't have that much say over your life."

"She does and she will." Her eyes darkened. "And I know Noah. He is overprotective to the extreme. If there's a slight chance that it would send her into the tailspin like before, he won't chance it. He hasn't even looked at me since she got here. And he won't. We're back to pretending we don't know each other and I'm only his employee."

I remembered their small argument the first night at her apartment. "That's what it was before?"

"Yeah. His mother is great. She always includes me with their family events, but I'm not their family, not really. Noah doesn't want me around his family. Brianna does, but not in the way I want to be there."

"With him?"

"Exactly."

"That sounds lonely." It sounded like me. Carter had been my family, and then it was gone when AJ died. I destroyed my second family as well.

"I'm fine." A hard edge was in her voice as she tossed back the rest of her drink. When she placed the glass back on the bar, she swayed to the side. I caught her, steadying her, but her head hung down. "Maybe I should go home."

"It's close to closing. Maybe we should all go."

Her hand found mine that was on her arm. She squeezed it. "Thanks, Emma. I can already tell that you're a good friend. Some days I think that's the only thing I'll get, good friends."

My voice was gruff. "Friends can be the best family sometimes."

"I know."

"What are you two talking about over here?" A sweet voice came from behind.

Theresa stiffened. "Nothing, Brianna. How's your night?"

Up close, her bright blue eyes were dazzling. With a small nose, the perfect tiny mouth, Noah's little sister resembled a pixie. Cute and adorable, but the feigned innocence in her depths shifted as she met my gaze. She let something dark slip for a second before her blinding smile rose a notch and excitement filtered through to cover it. The black staff shirt of Octave was tight on her, allowing a few inches to showcase the golden tan of her stomach. The uniform stipulated black shirt and black pants, and Brianna's black pants stuck to every curve she had. She stuck a hand out. "We haven't formally met, though Noah filled me in."

"Brianna, this is Emma. Emma, Brianna." Theresa waved her hand between the two of us.

When my hand took hers in the handshake, she held on a second longer than necessary. The warning was given. When my eyes narrowed, she let go. The smile never slipped a notch. "And you know Carter as well?"

Oh boy. My chest tightened. "I've known Carter all my life." I couldn't help it.

Her eyes widened. "Really?"

Theresa rounded to me. "Really?"

A hand curved around my hip at that moment and I was pulled into Carter's side. He was warm and embracing. My body molded to his, fitting perfectly, as he said, "I was best friends with her brother. Their couch was my second bedroom."

"I didn't know you had a best friend, Carter." Noah joined the conversation.

"I did." He dropped a soft kiss to my shoulder. "And with that little tidbit, Emma and I should be getting home."

Brianna's eyebrows shot up, as did Theresa's. Noah frowned.

Carter led me out by the hand. I glanced over my shoulder. Theresa mouthed to me, "Home?" I gave her a brief smile before we were out the door and hurrying down the darkened hallway. The guards fell into step around us, surrounding us, and we made our way through the club's maze. The few times I had been there told me that we weren't going to the usual side exit. However, I didn't ask where we were headed as Carter dragged me behind him at a fast speed. The men sensed his urgency and grew tense as we stepped through the tunnel that connected the club with the hotel behind it. I remembered the penthouse, but as we stepped out of the plush hallway, lined with red velvet carpet, we went to the side stairs and hurried downstairs instead.

We stopped at the door that opened to the basement parking garage. The men swept through, but Carter held me back. For a second, we were alone. "What's going on?"

His hand tightened around mine. "We need to get you to safety."

"Carter." Alarm slithered down my back. "What's going on?"

He didn't respond, only withdrew his gun and tightened his hold on my hand. The door opened and one of the guards gave him a nod. "It's clear, sir."

Carter went first but held my arm tight. When we crossed the few feet for the car, he stepped to the side and guided me inside with a hand over my head. He slid in next. I expected more guards to follow. There was room for three more, but was surprised when he shut the door. It was only the two of us. It wasn't long until we started moving.

It didn't seem like we had gone far when the car jerked to a stop.

My heart flew into my chest. Not again.

Unlike last time, he didn't wait to hear any information from the front. As soon as the car braked, Carter reacted. He had been sitting next to me. I had taken a relaxing breath. A few of the knots in my stomach had just loosened when he flew out of the car before I could even comprehend what was happening.

As soon as I had, the air outside was filled with screams, gunshots, and shouts.

"Gun!" someone yelled.

Another screamed, "Run!"

The next second, I heard a stampede. People ran past the car. The thud of people being shoved came next. "Get out of here."

Someone barked out, "Move away from there! Now!"

"Ahh!" a girl cried out. Another thud came and her scream cut off.

That was all it took. I scrambled out of the car. I didn't want innocent people to get hurt because of me. When I opened the door, more people were running past. A guy almost ran into me. He caught himself, bounced off the car, and rotated in a circle around me. He kept running.

"Get in the car!"

I looked around. Some of the guards were positioned around me, but half of them were gone. I saw Mike in the distance. He was fighting someone. Where was Carter? Panic started to rise when I couldn't see him. Then I yelled out, "Carter!"

"Move it—" someone cursed. A strangled sound came from him next and I whirled to see that one of the guards had grabbed his throat. The guy was lifted off the ground and tossed aside. "Hey!"

"Get going." The guard pointed down the opposite direction. "Now."

The guy stood, ready to argue, but saw the other two guards. He ran where he was told to go.

"Emma!"

I craned my neck. Theresa stood inside a doorway, not far from where the car had stopped. Noah was in front of her with a restraining hand across her stomach. He was scowling as he watched the herd of people in the streets.

Bang! Bang!

"Emma! Get over here." Theresa waved me over frantically.

"No." The guard closest to me grabbed my arm and started to push me back into the car. "Get inside, Miss Emma. Mr. Reed is coming back."

"But," I looked to my friends.

"It's safer." His hand tightened.

"Emma!"

I recognized the voice. Everything in me tightened with tension. Carter. He was there, running back to me and waving me to the side. When he saw I wasn't doing what he wanted, he yelled next, "Matthew, get her inside now!"

A woman screamed behind me.

"Carter!" Noah stepped out from their doorway. "Our car took off."

He waved them over. "Get in the car. Matthew, get her inside NOW!"

The grip on my arm doubled and I was lifted in the air. As I watched, Noah and Theresa started to cross towards us, but then I saw something else. Horror rose in my throat and my eyes bulged out. I couldn't stop it. I couldn't do anything.

Carter was covering the distance at a breakneck speed, but someone stepped out of another doorway. He was too far away for the guards to grab him, and not close enough for Carter to tackle him.

Scott Graham lifted the gun in his hand. It was small, but he lifted it with ease. He had done it many times before. Instead of the flashy Casanova impression he had given me before, a cold mask gripped his features. He was like Carter, a killer. Then he turned the gun towards me.

Everything stopped.

My heart stopped beating. I stopped breathing.

"EMMA!" Theresa yelled. A bloodcurdling scream ripped from her throat next.

He saw me, aimed, and his eyes narrowed. It was coming. It was a matter of seconds.

I readied myself. I stared at him, dead in the eyes, and waited. I was going to die. I knew it in that moment, and I couldn't do anything to stop it.

The guard whirled around in that moment, but Scott could still see me. He moved his gun to the side and steadied his hand once more.

All the sudden, Carter was there. He snaked a hand around his neck. Scott stiffened, but it was too late. Carter grabbed a hold of the back of his neck and twisted. It was a clean movement, lethal. His neck snapped and he let go of the body. It dropped at his feet. Carter didn't pause. He sprinted over it and was next to me seconds later.

He took me from the guard. Before I was shoved inside, I looked over again. Two guards had followed Carter. They swooped down and each grabbed one end of the body. Scott was thrown in a car before us, and it raced off.

Theresa and Noah were already inside the car, waiting for us.

"Where's your sister?" My heart was pounding in my eardrums.

"Employee exit. She's safe."

As we had talked, Carter slammed his door shut and our car took off again. The sister wouldn't have mattered anyway. Carter wasn't waiting. From the sudden speed of the car, I was thrown backwards. He still held me around my waist and pulled me to his lap. I sat there, huddled over him, as I couldn't close my eyes anymore. I almost died. I should've felt something, fear, shock, something, but I felt nothing.

TWENTY-ONE

I assumed we would take Theresa home, but was surprised when we stopped outside a remote cabin-like home. It was huge. When I climbed out of the car, I glanced over and saw two large wrought iron gates closing behind us. It locked and a bolt of electricity sounded. No one was getting in.

"Where are we?"

Noah answered Theresa's question, "We're somewhere safe. Don't worry. We're only here for the night." He frowned at Carter. "Right?"

There was no answer. Carter took my hand and led the way. When we stepped inside a spacious foyer, he pulled me into a back room and closed the door. "I need you to do me a favor."

"Why are we here? Why aren't we home?"

He stepped close and dropped his voice, "That's part of the favor I need from you. I don't trust your friend. I can't let her go on her own and I couldn't bring them to our home, so this was the next best choice. Everyone's on lockdown for the next twenty-four hours. There's no cell phone or internet connection here. I have one television, but that's it." He turned my shoulders so that I faced him squarely. "Emma, I need you to watch your friend for me."

"Theresa?" Alarm rose in me. "Why?"

"I killed a man. She was already in the car, but she could've seen. I need to know what she saw and what she's thinking about it."

"You mean if she'll report you?" No, she wouldn't. I frowned. She couldn't, this was Carter. My Carter. "She knows you're friends with Noah and she knows about us."

"You said yourself that she's never approved of my connections and she doesn't like my friendship with Noah." He frowned a little and touched my hip to pull me closer. His head dropped to my neck, his favorite spot. His lips brushed against my skin as he murmured, "I killed a man in front of her. I know she considered him a friend. I'd kill him again."

Shivers coursed through me, but they weren't the bad kind. They should've been, but they weren't. I held my breath, closing my eyes as his hand explored under my shirt. It traveled up, nearing my breasts. It stopped underneath my breasts. His fingers slid under my bra and rested there. My chest rose as I wanted him to continue touching me.

He grinned against my neck and moved back to meet my gaze. His eyes were lidded, heavy with desire. "I would do it again in a heartbeat. He was sent to kill you, Emma."

The image of him holding his gun flashed in my mind. A heavy feeling rested over my chest. "Why? He worked for you, didn't he?"

He hesitated, removing his hand and stepped back.

I was cold without his touch. "Carter."

He grimaced. "I forgot he was friends with Noah and Theresa. I had hoped to keep him away from you." He paused for a beat. "He was selling information to Franco."

"What? Why would you—how long have you known that?"

"It's why he was working for me. We were watching him and Octave was the best place for him to work. All of my businesses are legit, but he didn't know that."

"Wait. You stuck him at Octave so that he could give information to Franco?"

He chuckled, shaking his head. "No, we stuck him there because there *was* no information to give. Anywhere else and he would've been suspicious, but Octave doesn't strike people as being vanilla. That's what it is, though." His grin fell flat. "He's the one who told Franco where you were. He's why we were attacked the first time."

"But..." That meant that they had been looking for me...not Jeremy's body anymore...

"Yeah," he sighed. "They knew, Emma. They knew it was you."

Ben gave me enough money.

Ice ran through my veins. My mouth fell open as my breathing slowed.

He looked happy last week. He thought he was hot stuff.

I stopped breathing. It couldn't be, but it had to be. No way. I felt gutted. Someone had taken a knife and slid it across my throat before they reared back for one deep thrust. A sick sensation started to fill me and I began to tremble.

"Emma?"

I shook my head. It couldn't be, but he said it himself.

"Emma!" His hand grasped the back of my head. He forced me to look at him. "What's going on?"

"You," I gasped out. I couldn't talk.

"Me?"

"You said—it was Ben. Ben told them." *Ben gave me enough money.* Oh god. I closed my eyes. A raging headache had started. It was going to split me open. *Mallory and Ben are gone.* Panic overwhelmed me and I couldn't breathe. I opened my mouth to draw in oxygen, but none came. My lungs stopped worked. I pounded on my chest, blinded, feeling more and more panic suffocating me. It was taking over me. I couldn't see.

Carter cursed and lifted me in his arms. He was taking me somewhere. My mouth was gaping open as I desperately tried to draw in oxygen. Nothing. I started to thrash around. Oh god. Oh god.

Then water hit me. It was freezing, but it dosed the storm inside of me. Screaming, I lunged away from it, but Carter held me in place. He bent to change the temperature with his arms around me. His body trapped me in place and I tried crawling over him to get away. A second later the water warmed and my chest rose up and down at a steadier rate. I was calming down.

"What's wrong with her?" Theresa asked from a distance.

Mallory and Ben are gone.

I shook my head. I couldn't get Amanda's voice out of my head. It was him. He had sold me out.

Ben gave me enough money.

He gave her money to take care of my things.

My feet gave way as I realized what that meant. He knew—he wanted my things put away. He paid for my things, mine and Mallory's, to be stored away. Did he know what they were going to do? He had to know.

"Emma?" Carter held me now.

I looked up at the concern in his voice. He was gazing down at me, his eyes already knowing. What did he know?

"Emma? Are you okay?" Theresa stood at the shower door. She was pale and her bottom lip was quivering. She held onto the door handle, but her hand was shaking.

I spoke, raw of emotion, "You told me he would sell me out."

Carter closed his eyes. His shoulders dropped and a breath left him. He knew.

He'd been right. I had even hoped for it, but knowing it happened—feeling it now. It was different. I couldn't have been prepared for the betrayal.

"Who sold you out?" Her hand started to rattle the shower door know. "What's going on?"

I held Carter's gaze. The world fell away underneath my feet. I didn't feel the water anymore. "He told them, didn't he?"

He nodded.

Reaching for him, my hands held onto his shoulders and he lifted me from the shower. He walked us both out and into a bedroom. Setting me back on my feet, he walked into the bathroom. Theresa touched my hand, her eyes grew wide when she felt my coldness.

She whispered, "What's going on, Emma?"

Carter came back with towels. He handed one to me as he took a second to wrap around my body. Then he started drying off himself as he went back out the door.

"Emma?"

Ben sold me out. He was paid to sell me out, but what about Mallory? They were gone. Where had they gone? Was she okay?

Theresa inched closer and dropped her voice, "I know he killed Scott. Don't worry, Emma. I'm going to call the police. I know you're infatuated with him, but he's not good for you. I'm going to take care of it. I'm going to get you away from him."

I looked at her, but felt detached from myself. It was like I was watching us from a safe distance, outside of my body. I watched as I said to her, "He was going to kill me."

"No." She shook her head. "I won't let him. I won't let him hurt you."

"Scott Graham was going to kill me. Carter saved my life."

Her eyes widened. Then narrowed. "You're in shock. I can see that. You don't know what happened—"

My hand latched onto her arm and held it in a death grip.

She cried out and then tried to pry my fingers off her arm, one at a time. She glanced to my face and back again to her arm, back and forth, back and forth. Her eyebrows furrowed together and she bit her lip. "Emma, you don't know what you're saying. You think you're in love with him, but you're not. You're blinded by his looks and his power. He's dangerous, Emma. He's very dangerous."

"He's my family."

She got three of my fingers off, but they latched back on. She sighed. "Okay. Okay, Emma. I can see this is going to take longer than I thought. Don't say anything to him. He's going to come back any moment—"

"I killed someone."

My words silenced her. Her arm dropped to her side and she staggered back a step. "Wha—what did you say?"

"I'm protecting her."

She whirled around to see Carter in the doorway. A grim expression was on his face and he held dry clothes in his arms. Then he walked around me and peered close. "Her eyes are glazed over."

"She's in shock. She thinks she killed someone."

"She did," he snapped at her and tossed the clothes on the bed. "Leave and I'll take care of her."

She snorted. "Yeah, right. You might be buddies with Noah and you might've known Emma in a previous life, but I'm not leaving you alone with her. Not one second—"

"Noah." Carter turned to the doorway.

"What?!" she squeaked as she was lifted in the air. Noah had been waiting in the background. He stepped forward, grabbed Theresa, and left the room with her. Carter called after them, "She can't leave. Not yet."

"I know," Noah's voice lashed out at him, over his shoulder.

The door was slammed shut a second later, and I turned towards Carter. I was still detached from my body, but he lifted his hand to my face. He cupped the side of it and ran his thumb over my cheek before he murmured, softly, "Come back to me."

I shook my head. It was safer where I was.

"Come back to me." He moved closer. His voice was a sensual caress against my skin. "Come back to me."

I shook my head. It was better not to feel. There was no fear. No one betrayed me when I was like this.

Then he rested his forehead against mine and breathed out, "Please, Emma. I need you with me. I love you."

I closed my eyes and the hurt seeped back into me. Everything hurt at once. It was too much, but I opened them again and I saw the relief in his. His hand closed around mine, and he tucked some of my hair behind my ear. I couldn't handle it, not all of it, and I felt myself numbing again. Then I stepped back. I couldn't do this if he was touching me. And I knew that I needed to hear it all. "Tell me what's going on."

He nodded, a look of surrender coming over him. "You're not going to like some of it."

"I have to know."

"Okay." He waited until I sat and then he started. "I told you before that I had an inside man with Franco, but I stopped hearing from him right before our first attack. He texted me that Ben sold you out so I doubled your guards after that, but I don't think you noticed. Then when we were attacked, I knew something had happened to him. He would've let me know ahead of time."

"They killed him?"

He nodded. "His body surfaced yesterday. It was delivered to one of the Mauricio houses."

I sucked in my breath. There was more. I knew there was more. "What else?"

He hesitated, tense, and then asked, "Are you sure you want to hear all of this?"

"I have to." I had no other choice. "Mallory's gone, Carter. I'm *really* hoping that Ben took his money and split with her, but I need to know for sure. That means that I have to know everything. You have to tell me everything. Please."

He didn't wait another second. "Your friend Ben went to Franco and told him that you were the killer. He didn't know about me or what happened with the body, but they'd been looking for Mallory. They knew Jeremy Dunvan had been seeing a regular girlfriend. He knew it was only a matter of time before they found her, so he gave them your name for some money and her safety guaranteed." A hard look came over him. His wolf eyes turned into ice. "He was stupid. They're planning to kill him anyways, if they haven't already."

"You know this from your inside guy?"

"And we know that Scott Graham told Franco you were at the club. He didn't know that I'd be there too or that you'd be going home with me. They can't get to you when you're in my buildings. It's why we've been attacked twice on the streets. After the first attack, we were going to take Scott to the warehouse for an interrogation." He stopped for a second. "That's what we do before someone's killed."

They were going to kill Scott, but they didn't. "What happened?" I never blinked.

"We needed to know more and I figured my guy was dead so we left Scott where he was. He was being kept around to see if he'd be useful to us. His time ran up tonight. Gene came in to take him to the warehouse, but he got free somehow."

"Why tonight?" My heart sped up.

"Because everything was going to be done tonight."

"What?"

He started to pace as his hand raked through his hair. His wet shirt had started to dry, but it was lifted up from the movement. It stuck to his skin and remained there. As I watched him go back and forth, his muscles tightened with tension. Suddenly dread started to fill me. Aside from the attack and stampede that Scott's gun had started, there were other events going on. Events, I was starting to realize, that had been in the making for awhile.

I stood slowly, dismay filling me more and more until I was standing in front of him. I stopped him, holding onto his arm. "What was supposed to happen tonight?"

"Franco Dunvan was supposed to die tonight."

"By you?"

He shook his head, his jaw clenching and unclenching. "By his own family."

"Just tell me. Explain it to me."

"I've been in Chicago since last weekend." He paused for a beat. "Do you know who lives in Chicago?"

"No."

"It's the headquarters for the Bertal Family."

My heart kept pounding, stronger and stronger. "Okay, so you went there? Why?"

His hand touched my arm. His hold was gentle as he tugged me close. I could feel his heart through his shirt. He murmured, dropping his voice to an intimate whisper, "I went there to barter a truce between the Mauricio Family and the Bertal Family."

My heart stopped. "You did that for me?"

"I would do anything for you." His hand cupped the back of my neck. He tilted my head up to meet his eyes. They were hungry and dark. When I saw the demand in them, a flame of desire lit in me. It grew into a fire that blazed hotter and brighter the longer I held his gaze. "Both families have wanted peace between them, and I gave it to them. I didn't get the final decision until this evening, but I got it. I was called in to see the heads of the Mauricio family this afternoon. That's where I was before going to Octave, but it's done. By tomorrow morning, Franco Dunvan will be dead and you'll be safe."

"What'd you do? How could you do that? I thought the two families had been feuding for years."

"No." He shook his head. "They've stopped fighting. The only section that's continued the fight was Franco's. When I went to them, I told them my stake and that I wanted your safety. I gave them 2.5% of the wealth that I'll accumulate over the next five years."

"And your family was fine with this?"

"I gave them 2.5% as well. Five percent of my earnings will go to the families from businesses that are clean. I bought us out and I bought Franco's death. This is a small price to pay, but large enough so that both families will get along. That was the deal, that both families take the 2.5%. I'm the truce between them. As long as I make money with clean businesses, it looks good to them and their name. You want legal businesses to mask the illegal businesses, but I'm out with all of those other dealings. I'm out. And you're out from Franco's watch."

"But why did Scott try to kill me?"

"I think it was a last attempt. My guess is that the hits started today and Franco figured it out. He wanted to hurt me the only way he really could. You." A primal look entered his wolf eyes. "It's what I would've done if I'd been cornered like that. I'd strike where I'd do the most damage, but it didn't work. You're safe."

"People are dying tonight?"

He nodded. "Only Franco's business associates. The Bertal family is cleaning up. Franco's death is their gift to me. They're doing the rest because they have to cover their backs too."

All of this was for me. All of that bloodshed was because of me. I didn't know how I felt about that, but I hadn't started this for me. I did it for Mallory. "Carter," I rasped out. "Do you know where Mallory is?"

He shook his head. "No, but if she's alive, they'll find her. The new Head of the Bertal family in this city knows about her. They know why you shot Jeremy. They'll contact me when she's found."

I nodded. That was all that mattered, right? All of this was for her.

"Emma."

"What?"

He seemed unsure now. "You need to know something else."

"What is it?" My heart started to pound again.

"Jeremy Dunvan was known for breaking in whores for their sex slaves." He paused, still unsure.

"Tell me."

The hesitation slid away to reveal a deep resignation in him. "My inside guy told me that they thought Jeremy was breaking in your roommate the night you shot him. He wasn't going to kill her. He was going to use her as a sex slave."

His words hit me. They were cold and stabbing.

He was going to turn her into a sex slave... He was going to turn her into a sex slave... Carter's words were on repeat in my mind. I kept hearing them over and over. Suddenly, I didn't care that those people were being killed. I wished I had done more than just shooting Jeremy Dunvan. He deserved worse. He should've died painful and slow.

TWENTY-TWO

"Are you okay?"

Carter had told me hours ago what they had been planning to do with Mallory. I asked him for some time alone, and he gave it to me. I'd been sitting on the bed ever since, just sitting there and thinking. As I processed through everything and realized what Carter had done for me, I was grateful. He bought my freedom while he himself wasn't completely free. He said that he'd have to pay them for five years, but was that long enough? I didn't think they would leave him alone after that. Then again, I wasn't a part of this life. This was his life, his world. Judging by the power and wealth that he seemed to have, it was a world that he had thrived in.

I waited until he closed the door behind him. He gave me a glass of water and a plate of food. My stomach grumbled as I saw the sandwich on it, but I left it untouched. My stomach said otherwise, but I couldn't eat. Thinking of Mallory as a sex slave had taken care of that.

"Emma?" He sat beside me.

"How will we know if everyone's been taken care of?"

"It doesn't matter. Franco is the one with the vendetta. When he's dead, no one will be paid for your hit. You'll be safe."

"But not you." The words wrung from me. He wasn't free of them.

"Emma?"

"You won't be safe. You're still tied to them."

He pulled me against his side and ran his hand up and down my arm. "You don't have to worry about me. As long as I continue to do what I do, I'll be fine."

"And if you don't? If you stop making money for them?" It was my worst nightmare happening in front of my eyes as I imagined what they'd do to him. An image of his body flashed in my mind. It was like Jeremy Dunvan's body, slumped over with blood coming from him, except it had Carter's blue eyes. It had Carter's chiseled cheekbones, his sculpted body, but it was lifeless and cold. I shook my head. That couldn't happen.

His hand fell away from my shoulders and slipped between us to find my hand. His fingers laced with mine. "That won't happen. I'm not new to this, Emma. I've been working with the Mauricio family for years. My word holds weight with both families now. I will be fine." Then he grinned. "But it feels nice to have someone worry about me. I'm the one people are scared of, not scared for."

I looked up, torn on the inside. "They don't know you like I do." *They don't love you like I do.*

His gaze fell to my lips and he whispered, "No, they don't. No one knows me like you do."

When his head moved closer, I closed my eyes and felt his lips touch mine. There was a soft insistence from him and I opened for him. As his tongue swept inside and took command over me, it wasn't long before I was lifted over him.

I gasped as he lifted my shirt off, "Carter."

His lips found mine again. The need for him rose, threatening to take control of me. I shuddered as his hand slid up my side. My skin burned in its wake, sizzling for more. As he continued to explore my body, all the sensations and love I felt for him took over.

I needed this. I needed him.

I was blind with hunger as he switched our positions. He laid me down, poised above me, and his continued to taste every inch of me. Along with my shirt went my bra. Then my pants were next. As his fingers slipped underneath the straps of my panties, he slid them down with his thumbs brushing against the insides of my thighs as he went.

I pulled him down to me and I wanted his shirt gone. When it was, when I felt the deliciousness of his skin under my hands, I tugged at his jeans. Carter reared back, long enough to kick them off and then he was back. He was between my legs, kissing me, touching me. He loved me with every touch and caress from him.

When he slid inside of me, I held still, helpless against how my body trembled for him. Then he started to move and I came alive in his arms. As the rhythm grew and his thrusts went deeper and deeper, I wrapped my legs around him. I joined with him, in every manner. My body was his. He could do as he pleased, and as I skimmed a hand down his back, he trembled underneath my touch. His body was mine as well.

We belonged to each other.

As I felt the edge nearing, I held onto him as he continued to move inside of me. His hand curved around my leg and lifted it higher. I opened even more and he went deeper from the different angle.

"Carter," I whispered against his skin. My hand clung to him, holding onto him. I met him move for move. He thrust in, my hips went with him. We rode together.

His eyes were open, bearing into mine. I felt myself stripped open to him, my soul bared, as his hips upped the tempo. Then it was time. I felt him tensing at the same time my climax ripped through me. Waves of pleasure slammed into me and I rode out each of them. As I finished, he let himself go.

I skimmed a hand down his sweaty back, kissing his shoulder when he collapsed on top of me. "Carter," I murmured.

He let out a long breath. His body shook as it came from deep within him. His hand trailed up my arm and he lifted himself up, tracing my lips as he looked down at me now.

We didn't speak. I couldn't. This man was mine. This very powerful being, sculpted to perfection with eyes that were of a wolf's. He touched his lips to mine, a soft claiming as he whispered against them, "I love you so goddamn much, Emma."

"I love you too."

I was weak with too many strong feelings sweeping inside of me, too many and too powerful for me to name, but as I gazed up at him, I saw his strength. As I lay in his arms and as he turned for me once more during the night, our bodies moved together as one and I felt my own strength awaken inside of me. I had grown addicted to this beautiful man. He was mine.

I would always love this man.

I rose from the bed and pulled on a robe that hung from the bathroom door. When I went into the kitchen, I looked around and started the coffee pot. As it brewed behind me and I began to look for more food to start breakfast for everyone, I knew that I had changed. Maybe it was that I had almost been killed, that I had seen it with my own eyes, or maybe it was knowing what would've happened to Mallory if I hadn't pulled that trigger. I wasn't sure which it was, but I had been changed. The culmination had occurred inside of me. I wasn't quaking anymore. I wasn't whining about losing my freedom or the inability to join friends for drinks without being babysat.

None of that mattered anymore.

It was done. Men had died because of me.

I no longer cared. I should've, but I didn't.

Or maybe it was how I felt like one with Carter now. I felt his power inside of me. My body grew stronger as I thought of the last time. The primal way he had taken me still sent reverberations through me. It wasn't that I was protected or sheltered by him, it was being with him and being loved by him, that made me feel his power. It was overwhelming and intoxicating.

"Morning," Theresa yawned behind me.

I turned and saw her anew. I knew she wasn't different. I knew it was me, but she looked weak to me. She saw it too. Her hand had risen to scratch behind her ear, but when she locked gazes with me, her hand fell away. Her eyes widened and her mouth fell open slightly. Nothing else was said. She shook her head and her eyes narrowed. Then she pulled the ends of her robe tighter around her, crossed her arms over herself, and mused, "You look different."

I unwrapped the bacon and placed slices into a pan. The sizzling from the oil started as I glanced back at her. "Did you sleep?"

"Yeah, surprisingly." Another yawn came over her and she rested against a counter. "Did you?"

Images of our lovemaking flashed in my head and a jolt of pleasure rushed through me. A faint grin came over me, but I nodded. "I did."

"Is *he* still asleep?"

My hand tightened on the pan as I heard her derision. We both knew who she meant. My back straightened, but I took a calming breath. "Yeah. Is Noah?"

I heard a soft sniffle behind me before she replied, "I wouldn't know."

I turned now and saw the agony in her depths before it was masked. "I'm sorry, Theresa."

She shrugged. "Yeah, well, what can I do about it? Brianna made her wishes clear last night. Noah's not going to go against them. Even if we did almost die."

"You know that Scott Graham started that riot last night."

"I didn't, no."

I tensed as I heard annoyance in her tone.

"Is that what *he* said?"

Okay. Anger boiled up as I regarded her. I'd had enough. "You have some poor misconceptions about last night, Theresa. Let me correct them for you right now."

She straightened from the counter but remained silent.

The tongs I held in my hand came down hard on the counter

beside me. "You saw what you saw. You saw Carter kill your friend, but he was a man that was sent to kill me. And yes, Theresa, he *was* going to kill me. Scott Graham might've been nice to you when you went to Octave, but he was selling information to a man that wanted me dead."

"Stop," she hissed. She had grown pale with each word I said. Her chest rose up and down at a rapid pace. "Just stop, Emma. You sound crazy."

I was calm. I was cold even. "A little more than three weeks ago I came home and found my roommate being raped. He was going to kill her or worse. And he was going to do the same to me because I was there. I shot him, Theresa."

She flinched as I said this.

I hardened inside. I didn't care. She needed to hear the ugly truth. "And because I knew Carter and I trusted him, I went to him for help. He's been protecting me ever since because the man I killed is the son of another mobster."

Her eyes went wide, but I saw the thoughts flying in her mind. She was connecting the dots. It was a matter of time and when her eyes filled with renewed horror, I knew she had figured it out. The name Dunvan fell from her lips in a whispered gasp.

"I killed Jeremy Dunvan and his father has been looking for me. I think you can guess what he wanted to do with me when he got me."

"Oh god."

I waited. I needed to know what she'd do with all that information. If she went to the authorities, she'd be condemning me as well. Then a different thought came to me and I felt sick. The back of my hair stood upright and I looked over. Carter was in the doorway. I knew he was waiting like me. He needed to know how she would react now that she knew the rest of it.

When his eyes caught mine, darkness flashed in his depths.

That was when I knew that she wouldn't get the chance to go to the authorities. Carter would ensure my safety, no matter the cost. I turned back to Theresa and hoped against hope that she would let it go because if she didn't, she was going to die.

Carter would take her life to save mine.

"Stop asking questions."

Our heads snapped up and over. Noah stood in the other doorway, fuming with fisted hands at his sides. He jerked forward into the kitchen as his eyes were latched onto Theresa. "I told you to stop asking questions. You have to stop now! I mean it, Theresa."

She straightened in defiance. "And what if I don't?" She rolled her eyes. "What's the worst that could happen?"

A low growl wrung from him as he cried out, "Are you kidding me?"

She paused, caught in the headlights of his glare. Then she swallowed tightly.

"You're in a safe house of a guy you know has mob connections and you're being snide about seeing him kill another man?" His eyes flashed in fury. "What part of that sentence is ludicrous? The. Whole. Thing! Think about it, Theresa!"

She frowned at him.

"You've always known who Carter was to me. I owe him my life, Theresa. My life! But that doesn't make him any less dangerous. He's been good to me and I will always be grateful to him for everything he's done, but you're talking about him like he's five. He is a killer and she's spelling it out to you. She's leading you down the damn road, but you have to stop and think about what she's not saying." Noah stepped closer to her. He begged her, "Please let this go.

Please, Theresa. He loves her. He snapped Scott's neck because of her. What do you think he'll do to you?" He reached for her hands and gripped them hard. Her tiny hands disappeared underneath his. "He'll make you disappear and the only reason I'll know about it is because of this conversation, right here. He'll do it when you won't be expecting it or it'll look like an accident. I have no idea, but I know he'll do it and it'll happen because you're threatening her life. Don't you get that?" He lowered his head so he was eye-level with her. "Please get that, please, please get that, Theresa. Stop. Talking. About it. Just stop. That's all you have to do."

"But," she opened her mouth as tears flowed down. Nothing came out. Her eyes jumped to mine, and I didn't do anything. He was right. She needed to hear it. Then her mouth shut and she fell back into the counter. She would've fallen if Noah hadn't been there.

He swept her up and turned to Carter. "She won't say a word. I promise."

Carter narrowed his eyes.

"I promise, Carter."

He looked to me as if to ask if I should believe him. I didn't do a thing. I couldn't. I had no idea what Theresa would do or what she would think a month away, or even a year, or ten years, if she would remain silent. So I gave him no answer.

The corner of his lip curved as if to say 'thanks a lot', but his eyes were still flat.

"Carter?" Noah pushed.

He stepped back to let them through. That was the only response he gave to the unspoken plea from his friend. Noah's shoulders sagged in defeat and he hurried them out the door. A car was outside.

When they shut the door behind them, I commented, "He

thinks you're going to kill the woman he loves."

Carter watched me. "Should I?"

Twenty-four hours earlier and I would've been pleading for her life. She was innocent. She was pure. She meant no harm. But now I had changed. Theresa had become a friend, but everything shifted last night. Carter was my lover. He was my family. He was my only ally. And because of that, because she held a threat to his life, I told him, "I can't lose you."

Then I picked up the tongs again and turned off the stove. The bacon was burned by then so I removed the pan and left.

TWENTY-THREE

Carter never did anything with Theresa. I asked him one night what he intended to do. He had men watching her, but that was his only response. When I asked what would happen if she contacted the police, he shrugged. “I don’t see it coming to that. She cares about you and if she did anything, I’d take it to Noah first. I’m not completely heartless, Emma.”

She never did anything, which I had to admit made me relieved. After two weeks, nothing happened regarding Franco Dunvan either. He went missing and my gut told me that his body would never be found. There were no reports on the news about the upheaval that happened that night. It made me wonder how many other mob events happened that the general public had no idea about. I never asked about Franco, but I figured I was safe when Carter told me that I could go out with only two guards. That was fine by me. So much had changed, myself included. Work wasn’t the same. I had never chatted much with the other girls, but I chatted with them even less now. When I would go for coffee, I never looked to see who was in the breakroom. I got my coffee and returned to my office.

The new promotion was nice. I had more freedom over my hours and I didn't have Mr. Hudson breathing down my neck. In fact, I was his boss now and he had to report to me. I was lenient with him, but I knew there'd be a day when I would enforce those duties. However, that day wasn't now.

I worked closely with Theresa on the new account. Her excitement had waned, which made sense and I didn't take offense to it. That meant that she had listened to Noah's pleadings. One time I asked Carter if he still sparred with Noah in the mornings and he surprised me when he said he did. I thought their friendship would be strained, but it seemed like they went on as if nothing had happened.

It was the end of a week and I was about to leave. But as I stepped outside and saw the car waiting for me, I turned to Mike. He and Thomas stayed with me. They were the regulars. There were others, but I liked knowing who guarded my life the majority of time.

His hand fell away from the car door. "Maybe coffee today?"

I nodded and turned back inside. I went through the front lounge and headed for the café. Carter was gone again. Unlike the last couple times when he never told me where or why he was leaving, he explained to me the night before that he was going to Japan. He was brokering another business merger for a new website program. I nodded. I only cared about when he was coming back and I knew it would take at least a full day. It would be the longest we had been apart since the night he killed Scott Graham.

When I went inside the cafe, Amanda was behind the register. She signaled for someone to take her place and gestured towards a back booth. It was our old booth. When I saw that she grabbed two mugs and a coffee pot, warmth flooded me. It felt good to be falling back into our old routine. It made me feel like I still had one other friend.

"New threads?" she asked as she slid into the booth.

I waited as she filled both mugs. "I got a promotion. It requires better clothes." That was half true, but I wore the clothes Carter bought for me when I first went to live with him. After making love one time, I asked where the clothes had come from since they all fitted me perfectly. He said he ordered them when I came to him at Octave. He had known even then that I would be with him. My response was to pull him back down to me and it hadn't been long until he slid back inside of me.

Thinking about that night sparked desire within me. We hadn't slept much.

"So are you going to tell me about the new man in your life?"

I almost dropped my mug. "Excuse me?"

Amanda rolled her eyes. "Please, Ems. It's all over you. Even now you're blushing. I'm not an idiot. Who's the guy?" She shook her head. "Please tell me it's not Ben."

I grinned. "I'm going to have nightmares now. Can you imagine? Waking up and seeing him strutting around the apartment?"

She giggled. "With nothing on except his boxers?" She pretended to stick out her gut how Ben always would. He would rest his hands on the back of his hips and stand, trying to make his gut look bigger than it did. He was always trying to convince us that he wasn't just skin and bones.

Both of us groaned. I shook my head. "I think I threw up in my mouth just now."

"Me too." She giggled some more. "Remember the time he told

us he could join an MMA fight club but didn't because he didn't want to harm any of the other fighters?"

"You're right. He said it wasn't fair to the humanity of the MMA standards if he fought."

As she sipped her coffee, she shook her head. "He was such an idiot."

"Pretty much."

Then she sighed, "Am I pathetic for missing him?"

All of the amusement fled and I was left feeling empty. "I miss Mallory."

Amanda closed her eyes and lowered her head. She put the mug down on the table as she cleared her throat.

I heard the emotion there. I felt some of it as well.

She said in a quiet voice, "Mallory changed, Ems. What he did to her and what you did in front of her, I think it changed her. She wasn't the same Mallory before they disappeared."

Anger speared me. Mallory would've never left without a word before it happened. But I left first. I had no right to be angry with her. Then I admitted, "I think that changed all of us."

She wiped a tear from her eye. "It's never going to be the same, is it?"

Her eyes held mine. There was a spark of longing in them. She wanted me to tell her everything would be fine. The gang would be back to normal, but it wasn't the truth. I couldn't think of a way to lie to her and make it sound convincing. All I could say was, "We can still be normal."

Her eyes closed in defeat. "You're different, Ems. We can't be normal. You're not normal anymore. I think what you did changed you too." She opened them again and frowned at me, chewing on her lip for a moment. "It's like a part of you died."

A part of me did die. "I think that happens when you kill someone."

She wiped another tear away. The coffee had grown cold by then. "I've been thinking about moving, leaving this place."

"Where?" A pang stabbed me.

She shrugged. "Maybe back home. They offered me a teaching position and I could take care of my mom. It doesn't seem like there's anything here for me."

I didn't want her to go. I didn't want to lose another friend, another part of my old life.

She had been watching me. She asked now, "What do you think about that?"

I hesitated. "I don't want you to go. I wanted us to be friends again."

Pushing her mug away, she leaned back and sighed. "I don't know, Ems. I really don't know. Things are so weird now. I have to make new friends. I have no idea where-"

"I moved in with Carter Reed," I interjected in a rush. Then I blinked, startled, at what I had just said. Oh god. She knew. I waited, biting my lip, for her reaction. What would she say? What would she do?

A confused look came over her. "Um, what?" Her eyes lit up. "Carter Reed? He's hot!" She seemed awestruck then. "Wow. I mean-whoa. He's hot and rich. You're living with him? Holy shit, Emma. No wonder you didn't say anything. He's like the boyfriend of all boyfriends." Her eyes narrowed. "Wait, you are boyfriend/girlfriend, right? He's not tossing you around, using you for sex, is he?"

I shook my head, fighting back a smile. "No. I love him. I love him a lot." It felt good to be sharing this, talking about him to someone who didn't think he was brainwashing me. I admitted, "I've missed this. I've missed you."

Her hand reached out and she placed it over mine on the table. "Me too." A third tear slipped down her cheek. "Me too, Ems." She let out a timid smile. "Maybe we should do dinner every Friday night or something. No, wait, that'd be date night. Okay, Thursday nights. Let's do something then." She sat up. "Hey! Does that mean we can go to Octave sometime? That'd be amazing."

I laughed as my chest felt lighter. "He owns restaurants too. We can eat at any of them, any time."

"Oh man. Wow, Ems. That's great." She nodded, her lip quivering from emotion again. "That's where you went, didn't you? To be safe from Franco. You went to him and he protected you."

I nodded.

Her eyes grew thoughtful and she sighed again. She looked defeated now. "Ben didn't get that money from his job, did he?"

She didn't have to look at me. She already knew the answer.

"I'm sorry, Emma. I'm so sorry." Then she asked the question I couldn't answer, one that I wanted to know, too. "Where'd they go? Where did Ben and Mallory go?"

I didn't know, but I hoped against hope that Mallory was okay.

Carter came back the next night. He woke me when he slid into bed and I glanced at the clock. It was three in the morning. When his hand curved around my thigh, he tugged me close and rested his head into the crook of my neck. He pressed a kiss there and his hand explored my waist before it slid upwards. When it came to my breast, he spread his palm out and held me. His thumb rubbed back and forth over the peak as he murmured, "Japan was exhausting."

Desire pulsed through me. He felt my tip hardening under his ministrations. "I'm glad you're back."

He moved up and gazed down at me. His eyes darkened with lust and his gaze lingered on my lips. "Me too."

He lowered his head and my heart fluttered, ready for his kiss and ready for the hunger that always enslaved me. When he slid inside of me, I hoped that I'd never get used to how alive he made me feel. All of it took over me. It was later as he held me close and he had tucked himself around me that I wondered if he was healing that part of me that had died.

It was the next morning when he asked if I was alright.

I lowered the orange juice in my hand to the counter. "Why do you ask?"

"Because I know you. I know something's wrong."

A fierce surge of love rolled through me. It was overwhelming and sudden. I gasped from the intensity and couldn't speak for a moment. I wanted to protect him. I wanted to protect us and I would do anything it took to do that.

His saw what was in my eyes and took me back to the bedroom. As he lowered me to the bed, he gazed down at me for a moment. His hand slid through my hair and cupped the back of my head. "Do you know much I love you?"

The same feeling of protection washed over me again. I could only jerk my head in a nod. My throat was thick with emotion. It was suffocating me and I gasped as I pulled him down to me, "As much as I love you."

The next night he took me to one of his restaurants. It was one of his more exclusive ones and as he led me through to a back section, I wasn't surprised when I saw celebrities spread through the dining area. It seemed that everyone in the restaurant emanated money. When we passed by the restrooms and three women walked out, my mouth dropped open from how beautiful they were. One called to Carter, but he ignored her and pulled me to a small set of stairs. We went to a second level that I didn't know existed. I realized the second level was the most private area in the whole restaurant. There was only one long table for the entire level. We were able to look down over the main floor through a glass floor beneath us, but no one could see us. I remembered seeing a mirrored ceiling when we were below.

As we sat, the chef came to greet us. Carter did the introductions, but I was surprised as I watched him talk with his employee. He wasn't faking the warmth. He genuinely liked the man. After he left us and a server brought over a bottle of wine, I asked, "How do you know him?"

He waited until the server had left, after filling both of our glasses. "Remember when I told you when I went to the Mauricio warehouse? That was Farve."

Shocked, I murmured, "You said he was drinking buddies with your dad?"

Carter's smile thinned. "He never approved of what my dad did. I think he took me in to make up for not stopping my old man."

I shivered as I remembered some of the worst times Carter came over for our couch. "He could've protected you from him."

His eyes shot to mine. "You protected me from him."

I held my breath, captivated by him.

"So did AJ. You gave me a home when I needed one."

"You kept going back." The bitterness was still with me.

"Because I loved my father." Darkness flickered in his depths. "I was a fool, but because of him, Farve saved my life. He gave me a third home after I lost you and AJ."

"You never lost me."

His eyes held mine steadily. He said, softly, "I did. I let you go so you could be normal. I never wanted this life for you."

"This life?" I gestured around the restaurant, teasing.

"The life you would've had then, if I had brought you with me. For awhile there, it was hard. They had me do horrible things, Emma."

I knew what he was doing and I didn't care. I never flinched. I never looked away. Instead, I picked up my wine and sipped it before I replied, "I wouldn't have cared. I don't care now." He was warning me away, testing to see if I was scared. "I know who you are, Carter. I'm the only one who knows you."

TWENTY-FOUR

I told him about Amanda that night in bed. He nodded, replying, "That's good. You met her in college?"

I shifted down in bed, surprised that he knew that, but knowing that I shouldn't have been. He had men watching me all my life. He probably knew more about me than I knew myself. "No, not really. I didn't have a lot of good friends in college, none that stuck. I knew Amanda from freshman year. We were in this social club they did. They grouped a bunch of freshman together. I think it was to help jumpstart a social life. I stopped going to the club outings after the first night when I realized we didn't actually have to be there."

He trailed a hand up my arm, sending tingly sensations in its wake. "You didn't become good friends with her then?"

"No, it wasn't until I was hired at The Richmond. She teaches, but works at the café next to it during summers. We reconnected. I met Mallory before that. She was my only friend since college." I sighed, feeling some of the emptiness from those years again. "It took me awhile to learn what good friends were like. I never pledged to a sorority but I was friends with a bunch of them during college. We went to fraternity parties, and those were the worst. To be fair, I think it was just the girls I had become friends with. They were the stereotypical stuck-up girls. I don't even know why they were friendly with me."

His hand moved to my hair. He started brushing it back from my face. The light touches were comforting and the old emptiness started to ease away. He murmured, "Do you not know how beautiful you are, Emma?"

Jolted, I looked up and saw the somber expression on him. My chest rose, full of warmth again, and I couldn't speak for a moment. I saw the love from him and it took my breath away.

His thumb rubbed across my forehead and down my cheek. He cupped my chin and smiled down at me. "You have always been beautiful, Emma. I worried about you when you were in those foster homes. I was glad when they placed you with that last couple. The Jones were nice to you." When he saw my surprise, his smile widened. "Yes, even then I was watching and trying to help you. I asked the judge to move you to their home. He agreed that it would be beneficial for you. That was the only reason he approved the transfer."

I let out a shuddering breath. Nothing should've surprised me anymore, nothing when it came to him. Then I murmured, my voice hoarse, "You thought I was beautiful?"

He flashed me a grin. "If AJ wouldn't have killed me, I would've kissed you a long time ago."

"Really?"

"Really." Then he leaned down and pressed his lips to mine.

The hunger started in me and I opened for him. It wasn't long until kissing wasn't enough and he was shifting to lie on top of me. It was later, much later, that he asked about my friends in college. I curled against his chest and pulled the sheet to cover me. His hand caressed my stomach, running in small circles.

Feeling content, I murmured against his skin, "I don't even talk to anyone I knew from college."

He pressed a kiss to my shoulder. "You became friends with Mallory after you graduated?"

I rolled over and looked up at him. "What are you doing?"

He laughed. His hand traced down the side of my face and his thumb rested on my bottom lip. "I'm trying to understand your life, Emma. I was given reports, but that didn't tell me what you were feeling or what you were thinking."

"I think you have the more interesting life."

His eyes fell flat. "No, no I don't. I took a lot of beatings from my old man, but I never left. I didn't want to leave my best friend and his little sister. They were my family. When someone took that away, I did what I knew how to do. I beat *them* up. When that didn't make it feel better, I killed them and you know the rest. My life's not interesting at all."

"I think you're underestimating yourself."

His thumb rubbed back and forth over my lips. He murmured, "I'd rather hear about you."

As his hand ran down my neck and in the valley between my breasts, I closed my eyes as he cupped one of my breasts and caressed me there. I murmured, "I met Mallory at my first job after school. I got hired at The Richmond later and saw Amanda again."

"Tell me more." He moved down to kiss the valley between my breasts.

Desire flooded me. My heart pounded against my chest.

"Uh...we used to talk about guys a lot. All three of us. Mallory dated a lot of guys. Ben worshiped her, but she never gave into him. And Amanda," my breath hitched as his tongue swept the underside of my breast, "uh, Amanda liked nerdy guys. She said it was the curse of having a wimpy dad."

He moved further down my stomach. My hands slid into his hair and held on. I gasped, unable to speak. The ache between my legs grew with each nibble from him.

"It sounds like you had fun with her?" His hand moved to my hip and he urged me to my side.

As I did, he settled behind me. My leg was lifted and he fit between them. His arm reached around me so I was held against his chest. He started to nudge inside of me. I couldn't talk. The sensations were overwhelming me.

He murmured into my ear, pressing a kiss there, "Tell me about your friendship with her."

I struggled to concentrate and gasped, "We laughed about our dates. And Ben." He pushed further into me. My eyes closed and I rested my head against his. He began a slow rhythm.

His voice was husky as he murmured, "Why did you laugh about him?"

"Because he's funny." My throat closed off. I could only lie there as his fingers moved over my body and his hips thrust into me. "Carter," I gasped again.

"What's wrong?"

I heard his amusement. Twisting my head to the side, I caught his gaze. They darkened and a primal hunger burst over me. Pushing at his hips so he slipped out, I started to turn, but Carter grasped my waist. He lifted me over him and slammed inside of me in the same movement. There were no words after that. I folded over him, bending down so my chest was pressed against his as he urged my hips into a faster pace.

It was later, after we both exploded together and I was still curled over him. He was tracing my hair back, skimming his hand over my body in a soft caress before he'd move back to my hair and repeat the same motion. I was falling asleep when a thought came to me. "Do you have men watching Amanda?"

His hand tightened around my breast for a second. Then it relaxed. "No. Are you worried about her?"

"No." I had no reason to be. Then I looked up at him. "Could I invite her to Octave one night? It'd be fun."

"You can invite her anywhere you'd like." He gazed at me, a soft longing in his eyes.

My heart constricted. "What's wrong, Carter?"

He only gave me a sad smile. "I'm glad you have a good friend. This life with me is solitary. I worry about you when I'm gone."

"You don't ever need to worry about me."

He gripped my arms. "I do. And I will always worry, but it's because I love you. I will never control you, Emma. You can make your own decisions and go where you want and I will never say otherwise. But I need you to know that if I worry about you, it's because I love you. I want you safe. I will always want you safe, no matter who you are with or what you're doing."

The intensity on his face had me gasping again. No one had looked at me like that since AJ, since he told me to go as he faced down Tomino in that alley. That had been the last time I felt someone's love for me as much as I did from Carter now. He had said the words and I knew he meant them, but I felt them this time. I had no words. I had no way to express what I was feeling so I leaned into him and captured his lips with mine. It wasn't long until both of us were groaning again. I was home. I was where I was supposed to be.

The next month went by and I was happy. Carter tried to limit his travels to one day a week and when he couldn't, I knew he hurried so he could get back to me. Work passed uneventfully. I was still enjoying my new job and the parameters I was given, but Theresa remained withdrawn when we worked together. That was a damper on my good moods. After work, I began going to the cafe more and more. Amanda started to wait for me in our booth. She knew when my job ended and had a coffee pot waiting for us. We never discussed Ben and Mallory again. I shared with her little things about Carter, about a new restaurant he took me to or how he said we could go to Octave at any time, and she would tell me stories about her co-workers.

The last Friday of the month, I slid into my side of the booth and noticed she was different. Her head was down and she was wringing her hands together. Her shoulders were slouched down.

"What happened?"

Her head snapped up with horror. "I have a date."

I grinned. "You look ready to pee yourself. How is that a bad thing?"

Her hands kept twisting around each other and she let out a deep breath. "How did this happen? I keep asking myself that and I have no idea how it happened. I really don't. He was there. He was hot. He was asking for a bagel. I was giving one to him and then his hands touched mine." Her chest rose for another dramatic breath. "Then he kept coming in. I'm nuts. I know I'm nuts. My best friend is dating a mob hitman, okay-my only friend is dating a mob hitman. What am I doing? I can't go on a date. I have to call and cancel."

She dove inside her purse, fumbling for her phone, but I

snatched it away. “What are you talking about? You can’t date because of me? You can’t think that, do you?”

She froze.

I saw she did. I flung her purse back on the table, but grabbed her phone before she could. Then I pointed at her, her phone in hand, with each word. “You can date whoever you want. You can’t not date because of me. You got it?”

She swallowed. “He’s a cop.”

Oh.

I fell back in the booth. Her phone fell out of my hand. I hadn’t considered that scenario, but then I really started to think about it. I never told her anything specific. The only things I said about Carter were the good things, how he made me feel and normal dating stuff. I didn’t even know anything about his business connections. He said he was out, but he had killed in the past. And I knew about some of those, but I would never tell a soul. So I looked back up. “Date him.”

“Huh?” Her mouth fell open.

“Date him.” I shrugged. “Why not? You don’t even know Carter. You don’t really know anything about him. Why couldn’t you date this guy then?”

She continued to gape at me before she pretended to bang her head on the table, groaning. “You were supposed to agree with me. I can’t date this guy.”

“Why not?”

“Because!”

I grinned. This was the old Amanda and I said what I would’ve said then, “Just wait till Mals and Ben hear about this. You’ll hear all about-” I stopped. I couldn’t believe I had said that. I’d forgotten. I sat back, feeling the blood drain from my face. “Oh man.”

She shot forward and slapped a hand on the table. “Look at me.”

I'd forgotten about them.

She slammed it down again. "Look at me, Emma!"

I jerked my gaze up, my heart still pounding. Mallory.

She hissed at me, "So what?! Huh? So what. I know what just happened and it's okay. It's okay. Okay, Ems? Okay?! I know you're thinking that you forgot about Mallory and how could you, blah blah blah? Am I right?"

I couldn't think. My eyes were fastened to hers, but I couldn't deny the guilt in me.

"You're wrong. You're wrong! What happened was a horrible, horrible thing and you saved your friend. You did. You saved her, but when you did what you did, the game changed. Your man knew that. He knew right away that there'd be a time when it would come to you or her. Ben did a bastard move, but he did it to save Mals, and you forgetting about them just this second means that you're moving forward. Okay? That's all it means. You're moving on. We're all moving on. Wherever they are, they're moving forward too. You don't need to feel guilty about leaving her and I know you do. Be happy with that hot piece of ass and feel okay being happy with him."

I murmured, "How do you know all that to say to me?" Was it really that simple?

"Because I love you. You're my friend and I'm grateful that I still have your friendship." Her chin locked in place and she crossed her arms. "I'm pissed that Ben went to them, but I've realized that it had to happen. Your man was right, that's why he took you away from us. If you had stayed with us, you were a sitting duck. They would've found Mallory and Ben would've told them what you did to save her." She shrugged. "It had to happen. Your life or hers. Your man saved you and Ben did what he had to."

Some of my old humor sparked in me and I grinned. "Did you really just refer to Ben as a man?"

Amanda smacked her hand to her forehead and moaned. "He'd been so pathetic over her for so long. Always panting after her, being one of *those* guys. He was such a creeper."

I chuckled. "He would call the apartment when she was on dates. He always wanted me to tell him when she got home. I never did, but one time he even sent me a pizza. It was like he was trying to bribe me for information on her."

"Mallory was so stupid." She amended, "She was nice, but she was stupid. How could he not give her the creeps? He was her very own stalker that she treated like a friend."

I snorted, "Or like a brother at times. There were times when he'd come over and she'd hide in the bathroom. We even had it rigged where we could slip through the window. Ben never believed me when I told him she wasn't home. He demanded to search the apartment to see it for his own eyes."

"He was a little crazy about her."

"A little?" My eyebrow rose. "Try a lot, but she always said he was nice deep down. Guess she was right in some ways? He was there for her in the end."

"Yeah, I guess. He was like the pervy cousin that was always around."

I grinned. He was. Then my smile waned. "Why are we talking about them like they're dead?"

"Because they are."

My eyes shot to hers.

She shrugged, glancing away and sighing at the same time. "At least to me, they are. They're gone. They left us behind. At least when you left, you were still working. We still texted. But they're completely gone. No word. No call. No nothing. So to me, that's how I think of it. They're dead to me."

"That's perverse."

"Helps me from getting hurt by them. I locked 'em out. Maybe you should do that too."

"Yeah, maybe." I bit my lip as I looked away. "Mallory never texted me."

"Because stupid Ben destroyed her phone one night. He thought they could find her from its gps. You didn't hear him at the end, before he got all happy. He was sounding crazy. He thought there were men watching them. He thought someone was listening in on the landline and they could get into his computers. He was scared to leave the apartment. I mean, really, he took a butcher knife with him when we ordered pizza. I'm surprised the kid didn't drop a deuce on his doorstep."

I looked down. I couldn't stop myself. There *were* men watching them. Carter had sent them. I didn't know about the rest, but Ben wasn't as crazy as she thought. As I slid out of the booth, I mustered up a smile. "On that sanitary note, I think I'm going to head home."

"Tomorrow?"

I stopped, caught by the earnest hope on her face, and nodded. "Yeah. You know, let's do something fun. Maybe a night at Octave?"

Her eyes lit up. "Serious?"

"Serious. We'll have our own box too."

"Is your man going to be there?"

I shrugged. "I have no idea. He tries to come if he's not busy."

"So you're saying it could be just the two of us, in our own private box?"

"Is that a problem?"

"Nope. Just means I can get wasted and not worry about looking like a fool."

-CARTER-

When his phone rang, Carter inwardly sighed. It wasn't the ring he wanted to hear. He picked up his phone, "Gene?"

"You have a problem."

He didn't blink or react. It was how he assumed the conversation would start. "With what?"

"Our cops called. All of them said the same thing, your woman's roommate was found an hour ago."

He held back his grimace. He already knew it wasn't good news. "She's dead."

"Yep, beaten and strangled. Cops think the boyfriend did it, that one you said would be a problem."

"They know why?" Emma would want to know. She'd want to understand and then she'd blame herself.

"A butcher knife was taken to her stomach. They think she was pregnant and the prick didn't like who the father was."

Dunvan.

Carter sighed. "Okay. Thanks for letting me know."

"The boyfriend's still missing. Cops are canvassing the neighborhood for him, but right now they only think he was a crackhead. You know what'll happen if he's taken into custody."

"Crackhead?" But Carter knew that's what Franco had done. Get them hooked and they belong to you forever.

"Yeah," the older man sounded wary. "They were using an abandoned apartment in a warehouse. It looked like a usual crackhead's place. You know what's all there."

Carter nodded to himself. "Find the boyfriend before the cops do."

"What are you going to say to your woman?"

He never hesitated. "I'm going to tell her that her roommate died from a miscarriage and bled out."

"That's it?"

"She doesn't need to know the rest. She'll know the friend she tried to protect is dead anyway."

"Listen to you. You're going soft on us, Carter. Pretty soon you're going to be having emotions and shit like that."

"What would you feel, Gene? If the situation were reversed and it was your woman?" he asked, suddenly exhausted. He was stalling. He knew it and he asked the question anyway.

The other man laughed into the phone. "Fuck. I don't got no feelings, not after this long in the business. I'm surprised you do."

Did he? An image of Emma's heart-shaped face appeared in his mind and anger rushed to him. The damn boyfriend. The prick could hurt her. After all he'd done to keep her from harm, and now this. He murmured into his phone, "I've got enough feeling to know what I'd like to do to that boyfriend of her roommate's."

"I hear you. I'll be missing you around these parts."

"I won't."

Gene chuckled, low and gravelly, "Bye friend."

Carter's goodbye was a command, "Find the boyfriend." When he hung up, there was no regret or doubt. Carter punched in the number for her driver and told him to bring her home as soon as possible. When that call was done, he stood and left his office. He knew he would pretty-up the conversation as much as he could, but for the first time in a long time, he was scared. He wasn't used to being scared of anything, but that's all he'd been with Emma since she came back into his life. Terrified.

Mike waited beside the car next to the curb. I took two steps when I heard my name being called. Theresa was outside the hotel with her hand in the air. When she saw that I was waiting, she hurried over. "Hi! I bet you're shocked to see me like this."

To say the least.

My tone was cool, but I was curious. "What's up, Theresa?"

She nodded with her cheeks puffed out. "Okay. Here I go." A deep breath. "I've been a bitch. I know I have. I'm really sorry. I have no excuses. I really don't, but the idea of what he did and the whole story about what you did really had me confused."

"It wasn't a story."

"I know it wasn't. Trust me, Noah's hounded me for days when he found out that I've been less than friendly to you."

I narrowed my eyes. "You're doing this because of Noah?"

"No, no! I don't do anything because of Noah. Life would probably be easier if I did, but I'm too stubborn and thick-headed.

I'm doing this because it's taken this long for me to realize that I was wrong. If you did what you did, why you said, then you don't deserve going to jail and I understand why you couldn't come forward. I wouldn't have the courage to stay here and try to have a normal life after that. I get it. I do. I really do." She grimaced. "And now I'm babbling. I just wanted to say that I'm sorry for not being a friend. There's no excuse. I should've said this stuff to you a long time ago, not wait until a month later because I was embarrassed."

"You were embarrassed?"

"Yeah," she let out in big breath. "Big time. I'm an idiot and I know we weren't great friends, but I felt like we were going to be. Do you think I could have a do-over?"

Suspicion clouded over me and I couldn't help to wonder if she had struck a deal with the cops? Was she a plant now, trying to get information on me or Carter? "I won't talk about Carter."

"No, no. That's fine. I understand."

"At all. I won't talk about what we said I did."

"I know. I really do understand." She grimaced again, looking up and down the street.

Mike had closed the door to the car long ago, but he stepped away from it now. His presence was enough of a reminder not to mess with me.

Theresa grinned at him and waved. "Heya, Mr. Bodyguard-Whose-Name-I-Never-Learned. I'm not going to hurt her again." She turned to me, a small plead in her eyes. "I'm really not. I know I did when I turned my back on you. I won't do that again. I was lucky enough to find a genuine friend. I'm not going to screw it up." She chuckled, "You're one of the only friends that I could hang out with Noah too. I was surprised when he told me that he and Carter still work out together."

"Me too," I admitted.

"So am I pressing my luck by asking if you'll give me another chance?"

I wasn't going to trust her, but it wouldn't hurt to have a friend to talk with at work or the potential night at Octave. And at that thought, I suggested, "I'm heading to Octave tonight with a friend. Do you want to come?"

Her eyes got big. "Really?"

I nodded. "Why not? As long as you don't judge my friend when she gets wasted."

"Have you not seen me when we've gone out?" She laughed. "I tend to drink more than I should. Noah's always on me about it, but I like to blow off steam."

"Okay. Yeah, we'll see you there. I'll text you later what time we're heading."

"Are you going straight from your place or...?"

I hadn't thought about it, but I ducked back inside the cafe. Amanda was behind the front register. "Do you mind if a coworker of mine comes with tonight?"

She shrugged, but she looked surprised. "Sure."

"Should we get ready at your place?"

"Oh. Yeah." She nodded more vigorously. "We can drink wine and get ready together."

Our eyes met and I knew she was thinking the same thing. Just like old times. She flashed me a grin. "Eight tonight?"

"Sounds good." I waved before I ducked back out. "See you at eight."

Theresa had been fidgeting as she waited on the sidewalk. Her head popped back up when I came out. I told her, "Pick you up at 7:30 and we'll get ready at my friend's place. She'll want to drink wine before we go."

"Sounds like my kind of friend."

Mike stepped close to me. His low baritone sounded behind my ear. "Emma? There is a call for you."

I nodded. That was his reminder that we needed to go. I waved to Theresa. "7:30 tonight."

"7:30! See you then. I'll have everything ready to be ready."

"Okay."

As I got into the car and Mike sat up front, he'd been doing that since I now only needed two guards, I couldn't wipe the smile from my face. So many ups and downs, but Amanda was right. It was time to move forward and not feel guilty because of it. Wherever Mallory was, I hoped she was doing the same. A night out with Amanda and Theresa would be interesting, but I knew it would be fun. Then I stopped thinking about it as we drove home. The usual excitement to see Carter kicked in.

When we got there, he was waiting in the kitchen, and I tossed my purse on the counter and threw my arms around him. Pressing my head into his neck, I exclaimed, "I'm going out with the girls tonight. I hope that's okay. Theresa extended an olive branch and she seems genuine. I don't know if she is, but tonight will be fun anyways. Amanda's going too. We're going to go to her place to get ready..." I looked up and my voice faded.

Something was wrong. Very wrong.

"Carter?"

He never hugged me back. Every muscle in him was tense and rigid. He could've been a statue made of stone. His jaw clenched as he gazed down at me.

"Carter?" I asked again. My heart picked up as I looked into his eyes. There was something—no, it couldn't be. My arms dropped as if burned and I stepped back. I started to shake my head. No way.

But as he spoke, he said what I knew he was going to say.

My gut felt kicked in. I was sucker-punched as he said, "They found Mallory today."

I kept shaking my head and moving away. I wanted to detach again. I wanted to go anywhere else. This wasn't happening. "Don't," gurgled from the bottom of my throat. She was safe. She was away. She wasn't what he was going to say. There was no way. Ben never would've allowed that to happen.

"Emma."

"No."

"She was pregnant."

Oh god.

I fell to my knees, or I would've. Carter caught me. He cradled me to his chest and he tucked his chin into his favorite place. His lips brushed against me as he said it, "She miscarried and bled out."

She was dead. He was telling me she was dead.

I looked away. I tried to be away. I didn't want to hear this.

"Emma," he whispered as he brushed some of my hair down. "Emma. Look at me."

I didn't. I wouldn't.

"Emma."

"NO!" I ripped out of his arms and staggered back. When he reached for me, I batted him away. "No, I said!"

His arm fell back to his side.

I killed him for her. She was going to die and I stopped it. I killed him. I took him away so she could live and now he was telling me—I refused to believe it. I shook my head again. "No. I don't believe you."

"The police found her."

"Where?"

His eyes narrowed. "You can't go there."

"Why not?! She was my family." She left and I thought she was starting over. That's what Amanda said. Amanda was always right. They were starting over. I was starting over. We had all survived. And now Carter was saying that all of us hadn't survived. Not her. I looked at him and whispered, "It should've been me."

He jerked me against him and wrapped his arms around me. "Not you."

"It should've been me."

His arms tightened around me. "Not you. I'm sorry. I'd kill every single person to keep that from happening."

"Well, you did." I pulled away. "I got out. That's what you wanted. You wanted me here and safe. So congratulations. I'm alive, but if I had stayed there, they could've traded me for her. She would be alive and I'd be dead instead—"

"Her boyfriend killed her!"

I froze. Ben? There was no way, but as I turned and stared in Carter's cold eyes, I knew it was true. He would never lie, not about this. "What did you say?"

"Her boyfriend killed her. He went nuts, Emma. She was pregnant. Whose kid do you think it was? I'm guessing not the boyfriend's."

I reared back as if slapped. His cold tone whipped at me, but it was true. What he said was true. I shook my head. "Ben would never hurt Mallory."

"He would if he was high on something," he clipped out. "My guess, Franco got him hooked. He didn't want all that cash to walk away. When the boyfriend found out that she was pregnant, he snapped. It wouldn't be the first time a guy went into a rage."

From the knowing tone in his voice, I stopped dead. My heart even held for a moment. "Have you done that?"

"To the woman I love? No. To those who would hurt her? Yes."

I was struck speechless again. Carter hadn't blinked an eye when he responded. He seemed calm even. He was, I shivered, the cold-blooded stranger to me again.

"That boyfriend of hers-"

"He wasn't really her boyfriend. He never had been."

"He wanted to be. I'm guessing he was pissed when she dated Dunvan. I'm guessing he thought he had put in his time, waited it out for her to finish with the last guy and he was next in line. Then when she started dating Dunvan, he was over all the time. He was calling? Maybe even stopping by the apartment when she was out with him?"

How did he know this?

Carter continued, "When you went to him, he was able to be the knight in shining armor. I bet he loved that. He had it in the bag. He probably convinced her that first night that she couldn't stand the feel of Dunvan's touch, she wanted another man's touch."

"She didn't want to feel him anymore. She wanted to feel me. She wanted another man's touch."

I remembered Ben's words and the scratches down his back. He hadn't even looked remorseful except that she was crying. He had made her cry again.

"Emma?"

I focused on Carter again and blinked, startled. Why did he have to be so beautiful? And his wolf eyes, icy blues. Why did he have to save me? I murmured, "You should've left me alone."

He drew in a deep breath.

I kept going, numb now. "You should've let them kill me back then. I could've been with AJ all these years. You would've been fine. You were going places. You got accepted to college before. Why didn't you go?"

He leaned back against the counter. His arms slipped to my hips and he held me loosely between his feet. "You want to have this conversation now?"

"Indulge me."

He stared at me, studying me. "Why now?"

I shrugged, turning away.

He caught my chin and pulled me back. "Why, Emma? What's going on in that head of yours?"

I didn't move from his hold. I wanted to lean into him. I wanted him to wrap his arms around me again and I wanted everything to go away. But it wouldn't. She was dead. I had felt it. I knew something was wrong, but Amanda convinced me everything was fine. I had bought it. I really thought Mallory was happy somewhere, off with him, but Carter was right. Ben had done all of those things.

"You're right."

"About?"

Everything hurt. "About Ben. He said she wanted another man's touch. I thought he really loved her."

"He was sick in the head." He tugged me closer to him. I closed my eyes when he moved to my neck and pressed a kiss there. I belonged to him. Why did I even fight against it sometimes? A feeling of being claimed, liking it, was mixed with emptiness. Mallory should've been alive. She wasn't. I was, and I was with Carter. I was with my soul mate while she had her baby cut out of her.

He murmured against my skin, "You tried to save her, but you can't give your life for hers. She's gone, Emma."

A shudder went through me.

"She brought Dunvan into your lives. You were all doomed the second that happened." He pulled on my arm. "You know I'm right. Somewhere in there, you know I'm right. You can be angry at her."

My head whipped to his. "She *just* died."

"She died a long time ago," he said flatly. "You know that. You've always known that."

I shook my head. "This is why you should've let me go. None of this would've happened. She might not have met him. I wouldn't have even been her roommate. Maybe I was supposed to die, Carter. Maybe you weren't supposed to save me or kill all those guys for AJ-"

"I killed them for you. They were looking for you. I wasn't going to let that happen."

I shook my head. I couldn't stop shaking my head. "It wasn't supposed to happen like this. She shouldn't have died like that. I should've stayed-"

He gripped my arms and anchored me in front of him. "Stop it, Emma. Stop it right now."

"No. She shouldn't have died—"

"Stop!"

"I handed her to him!" I yelled, yanking away from him. "I saved her from one monster and I gave her to another. She never had a chance. She never had a chance, Carter. How am I supposed to be okay with that? She was my best friend. She never drank. She never smoked. Guys were her thing. She went from one guy to the next. She was never loved and I..." I hadn't stopped any of it.

"She wasn't your responsibility."

I glared at him. "Then you're not my responsibility. Then I'm not your responsibility."

A scowl came over him, but he remained silent.

"I loved her. She was family. She was my responsibility. She was broken. You have no idea."

His eyebrow lifted. "I don't know broken people? Bullshit."

I froze at his anger.

"You've been broken since AJ died. You were broken even before that, when your parents died."

I turned away. I didn't want to hear this.

An arm came around my waist and he trapped me, pulling me backwards against his chest. He continued, speaking into my ear, "Maybe this isn't the right time for this speech, but you're not responsible for her. You never were. You cared about her and you tried to help her, but that's all you could've done. You're not a god. You're definitely not her God. You did what you could do. You went above and beyond for your friend, something I'd be lucky to have. And I'm guessing that she knew it. She knew you were a good friend, but she probably knew you needed to save yourself. You did that. You can't blame yourself."

I whispered, "Why are you saying these things to me?"

"Because you can't mourn her if you're blaming yourself. I don't want you locked there. You mean too much for me to let you do that to yourself."

"Stop, Carter."

His arms tightened, and he started kissing the back of my neck. His hand spread out and started caressing my stomach. "I won't stop. I won't ever stop. Don't ask that from me. I love you, Emma."

I loved him too. The power of that emotion swept through me and I sagged into him. He caught me and held me in place. He continued to kiss my neck as he whispered, "You're mine. I won't let you go. I won't let you blame yourself for her death. You did what you could. It's not your fault. It's not."

He held me as the tears began to fall. Carter carried me to bed and he stayed with me for the rest of the night. He got up at some point and I heard him on the phone. When he returned and got behind me again, he pressed a kiss to my shoulder. "I called Noah and told him what happened. He'll tell Theresa you can't go out tonight."

Theresa.

I sat up. Amanda.

Carter sat with me. "What is it?"

"Amanda doesn't know. I have to tell her." A whole new storm started inside of me. I'd have to tell her what he did to Mallory, then I realized he never said what happened to Ben. "Did the police get him?"

A wall slammed over his gaze. His jaw clenched. "No. My men are looking for him."

"Oh god." He knew what I did.

Carter pulled me close. "My men will find him."

And that meant Ben had to die. One more person. No matter what Carter said, I was responsible for all of it. Mallory was dead because of me. Jeremy Dunvan was dead at my hands and now Ben was going to die because of what he knew about me.

"I have to go to her now."

"Amanda?"

I nodded, feeling a heavy burden on my chest.

"Okay." Carter kissed my forehead. "But I'm coming with you."

As we left, our hands were laced together.

TWENTY-SIX

When we got to Amanda's building, Theresa was already there. She waited for us outside the front door, panting. She straightened and wiped her hair back as she tried to catch her breath. "Hi." A deep breath. "Noah told me your friend died and I didn't know which friend, but I figured you might be here. I didn't know for sure. It was a crapshoot, but I made Noah look up your friend's address."

"What?" How?

"I remembered her name when we met in the bathroom awhile ago. Do you remember?" She bent over and took more deep breaths. "I booked it over here. I kept thinking I needed to be here for you."

"How did you get Amanda's address?"

"Oh, that." Her cheeks reddened. "The cafe is owned by The Richmond. I made Noah look up her address."

Carter and I shared a look. She already knew some of it but knowing it and hearing more about it were two different things. "Theresa, that means a lot to me, but-"

She waved it away. “No, no. I’m here for you. I want to support you. I do.” She turned to Carter, who still held my hand. “And I’m glad you’re here too.”

“You are?”

She nodded, so earnest. “I do. I am. I was hoping, anyway. I want to apologize for my behavior before. I was in your home and I acted atrociously towards you. You saved Emma’s life, in more than one way. The only thing I should be is grateful to you. So thank you.” She threw her hand out and waited.

Carter glanced at me from the corner of his eye, questioning, but shook her hand.

She pumped their hands up and down in one firm handshake. “Thank you for doing that.”

“For what?”

“For accepting my apology. That means a lot to me.”

“You must really like Emma.”

“I do.” Her whole face lit up. “I really do. She’s very loyal and she doesn’t use me for anything. Do you know how hard that is to find in a friend?”

Carter looked at me, as if to say ‘is she serious?’ before he remarked, “I have somewhat of an idea.”

“Oh, right.” She flushed again. “I forgot who I was talking to. You’re not that imposing in person, but I think it’s Emma. You seem, I don’t know, lighter? Maybe happier when you’re with her? Not like in the meeting or when we saw you without her. You were all dark and intimidating. I still laugh when I remember Allison’s reaction to you in that meeting. You’re all lethal and hot. I think she dropped her panties the second she walked through the door.”

“Theresa.” I was not in the mood for this.

“Hmmm?”

"My friend died and I have to tell my other friend the news. Can the Carter Fan Moment wait for another day? Maybe never?"

"Oh, sure. Sorry."

Carter touched the small in my back. "Maybe we should head inside?"

When I pressed the buzzer for Amanda's apartment, she let us in right away. She didn't say anything over the intercom and as we got into the elevator, I couldn't shake an odd feeling. That wasn't normal. Amanda usually had something to say, but I pressed the button for her floor and shook it off. Maybe it was me. The entire day had sucked.

"You ready?" Carter asked me.

I nodded. She had to know, but I wasn't ready to feel ripped down the middle again.

When we got to her floor, I knocked on her door.

After that, everything happened in fast forward. The door was swung open, but no Amanda. It was Ben. The only thing I had time to notice were that his eyes were wild before he jerked me against his chest, turned me around, and held a knife to my throat. He swung his other hand in front of me and pointed it in Carter's face.

My nightmare was happening in front of my face.

He had a gun to Carter, who started to lunge forward.

Ben yelled out, "I don't think so, buddy. I'll slice her throat. Even if you can wrestle the gun from me, I'll cut her open. You know I'll do it." A maniacal laugh came from him. It was high and shrill. "I believe you've seen my handiwork already, huh, Mr. Bigshot-Man-In-Charge! HUH?!"

Carter stood still for two seconds. His eyes narrowed as he looked at the barrel in front of him. Then his eyes slid to the knife at my throat before he barked over his shoulder, "Run. Now."

Ben tightened his hold on me as he tried to see who was behind Carter, but as he did, Carter reached for him. He grabbed the inside of Ben's wrist and slammed it against the wall. The gun fell free at the same time he ripped the knife from his other hand. Surprised from the speed, Ben froze for a second. In that second, Carter punched him in the face, shoving him backwards from me. Then he twisted the other wrist. As it snapped, he pulled me free. I was shoved behind him and he kicked at Ben's chest. From the sudden pain and force, Ben fell to the ground. He only had another second to look up before Carter knocked him unconscious with one blow to the head.

I ran inside and found Amanda on her bed. Her hands were tied behind her back with tape. There was more tape around her mouth. Dried tears left streaks down her cheeks, but as she saw me, fresh tears burst forth. She started yelling something, muffled, and I ran to her.

"Amanda, are you okay?"

She turned to her side for better access at her hands, but I couldn't tear the tape off. I cried out in frustration, feeling panic. This wasn't right. He could've killed her too. As the panic started to blind me, Carter moved me back and used the knife he'd taken from Ben. He cut the tape free and pulled the other from her mouth.

She shot forward, scrambling into my arms.

I fell back onto the ground with her, and we held each other.

She was weeping as I kept her close. I didn't want to let her go.

"Emma," she sobbed. Her head was buried into my shoulder.

"Shhh. It's okay. It's over."

Her arms shook. Her entire frame was trembling.

"Oh my god," Theresa gaped behind us. She stood in the doorway with a hand over her mouth. Then she shook her head and resolve came over her. She came over and knelt beside us. "What can I do?"

I opened my mouth, but I had no idea. I was only holding Amanda. I had no intention of letting her go, but Carter plucked her out of my hands.

"Carter." I jumped to my feet and wiped my palms down my face. They were wet, from either Amanda's or my own tears. I tried to quickly dry them but gave up. I was covered in tears. "Don't."

He handed Amanda to Theresa, then pointed to the door. "Take her. I have a man in the hallway. They'll get you to the safe house."

"That place from before?"

"That place from before."

"Okay." She tucked Amanda under her arm and asked, "You got everything you need?"

Amanda turned to me.

My heart melted. She looked lost and fragile. It was a six-year-old version of my friend that stood in that doorway. I nodded. I already knew what she needed. "I'll pack a bag. I'll bring it with me."

Theresa chewed on her lip as she eyed Carter up and down. "That might be awhile, but I remember that there were other clothes at that place. We can use something there until you come."

When they left, Amanda held my gaze the entire way. At the last second, before Theresa pulled her through the door, she glanced at Ben who was still unconscious on the ground. She hardened then and stopped in her tracks. She gazed down at him, almost in a sad way though. "I know what he did. He told me."

Theresa whirled back to face me. I knew she was unsure what to do. But I knew. I stepped forward and touched Amanda's hand. "Did he tell you that she was pregnant?"

"She was?"

I nodded. Everything seemed so bleak. Mallory shouldn't have died the way she did. I should've saved her, but I didn't know. Carter was right. I hadn't known. "They think it was Dunvan's baby."

"It wouldn't have mattered." Amanda was insistent. "It wouldn't have mattered, not to Mallory. She would've loved that baby so much. I bet she was happy when she found out. She wasn't alone. She had someone to love..." She grasped my arm tightly. "Make him pay. I don't care if he was our friend. He killed her. You make him pay, Emma."

"I—"

"Promise," she hissed.

Carter took her hand from my arm and transferred her to Theresa again. He moved so he stood between us. "Take her to the safe house. Emma will follow in a few hours."

Amanda's eyes still held mine as Theresa dragged her out. "Promise, Emma. Promise!"

Mike was in the hallway. He reached to close the door, but his eyes flashed me an apology before he did.

I was frozen once they were gone. A new storm had been awakened inside of me. Amanda wanted vengeance, but didn't she understand that I was the one who messed up. I brought Mallory to him.

TWENTY-SEVEN

"Emma."

I looked up. Carter had been watching me. He had an unreadable mask over him again. I shivered as I knew I was in the room with the Cold Killer again. He gestured to Ben. "What do you want?"

I licked my dry lips. "What do you mean?"

"What do you think?" He kicked Ben's feet. "This is your decision. What do you want done?"

"I..."

The memory of walking into my apartment rushed back to me. I was back there, all over again as Dunvan was raping Mallory. She was whimpering, trying to fight, but he only hurt her more. He wouldn't stop. So I had to do it.

I made the decision then. I wasn't sure if I could make it again.

"Carter," I rasped out. "I..."

"What do you think would've happened to Theresa had she talked?"

My eyes snapped to his. A surge of possession rose in me. "That was different. That was you. This is-"

"He's already killed her. He sold you out and then he got out of Dodge. Franco got him hooked. I bet he needed something to take the edge off, he was ramped up from selling you out and everything. Franco gave him something, said it was free and it'd calm him down. Stupid shit. He was hooked after that. When he wakes up, he'll be off his high. You're going to have a different Ben then. He's going to be crying. He's going to be begging for your forgiveness. What are you going to do?"

I flinched from his tone. "Why are you talking to me like this?" He was so harsh.

Carter reached down and dragged Ben further inside. He threw him into the middle of the living room. "Because when he wakes up, he's still going to be the son of a bitch that killed your friend. He came here for a reason. Why do you think he came here?"

"I..." I shook my head. I didn't want to know. I really didn't. "He's sick, Carter."

"Yeah," he laughed. It was an ugly sound. "He is, but he's smart. He's a survivor, Emma. He survived that whole situation with Franco breathing down his back. He prospered, getting money out of the deal. What does that tell you?"

"Stop it."

"No. You need to see the real Ben. He's going to wake up, blubbering like a baby and you can't buy into it. He'll say a lot of pretty words, how he's sorry for what did he do to his woman, but you can't fold. I'm trying to help you see the real Ben here."

I turned away, but he was there. He wrapped his arms around

my waist and held me over Ben's body. I tried kicking, but he shifted his hold so I couldn't move anymore.

His voice came from behind my ear. "You need to stop blaming yourself for everything that happens to your friends. You need to know what kind of animal this guy really was. Now look at him. Look at him, Emma."

I refused.

He jerked my head down. Fine. If this is what he wanted, fine. I didn't see anything, just Ben. He was unconscious, but I couldn't shake the image of his wild eyes. He wasn't moving. He was just lying there.

Carter held me tighter. "What do you see, Emma?"

"Nothing. Him."

"Look at him. What do you see?"

What did I see? Nothing.

"Tell me what he's wearing."

"What? He's wearing baggy pants. So what?" I tried wiggling out of his hold again. "Carter, stop this."

"What's in his pants? Look, Emma."

Anger rose in me, but I looked. Then I saw it. There was a bag in his back pocket. "Is that what you're talking about?"

"What's in it?"

"I can't see it."

"Look. Yes, you can."

"Fine!" Then I saw the corner that peeked out of his pocket. "White stuff. You already said he was on drugs."

"Keep looking."

I noticed a bulge in the same pocket and moved to get free. Carter let me go this time and I knelt closer to Ben. I pulled the bag of white powder out. Another knife came with it. His phone was in the other pocket, along with a set of keys. "What does this all mean?"

"Why did he come here?"

"What are you doing?"

"He butchered your friend, Emma. He should've run, but he didn't. He came here. Why? To break the news to your friend? I doubt it. Open his phone. Look at the last number he dialed."

I didn't recognize it. "There's no name saved to it."

"Read it to me." When I did, he said, "That's the same number Graham dialed. My guess, it was his last connection to Franco."

"Franco's dead."

A groan came from Ben and Carter hit him in the head again. No more sounds came again.

"I want to talk to him."

He shook his head. "You're not ready."

"Why are you doing this?"

His nostrils flared as he pierced me with his eyes. "Are you kidding me? All you do is blame yourself for your friend's death. I get it. You just found out today, but I'm not going to let you keep blaming yourself. That'll screw with your head. I want you to mourn your friend, but you have to have the facts straight. You need to start doing it in a healthy way and your head's not clear, not when it comes to your roommate. I'm trying to help you with this guy. He's scum, but he was scum that your roommate brought in. You had no say over him. She brought him in. She stayed with him. She chose to go to him. Not you. I want you to be clear - you couldn't have stopped her from going to this guy. You can't blame yourself for that."

"And making me take inventory on Ben is going to help that?"

He lifted his hands. "It's a start. You need to really look at him for who he is. You never did. I heard you interact with him before.

You thought he was annoying and stupid. You laughed at him. You never took him serious. You did what most girls do, you only see the surface. Every person gives you an image of what they want you to see. This asshole looked pathetic to you, maybe lovesick?"

Everything was swirling inside of me. I was confused by what he was saying, but I only wanted to yell at Ben. He took her from me. He shouldn't have taken her from me. *"Make him pay, Emma. Promise!"* Amanda's shout came back to me and I shook my head. She was right. I was tired of Carter's lesson.

I started forward for him, but Carter hauled me back. His hand stayed on my arm. "What were you going to do?"

"I..." I had no idea.

He sighed in frustration, raking a hand through his hair. His shoulders bunched as he lifted his arm and the sleeve of his shirt slid down. His bicep doubled in size before his arm went back down. For some reason, I couldn't look away from his arm. His muscle folded back into place, but every part of him was sculpted to perfection.

"Are you checking me out?" His tone held a trace of amusement.

"What? No." But I was. My cheeks warmed and I hung my head. How could I do that? At this time, at this place?

He chuckled, "Don't beat yourself up. You're stalling. I'd stall too." He sighed as he hooked a foot underneath Ben's stomach. He flipped him over. One of his arms hit the couch and stayed there. It couldn't slide back down from its awkward angle. Then Carter gestured to him and stepped back again. "Okay. Look at him again. Tell me what you see."

I had no idea. Nothing. He had on a nice shirt. There was cash in his front pocket. His jeans didn't look as baggy from the front and there were no stains. Even his shoes seemed new. Wait. His shoes were new. He was clean-kept. He had money. He had a working phone. He had drugs. My mouth dropped open.

"Getting it now?"

"He was high. I thought-"

"You thought what?" He was calm.

"I thought he was desperate and sad. Maybe he didn't know what he had done when he..." I couldn't say it. I should, but I couldn't. It was too soon.

"He gutted your roommate. He murdered her and he's not desperate, Emma." Carter grabbed the phone, pulled out the money, and picked up the knife. "He's got keys. That tells me he's got somewhere to go. He's got money, so he's not here to score quick cash. He's got drugs. That means he's got his next hit already with him. And he's got a second knife. My guess is that this is his favorite one. He used Amanda's knife on you, and he came with a gun. Where'd he get the gun?"

I shook my head. "It might be the one I used on Dunvan."

"Nope," Carter negated that. "My men took care of that one. This was his. He came here with a gun of his own, Emma. Put it all together. What are you getting?"

I shrugged. I was so tired, so damn tired of it all. I felt myself growing numb again and shutting down. He murdered Mallory. The son of a bitch killed my friend and took away her baby. We could've, at least, had the baby. I wouldn't have cared if it was from Dunvan. It would've been half Mallory. She was a good person. The child would've been a good person too.

I wiped a tear away and sat on the other couch.

Carter sighed. His tone softened, "I'm sorry if I'm hurting you, but I'm helping you too right now. I'm trying to get you ready because he's going to wake up soon. Right now you're thinking that he didn't know what he did and he's going to use that on you. He's going to beg and plead. He's going to cry. He's going to use every trick he can think, but that's not the truth. None of it is. He knew what he was doing, Emma. He killed her and he bragged about it. You heard him. 'We saw his handiwork?' He wasn't here to kill Amanda. He could've done that right away. He was waiting for you. He knew what he was doing. Look past his surface and get a feel for him inside. What do you feel? Use all of it. Add it all up in your mind."

I shook my head. I couldn't. He was pushing me too hard. "Why are you doing this to me?" I started to turn away.

He caught my arm and pulled me back. "Because you need to know everything and have all the facts in your head. I won't let you walk out of this apartment with regrets. Those will eat you up inside and I love you too much to watch you go through that. You're going to make a decision on what to do with him and you're going to own it. You have to know everything first."

I shook my head. I didn't want to do this.

He pulled me over to Ben's things. His voice was hard now, cold again. "Look at his shit. He broke in. He tied up the owner of the place. He has drugs. He has a gun. He has a knife. He has a phone. He's wearing good clothes. He's got keys to go somewhere. A person has an agenda when they go somewhere. They have a reason for everything they do. He's not looking for an immediate score. His last phone call was to Franco's guy. He was waiting for you. What was he doing? When he wakes up, it'll still be his goal. When you figure out the agenda, you figure out the person."

It was too much. Too many things were being stirred inside of me.

Carter broke. He said in a soft voice, "He already sold you out once and he was awarded for it. What do you think he was here to do? Again?"

My eyes got big and my heart paused. He was going to do it again. Carter was laying the groundwork. He wanted me to figure it out for myself. He was right, Ben would've convinced me. He would've cried and begged. I would've felt bad for him. Hell, Amanda and I always felt bad for him. We made fun of him, but we thought he was pathetic for how much he loved Mallory and pined for her.

Carter was right. I would've bought it.

"He's setting up long-term. He was here to grab you for Franco, or kill you himself." Carter went over and kicked at his feet. "My guess is that he was going to grab you, then call Franco and ask what he wanted him to do. He probably doesn't know that Franco's dead, no one does unless they're in the family."

"What would've Franco said?"

He shrugged as he kicked his feet again. "Franco would've had him bring you in, then he would've killed the guy. Your friend would've thought he was being so smart, that he had it all figured out. He was going to get a big reward this time, bigger than just telling him who the trigger had been."

"It sounds so easy to him, killing me like that." I shuddered. My voice trembled, "Did he kill her that easy too?"

Carter had bent down and was untying Ben's shoes when he stopped and looked up. He stared at me for a minute before he replied, "This guy sounds like a normal controlling and abusive asshole. He probably had a lot of fury built up over the years. He watched her with other guys?"

I nodded.

"Okay." He nodded to himself, like he had come to a decision. "You're not going to like hearing this, but this is what I think happened. The guy wanted your friend and he finally got her. And he got her all to himself. I'm sure he put on a whole show, how he didn't want you to go, but then, in truth, he liked that you were gone. He had her to himself. But once he did, I don't think it went how he thought it was going to be. Life spent in hiding ages a person. It was wearing on him. Franco got him hooked on drugs so he was getting high, he had a bunch of cash, and your friend started looking different to him. He started thinking about what he could do on his own. He started feeling more and more trapped by her. If it hadn't been for her, he could be living life grand. He knew I was with you. Someone told him at one point so he was hiding from me too. He blamed that on her too, since you were her roommate."

With each word, I felt more and more sick. My stomach had climbed into my throat by his last words. "Why are you telling me all this?"

"Because I'm painting you a picture so you understand that when he got high, he got angry, they probably got into a fight, and he killed her. He probably didn't even care that much anymore. She was a burden to him by then."

"How do you know this?"

"Because this is what I do. I figure people out. I figure out their agendas. And your buddy here, he's not some mastermind. He only thinks he was." He had Ben's shoes off and ripped off his shirt next. His pants were last before he stood up. "Are you ready?"

"Why did you undress him?"

Carter flashed me a hard grin. "You don't want to know that answer. Alright, here we go." He started shaking Ben again, kicking more at his feet. At first there was no response, but after a few more vigorous slaps on the face, he started to wake up. He sputtered and threw himself backwards. When he came up against the couch, he scrambled to his feet.

Carter pushed him back to the floor. "You stay there. Okay?"

Trembling, Ben nodded. His face looked drained of all his blood. And then he turned to me. His eyes widened, remorse filled them, and his lip started to quiver.

I looked away, sickened to the point where I was revolted now. Carter was right.

"Emm-Emmm-Emma," he stuttered out. "I'm so sorry. I'm so sorry. Oh my god. Oh my god. Oh my fucking god. I-what did I do? Mallory," he choked on her name. "What did I do to her? What did I do, baby? What did I do to you? Oh my god."

I couldn't hear it. I didn't want to. Without thinking, still hearing Amanda's shout in my head, I picked up his gun and swiftly turned in the same movement. I shot him. The sound went off, but I never heard it. His body slumped back down and his mouth stopped moving.

He was dead.

I had avenged Mallory.

Then I turned and left. I never looked back.

TWENTY-EIGHT

I left Carter in that apartment. There was a car downstairs waiting for me and I was driven to the safe house. Amanda and Theresa were at the dining room table, a huge glass of wine in front of both of them. When they saw I was alone, each gave me tired smiles. I showered before I joined them, but when I did there was a huge glass waiting for me. I needed it.

We sat together the rest of the night. None of us wanted to go to sleep.

They never asked what happened. They knew.

Noah arrived when it was nearing six in the morning. He looked exhausted as well. I wasn't sure why, but I didn't want to know. Theresa tipped her head back, as if waiting for a kiss, but he knelt and folded her body against his. He stood and both disappeared down the hallway.

Amanda lifted her eyebrows.

I yawned, "My boss. They're complicated."

We didn't speak another word, and Carter was the next to come in. He didn't pick me up as Noah had, but he took my hand and led me to our room.

I looked over my shoulder, but Amanda had her head down. She was resting it on the table. I knew she didn't want to sleep or she would've asked for a bed.

After we showered, Carter lifted me and took me to the bed. He put us both under the covers and we lay together. When I started to reach for a shirt, he shook his head. He wanted only our skin against each other.

We never talked about what I did, between any of us.

Amanda didn't want to go back to her apartment, so she stayed at the safe house. She lived there, and this time it was my turn to pack up her belongings. I had all of it put into storage. She only asked for a few things, mainly clothes and her computer.

Since Amanda stayed at the safe house, so did Theresa. I didn't understand why, but she told me that Amanda reminded her of her mother. A bond formed between the two and after three months at the safe house, Theresa took her in. There was no question, no discussion. We were all having dinner one night, Noah and Carter as well, and Theresa put down her fork, tilted her head to the side, and told Amanda she was moving in with her.

The next day, the little belongings Amanda had were packed up and both of them left.

I wasn't sure who was more relieved, Noah or Carter. Since both of my friends were at the safe house, I wanted to stay there as well so Carter stayed with me. Noah was the only one who didn't stay all the time, but he was around more often than not. Amanda asked me one night if it was weird that I was almost living with my boss, but I shrugged. Nothing seemed weird anymore.

There was no name on Mallory's headstone. She had no family.

Ben was listed as her emergency contact so she was never identified officially. I was taken to the morgue after hours one time and saw that it really was her. I knew it was, but Carter wanted me to make sure. Amanda hadn't wanted to come.

We never talked about Mallory, not at first. After Amanda moved in with Theresa, it was another three months before her name was brought up. We started a new tradition for the three of us. We spent every Friday night at their apartment. It was spent talking, laughing, and drinking wine. Lots and lots of wine. A pizza was usually ordered as well. The nights were meant for only light conversations, but that night Amanda asked if we could have our own memorial for Mallory and the baby.

She started crying after that.

By the end of the night, all three of us had each used a box of Kleenex. I was a mess when I slipped into bed with Carter that night, but I relayed what Amanda had asked and explained that the rest of the night was spent sharing Mallory stories. We even talked about how pathetic we thought Ben was. Carter shook his head, kissed my forehead, and pulled me over him. He liked to sleep with me on top of him. He ran his hand up and down my back. It was only later that I realized that he didn't sleep. He held me. Carter didn't need much sleep. The first time I noticed, I woke to him pacing in the room. He was a caged tiger.

When I felt tension in his body, I slept naked and on top of him. It soothed him for some reason.

Over the next couple months, the three of us formed a tight bond. Besides the Friday Wine Nights, there were many others spent at Octave. Noah came some of those times, though he was annoyed most of the time. Brianna continued to work at the nightclub, and she still didn't approve of a romantic relationship between Noah and Theresa. That pissed Theresa off.

I asked Amanda one time about the cop she was going to date, and she looked at me like my head exploded. "Are you kidding me? After what we did?"

I never pointed out that she technically didn't do anything, but a part of me was glad she considered herself part of it. It made the guilt fade a little. Killing Ben never made me lose sleep, but I still had nightmares about Mallory. No matter what Carter tried to get me to think, I would never be rid of that guilt. It had been my job to protect her. I had failed. I had avenged her, but I had failed her. I had failed her child as well.

However, I was learning to live with that guilt.

It was the only point of contention between Carter and me.

Theresa and Amanda had each other. Theresa sort of had Noah, but Carter and I had become a team together. We grew so close that we didn't need to speak half of the time. We knew what each other thought.

This night was one of those nights.

We were at Octave, in Carter's private office with his patio dance floor. Amanda and Theresa were dancing together while Noah was discussing our latest business venture from The Richmond. I stopped listening to him and glanced over at the door. He was there. The hunger started again. I had grown used to that as well.

Noah stopped talking and grinned. "I know that look."

His eyes found mine immediately, a slow smile growing as he closed the distance between us. They darkened, full of promises, as he murmured, "Hey there."

"Hi."

He grinned and took my elbow. He moved so that he was

leaning against the counter. My back was against his chest and he wrapped his arms around me. He tucked me close, between his legs. Then he turned to Noah. "Are we sparring tomorrow again?"

Noah shook his head. "You two."

Carter laughed, his voice low smooth against my ear. "I believe your other half is just on the other side of those doors if you choose."

He groaned, "Don't get her started. Brianna's on tonight. I don't need another lecture."

"It's like that?"

"It's like that." Noah looked to the dance floor. His tone lowered, "I'm going to need a full hour in the gym tomorrow, if you're game."

"I'm game." Carter pressed a kiss to the back of my neck. "But it might be worth taking what you want before someone else does."

"Not you too. That's all Theresa harps on me now. 'I got asked out for a date today.' 'I'm going to dinner with so and so.' Oh, and then my favorite, 'One day I'm going to get sick of waiting, and you'll regret that day ever happened, Noah John Tomlinson.'" He pretended to hit himself in the forehead. "Believe me, I am aware my chances are dwindling each day."

I turned, unable to help myself. "So why don't you? She loves you."

My boss went still at my words. Then he choked out, "She does?"

I snorted in disgust. "She wouldn't be waiting for you if she didn't. Forget your sister, Noah. You get that love once in a lifetime, if you're lucky."

He didn't wait another second. He put his glass down and went on the dance floor. Amanda danced by herself for the rest of the night.

Carter tightened his arms around me and kissed the back of my ear. He caught my lobe in his teeth, sweeping his tongue against it, as he murmured, "Once in a lifetime, huh?"

I turned around and wound my arms around his shoulders, then grinned as my lips found his.

It wasn't long before Carter said our goodbyes for us and took me home. Our departure was barely noticed. They all knew it was never long before the two of us left. As he carried me to our bed, I couldn't help to think about our own family. We found each other after so many years apart and came together, as he slipped inside of me, as one. Our hips moved together in perfect rhythm. I gasped, falling back onto the pillow, as he moved over me. My hands skimmed up his arms and he looked up, his eyes falling into mine.

There. Right there.

He was all I needed and I was all he needed. This entire experience had changed me, hardened me. I had killed two men. And as Carter continued to thrust inside of me, I knew I would do it again if anyone tried to take him away from me.

It was early the next morning when Carter woke me up. He nudged me in the side. "I want you to get up with me."

"No." And I rolled over.

After a soft chuckle, he said again, "Come on. I want you to go to the gym with me."

"No."

My pillow felt wonderful. Too wonderful to get sweaty and

whatever else he had in mind. I wasn't moving and hugged my pillow tighter.

There was no warning.

Carter flipped me over. He hooked a hand around my leg and slid his other under my arm. I was lifted in the air like a rag doll. With a gasp, I clung to him to keep from falling and was carried into the walk-in closet. He deposited me on the bench as my shirt was taken off in record time. Workout clothes were tossed to me before he went to get his clothes.

"What is this?"

He flashed me a grin. "You're going to train with me and Noah."

I snorted and threw the clothes back to him. "No, I'm not."

"Yes, you are." His grin turned wicked. "I think it'd be good for you to learn some moves, just in case."

"I have how many bodyguards?"

The grin faltered. "Guards can die. You should still learn how to defend yourself."

"Oh." There went that argument. "Noah is my boss and an MMA champion."

"So?"

"So. It's awkward. And inappropriate."

Okay, I was grasping for straws here.

He shook his head, but tossed the clothes back to me before he pulled off his own shirt.

Oh. Consider me distracted. I sighed as I watched his back muscles bulge and stretch when he pulled a different shirt on. This was a tight tank but torn down the middle as if someone had grabbed for it and ripped it. Then he pulled on some pants and I was even more distracted. His obliques stuck out, rippling under his skin, and when those workout pants covered him, they clung in all the right places.

The throbbing began again. My mouth went dry. I wanted a different workout.

"Noah is the same boss that you've given love advice to and have gone drinking with. If anything's inappropriate, that's inappropriate."

I sighed. "He's my boss."

"And you're my woman." He stopped and glared.

A thrill went through me. A primal possessiveness was in his gaze. His lips flattened, though my own still tingled to touch his.

He continued, "I just think it's smart for you to know how to fight. And I want to make sure you learn the right way. I trained Noah, Emma. I'd like to train you as well."

All fight fled as he looked at me like that. His wolf-like eyes were tender and loving. My desire for him only magnified, but I contained it. Carter was waiting for me in the basement garage after I finished dressing. A car was already there so I slid into the seat beside him, and he reached over for my hand, kissing the back of it. "Thank you."

I sighed. He was so damn wonderful.

It was nearing six in the morning, way too early, and when we got out of the car in another basement garage and went through a single black door, I saw that we had it to ourselves.

Carter crossed towards a fighting ring, but I lingered behind. The entire front hallway was covered in pictures of Noah. Most of them were when he was an MMA fighter. He stood in his bright red shorts with other fighters. Some pictures were with other people, whom I assumed were his family. I recognized Brianna in a few and Theresa in others. There were even photographs of Noah and Carter. One caught my eye. It was dated a long time ago, six months after AJ died.

"Carter?"

"Yeah?" He straightened from stretching.

I pointed to the picture. "How long have you known Noah?"

He came over and stood behind me. One of his hands rested on the side of my hip, but he didn't pull me in. It was just there. His chest skimmed against me lightly as he took a deep breath. "That wasn't long after-"

"After AJ died."

"Yeah." He sounded sad. "He was some punk kid coming in, looking for a job."

"Really?" I glanced over my shoulder.

His eyes were lidded, going through past memories. He laughed, a hollow echo to it. "I was there when he approached one of the new guys. It was a bakery downtown. That was where some of the product was hidden. I was collecting money for Farve, who laughed when he saw Noah. He pulled up in a fancy car, wearing khakis and a purple vest. He looked ridiculous. Rich punk with daddy issues. That's what Farve said when he pointed him out."

"What'd you do?"

"Nothing. Well, nothing to him. I told our guy not to give him a job. Then I was notified a month later that Noah was back demanding a job, so I told the guys to bring him to me. I think Farve thought I'd lost my mind. I wasn't high on the ladder yet, but high enough with enough clout by then for people to do what I said."

"What happened?"

He laughed again. Fondly. "They brought him to me and I told him if he wanted a job, he needed to take me down. He mouthed off, said he could do whatever he wanted. That's when I told him that I was the guy who'd be coming after him if he didn't make the right payments so he better know what he was getting into."

"Did he take you down?" I grinned as I asked. I already knew he couldn't, not then.

He chuckled and shook his head. "No. He still can't. He can overpower me, but I'm quicker."

"Like hell you are."

Noah stood there, a wide smile stretched over his face, as he held a gym bag over his shoulder. He wore a similar shirt like Carter, ripped in places and looking like something he bought from a thrift store. His pants were even worse. Gray, faded in places so much that his skin shown through. The pockets looked like they'd been ripped out long ago. A deep chuckle reverberated from him. "Those are fighting words, my son."

Carter chuckled. "That's what I said to him all those years ago."

It took a moment before I realized Carter had addressed that to me. He nodded towards Noah, who stood next to me now. "She asked about this picture. I was telling her how we first met."

"Yeah." A dark haunted look appeared over Noah as he sighed. "That was around the time Theresa's parents died. I was close to her dad and was fucking angry at the world. I wanted to do damage. I don't know if it was to myself or to others. Anyways," he blinked a few times and the darkness disappeared. He forced a smile instead. "Don't matter now. This man never let me anywhere near that lifestyle."

Carter had been watching as well but caught my gaze and squeezed my hip. "I paid for his first fight."

A genuine laugh rippled from the bigger guy. "And all the rest since."

"You were his sponsor?"

"More or less." Carter shrugged. His icy blue eyes grew

thoughtful again. A shiver went over me. He was remembering AJ. I didn't know how I knew it, but I did. He murmured, "He reminded me of your brother. Same look in his eye, angry and hurting. Ready to fight. When I saw the kid had talent, I knew he had a different future for him."

"Kid?" Noah reached around me and punched his shoulder. "I'm two years older than you, man."

"Age doesn't mean a thing. I'm older and wiser." Carter winked at me. "I'll always be older and wiser."

"My ass, you will," Noah griped, but the fondness was evident between the two. As they moved for the fighting ring, I studied more of the pictures. There were more of the two dressed in business suits and still more of action photographs. Noah was in the ring, a feral snarl on his face, his biceps bulging as his fist was clenched and ready to make contact with his opponent. The word "Knockout!" was written underneath. My eyes drifted over the photograph and I sucked in my breath. Carter was in the background. A large and imposing man was next to him. This man sent chills down my back. If I ever saw him in person, I would've been terrified. A scar ran across the entire length of his forehead and his eyes were dead.

I glanced to Carter now. He and Noah had moved to the ring to stretch together.

That was his life then. Sometimes I forgot about whom he worked with and what he had done. That was the stranger side of him, the side he kept hidden from me. It came out. I glimpsed it at moments, when we had been ambushed by the cars and with Ben, but it was different. Those moments had been in-the-moment. He had been defending me, but there were times when he didn't have to defend people.

I drew in a ragged breath.

My heart felt like a hand was squeezing it tight.

I couldn't forget that side of his life. But then he glanced over and his gaze pierced mine. The hand tightened once more of my heart before it pounded with renewed vigor. It broke free of whatever hold that was and a different sensation flooded me.

Addiction.

And something else. A dark strength.

No matter what path Carter would take us, I'd go with him. I was becoming like him.

"Emma. Come over here. I want to teach you this move."

I turned and followed. I'd always follow.

TWENTY-NINE

-CARTER-

The bigger man was waiting when Carter stepped out of his car. They had picked their old meeting place for a reason. No one would be around the abandoned warehouse, but three cars circled the block. Men got out and spread around.

Carter nodded in greeting. He hadn't been thrilled to hear from his old colleague, but he wasn't surprised. There'd been no word on Franco's body. There should've been word. The radio sounded from his man. "All clear, sir."

No time was wasted. Carter asked, "What's the reason for this, Gene?"

The older and bigger man grinned, but it looked like a sneer. The scar across his forehead stuck out that night. The moonlight illuminated it, casting a shadow over the man's eyes. Carter didn't need to see them. He knew this man too well and he knew his comrade was troubled.

"Why couldn't I have called just to catch up?"

"I'm out." Carter's eyes flashed a warning. "What's happened?"

"You're not that out," Gene sighed. His wide shoulders hunched forward as he slid his hand into his front pocket. He pulled out his phone and checked the time. "You know why I've called."

"His murder was called in." Carter's jaw clenched. "What happened to the caller?"

"Disappeared."

"What do the Bertal Elders say?"

"They aren't saying anything, which is why I need you to come back in."

"No." The answer was swift.

Gene growled, "Check your attitude, boy."

"Check yours!" Carter snarled back. "You're not calling the shots for me. You haven't for a long time."

"Fine," the older man bit out, his teeth ground against each other as his hand fisted around his phone. "We'll do this your way."

"I want a meeting."

"That's not smart."

"They didn't hold up their end. A body was supposed to be delivered to me. It hasn't and now their man disappears?"

"Franco is probably alive. You know that. It doesn't mean they've reneged."

"I don't care," Carter lashed out. His eyes took on a murderous glint. "I've held up my end. I've already given them their royalties. If they don't agree to a meeting, I'll go to fucking war."

He started back for his car.

Gene called after him, "You'd do that for her?"

"I'm doing that for everyone. You, included. The Bertal family will either work with me or I'll go against them. It's their choice, but they will be told of my intentions."

"You're going to stir up a shitstorm. You know that, don't you?"

Carter went to his car. The door was opened for him, but he turned back. A dead calm was in his gaze as he met his friend's. "Shitstorm's always been there. If we have to, it's time to take them down. We know they're weak right now."

Gene sighed as Carter got into car and left.

The man beside him asked, "What are you going to tell the Elders?"

"To prepare for war." Gene cast a shrewd glance over the younger man. He was new. He didn't know the lengths Carter Reed would take to insure his win. And this woman of his had only made him even more lethal, no matter how often he teased him about going soft.

Getting out of the car, Amanda was right behind me. I glanced back to make sure she followed the rest of the way inside Joe's and she was. Biting her lip and tugging at her sleeves, she rolled her eyes. "Why am I here? I don't work at The Richmond."

"You're my friend."

"But I don't work at The Richmond. I'm not going to fit in."

"Come on. You'll be fine. Theresa's already here. She's holding the table."

"Oh my god," she groaned as we went through the door. "You are both nuts for making me come here."

I shrugged. "It's Friday Wine Night."

"No, this is not Friday Wine Night. That happens at home, with pajamas, with the three of us, lots and lots of wine, and pizza. Not here. Not with your stuck-up co-workers and definitely not with your boss here. He's my boss too. It's still uncomfortable for me. Noah owns the cafe, remember?" She inched closer and hissed again, "I shouldn't be here!"

"Oh, hush. You're here. You're going to have fun. And you're teaching again."

"I'm going back over the break. He's still my boss." She grumbled again, "Seriously, Emma. I feel so out of place."

My hand grabbed her arm and I latched on. "You're coming."

She had to, she was my plus one. Carter would've caused too much of a commotion. Since getting free from the Mauricio family, his name and image was everywhere. The media's interest in him hadn't lessened. It'd been leaked that he had been released from his mafia connections. The news spread fast he'd been made into the poster boy for redemption.

I had a gut feeling that the news loved to report on him. He raised their ratings every time, but when Noah asked if he'd come since Theresa had somehow blackmailed him to going to Joe's for Friday Karaoke, Carter had laughed before punching him.

They'd been sparring.

As we went inside, I wasn't surprised to find the place full. Most of the workers from the hotel were inside. Varying expressions of nerves were on most of them, a few were eager and another handful determined—I wasn't sure for what, but the night would be interesting. Noah Tomlinson was going to make an appearance at Joe's. The rumor had gotten out. He was rarely in the office since he preferred to work from his home office so it was the first some of the workers met the Big Boss in person.

Theresa popped up from a stool and waved us over. She almost slipped off her stool and pitched forward. Noah grabbed her arm, sitting her back down with a deep scowl over his face.

Amanda started giggling behind me. "He looks miserable."

"See." I threw a grin over my shoulder to her. "Nothing to worry about."

"So says you whose boyfriend is even more intimidating than the boss." She nudged me with her elbow. "We should go over. Theresa's going to come over and get us if we don't march over there." She paused as we watched our friend start laughing. She hit the table with her hand and kept laughing, even as she spilled some beer from her pitcher.

Noah grimaced as he lifted the pitcher out of reach.

She kept laughing.

Amanda amended, "That's if she can walk."

I shook my head. "Let's go."

Leading the way, a few people said hello when we moved past. I extended a polite greeting, but I never wavered. Since my promotion people had been friendlier, but there'd been a time when they froze me out. I wouldn't be forgetting that.

As I rounded the table of girls that I once considered casual work friends, it was the same reception. All of them were warm and a couple gushed to me, but they'd been the worst.

Bitches.

I wasn't blind to their keen gazes as they watched us approach Theresa and Noah's table.

"Hey!" Theresa threw her hands in the air again. The glass she'd been holding emptied onto a person walking by. They stopped, but saw Noah's hulk size and kept going.

They were smart.

Then Theresa hollered, “My friend and roommate! You’re here.”

Amanda and I shared a look. This night was definitely going to be interesting.

Noah’s head leaned back. He gazed up at the ceiling, groaning at the same time.

“Heya, heya. Sit here.” Theresa padded the empty stool on her other side. She jerked her hand to Amanda. “Now.”

I nudged her this time. “You heard your roommate. Get going.”

“Emma,” Theresa wasn’t finished. She leaned forward. Her elbow grazed the top of the pitcher. It started to teeter as she commanded with a wide smile, “You sit there.”

Noah’s hand darted and he scooped up the pitcher before it spilled anymore.

“Good catch.”

He grunted in response and passed the pitcher to a waiter walking by. She started to ask him a question, but he turned his back to her. A scowl came over him and he scanned the room. “When is this over?”

I laughed, taking my seat. “It hasn’t even started.”

“Oh god.”

Theresa was whispering in Amanda’s ear. I gestured to her and asked him, “When did she start?”

“Don’t get me on that. She’s been going like this since I picked her up.” As his jaw clenched and his shoulders stiffened, I knew there’d been another fight between them.

“Are the two of you a two anymore?”

“We never get to that point. Something always comes up.” He shot me a dark look. I didn’t take offense to it. Ever since the sparring lessons, I’d gotten to know my boss a bit better.

“I thought you were going to be? I thought you told her how you felt."

"What are you two whispering about?" Theresa's voice jarred from across the table. Her eyes were narrowed, studying us, but she teetered on her chair again. Amanda caught her this time.

"You."

Her eyebrows shot up. "Really? What are you saying?"

Noah leaned back and locked gazes with her. "I was about to tell her that you've drank way too much for the night. I should take you home."

"No." She pounded a hand on the table. "You said you'd stay for Karaoke. It hasn't even started."

"Fuck Karaoke." He glanced around the bar. "Look at this. I'm a damn freak show."

"No, you aren't."

"Yes, I am. I shouldn't be here. I'm everyone's boss. This isn't appropriate."

Theresa shot her hand out and pinned his arm to the table. She leaned close, lowering her voice, but not enough. "You promised me you'd do this. I don't care whose boss you are. Co-workers party all the time together."

"Yeah," he said. "At holiday parties."

"Noah."

He shook her hand off and stood from the table. As he reached for his wallet, he glanced up and froze. His eyes rounded and his mouth opened. Then a hush went over the room. I closed my eyes as tingles raced over my skin. I felt him coming. I knew he was there, and as I turned around, Carter stood behind me. A slight smirk was there.

He wore a hooded sweatshirt over custom-fitted jeans. I knew he aimed to look casual, but it only made him look younger and innocent. And everyone in the room knew Carter Reed was no angel, though his face teased at the image. His eyes were filled with dark promises as he skimmed over me. I hadn't thought he was coming, but I was glad Theresa made me promise to dress up. I wore shimmering black pants, loose, but they rested low on my stomach. They matched the black top I wore. It was sleeveless and the ends tied around my neck. There was no back. It ended under my sides. That was it. His hand touched the small of my back as he sat beside me. A fresh burst of sensations shot through me. As his thumb rubbed over my skin, he leaned forward to kiss underneath my ear. It looked like he was saying something to me, but he wasn't. He was nibbling.

I bit my lip to keep from groaning out loud. As if he sensed my battle, he swept his tongue against my earlobe and whispered, "If this is how you dress going to these things, I don't think you can keep me away."

I grinned. Our eyes met and held for a sizzling moment where he was close enough to kiss. Then he moved away, but not before he skimmed a tender hand from my hair down my back to rest on my waist. He pulled me closer to him as he turned to Noah. "Karaoke?"

A grunt, followed by a curse was his response.

Theresa and Amanda were both wide-eyed as they witnessed the exchange.

They'd been around Carter, but I knew both were still frightened from conversing with him. Theresa had gotten over her disdain for him long ago. She seemed tongue-tied around him, even after Ben's death and staying at his safehouse until Amanda was ready to move out. They murmured quiet hellos to him but conversed with each other after that. The drunken loud state Theresa had been in was shot down, way down.

I frowned. They should've been comfortable enough to say more than hello to him, but that wasn't the case. When Carter showed up, he talked to me or Noah. Amanda confessed she was still scared of him, and Theresa confided that she didn't know how to talk to him.

Theresa said something now and Noah looked over. As he was pulled into their conversation, Carter moved his hand up and down my back again. He murmured, "I hope I don't have to sing because I came. I don't think that'd be good."

I sucked in my breath. Too many lustful temptations were going through me as his hand continued his caresses. "No." Sneaking a glance around the room, it was how I thought. Most everyone was watching our table, but the attention was no longer on their boss. It was on Carter.

I couldn't blame them. I couldn't even blame the media. Their obsession wasn't dying down.

"So," Theresa spoke up. The brave one. Her smile teetered as she caught my gaze, but she pushed forward, "Carter, I hope you're not trying to be incognito with that get-up."

He stiffened but glanced down.

I burst out laughing. "He was."

He grimaced at me. "Didn't work?"

Theresa was building more confidence. She laughed with me, shaking her head. "I don't think you can go anywhere in this city with that face and be invisible."

I sucked in my breath.

Carter threw me a look from the corner of his eye, but he shrugged. "I thought I'd try to fit in with The Richmond work force."

"Good luck. That's not going to happen," Theresa teased him. "Too mysterious and too gorgeous."

Noah frowned at her. "I thought you were my date."

"We're not on a date. I work for you."

"Because I'm stuck with you," he shot back, but the grin that appeared took away any negative connotation.

She gasped and hit his arm.

And the two went back to their pseudo-flirting/bickering again.

Amanda shook her head as she watched them. She caught my gaze and pretended to roll her eyes upwards in annoyance. We both knew better. She only wanted Theresa to be happy. I did too, but it was more for Amanda. She'd been brought in from the cold. Theresa and Amanda would be attached at the hip from now on. I wasn't worried because no one understood how cold it was on the outside like I did. I'd been there, right alongside her.

My chest lifted as I took a deep breath.

Things were better.

They were going to stay that way.

There was no reason to think of the past. It wasn't going to happen again.

"You okay?" Carter asked, touching my arm.

I nodded. "Yeah." Managing a tentative grin, I meant to reassure him. It didn't work. His eyes sharpened and he knew something was wrong. "I mean it. I'm fine. Just thinking of past demons."

An hour later, the karaoke was in full effect. So was the drinking. Even Noah seemed a little friendlier than normal. And because of that, the rest of the coworkers sensed it and grew brave. A few approached the table. We moved to a back corner and Carter was positioned at one end. Noah was on the other end so the coworkers approached his side, but they couldn't stop from glancing at Carter.

They all noticed the hand he held over mine on the table. None spoke to him. I didn't think they dared, not yet, but they were curious. Correction, they were fascinated. After the seventh person, this time she was openly staring at Carter, I grew restless. Nudging him in the leg, I gestured to the aisle. "I'm going to refill the pitcher."

His eyes narrowed. He knew what was going on but folded out from the table. The girl squeaked and scrambled away. She must've not have been expecting that he would move.

He's not a statue, you moron. My inner bitch was raring to go, but as I started to move past him, he took my arm. Holding me close, he murmured in my ear, "It's okay. You don't have to protect me."

I bristled, "I know, but you're not a goddamn animal from a zoo that got loose."

He chuckled, the sound brushing against me. It warmed me and a surge of desire flooded inside. Just like that, one laugh and I wanted him.

"If that's the case, they should be running in the other direction."

I snorted. "Yeah, well, I'm worried a few will go into heat and start throwing themselves at you."

He laughed again. "And you have nothing to worry about in that case either."

I sighed. I knew he was right, but at that moment some of the girls I used to consider casual friends came over. The interest was in their eyes, along with their own desire. I bit back a growl.

Grabbing the empty pitcher, I gestured to the bar and slipped from his hold. As I did, I glanced back once I got to the bar. A sneer came over me. Carter was watching me, amused as he folded back into the seat. My eyes darted to the two girls that stood next to Noah. They were talking to their boss, laughing with him and even Theresa, who thought everything was hilarious by then, but their gazes never left Carter for long.

"Hey."

I turned. The bartender was gazing at me with frank approval. He lingered on my cleavage before catching my eye. Gesturing to the pitcher I had placed on the counter, he asked, "Refill?"

"Yeah," I murmured, distracted as I looked back to the table again.

"Here you go."

I reached for my wallet and handed a ten dollar bill to him, but it wasn't until his hand covered mine that all my attention snapped into focus. The bartender ran a finger over my wrist and palm before he closed my hand over the money. He winked. "It's on me."

He was hitting on me.

I couldn't believe it.

Mistaking my shock for interest, he continued to run his hand over my arm. He went up and down before I jerked it away.

"Do you need anything else?" His eyes were saying something else. Do you want anything else?

I sucked in my breath before a calm settled over me. Leaning close, I gave him a sultry grin and saw him light up. He leaned closer as well and I whispered, "You see the guy behind me?"

His grin grew. "There are lots of guys behind you. Is one of them your boyfriend?"

I nodded. My smile stretched. "You see the head honcho at the back booth?"

Wariness started to filter in. His grin lessened, only a bit. "Yeah?"

"You see the guy across from him? In the black hoodie."

His grin vanished and he straightened.

"You recognize him?"

His Adam's apple jerked up and down. Panic came over him. Oh yes, he did.

I patted his arm. "Don't worry. I don't think he'll kill you for hitting on me."

The bartender moved his hand away and slammed against the counter behind him as if he'd been burned.

I didn't look over my shoulder, but I knew Carter was watching. He'd been watching the whole time. This guy seemed ready to piss himself as he stuttered out, "Uh-I-I have more customers." And he hurried to the farthest end of the bar.

"Did you enjoy that?"

Two arms came around me and rested on the bar. Turning in his arms, Carter smirked at me. His eyes full of humor and something more. They were dark, a primal stirring underneath. My body reacted before I comprehended what he said. Then my heart slammed against my chest and I drew in a deep breath. He leaned closer.

I knew so many were watching this. Sliding a hand up his arm and encircling his neck, I ceased to care. I pulled him closer.

His lips lingered over mine, brushing against them. "Are you ready to go home?"

Nodding, I wound my arms tighter and surged upwards. My chest was pressed against his and he wound an arm around my back. Lifting me in the air, he carried me out of the bar. We must've looked ridiculous, but I didn't care. The need for him would never lessen. It grew with each day and as soon as we were outside, Carter placed me into the car. He was right behind. I was barely aware of anything else. His lips covered mine and that was all I needed.

The world melted away.

THIRTY

A week later we were back in that car, but instead of leaving a work event we were heading towards one. It was The Richmond's Christmas party. Noah had opened three more Richmonds across the nation so each hotel across the nation and a few internationally were sending employees to our corporate headquarters. In short, this party was a big deal.

Carter was dressed in a tuxedo and I wore the white dress Theresa had once forced me to wear. The fabric was sheer and shimmery. It was layered so nothing could see through, and the two lengths were tied around my neck again. The ends were long enough so they were draped over my shoulders and decorated with diamonds. My hair was another matter. I had tackled the dress on my own without difficulty, but Amanda insisted on doing my hair. So we had all been picked up from their apartment. Noah was already at the party, but my friends were dressed to impress.

Their eyes got big when Carter came to the front lobby. Even

Amanda seemed to have held her breath for a second.

I couldn't blame them. He was dashing.

I wasn't sure if it was the rich lines from the tuxedo that molded over his lean physique or it was his eyes. An extra amount of chill was in them that evening. They seemed ready to tear into anyone, which emphasized the aura of danger that always clung to Carter.

I patted his hand once in the car and asked in soft voice, "Are you okay?"

A soft kiss to my cheek was my reward. He patted my hand back. "I am fine. You look ravishing."

His answer didn't appease me, but I sighed. This would have to wait. I knew Carter well enough to know when he was lying to me. No one else would be able to tell, but I also knew that he wasn't going to confide in me with my friends in the same car. And I couldn't stop remembering a phone conversation that he had. He'd been in his office at home, but the door was open. I hadn't intended to eavesdrop, but when Franco's name had been said, every alarm went on full alert in me. I hadn't heard much, but I knew enough to know that Carter was keeping something from me and that it was related to Franco.

After the night when he was supposed to have been killed, I never heard actual confirmation. I didn't know if I should've. Carter pulled most of the guards around me so I assumed everything was fine, but I couldn't ignore the knot in my stomach. Maybe things hadn't ended as well as I had assumed?

"Emma, did you hear about Tamra?"

I lifted my head and turned to Theresa. She was even more beautiful than normal. Her dark blonde hair had been swept up into multiple tiny braids. Amanda worked miracles with them as well. The same diamonds that had been added to my dress were also in

Theresa's braids. They matched the shimmery gold dress she wore.

Giving her a smile, I forced those nagging thoughts to the back of my mind. They'd have to be dealt with on another night. "What about Tamra?"

"She got promoted. She's going to a branch in Minnesota to head it up." Theresa giggled, her cheeks were flushed from the wine we had in their apartment. "I think she's pissed. She wanted your old job, under Mr. Hudson, but her supervisor booted her ass. Can you believe that?"

I grinned. It was karma. Tamra had been one of the queen bitches who froze me out awhile ago. I wondered what she had done to piss off her supervisor. A transfer to Minnesota wasn't really a promotion. Everyone would've preferred to work their way up the ladder in our corporate headquarters. That was here, not there.

Amanda frowned. "Weren't you friends with her, Emma? Didn't she come out once with us..." And she faded because this was the awkward moment. Tamra had gone bowling with us. Ben, Mallory, and the current boyfriend had been there as well.

Theresa grimaced. "Speaking of the dead..."

"Theresa!"

"What?" She shrugged her shoulder and ignored her roommate. "You guys never talk about her. It's been long enough. I don't think Mallory would've wanted you to never talk about her. One night of bawling over her doesn't cut it. It's good to reminisce about old times. You're honoring her memory."

Amanda grew red in the face and she turned towards her window.

Theresa rolled her eyes. "I know what I'm talking about. My parents are dead, remember?"

Carter looked over then. He'd been content to be quiet and stay in the background, as much as possible for him. His eyes narrowed now. "Everyone grieves differently. I doubt you were laughing about your parents five months after they were ground into cement."

"Carter," I murmured.

Theresa paled. "That's a horrible thing to say."

"Their friend was gutted. The other was killed by Emma." His wolf-like eyes grew in hostility. "Sometimes silence is being sensitive." Then he turned away again. It was obvious the conversation was done.

Frowning, I watched Theresa to see how she would handle that efficient dressing-down. Her head went down and her hands folded together in her lap. Her shoulders drooped as well. I exhaled a soft breath. It wouldn't help for my one of only two friends to remember her previous disdain for Carter.

But when we got to the party and stepped out, Theresa stopped both of us. She looked from Amanda to me. "I'm sorry, guys. Sometimes I speak before I think."

Amanda threw her arms around her roommate. "Oh, we know!"

Both laughed and pulled me in for the hug.

"You guys are some hot mamas. Let's party!"

Biting her lip, Amanda's cheeks grew rosy again, but I caught the surprise in her gaze. I agreed with Theresa. My oldest friend was a serene vision. She wore a very soft pink dress. It was a strapless A-line, hanging down to her toes. She resembled a Greek goddess.

Remembering the cop who wanted to date her, I kissed her cheek and whispered, "It's your turn."

Her eyes held mine and a promise passed between us. It was her turn to be happy. She knew what I meant without another word of explanation. Theresa and Noah would eventually figure it out. They had to. They loved each other and I had Carter. It was

Amanda's time now.

The event was held in the largest banquet hall, but that wasn't big enough. The lobbies surrounding were filled as well, with liquor and food stations every few feet. The party seemed in full swing when we arrived, but as we stepped inside, I sensed the attention. One by one they turned to us. It wasn't like at Joe's. It was more. That's when I realized that I'd been secluded at work the past week. Theresa wanted me to work with her in a private conference room. She got the coffee for us. She paid for the food and had it delivered to her office. The times we ate out, she suggested a cafe a few blocks away. It was starting to make sense now.

I caught her gaze. "How bad was it at work?"

She grimaced. "It would've been too much for you."

I sensed the avid attention and knew she was right. I wanted to hit myself in the forehead. I should've known. Carter was at Joe's. They all saw and they had a week to comprehend it. The interest had been heavy that night, but it was more tonight.

With his hand in mine, he led us through the crowd until it opened to a group of tables that had been sectioned off from the main crowd.

"Ah!" Theresa grinned. "VIP. I like it."

Recognizing a few of the security guards from Carter's own group, I knew he had planned ahead. Mike even nodded to me with a friendly smile. Progress. Once we stepped past the divide, all bets were off. Older and distinguished-looking men approached Carter in waves. They wanted to shake his hand, talk about the hotel, and that was when I figured it out—they knew him from the board. These were my bosses, or my other bosses. Seeing that he would be busy, Theresa tapped my arm and pointed to a back table. She leaned close. "Let's grab that one. Noah's already here, but I'm sure he'll want to sit with us."

I nodded. Anything to get away from the prying eyes.

As we settled in, Theresa went to the bar and returned with three drinks. A waiter followed behind her with two bottles of wine. Another came over with a platter of food. We were munching on fancy hor d'oeuvres, and I wasn't sure I wanted to know what was in them. It didn't take many of them before I was full and left the rest on my plate. Theresa snagged them later on and Amanda nibbled at hers. That's what she always did.

We were able to watch the crowd and they weren't able to approach us. The other people in the VIP section were the older men and their dates, and those women knew each other. They cast shrewd looks at us, but no one approached. I was grateful. Theresa called them Snobby Social-nators. Again, I was grateful they remained away. After awhile, Theresa pointed to a few guys and asked Amanda to rate them. The conversation soon went in that direction. We were busy picking out the Mr. Amanda-To-Be the rest of the time. It was surprisingly fun.

The fun ended an hour later.

Carter had been talking to the board members the whole time when a man went over and whispered something in his ear. I stood up without thinking. The conversation at my table stopped and Amanda asked, frowning, "What's wrong?"

Theresa turned towards Carter. "Where's he going?"

I couldn't answer them, but my gut had dropped out of me. Something was wrong. Something was happening. We watched as he turned for a side door. The man went with him, but gave him one final nod before he turned away and went through a different door.

I started forward.

"Emma!" Amanda hissed at me. Her hand grabbed onto my wrist. "What are you doing?"

"Something's wrong."

"So let it go. Carter knows what he's doing."

I frowned at her. What was she doing? She'd never questioned me before, but I only pulled my wrist away. "Watch my purse." Then I hurried after him. When I got to the hallway, I couldn't see him, but I turned to the farthest corner. There was something about that man. He wasn't dressed like everyone else. He wore a suit, not a tuxedo. His hair hadn't been slicked back like most of the other men who were dressed to impress that night. There was nothing about the guy that should've made him seem out of place, but a lightbulb clicked. That was it. He was nondescript. He looked like he wanted to blend in and because of that, because I'd been around Carter's security guards enough, I knew he'd been one of his men. He hadn't been a guard though. If he had, he would've returned to his post, but no—the guards were all dressed in black suits. This guy wore a brown one.

He was mob. I knew it.

I turned another corner and stopped short. The guy was there, at the far end. He was looking out the window with his phone pressed to his ear. He was talking into it and as he seemed to be following something outside, he was relaying instructions over his phone.

I started for him. If Carter wasn't around to give me answers, he would, but I was pulled into an empty conference room.

Gasping, I was pushed against the wall and a hand covered my mouth. A body pressed against mine. All the tension left me. This was Carter. My body reacted before I realized it was him and it softened. My legs parted for him and he bent closer, nuzzling under my neck, before he whispered, "What are you doing?"

My eyes snapped open. This wasn't my Carter. This was their Carter. I pushed him away. "I was following you."

He leaned back, but his body kept mine anchored to the wall. His eyes were hard and aggravated.

I didn't care. I kept my hand on his chest. I needed to feel his heartbeat, to know when if he was lying to me. "Where were you going?"

"To the bathroom."

His heart didn't skip a beat. Nothing. It was steady, but I knew he was lying. I saw it in his eyes. "This isn't the bathroom."

A grin teased at the corner of his mouth. Then his eyes switched. They darkened and lust began to fill them. "I was coming back."

"You were leaving."

The lust vanished and he took a step back now. The air felt cold without his heat, but I stopped myself from feeling it.

His eyes narrowed, but he murmured as his hand began to caress the back of my neck, "You don't believe me."

I shoved his hand away. "Stop manipulating me."

All gentleness vanished. A hard wall came over him now. "You stop it, Emma."

Sucking in my breath, I hadn't expected that harshness to come at me. Blinking back tears from the shock of it, I geared myself to be strong. I had to stick with the truth. That was the hand I had and I needed to use it. "Who was that man?"

"What man?"

"Stop lying to me," I hissed, gritting my teeth.

His eyes closed to slits now and I knew he was reassessing me. I didn't care. I snarled at him, "I know you're lying so stop it. I know something's going on. I know that man came to you and said something to you. I know he's with the mob."

There.

My heart skipped a beat.

I tossed out the first card and I waited.

It was now his turn. Would he continue to lie or would he tell me the truth? I needed the truth. I was realizing that. He had protected me for so long, as I tried to protect my loved ones, as I tried to protect him when we were children, but it would have to be different now.

"He is."

Relief rushed through me and my knees sagged, but I wasn't done. I forced myself to stand firm as I said the rest, "I know that Franco is alive."

Okay, that was a total bluff, but it'd been bothering me for the past few days.

He didn't react. Nothing.

I frowned. What did that mean? But then he took a deep breath and pressed his lips together. The ice in his blue wolf-like eyes dimmed a little and he glanced away. His jaw clenched as he swallowed, taking a breath at the same time, but then he turned back. It was there. I was bowled over with the realization. Franco *was* alive. I saw it in his eyes. Releasing a ragged breath, I couldn't talk for a moment. No words could even formulate in my mind. Where did I go from there?

"You should go back to the party."

I reared back. That was it? "Are you kidding me?"

He grew weary.

I shook my head, a bitter laugh spouting from me. "I can't believe you. Franco's alive and that's all you say to me? I should go back?"

"Emma."

He reached for me again. I slapped his hand away. "No!"

"What do you want me to say?" he bit out now. The chill had come back. It doubled as he snapped, "You're not involved with this. I'm doing this to protect you—"

"That's bullshit."

He stopped, his chest starting to heave now. "Are you fucking kidding me?"

"No!" I didn't hesitate now. "I am involved with this. You and me. We're together. I won't stand by anymore."

"Not with this! Not with my ties—"

"You said you were out."

"I am out!"

"No, you aren't," I yelled back.

Suddenly his hand came up and pressed against my mouth. I was moved back to the wall and he rested his body on mine. His head was beside me and I could feel his deep breaths. His chest moved against mine, but his breath teased over my neck. My heart began to pound again, but I tried to listen over its loud thumping.

We heard through the door, "We'll set up in a back suite. Reed wanted this meet. We'll give him what he wants..." The voice faded as the man moved beyond the door.

Carter didn't let go of me and I grew aware of the shadows that flickered past the door. We could see them as they followed whoever that man was. Then a sick feeling came over me and I whispered around his hand, "Was that Franco?"

He was tense, but he shook his head.

"Tell me what's going on." The need to protect him surged inside of me.

It was there. He was considering it. I could feel it, but then he let out a deep breath. It was gone. An apology flashed in his gaze. "I can't."

"Carter."

"Emma," he whispered, bending close again.

I closed my eyes as I felt his lips move against mine. My heart was beginning to break. I didn't know what he was going to do.

He added, "Go back to the party."

"And you?"

He began to step back, but I didn't let him. My hands were fisted into his tuxedo and I kept him against me. I didn't want to let him go.

His eyes flickered down to my hands. He didn't fight my hold, but he gave me a tentative smile, cupping the side of my head. His thumb brushed some of my hair back. "I need to make some phone calls and then I'll come back."

"You promise?"

The need to believe him was so strong, but my gut was stirring. He was still lying to me.

He nodded. "I promise." Then he pressed his lips to my forehead and again to my lips. "I love you. I'll be right back."

"Carter."

"I will." His eyes were reassuring now. "I promise."

I let him go. I had no choice. I knew that now. He was going where he was going and I drew in a shuddering breath. My heart wouldn't calm down. I had no idea what to do, but he was gone in the next second. Even if I went after him, I knew he'd be gone. This was what Carter did. He was a ghost, but I had no idea what to do.

My legs couldn't move.

I was beyond scared now.

I went back to the banquet room, unsure what to do. This was what he did. That was who he'd been for so long, so I should trust him, but not this time. A nagging voice kept saying to me. *'Get up and go after him! What are you doing?!'*

The award ceremony had started, but I struggled to hear any of it. The voice kept yelling at me to get up and go.

"Finally," Theresa exclaimed once Noah gave the last speech of the night. He thanked all his employees and gave the normal 'This hotel wouldn't be what it is without the people in this room' message. A collective 'Aw' went around the room as people felt moved by it. Then he announced that all the liquor stations had been restocked and hurried off the stage. Coming towards us as everyone else headed towards the stations, he was only stopped by two board members. When he broke free from them, he collapsed into the chair beside Theresa. "Shit," he grunted. "That took a lot of time." He reached for Theresa's glass and drained it.

"Hey, that's mine!"

He put it down and reached for mine.

"That's Emma's!"

"She hasn't touched it all night. I've been watching you guys."

"Do you know where Carter is?" I asked now. My soft voice was clearly heard, and Noah stiffened before meeting my gaze. He was guarded. He knew. That was all I needed to know before I stood up. The voice screamed at me, *"GO!"* My mind was made up. "Nevermind."

I was going after him.

"Emma, where are you going?" Theresa stood with me.

Amanda stood as well, but she remained silent. She was waiting for what I said next.

A fake, but polite smile plastered over my face. "I think I have to go to the bathroom."

An eyebrow lifted as Theresa asked, "You think or you have to go?"

"Yes." I nodded to myself. "I need to go to the bathroom."

"Mind's made up, hmm?" Her grin turned knowing.

Noah set his glass–my glass–down on the table and regarded all three of us with caution. "What's going on?"

"Emma has to go to the bathroom."

"Okay. Go." He kept skirting between us. "Do you all have to go? Am I supposed to watch your purses?"

Theresa snorted again, but in disgust. "Yes, Noah. That's what we're doing. Would you watch our purses for us?"

He gestured to the table. "Sure. Leave them, but don't you guys always take them with?"

Theresa opened her mouth to keep arguing, but I clutched mine and headed towards the nearest exit door. Amanda followed behind. Theresa remained at the table. Her arms went up in the air–all the signs of another Noah/Theresa fight about to happen.

Amanda snickered. "You know they're going to find a room pretty soon."

"Yeah." I shook my head. Their sexual chemistry fizzled at times, but was combustible at others. It was nearing the explosion mark now. "Wish they'd get together once and for all."

"Yeah," Amanda sighed beside me as we went through into the hallway. It was empty except for a few drunken employees.

"Emma!" someone called out.

Oh god. It was Tamra. She had a fake smile as she gripped her drink. A purse was stuck underneath her arm and her free hand held up the front of her silver dress. Even in high heels, she hurried to us and didn't seem to break stride. I would've been impressed if I hadn't been so irritated. She was keeping me from finding Carter.

"Hi, Tamra."

"Hi!" Her red lipstick was smeared to the side and a few strands of her beautiful sleek hair slipped from the fancy bun. "Did you hear about my promotion?"

I shrugged. "Yeah. Congratulations."

"I know. I'm going to be heading up an entire hotel. I think Mr. Tomlinson wants me to prove what I can do. Once I do that, I'll be back and higher than ever. This is a great opportunity."

"I'm sure it is."

"Yeah. I know it is." Her smile never wavered, I had to give her that, and she even smoothed back the frayed hair strands. "So," now her eyes snapped to attention. She was going in for the kill. "I didn't believe it when I was told, but tonight I saw it for own eyes. You and Carter Reed. Imagine that."

"Yeah," my tone chilled. "Imagine that."

"That's great. Well, if the reports are right. You know, if he got out of the mob and everything. But damn, Emma. I'm so proud of you."

My smile was stretched thin. Did I have time to hurt this girl? "Proud of me?"

"Yes. He's gorgeous. I mean, I know what he looks like, but he's so much more in person. I can't believe it." Then a look twitched in her eye. Revenge? Anger? "And I heard that your brother was his best friend. That's so nice of him to reach out to you, you know, to honor your brother's memory. The media should really report how generous he must be."

Nope. I caught it now. A smug pretentious look, that's what it was.

"Really?" My eyebrow went up. My hand turned into a fist.

Amanda moved first. Damn her. She pushed me back. "I'm really sorry, but we have to get going. I'll make sure to tell him your message."

Tamra blinked. Her mouth opened a fraction.

Amanda finished, "I'm sure he'll see it that way, that's he's being generous by being with his best friend's sister. I'm sure he won't take offense to that at all, but that's my opinion. All I know is that he really loves Emma so I'm sure he won't take it in the degrading way you actually mean it to be."

A small growl came from me.

Amanda turned and pushed me back. "We're going to the bathroom, remember?"

Yes. I had things to do. I'd never been friends with Tamra before, but now I wanted to yank her hair and slam her against the hallway. We were that type of friends now. And I knew there were so many others girls just like her.

"Let's go."

"Fine." My teeth ground against each other. As we went further down the hallway, we came to another one and paused. I glanced over. "You know we're not going to the bathroom."

"Do we know where we're going?"

"Nope" I answered.

"Okay." She nodded. "Do we know what we're doing?"

"Nope."

"Is he doing mob stuff?"

"Yes." I didn't falter. She deserved to know what she was walking into.

"Glad we're on the same page."

I caught the disapproval in her tone and pulled her to a stop.

Then I faced my now oldest friend besides Carter and hoped she saw how much this meant to me. "I love him."

"I know." But she faltered.

She didn't. Or she didn't believe it. I touched her arm again. "I grew up with him. He was family to me."

"He abandoned you."

Now the truth was out.

"No." I shook my head.

"Yes, he did." Her eyes grew hard. "I defended you just now, but he left you. And I know that he's not with you because of your brother, but it still pisses me off that he left you in the first place. You told me stories about the foster homes, Emma. You've never mentioned Carter Reed at all, not until," her voice lowered and she moved closer, "you know. So no, I don't think he's family and I don't think he loves you."

My mouth fell open. How could she think any of this? Thoughts and betrayal raced through me when she continued, "I think he wants you. Yes. I think that. But he wouldn't love you because he wouldn't have let you grow up alone. You were alone when I met you."

"I had Mallory."

"Who you took care of, all the time. You were alone."

My eyes got big. I couldn't believe Amanda said that.

She wasn't finished. "I loved Mallory. I did. And I loved the group we had, all four of us, but you were my friend. I took care of her when you left. I did it for you. Mallory's never taken care of you back. It's always been one-sided, and I think you were just grateful she allowed that. So yes, Emma, you were alone until we became friends."

I opened my mouth.

"And I haven't left you now either. I know I'm roommates with Theresa. I know she's taken me under her wing and I'll always be grateful, but you are my best friend. You are my sister. That's how it is, so even though I don't approve of whatever you're about to do, I'm still with you. I'm here. I'm with you."

She ended it with a dramatic nod.

"Okay." I didn't know what else to say.

Her eyebrow arched up.

"Let's go find Carter then."

And she gestured for me to take the lead.

So I did.

A large group stumbled past the hallway to one end. I went the other.

THIRTY-ONE

Amanda and I looked all over the hotel. They could've been anywhere, but just as we began to head back in defeat, I saw some big muscle-bound guys at the end of one hallway. It was where the larger suites were located. I touched Amanda's arm. "Let's go to my office quick. I have a master key that'll let us in."

An eyebrow went up. "You think we'll have to break into a room?"

"No. That's why I'm getting the master."

"Oh." She nodded. "You go. I'll stay in case they leave."

"Okay." I hurried off, but when I returned there was no Amanda. The guys were still there. Their hands were inside their suit jackets and a bulge was underneath, as if they were holding their guns close. I started forward. I could go into the suite beside that one. It was empty and I knew the patio was right next door. If I couldn't hear through the walls, I would have to try the patio. As I started forward, my heart pounding in my ears, a hand wrapped around my arm and I was lifted backwards.

Before I could scream, a hand muffled it. My eyes got big. I couldn't fight back. It happened so quick, but I was shuffled into a different room. There were guys everywhere. Mike. Thomas. These were Carter's guys. Sagging in whoever had a firm grip on me, I didn't fight as I was carried into another adjoining room and then dumped on a bed. Amanda gave me a shaky grin from the bed beside it. She was rubbing her head, but her eyes flitted up and locked on whoever had been holding me. Color warmed her cheeks before she jerked her gaze away.

Frowning, I looked up and froze. It was the guy from Carter's photograph. The scary one. The one with the scar that ran horizontally over his forehead. He was glaring down at me, even more intimidating in person than over the image. If I didn't know he worked for Carter, I would've been sure my life was done.

I rasped out, "Where's Carter?"

"Where do you think?" he grunted back, going back to the other room.

As he left us alone, I asked Amanda, "Are you okay?"

She nodded, rubbing the back of her neck this time. "He grabbed you too, huh?"

"Yeah."

She grimaced. "It was more shocking than anything. Who is he?"

"He works for Carter."

"I work *with* Carter." He had returned, his hostility barely in check. Raking me from head to toe, I felt as if he could read my thoughts and felt all the nerves inside of me. It was disconcerting. Carter did that as well, but it was more from him. This guy made me feel violated. I crossed my arms over my chest and glared back.

A small smile flitted over his face. It was gone as quick as it appeared and I wondered if I'd even seen it in the first place. Maybe I was searching for a sign of friendliness? Either way, his silent stare wasn't helping Carter at all. I demanded, "Where is he?"

"He is in a meeting."

"I know. Where?"

The guy went to the window and peered out.

"It's none of your bus-"

"Gene." A guy poked his head in the room. Grim. "It started."

This was Gene?

Grabbing a gun that'd been on a table, he held a radio in his other hand and rushed from the room. All the guys except Mike followed after him. When he stopped in our room and gave me a tentative grin, I sighed. He didn't know it, but I wasn't going to let him baby-sit me.

He caught the defiant look from me, but took his post by the door.

"What's going on?" Amanda sat on my bed. She kept wringing her hands together in her lap. "What if Theresa comes and looks for us? You don't think she's going to walk into that, do you?"

Theresa was the least of my worries at that moment. Standing up, I went to press my ear against the wall behind us.

"What are you doing?"

I waved her off. I couldn't hear if she talked. But it didn't matter. I still couldn't hear much. So I grabbed a glass from the coffee station and pressed it against the wall. I heard a little bit more. Shouting. Cursing. The sound of someone getting hit. Then I heard someone say, "You're going to die, Carter Reed."

That was all I needed.

I ran from the room into the middle one and darted for the

patio. They were close enough so I could climb over, but as soon as I stepped foot outside, a guy from the adjourning patio barked, "Hey!"

I wavered. My heart was pounding. The blood was rushing to my head, but I couldn't get that voice out of my head. Carter was in danger.

"Emma," Mike hissed from the room. He jerked his hand inside. "Get back here."

I couldn't. The guy already saw me and had his gun drawn. I had no other choice except to climb the patio. If I darted back inside, he'd follow. Mike and Amanda would be in danger, so with my chest tight, I started to climb over. The other guy grabbed me around the waist and carried me inside.

My heart stopped when we got there.

Carter was on the floor. Blood was all over him and as he raised his head, he paled when he saw me. His skin was already sickly white and one of his eyes was swollen shut. His nose looked broken, but when he started to rise, a guy delivered a swift kick to his side. He fell back down, holding his arms over his ribs for protection. It was minimal. The guy kicked him some more and a third clipped Carter underneath his chin. His head reared back and his entire body flipped over from that last hit.

He was unconscious.

A shrill laugh came from the corner of the room.

I sucked in my breath and turned. This guy, whoever he was, was going to die. He wore a tuxedo, with his belly extending over his pants. With thin graying hair, he narrowed his eyes at me, but he looked back to Carter. Sick enjoyment was in his gaze as he reached inside his breast pocket. A phone came out and he dialed a number.

No one moved.

My gaze skirted between the sick bastard and Carter. This guy was a guest of the Christmas event. I saw the invitation sticking out of his coat when he had pulled the phone out. He was Noah's guest, Carter's guest, and he did this to him?

I jerked forward, but my captor held me close. He scooted back.

NO!

This wasn't going to happen. Not to Carter. Not to me. This was not happening.

A surge of adrenalin came over me. I couldn't wiggle out. I couldn't kick or hit so I sunk my teeth into the guy's meaty arm. I went as far and as deep as I could. The guy yelled out and dropped me. Cursing, he scooted back and I was free. Rolling to my feet, I felt a second guy reach for me and I spun away. They were all shouting now.

"Get her!"

One reached for my arm, but I slammed my foot on his and then brought my knee up into his groin. He groaned and fell away. A fourth guy came next. I brought my elbow up, but he only chuckled and ducked. I twisted to the side. It didn't matter. He dodged all my hits and wrapped his arms around me. I was held in another paralyzing hold again with a book shoved between my teeth and his arm now. "We're not all stupid, honey."

I seethed and fought back. Nothing. My heart was pumping. My blood was racing. I had to get free. I had to protect Carter.

"Oh, she's a fighter, huh?" The leader chuckled some more but turned his back to me. He was completely disinterested with me as he spoke into the phone, "We've got him. And her too. We got them both." He paused before nodding. "Yeah, sounds good. Be there in ten." He turned back and waved a hand to the room. "Pick him up. He wants them both."

It was then that I looked around the suite. It was filled with men, all in black suits and the same bulges underneath. I knew it was his men that were in the hallway. As two guys moved forward to pick up Carter, the guy laughed to himself. "He's a fucking idiot, showing up alone to this meeting. Carter Reed, thinks he can take on anyone. Not me, you punk kid. Not me."

As the guys reached down and one touched under his arm, Carter moved like lightning. He grabbed the guy's hand, stuck something in his chest, and threw his body into the second man. Jumping to his feet, he pulled out a gun and shot at the three men in the room with me. The leader's eyes got big, a strangled chortling sound came from him, but he backed against the walls with his hands in the air. At the same time, doors were kicked open. More men flooded into the room with guns already drawn. Mike and Thomas came in from the patio. A hand chopped at the neck of the guy who was holding me. I was released as he fell to the ground, but Mike caught me. He carried me from the room, back out onto the patio and over to the other room.

"Emma," Amanda cried out and rushed towards me. Mike released me as soon as we were in the room and it was then that everything clicked in me.

Oh my god.

My knees buckled and I slipped to the couch beside me.

"Emma." Amanda caught me and helped me sit down. She took my hands in hers. "What happened? What were you thinking?"

"I..." I couldn't even answer that. What had I been thinking? "I wasn't." Carter was hurt. I went for him. That's all I had thought, but I blinked as I realized there was more. I would've traded my life for his. My chest swelled and my heart tried to burst from its place. I would've given my life for his.

The image of Carter being kicked flashed before my eyes again. I flinched and reeled backwards.

Mike stepped forward, his hand to his ear. "We're supposed to move you back to the house. Emma, would you please come with me?"

I stood without thinking. Carter had been beaten senseless and he got up. All his movements were precise, as if he knew what he was doing, as if he was waiting...Horror filtered in now. What had I interrupted?

"Emma."

I should've trusted him.

Amanda helped me stand. My legs still wavered when I got up from the couch. She held onto my arm. "I'm coming with her."

He frowned but nodded. "Fine."

And then we were shuffled into the hallway and down the back exit. As we headed into the back elevator, I glanced to Mike. They knew the hotel inside and out. They had gotten help from someone, who knew all the back hallways and staff shortcuts. We were bustled through the storage doors and into a SUV. Mike got into the back seat with us. It was large enough for four more people. The doors from the front opened and two more guards got inside. Mike touched his ear, "Clear."

The SUV shot forward.

I glanced back, as if to catch a look at Carter, but there was nothing. The storage doors to the hotel had already closed by the time we turned a corner.

When we got to the house, I turned to Mike. "Is he okay?"

He nodded and gestured inside. "He'll be back as soon as he can. Your other friend was notified of your departures." Mike glanced at Amanda as well.

Understanding dawned over her. "Oh, to Theresa. That's good.

She would've worried."

He nodded again, a silent clip of the head.

I sighed. That was all we were going to get, so when we got back, I led the way inside. Amanda trailed behind me and as we went through the gym to the kitchen area, I heard her gasp behind me. This was the first time she had seen my home, my new home.

"Is this where you live?" She was breathless.

I nodded. "It's Carter's place." But that wasn't true. It was now my place too. There was no energy to enjoy this moment. Amanda was my first and would probably be the last to see the inside of my new home. I should've been proud, but all I could think about was him.

"Is there a bathroom?"

I nodded and showed her the one on the main floor. Then I went to the bedroom and changed clothes. My dress dropped to the floor. I didn't care about picking it up. Carter was supposed to have been there to undress me. We were supposed to have spent the night making love and I had no idea where he was. After I pulled on sweats and a baggy sweatshirt, I grabbed another pair of each for Amanda. When I went back to the kitchen, she was searching through the cupboards. She gave me a sheepish grin. "I was going to make coffee."

I lifted the clothes for her. "Yeah, I can make some. That's a good idea."

"Thanks for the clothes, not that I wouldn't mind sitting around in this ball gown." Giving me a crooked grin, she slipped past for the bathroom again. The coffee had started by the time she returned and it wasn't long before I poured cups for both of us. And like my routine on the other mornings when Carter was gone for business, I took some coffee to Mike. He told me more guards had returned and taken point around the building so I filled up a thermos and climbed to the top floor. The guards didn't even act surprised anymore. And then, I slid onto a seat beside Amanda at the table. We waited.

It was hours later when people arrived, but they were the new guards. Mike went home. A different Mike took his place. He was positioned in the garage. The only reason I knew of the change was because the first Mike came in to warn me of the shift change. He gave me a tight but reassuring smile. "I didn't want you to be alarmed."

"Any word from Carter?"

He shook his head and left.

Amanda asked once he was gone and we were alone inside, "Would he tell you anyway?"

"Probably not," I sighed.

"Emma, I'm sure he's fine."

"I know he is." But that wasn't the point. I wanted to speak to him. I wanted to feel him, taste him. I wanted to hold him in my arms again. The images of him being beaten hadn't stopped. I kept seeing them over and over again. And I hadn't been able to stop it. Arms of cement held me back. It sent a chill down my back because there would be another time, but Carter might not be able to get out of that one like he had this time. Whether he told me he was out or not, it didn't matter. I knew that Carter would always be connected to the mob.

I'd been kept in the dark. It was terrifying.

I wouldn't for the next time.

"Look," Amanda said. "Maybe I should head home?"

"No, stay." I grabbed her arm when she started to stand. "Please."

She caught my gaze, saw the pleading, and bent down. She pressed a kiss to the top of my forehead, skimming her hand over my hair. "It's not the same, you know."

"What isn't?"

"Carter and Mallory."

My mouth went dry. I hadn't realized I'd been putting the two together, but she was right. I lost Mallory, even though I'd been reassured she would be fine. I swallowed over a big ball of emotion in my throat. I was scared of the same thing happening to him.

"Mallory was doomed from the beginning."

Tears pricked at the corners of my eyes. Amanda had never spoken like this before. She sounded resigned as she pressed another kiss to my forehead. Turning, she rested her cheek to the top of my head and murmured, "She knew who Jeremy Dunvan was when they started together. And she knew he was a bad guy. That's all she picked. She's not the same as Carter."

I blinked back the tears.

"And he's not like her. He'll fight for you." Amanda stood. The corner of her lip curved up, but she was haunted. I knew it because I was the same. We were both haunted. She continued, "I was wrong before. Carter loves you. That's obvious and if anyone's going to get out of the mob, it'll be him. That man isn't one to be crossed." She patted my hand again. "He'd move heaven and earth to keep you safe. I don't agree with how he kept you safe before, but I know the lengths he'd go for you now." Another yawn escaped her. "You should try to get some sleep too."

Later, we both snuggled into couches in the downstairs media room. I knew I wouldn't be able to sleep, but Amanda wasn't having that problem so we compromised. She made me promise to try so we put a movie on. It was a tradition we used to do when we'd go drinking with Mallory and Ben. Mallory usually ended the night with some guy. Ben would storm home and Amanda stayed the night on the couch. We would both fall asleep to a movie.

But I didn't that night. I was awake for hours when a silhouette finally appeared in the doorway, and I almost cried out in relief.

Carter came and took my hand. He led us to our room.

THIRTY-TWO

When we got there, he let go, but I took his hand again and led him into the bathroom. His face had been battered from the beatings. There was dried blood over him, in his hair as well, and he stood there watching as I inspected every wound. He winced as I probed his ribs, so instead of having him lift his shirt over, I took a firm hold at the top and ripped it. It fell to the floor. My eyes took it all in. His chest and ribs had taken the brunt of the kicks, at least the ones I saw. The tips of my fingers softly grazed over him, and he hissed from the pain.

My eyes caught his. I saw the pain and took a deep breath. Strength surged inside of me. He needed mine so I pointed to the counter and murmured, "Sit." My voice came out hoarse, and I bit down on my lip. Pain sliced me when he made a motion to vomit. When he didn't, I let out the breath I'd been holding and warmed some washcloths.

Pressing it to the cut on his nose, the washcloth immediately turned red from the blood. He hissed some more when I continued to his swollen cheek, then his swollen eye.

"You should see a doctor."

He nodded, closing his one eye. Slowly, he leaned forward and rested his forehead on my shoulder. His lips moved against my skin as he answered, "I had to see you first."

My hand lifted to cradle the back of his head. I drew another deep breath in and rested my head against his. My eyes closed. I felt his pain and I hated it. He shouldn't have been hurting, but I knew he put himself in that situation for a reason. So many questions flew in my head, but I refrained from asking. My fingers began to massage the back of his head, delicately at first and they grew stronger when he didn't grimace or flinch away. Instead, his hand moved to the small of my back and he pressed me tighter against him. As I kept massaging, he grew more and more tired. His weight leaned on top of me until all of it was there. He had fallen asleep. I was holding him up and I stood there. I continued holding him. I would've stood there for hours, standing for him but a small movement caught my eye and I looked up.

Amanda had a hand to her mouth. She watched from the doorway. As she did, a lone tear slipped down. Then she mouthed, "He's asleep?"

I nodded. The woman in me didn't want to move, but logic kicked in. He needed medical attention, sooner rather than later, so I whispered, "Go out the doors and have them call a doctor for me."

She nodded, disappearing again.

Carter groaned and stiffened on me. He lifted his head up, holding it in the palm of hand as he grunted. His eye was pressed tight. "I fell asleep."

He didn't move all the way back, just enough so he could sit upright. Sliding my hands up his legs, more to test if there were wounds, I urged them apart and stood in front of him now. Front and steady. Then I began cleaning the rest of his blood. I started with his head first. Since there was so much blood, I went slow and dabbed so I wouldn't reopen already healing cuts. When that was done, I got more washcloths and started on his chest.

Carter sat there the whole time. His hands rested on my hipbones. As I continued to wash him, his eyes closed and his head bobbed down. He slumped forward, as if he'd fallen asleep. But when I moved to grab another handful of washcloths, his hands tightened on my hips to keep me anchored in front. I skimmed a hand over his cheek, cupping the side of his face, and his eyes opened to mine. He was drowsy, but he moved to the side and kissed the inside of my hand.

"A doctor should be coming," I murmured, my voice thick from so much damn love for this man.

His eyes closed again, but he kept a firmer grip on me.

Amanda came back and gave me the five minute signal. I wasn't sure if we were supposed to leave or if the doctor would come to us, but I nodded. She left again and I took Carter's hand. "You should shower and get different clothing on."

He nodded. When he moved to unbuckle his pants, I brushed his hand to the side and did it for him. His pants and boxer briefs dropped to the floor. Before I could take him into the shower, he stopped me. His fingers came to my clothes and he lifted the sweatshirt off. My sweats were next and then we both stepped under the water. As it drenched us, more of his blood trailed down. The red circled the drain on the floor, turning the water pink. That seemed symbolic to me. Things were healing.

Skimming a hand down my arm, he tugged me against him and

hugged me. Then he murmured, "I almost lost it when I saw you being carried into that room."

My hand raised and slid back into its place, on the back of his head. My fingers dug in and grabbed a hold of his hair, but it was to hold him against me. I was cautious of all his bruising. "I'm sorry. I wasn't thinking."

"He could've killed you." His hand gripped me tighter. "He could've shot me and taken you instead. Franco wanted you too."

I didn't say anything. He tried to keep me away. I should've trusted him.

He growled into my shoulder. His other hand pressed me against him harder. "It's why I didn't tell you what was going on. I couldn't have you anywhere near the situation. I needed you where my men were watching you." A soft curse slipped from him. "I had to wait until he made that phone call. I needed to know Franco's location. You could've been killed."

The horror from before rose in me again. I blinked back the tears at what I had almost done. "I'm sorry. I'm so sorry. You were hurting and I couldn't handle it. I reacted without thinking. No one will take you away from me. I won't lose you again, not now that I have you. My brother. Mallory. Not you too."

His lips moved against my skin, pressing a kiss there until he lifted his head. I gasped as I saw the agony in his depths. Pure agony. He choked out, his chest rising for a deep breath, "He could've killed you. You shouldn't have been anywhere near that room. Why didn't you just listen to me and stay away?"

"Because I was looking for you."

"I told you I would come back."

I stepped back and gazed at him, stupefied. "There was a time when you didn't come back for me. I can't lose you. You've been protecting me, but it goes both ways. I will protect you too. It's not just you in this relationship. I love you too. And I knew you were lying to me. That killed me the most. You didn't trust me to tell me the plan—"

"And if I had?"

I stopped. If he had? My eyes went down. "I would've done what I did anyway."

"Exactly." He closed his eyes, holding my hand to his chest before he lifted it for a kiss. "The Bertal family knew an Elder was working with Franco. They knew he had been tipped off before the initial strike. I was supposed to wait until they found out who that was. When I got word, I demanded a meeting and the timing was perfect. The elder's daughter works at The Richmond in Chicago. She was given three tickets and he volunteered to be the one for the meeting."

"You knew all of that was going to happen tonight?"

He nodded.

"And you never told me."

"I made a call." His eyes grew hard.

I didn't care. I didn't care what I would've done. My chin rose and I stepped even further back. "I won't have that in this relationship. Take it or leave it, Carter. If you're going to intentionally put yourself in danger, I need to know. I can't be kept in the dark, not anymore. I love you and I will always protect you, no matter the consequences to me. And it'd be smart for you to acknowledge my side."

His eyes clasped shut and a soft curse slipped from him. Then he sighed again, "I forgot how much fight you have in you." A crooked grin appeared. "I love you for it."

"Really?"

He nodded, tugging me against him again. He bent down and teased me with a soft kiss. "We didn't know who else was supporting Franco, even on my side, so I kept most everyone in the dark."

"Your men knew."

"Not until the last minute. Their calls were being monitored to see if they would send an alarm to Franco."

I bit my lip. "Did they?"

"No. Everyone was loyal. They could've taken you, another reason why I didn't want you to know. You were supposed to stay at your table." He groaned and swept me tighter against him. I could feel every inch. The water slid over us, increasing the arousal in me, but I held back. He was too damaged for that. He needed to heal.

He continued, hugging me so tight, "The plan was for the Elder to think I was almost dead. Once he made the call, we had him. We could locate Franco from the number."

"Did you?"

"Yeah. He had no idea. It's over. Franco is dead."

I frowned but didn't move away. His arms clenched me tight, making his biceps bulge from the movement. I hadn't known Franco wasn't dead. "But the guards? You only put two on me."

He shook his head. "No, they were always there. They just followed you from behind in case Franco tried to snatch you. I didn't want to alarm you."

"Carter." I was so pissed at him.

"What?"

"You should've told me all of this." He drew back, capturing my gaze and holding it. I couldn't look away. I didn't want to. He needed to see how I was affected. "I thought I was losing you. Do you know what that did to me?"

He grinned. "Yeah, it made you act crazy."

Rolling my eyes, I almost punched him in the chest, but pulled back at the last second. His grin widened at that. I shook my head. "You can't keep me in the dark anymore."

"I won't."

My eyes caught his again and I searched inside of him. When he saw my suffering, he softened. He whispered, "I promise."

I nodded. "Okay."

Then he kissed me and he put all of his love into it.

I stood on my tiptoes and hugged him as much as I could. He didn't seem to mind his wounds, but I did. After showering, we dressed again and left to see the doctor.

When he was being prodded, Amanda came over and stood beside me. She had put on a fresh pot of coffee since it was the middle of the night. She yawned as she flashed me an apologetic grin. "I am sorry again. You deserve to be happy and he's the guy for you, no matter what anyone says. This is right. The two of you. You're right together."

Warmth rushed up in me and I swallowed thickly. I was choked up with so much emotion, and all I could murmur was, "Thank you."

She patted my hand and kissed my cheek before whispering, "You deserve your happily ever after. He's it. This is it."

I grinned, blinking back more tears. "Even with the mob connections?"

"Even with." She pulled me in for another hug.

I was too touched to respond. The cynical side would've joked when had she turned into a hallmark card, but the sentimental side was too moved to even speak. It meant a lot, especially through all we'd been together. This was a friendship I didn't want to lose.

"Okay." She pressed her hand against my arm again. "Do you think I could get a ride home?"

My hand took hold of her arm before she could venture far. I pulled her back and shook my head. "You're better off staying here."

"Why?"

"I am pretty sure Theresa's not home alone."

"Oh. You're right." She sighed. "They can get loud. Alright. Can I sleep in a room this time?"

Laughing, I showed her to a guest bedroom on the second floor before returning back to the kitchen. The doctor was finishing up his assessment. He lectured as I drew clearer, "You need rest, lots of it. That means no nothing, Carter. No sex. No fighting. No nothing. If you can work from home, I'd recommend it. And I mean it about the sex. Don't think I didn't see that cute honey standing looking all concerned before. No sex."

Carter pushed him back a little. "Don't start, Doc."

"Don't start," he sniffed. "Don't start he says. He only woke me up, had his men come and transport me here, and now he says 'don't start.' I'll start all I want. You have a broken rib. It needs to heal!"

"Yeah. And it will."

I turned the last corner. The doctor saw me and graced me with a smile. He lifted his notepad in my direction. "Make sure he rests and don't have sex with him. Even if you're doing all the work, it'll still strain his ribs." He clapped Carter on the shoulder, giving both of us a polite salute of the hand before he picked up his bag again. "And now I'm hoping that same transport will take me home?"

Carter waved his guys to do his bidding.

Later, as I helped Carter into bed and curled up next to him, I asked over a yawn, "Is everything done now?"

He pulled me closer to him, tucking his head into the crook of my shoulder and neck. His hand went to my breast and simply held it. "Yeah. I think so."

I nodded, my eyelids already drowsy. "Good."

He kissed my neck where he was nuzzling me. "Good?"

Reaching up, I laced my fingers with his and breathed out a deep breath. Everything was how it should be. Amanda's words. Franco's death. Carter beside me. I knew that no matter what came at us, things would be fine. I breathed again in relief, feeling the first flutter of peace in my chest. My lips curved up as I rested my head against his. "Yeah. Everything's good."

"Good." He pressed his lips to my neck again, one last time.

It wasn't long until I heard his deep breathing and knew he'd fallen asleep. Then I closed my eyes. Everything would be fine. I'd make sure of it, no matter what challenges came at us.

Everything was perfect.

For more information about this author, please go to
Tijan's Books on Facebook.
https://www.facebook.com/TijansBooks

Other books by this author:

Fallen Crest High

Fallen Crest Family

Fallen Crest Public (soon to be released, end of December 2013)

The BS Series:

Broken and Screwed

Broken and Screwed 2

Braille (to be released)

Elijah (to be released)

ACKNOWLEDGEMENTS

Oh boy. I've got a list here. Lisa Jordan, you're so great to work with and I'm so glad I snatched this cover up as soon as I saw it! Obviously, I need to give a big hug to Amanda and Jocelyn for helping to edit this monster. A huge thank you to Cami Hesnault and the Crazies R Us Book Blog. They are organizing this blog tour, but Cami's been amazing and so helpful to me! I know you're a super busy woman too! Other big thanks to Megan Smith for being a beta and big congrats on your huge success! Another thanks to Jean Love, Maura Murphy, and Keara O'Neil. These ladies have been always willing to do a quick read for me. I'd like to send some love to Mari Brown at the Keepin' It Real Book Blog, Stacey at the Stay Blu Reads, and also Tamsyn Bester at The Secret Book Brat Blog, author of *Beneath Your Beautiful.* And lastly, to my sister in law, Mandy. Thanks for the support. Truly means a TON to me. I already dedicated this book to my other half, but I'll still mention him here. Tough times and good times, he's stuck with me. That means more than I can ever write here.

CPSIA information can be obtained
at www.ICGtesting.com
Printed in the USA
LVHW050604250621
691049LV00012B/1652

9 781951 771188